Crossing Paths

Violet Howe

www.violethowe.com

Cover Design: Elizabeth Mackey Graphics
www.elizabethmackeygraphics.com

Published by Charbar Productions, LLC
(p-v1)

ISBN: 978-1-7321215-4-6

BOOKS BY VIOLET HOWE

Tales Behind the Veils

Diary of a Single Wedding Planner

Diary of a Wedding Planner in Love

Diary of an Engaged Wedding Planner

Maggie

The Cedar Creek Series

Cedar Creek Mysteries

The Ghost in the Curve

The Glow in the Woods

Cedar Creek Families

Building Fences

Crossing Paths

ACKNOWLEDGMENTS

To my team: Bonnie, Sandy, Teresa, Tawdra, Lisa, & Melissa –
Thank you for your time and your insight. It is a wonderful gift to be
able to trust my content with others, knowing they will treat it with
the greatest of care but deliver the most valuable honesty.

Johanna – Thank you for advice on Cat's post-hospital medical care!

Nikole – Thank you for your knowledge and guidance on bringing
my turtles to life and ensuring their rescues were accurate.

CHAPTER 1
1982 - Catherine

"Look! Do you see it?" William's voice was low, and I couldn't understand why he'd suddenly chosen to whisper when we were all alone on the beach.

"See what?"

"Shh!" He put his finger over his lips as his eyes grew wide. "We have to be very quiet. You can't let her hear you."

"Who?" I whispered, scanning the surf and the sand.

He leaned in closer to me and pointed toward the waves, and I squinted as I searched the dark, inky water with its frothy white caps gleaming beneath the full moon.

"There!" he whispered, and at last, I saw her.

She looked like a log at first, rolling onto the shore as the waves crashed over her, but as she emerged from the surf, the moonlight reflected off her huge shell.

"Oh, wow! A turtle," I whispered, barely able to contain my excitement. "Can we go down there? Do you think she's okay?"

He motioned for me to talk quieter, though I swear I was being as quiet as possible under the circumstances.

"I think she's fine. She's probably coming on shore to lay eggs."

"Should we help her?"

He smiled and shook his head.

"No. She definitely won't want our help. But if we're quiet enough and still enough, we might be able to see her dig her nest. Do you think you could be quiet long enough for that?" William's grin told me that he doubted it, and we both knew it was unlikely, but I was willing to try. Moving to a crouching position, he motioned for me to step off the blanket. Then he tucked it under his elbow and took my

1

hand before leading me behind the dunes.

"Where are we going?"

"Shh." He turned and made his way to the top of a dune, peeking over its ridge before laying the blanket on a bare patch of sand amid the sea grass. He pulled me down with him to lie on our bellies as we peered over the dune at the turtle, who was now almost directly in front of us.

"She's headed this way," I whispered against his ear.

He nodded and motioned for me to be silent.

Her journey across the packed, wet sand was slow, but it was nothing compared to her laborious pace as she made her way into the looser drifts. I thought I would self-combust with excitement and the effort to remain quiet by the time she reached the base of the dune. But once she found her ideal spot and began to scoop out a nest with her massive fins, the wonder of it all so enthralled me that I lapsed into a speechless stupor.

When she'd gotten herself situated, she sat gazing out toward the gulf, and I realized my eyes were wet with tears of amazement.

William smiled at me as I swiped them away with the back of my hand, and then he kissed me, and my heart nearly burst.

How could one night be filled with so much love and joy, and yet be overshadowed with such sadness?

I stared into his eyes, trying not to think about what tomorrow would bring.

Our summer had come to an end all too quickly, and I couldn't bear to consider what my life would be like with him away at college and me stuck at home for another year.

I looked back at our mama friend, determined not to ruin the time William and I had left together with fears of what might be. We sat in silence as she finished laying her eggs and secured the nest, and then she headed back to the water, leaving a trail of swept sand behind her.

William pulled me into his arms as he shifted to lay on his back, and I nestled my head against his shoulder and stared at the stars above us.

His chest expanded with his loud yawn, and I looked up to see him smiling down at me.

"Well, that was pretty cool, but we'd best get on the road," he said as he pulled me closer. "We've got a long drive back, and I'm already feeling sleepy."

"Not yet," I pleaded. "Please? Can we stay a little while longer?"

I buried my face in his neck and swallowed hard against the tears that burned my eyelids, so different from my happy tears of minutes before.

This was it.

This was our last hurrah. Everything would be different once we got back home. He'd move to Gainesville and into the dorm, and though he'd promised time and time again that it wouldn't change anything between us, I knew it would. How could it not? He was leaving me behind, and a whole new world waited for him on campus.

"Please, William. I'm not ready to say goodbye."

He tucked his thumb under my chin and lifted my face to search my eyes with his. "No one's saying goodbye, Catherine. It's only forty-five minutes from Ocala to the university. We'll figure out how to see each other. I'm definitely going to come home for the weekend of your birthday."

"But that's two months away! That's so long. I'm used to seeing you every day. Talking to you every day. Kissing you every day."

"Okay, well, we won't be able to do that, but I'm telling you, there's no reason to be all upset. Nothing is going to change my feelings for you. I love you. I love you with everything in me. We have plans, don't we? I'm going to school now, and you'll join me next year. And then when we both have our degrees, we'll get married and start our own farm."

"And we'll name it Turtle Crossing," I said, grinning despite the thick lump in my throat.

He rolled his eyes as he always did when I insisted on that name.

"We've been through this a hundred times. No one is going to see the name Turtle Crossing and realize it's a horse farm."

"Because it's not just a horse farm. You'll raise horses and nurse them back to health, and I'll rescue turtles and tortoises."

He shook his head as he laughed. "I know what we're doing, but that name makes no sense."

"It makes perfect sense. Please? For me? Just tell me we can name it that. It'll make me happy."

He leaned back to get a better look at me. "Oh, like everything else that happened tonight wasn't enough to make you happy?"

A warm blush crept into my cheeks at the memory of what I'd convinced him to do earlier, and I smiled, not wanting to concede so easily but aware that he made a good point.

"Then, let's just agree that Turtle Crossing isn't off the table, all right? It can still be considered."

"Agreed," he said. "Now, let's get on the road."

He moved to sit up, and I pushed him back down with both hands.

"No! Not yet. Hold me in your arms just a little bit longer. Just a few minutes more. Please?"

I couldn't hold back my tears any longer, and they flowed down my cheeks as he frowned.

"Oh, babe, please don't cry. Please. You know I can't stand to see you cry."

He cupped my cheeks in his hands and brushed away my tears with his thumbs.

"Then hold me," I whispered. "Hold me a little while longer. I'm not ready for this night to end."

He kissed me and pulled me onto his chest, wrapping his arms tightly around me as his heart thumped beneath my ear.

I never considered that we might fall asleep. It never even crossed my mind.

We'd been sneaking out at night for weeks, stealing forbidden moments while my parents slept. But we'd always made it back home in plenty of time for me to be safely in my bed before my father woke for his coffee.

When my eyes fluttered open to see the sky turning pink on the horizon, my heart filled with a panicked dread like I'd never known.

I'd been right to worry. Everything *would* change as soon as we got home, but in a more devastating way than I'd ever thought possible. Neither of our lives would ever fully recover from what we set in motion that night.

CHAPTER 2
2018 - Caterina

S omewhere in the hazy fog inside my brain, I sensed someone watching me. I struggled to open my eyes, but it was as though the lids were held shut by a great weight. I lifted my hand thinking I could move the weight away, but the sheer effort of motion was too much, and my fingers fell back to the soft surface beneath me.

Something was covering my face. I hadn't felt it before, but once I became aware of it, a panic welled up within me. Fearing I would suffocate if I didn't remove it, I tried to force my hand up as I pushed at my eyelids again. I got them open, but the light seemed to pierce my brain, and I retreated back into the darkness just as a hand covered mine and gently pushed it away from my face.

"Careful," a male voice whispered. "Don't mess with that, okay?"

I opened my eyes again, determined to see who was with me as I squinted against the light.

I realized then that I must be dreaming, because somehow, I had conjured up the only man I'd ever loved.

It didn't surprise me to see him there. William had appeared in my dreams countless times in the years since we'd parted.

But this was different.

His fiery red hair held gray I'd never seen before, and the lines of time had etched his face so that he appeared far older than seventeen. His jawline was as strong as ever, and his eyes were the same brilliant blue, but a haggardness lay over them like a filter, and the skin surrounding them had crinkled with age. He wasn't as thin as I remembered. He was lean, but more muscular than the boy I'd known. He was still tall, but this changed version of him slouched a bit, as though he carried something heavy upon his shoulders.

I closed my eyes to dispel this older apparition, preferring to remember him as he was the last time I saw him—young and strapping, full of life, and brimming with hope. Of course, we had both been filled with hope back then. Back in the glory days before life revealed how cruel it could be.

"Catherine," the voice whispered, husky and thick with emotion.

My heart clenched at the sound of him saying my name, and I opened my eyes again, willing to give myself over to the dream if it meant I could be with him, even for a moment.

My mouth was so dry that I didn't have enough saliva to swallow, and I moaned as I tried again to remove the obstruction from my face.

Dream William took my hand in his and squeezed it gently, and I marveled at how strong the sensation of touch seemed. Never in my dreams had he been so real. The smell of horses on his skin. The roughness of his callused hands as they held mine.

I looked down and realized there were rails on my bed, and I lay under blue sheets that I didn't recognize. A thin tube protruded from my hand, and I followed its path to look up and see an IV and monitors.

Why would I dream I was in a hospital bed?

I blinked several times to try to bring the world into focus, searching my memories for any clue as to what had happened.

No matter how much I blinked, he was still there, and as my vision cleared, I stared at him, wide-eyed.

There was no way. It was impossible.

It had been thirty-six years. Thirty-six years since I'd said goodbye to him in the early hours of the morning and then disappeared without a trace, never to speak to him again. Thirty-six years since I'd carried a child he never knew existed.

"So, it is you," he whispered, bending to look closer at me. His eyes glassed over with tears. "I never thought I'd see you again."

I tried to speak but no sound came. The dryness in my mouth and throat burned, and I winced and squeezed my eyes shut as I forced a swallow.

"It's okay," he whispered. "Don't try to talk."

Perhaps I was dying. That had to be it. Something terrible had happened to me, and though I'd landed in the hospital, it was too late. It was the end of my life.

How else would William be there?

But if he was standing at the gates of eternity to greet me, it could mean only one thing. He had already passed, and tears escaped my closed eyelids as I realized he'd lived his entire life without ever knowing the truth. Without ever knowing how much I loved him, or that we had a daughter he'd never meet.

Then, a new realization dawned. If he was here, if he was greeting me in the beyond, then evidently, we'd been granted in death what was forbidden in life, and my eyes flew open with the hope of eternity by his side.

It was all wrong, though. Why would there be pain in the afterlife? Why would my face be covered with a claustrophobia-inducing mask? Why would I have an IV and be in a hospital gown?

The more I considered the facts, the more the truth became undeniable.

I was in real pain, in a real hospital, and that meant William had to be real.

I forced his name from my lips, but the effort set my throat on fire, and I clamped down on his hand.

He squeezed back softly but then released me.

"You look like you're in pain, so I'm going to get a nurse, okay?"

I shook my head and grasped for his hand, gripping it tightly as I tried to beg him with my eyes to stay since I couldn't with my voice. This couldn't be it. There couldn't be this brief reunion only to be met with another goodbye.

There was too much to say. Too much to tell him. So much that had been missed.

I tried to speak again, but he shook his head.

"I'll be back," he said, pulling his hand free as he placed my hand on my stomach. "You rest."

He cleared his throat, and with a brief nod, he was gone, and my heart wrenched anew with the pain I'd carried my entire adult life.

The door swung open within a couple of minutes, and a nurse in burgundy scrubs appeared with a huge smile on her face.

"Well, hello there, Ms. Russo. It's so nice to see you alert."

I certainly didn't feel alert. The blurry edges of my dream state were coming in and out of focus as I looked around the room.

The blinds were shut, and the lights were dim. I didn't know if it was morning or night. I had no idea how long I'd been in the hospital or how I'd gotten there.

I reached for the mask over my face, and the nurse pulled my hand away.

"Oh, don't touch that," she said. "You have to leave that in place. It's helping you breathe. I don't know how much you remember, but your lung infection worsened, and we've had you heavily sedated while the antibiotics did their job."

I tried to ask her how long I'd been there, but she gently admonished me for making the effort.

"Don't try to talk just yet. You need to rest a little longer."

Another nurse entered, followed by a doctor I remembered from a previous stint in the hospital.

They all seemed excited that I was awake, but their enthusiasm only added to my confusion. I had no memory of arriving. No memory of what had happened to trigger the ambulance ride they said I'd taken. The doctor told me the bronchitis and lung infection I'd been battling off and on for months had worsened. I'd been sedated for almost two weeks while they tried to find the right cocktail of antibiotics. It all seemed surreal. How could I have lost that much time?

I wanted to ask them how William had found me. How he'd come to be in my room. But I couldn't ask anything. I couldn't speak. I could only nod or shake my head in response to their barrage of questions.

The entire ordeal was overwhelming, and my eyelids grew heavy again as my energy depleted.

"We'll be back to check on you soon," the doctor said. "In the meantime, rest and let your body recover."

I let my eyes fall shut, and the room faded away.

One thought burned brightly in my mind as all else went dark.

William Ward had been there. He had been in my room. He had held my hand.

And he'd said he would be back.

CHAPTER 3
Caterina

I spent the rest of the morning in spurts of wakefulness and sleep without any real concept of time. Each time I woke, I was less fuzzy and more aware of my surroundings. I still couldn't remember anything about the day I was admitted, and it blew my mind to think that I'd lost so much time while I was under.

They'd removed the horrible mask from my face and replaced it with a tube in my nose, which was still uncomfortable, but infinitely better. I'd been able to sip water and ice cubes, which had helped soothe my parched lips, mouth, and throat.

The memory of seeing William by my side became more distant as the day went on, and I began to think it must have been a dream after all. The nurses had cautioned that I might be disoriented and that my mental focus might come and go in the after effects of the heavy sedation, which was probably what had caused his apparition.

Still, I looked to the door each time it opened with a flicker of hope that it would be him, but each time a nurse entered instead, I became more resigned to reality.

I had just closed my eyes and begun to drift off once more when I heard the door open.

It wasn't William, but my heart still leapt with joy to see Patsy— my dear friend, neighbor, co-worker, and stand-in mother figure.

It felt so good to see a familiar face. I hadn't realized until that moment how lonely and forlorn I'd felt all day. My smile was too big to contain, and so were my tears.

"Hey, darlin'," she said with her sweet grin, her blue eyes sparkling with moisture. "It's about time you woke up." She leaned to kiss my forehead, and I reached up to squeeze her arm, wanting so badly to hug her and have her wrap her arms around me. I tried to greet her, forgetting in my excitement that speaking hurt.

"Don't talk, don't talk," Patsy said. "You've had all kinds of stuff shoved down your throat. You don't need to talk." She sat on the edge of the bed, and a movement near the door caught my eye.

I'd been so elated to see Patsy that I hadn't realized she'd brought someone with her.

The woman looked vaguely familiar. I felt like I'd seen her before, but I couldn't place where or who she might be. She was staring at me wide-eyed with an expression that seemed both alarmed and pleased.

I nudged Patsy, hoping she would fill in the blanks for my foggy mind.

She glanced over her shoulder and motioned for the woman to come to the other side of the bed.

"Do you remember us talking about your baby girl?" Patsy asked.

The realization hit me with the force of a tidal wave. I had told Patsy my most guarded and precious secret, and somehow Patsy had found her. Caroline!

I stared at the woman I'd given birth to thirty-five years earlier.

My baby girl. My daughter. The purest part of my heart that had been set free and lost to me.

I opened my mouth to say her name, but only a whisper escaped. I reached out to touch her, needing to feel that she was real.

She moved to my bedside, and I grabbed hold of her hand, relieved to find she was flesh and blood and not some mental mirage. Our contact was like an electrical jolt passing through me, and a maelstrom of emotions hit me all at once. Happiness. Sorrow. Joy. Regret. Love. Relief. Pain.

She smiled back at me, her own eyes filling with tears as mine flowed.

"Hi, Caterina. My name is Caroline."

I wanted to throw my arms around her. I wanted to say how sorry I was that I gave her away. I wanted to tell her I loved her, that I had always loved her. That there had never been a single day I hadn't thought of her, wondered where she was and what she was doing. If she was okay. If she was happy.

Luckily, I held all that at bay and managed to simply nod, though I think I was probably squeezing her hand hard enough to cut off the circulation with all that angst and energy channeled into one point of contact.

"Do you remember Caroline was coming to have lunch with us before you collapsed?" Patsy asked.

Lunch? We were having lunch with Caroline? Surely, I would remember something that important. Why couldn't I remember? How could I forget finding my daughter? Had we met before today? How much had I forgotten? How much had I missed?

I looked to Patsy for answers.

"We found her, and I called and invited her to lunch. But then you got ill before she got here, and the ambulance came and took you to the hospital. They said the medications may affect your memory. It's okay."

I stared back at my daughter, trying desperately to clear the fog and remember what had happened.

"Caroline has been at the hospital as much as she could waiting for you to wake up," Patsy said. "She's been a rock for me. Just like you are. She's your daughter, Cat."

The first time I'd seen her, she'd been a tiny bundle; her face all scrunched up as she'd cried and her head adorned with a beautiful patch of William's red hair. I'd memorized that baby's face, and though the adult looked much different, she was still the most beautiful thing I'd ever seen.

I traced the outline of her face with my finger, trying to find that precious baby in the woman who sat before me. Only her hair was the same, but much longer, of course. I picked up a lock and twisted it around my finger, marveling at the fact that this was her. This was the baby William and I had created in love and carelessness.

I stared at the vibrant strands the same color as her father's and whispered, "Red."

There was so much I wanted to say. The words all tumbled over each other in my mind, and I cursed my voice for failing me at such a crucial moment.

Words! I could write the words. I motioned to Patsy, and as usual, she knew what I needed at once.

"Oh, yeah. That's a great idea. Let me find a piece of paper."

She dug into her bag and found paper, and Caroline offered me a pen. Patsy brought the table of the bed over my lap as I moved to a sitting position, and I forced myself to write slowly and legibly, choosing which words to bring forth first and pour out onto the paper.

"You're left-handed!" Caroline said. "Me, too!"

I smiled, thrilled to see her excitement at finding we had something in common.

I handed her what I'd written and waited as she read it.

"You had red hair the first time I saw you. I'm so happy to meet you!"

She smiled even wider and wiped at her tears.

"I'm happy to meet you, too! I've wanted to meet you for so long."

Relief settled over me like a soothing balm on an open wound.

She didn't hate me. She didn't resent me. She'd wanted to meet me.

I took the paper back, anxious to ask the question that had burned in my heart every single day since the moment she was taken from me.

"Has your life been happy?"

The joy in her face answered the question before she did.

"Yes! Yes! A thousand times, yes. I have a mother who loves me, and who is so thankful to you for your sacrifice. I have two beautiful children I adore. I've been loved. I've had a full and happy life."

The floodgates opened, and the intensity of the overwhelming emotions broke free.

I couldn't hold back my tears, my relief, my love, my sorrow. It all came pouring out of me in a deluge, and suddenly, my body was taken by a coughing fit that racked me with spasms and deprived me of oxygen.

The monitor next to my bed started screaming an alert, and I fought to catch a breath between coughs. Patsy and Caroline both looked alarmed, and though I wanted to tell them I was okay, I couldn't. I was worried myself. I couldn't stop coughing, and I couldn't breathe. I didn't want to lose consciousness again. Not when I finally had the opportunity to talk to my daughter.

CHAPTER 4
Caterina

"Okay, what have we got here?"

The nurse's voice was calm, but her movements were urgent as she rushed to my side and pressed a button to silence the monitor. She helped me sit up further and gave me a cup of water to drink, rubbing my back as I got the coughing under control and managed a shaky breath.

"I don't know what's upset y'all, but this lady needs some rest," the nurse said. "She can't be taking on stress, you hear me? She needs rest. She needs calm. So y'all gonna need to think of something to keep her happy, or you'll have to let her be."

I worried she was going to send them away, and I tugged at her hemline to try and explain why she couldn't do that.

"That's ... my ... daughter." It was all I could manage to get out.

"Well, no matter who she is, she can't be in here upsetting you," the nurse said. She turned to face Caroline and Patsy with her hands on her hips. "This lady doesn't need to talk right now. Her throat is raw, and her passages are dry. It makes her cough to try and speak. The best thing for her is rest. There's only supposed to be one of y'all in here at a time anyway."

She must have been feeling merciful, because she didn't make them leave, and I let out a sigh of relief when she was gone. Patsy and Caroline came back to my bedside, and I reached for Caroline's hand, determined to keep talking to her.

"Beautiful. Beautiful."

"Thank you," she said with a smile. "You are, too."

"You get some rest now," Patsy said. "We'll be back after a while."

I shook my head, unwilling to let go. I'd let go of William, and he hadn't come back. He'd become a dream. In that moment, Caroline

13

was real, and as long as I could hold onto her, I would.

"Stay," I whispered. "I want to talk to you."

The spasms gripped my throat again, and I coughed a couple of times, but Patsy was quick with the water.

"I'm gonna step out and leave the two of you alone," she said when my coughing had subsided. "But try not to talk, Cat. You have plenty of time to say whatever you need to when you're better. The important thing now is for you to rest and be able to get out of here."

Caroline and I stared at each other in an awkward silence as Patsy exited, but then I set my pen to paper once more.

I had so many questions. So much I wanted to know. Her life. Her childhood. Her teenage years. Her present circumstances. Her hopes and dreams. Her disappointments. Her failures and heartaches. I wanted it all.

Unfortunately, I was still in the ICU unit with visiting limited to half-hour time slots, but we made every second count as we continued our conversation broken into small chunks throughout the day.

She was generous and forthcoming as she shared with me the details of her life.

I discovered I was a grandmother, which I'd often wondered about, given her age and the amount of time that had passed

"Eva's fourteen and in full-blown teenager mode," Caroline said with a sigh as she scrolled through her phone and showed me a picture of my granddaughter.

She was a beautiful girl—her dark hair, olive skin, and emerald green eyes much different from Caroline's fairness. Eva had perfected a teenage smirk in the photo, and the attitude in her eyes and the set of her jaw reminded me of the girl I'd been long ago. Even our coloring was similar.

Looking back on what I'd put my mother through when I was a teen, I felt for Caroline, for what she'd been through already and was likely still to face from Eva.

"Ethan is ten," she said as she took the phone and found a picture of my grandson. "He's more interested in soccer than anything else. Well, other than ice cream. He's a sweet boy, but he can be rambunctious at times."

He had Caroline's red hair, blue eyes, and freckles. His mouth gaped open and his nose scrunched as he laughed in the photo, and my heart smiled to see such joy.

I couldn't wait to meet them. I loved them already.

Caroline smiled as I handed the phone back to her.

"They're good kids." She crossed her arms and glanced toward the window. "They probably both get away with more than they should, but I've had a hard time being consistent with my parenting since the divorce. I feel sorry for them, and I think I go too easy as a result." She frowned, but when she looked back at me, her smile had returned. "I'm working on it, though."

I asked how long she'd been divorced, and as she described the marriage and the detachment that led to its demise even before her husband cheated, I felt relieved for her to be out of it. This Brad guy seemed like a real ass, but I could tell Caroline was trying her best to minimize the emotional damage for the kids.

"I've always been a stay-at-home mom, and knowing the divorce would already be a big adjustment for them, Brad and I agreed that I'd continue to stay at home. It made sense at the time since he'd always paid the bills. The house is in his name, and he pays the mortgage. The car, too." She chewed on her bottom lip as she looked out the window. "Lately, I've been reconsidering that arrangement. He got promoted to partner at his law firm recently, and I agreed to follow him to Orlando so the kids can stay close to him. But they're old enough now that I could work while they're in school. I think I'd rather have some independence and pay for things on my own, you know, with no strings attached."

I'd seen what complete dependence on my father had done to my mother, and I was relieved to hear Caroline say she'd been considering a return to the workforce.

I wrote her words of encouragement for seeking her own income, but other than that, I refrained from saying much at all other than the questions I penned. I wanted to know about her, and I didn't want to stop the easy flow of information by interjecting with unwanted advice or critiques of her life choices. First of all, it wasn't my place to do so, but I also knew that any change in direction to focus on me would bring up topics I wasn't ready to discuss.

Memories I wasn't prepared to revisit just yet.

At times, I had to force myself to listen to her words, because I would get lost staring at her. The tilt of her head when she was concentrating. The deep-throated rumble of her laugh. The curve of her smile. The wave of her hand as she dismissed a topic as unimportant. The way her eyes looked upward when she was uncertain of her words. I could see William in her eyes. They shared the same color and held the same vibrancy.

I wanted to memorize every detail of her face. Her mannerisms. Her voice and her gestures. It was all fascinating to me. I'd imagined her so many times at so many ages, and to see her in front of me was a surreal and euphoric experience.

Occasionally, the fog would thicken in my brain, and my eyelids would grow heavy. But no matter how difficult it became, I forced myself to stay awake, to remain in the moment and not forsake a single second with her. I'd sleep as soon as our visit time was up, and then when I woke, I'd put more questions to paper while I waited for her return, not wanting to forget anything in our rush to connect in the half hour slots we were allowed to have.

The baby I'd mourned had become a full-grown woman who was funny, articulate, sensitive, intelligent, caring, and compassionate. My heart swelled until I worried my chest might not be able to contain it, and yet I wanted more. I was voracious in my appetite to know her. I couldn't get enough.

I held my hand on my throat and tried not to laugh as she told me about the man she'd met on her way to see me that fateful day I was hospitalized.

"There I was, standing in the middle of this auto repair shop, already pissed at the delay the blow-out had caused, and the mechanic can't tell me where the car is! Now, remember, this isn't even my car! It's Brad's stupid convertible since he had to borrow my Tahoe to take the kids camping. If I hadn't been so excited to come and meet you, I probably wouldn't have cared that his car was missing!" She laughed, and I chuckled with her, despite the pain it caused. "But when Levi came in and told me that he'd accidentally stolen the car and had arranged to have it put on top of a barn, I nearly lost it. I whipped out my phone and dialed the cops with both Levi and the mechanic protesting the whole rime."

The humorous ordeal had been frustrating, for sure, but there was a spark in her eyes and in her voice as she spoke of Levi. I wondered if he was as enamored of her as she was of him. I truly hoped so.

When she left me that evening to meet him for dinner, I cried again, unable to escape the feeling of her being taken away once more. But this time was different. I knew she'd be back. I knew we'd have more time together. Happiness outweighed any sorrow. My heart was full. My soul was at peace for perhaps the first time in my life.

Well, not completely at peace.

Someone was missing from the happy reunion, and though his apparition had been kind toward me, I doubted reality would be as forgiving. He had deserved to know her, too, but I had robbed him of that opportunity.

As painful as it was, I knew it was best if I never saw him again.

CHAPTER 5
Caterina

Caroline hadn't been gone long when Patsy came back in, peeking around the door with a tentative smile that grew when we made eye contact.

"The nurse said she thought you might be awake. I was getting ready to head home, but I wanted to say goodnight before I left."

I grabbed the paper and pen to scribble out my gratitude.

"Thank you, Patsy. Thank you for everything. For getting me to the hospital. For staying with me. For finding my daughter and taking care of her this past week. I can't thank you enough."

"Oh, honey," she said, perching on the edge of my bed and patting my arm. "You'd have done the same for me. I'm just so happy we found her, and that you've gotten well enough to wake up and talk to her. I was so worried about you, Cat. You scared the daylights out of me this time. I think my head has more gray than it did before."

I smiled and took the paper back from her to write more.

"Isn't she beautiful? Isn't she wonderful? I can't believe it."

Patsy nodded.

"She is. Just as sweet as can be, too. Although I declare, the girl has so much on her plate, I don't know how she knows whether she's coming or going. She's been driving down from Gainesville to see you and driving back to take care of the kids and get Ethan to soccer. It sounds like their dad doesn't help out a whole lot."

"She told me a little about the ex-husband today. Sounds like a real jerk. Have you met the kids? Grandkids! Can you believe I'm a grandmother?"

I rolled my eyes as I handed the paper to her, and then waited to smile with her as she read it.

"Yes! I've met Eva and Ethan, and they are both delightful. I can't wait for you to meet them. And yes, this Brad character needs someone to knock a knot on his head. But did she tell you about Levi?"

I nodded and motioned for her to say more.

"Oh, he's a dreamboat. Dark brown hair, dark brown eyes, and muscles for days. And I tell you what, he sure seems to adore our girl. His eyes light up when he looks at her. Did she tell you how they met?"

I grinned as I took the paper back with a nod.

"It's a wonder they're even speaking to each other after that rough start!"

"I think they have you to thank for that! When he drove her to my house and found out you were in the hospital, he just drove her right on up here and refused to leave until she was settled. Then he came back. Several times. I'd say he's quite smitten."

My smile widened, and I lay back against the pillow, my heart overflowing with the thought of Caroline being happy.

"You look like a kitten who's gotten her fill of milk. So content."

I nodded.

She looked at her watch and frowned.

"I need to go. George will be expecting me for dinner. The nurses said you'll likely be moved to a private room in the morning, so we won't have these time limitations on visits. I hope you were okay with me not coming in again this afternoon. They try to keep it to one visitor in the room, and I figured you and Caroline needed that time together."

"It was wonderful," I wrote. *"She answered all my questions and shared so much. It was a dream come true. Thank you."*

"She told me before she left to have dinner with Levi that you'd had a lot of questions for her. She said she held off asking any questions of you, but you know you can't avoid that forever, right?"

I picked up the pen again.

"I'll answer whatever she asks. I don't intend to hide anything from her."

Patsy arched an eyebrow, her expression stern.

"Even if it's about her father? Because you know that's going to be one of her first questions."

I nodded with all the reluctance I felt. I had known from the moment I tried to find her that if we connected, it was inevitable that she would want to know about him. Undoubtedly, she would want to find him, too. I couldn't bear to think of the confrontation that lay beyond that when he discovered the secret I'd kept hidden. But she deserved to know, and so did he.

"I know it can't be avoided."

"You told me when I asked before that you didn't want to discuss him with me, and I can respect that. You don't have to tell me anything, but I think you should know that—"

A nurse came in and greeted us, and Patsy's words fell away.

"Guess what, Ms. Russo? You're getting sprung! No more ICU for you."

She was joined by a couple more nurses, and Patsy stood and gathered her purse.

"I'll head out and let them get you settled. I need to go home and get George some dinner, but I can come back up and spend the night if you'd like."

I shook my head as I wrote out my answer.

"No, that's okay. You've been here plenty long enough. Go home. See George. Take a bubble bath."

She smiled and put her hand over mine with a gentle squeeze.

"I'll see you in the morning, then. Sleep tight, and sweet dreams."

I thanked her, but I was pretty sure there was no way my dreams could be any sweeter than my day had been.

CHAPTER 6
Caterina

I woke to the sun streaming through the windows of my hospital room and my life looking brighter than it had in years.

While I still wasn't out of the woods completely with the lung infection, the doctor seemed pleased with my progress, and I felt better with every passing hour. I had more energy, I was more alert, and I was able to talk for brief periods without coughing.

Much of my excitement could be attributed to Caroline. I had a whole new set of questions that had come to me since she left.

My first thought upon waking had been fear that she might have been a dream, but when the nurses mentioned her and Patsy visiting, I sighed with relief and rejoiced at my good fortune.

For years, I'd fantasized about meeting my daughter again. Of a tender reunion where I was able to express my love and tell her I was sorry. The reality had been much sweeter than anything I'd pictured, and I couldn't help daydreaming about what the future might hold for us. Would Caroline and I become friends, or perhaps more? I didn't dare think I'd ever assume a motherly role in her life. I might have given birth to her, but she had a mother who had raised her when I couldn't, and I knew I'd never take that place. I had no desire to. Still, I couldn't squelch the hope in my heart that we might be close.

Be like family in some way.

I still couldn't believe I had grandchildren. I closed my eyes to recall their faces from the photos, wanting to commit each feature to memory. I longed to meet them, and I hoped they would accept me in their lives.

The door of my room creaked, and I opened my eyes, expecting to see a nurse, or perhaps Caroline or Patsy.

My breath caught in my throat at the sight of him, and I knew that the little voice of hope in the recesses of my heart had been right all along. William's visit had been real. He wasn't a dream or a hallucination.

I sat up, my hand immediately going to my hair in some ridiculous concern over my appearance. I was in a hospital gown, fresh out of a medically-induced coma. He'd already seen me the day before in a bipap mask, and the last time he'd seen me before that, I'd been sixteen-years-old. Now, I was over fifty, and no sweep of my hair with my palm was going to erase the march of time or the effects of a two-week hospital stay.

"You're awake. You look like you're feeling better," he said, and his voice sent quivers rippling over my skin.

How was he here? How had he found me?

And more importantly, *why* was he here?

I stared at him, dumbfounded, unable to comprehend that this moment was really happening. I suppose that given the events of the past twenty-four hours, nothing should have surprised me, but I was speechless. I had no idea what to say.

He walked over and stood by my bedside, and I pushed myself up to sit taller. The movement made me cough, and as I reached for the cup of water on the table, he leaned over and retrieved it for me.

"Thank you," I whispered once the coughs had subsided.

The tenderness in his gaze as our eyes locked surprised me, and my heart pounded with such intensity that I was sure he could hear it.

A tiny door deep within me sprang open—a door that had been long locked and barred—and forbidden memories rushed forth from their hiding place behind it, filling my head with him.

William on the beach in the glow of the setting sun. William in the saddle with his head tossed back in laughter. William's fingers trembling as they grazed across my skin. William's lips crushing mine. William's sleeping form that morning the sun rose too early.

My eyes filled with tears, and I blurted out the words I'd longed to say to him for most of my life.

"I'm sorry."

He shook his head and looked down at his hands.

"Don't."

"I'm so sorry," I said as my tears flowed down my cheeks.

He pinched the bridge of his nose between his thumb and forefinger and squeezed his eyes shut. "Now's not the time. You need to rest. You need to get well."

"How'd you find me?" I asked, my voice breaking.

"It's a long story, but don't worry about that right now. You need to focus on getting better."

He looked at the ceiling and blinked several times, and then he met my eyes again.

We stared at each other, his eyes glassy with unfallen tears as mine continued to fall.

"I'm sorry," I said again.

It was all I could say. The only words I could muster. I meant it with every fiber of my being. Every ounce of my soul. And yet, it would never be enough. The past could never be undone. But it was what I had needed to say to him a million times over the years, every instance he'd crossed my mind. Every time I saw a turtle or a horse or a daisy. Every time I saw a redhead or picked up a book. Every time I thought of love or loss. It was all I had to offer him.

"I'm so sorry."

"Catherine, stop. Don't. We don't have to do this right now."

Hearing my name on his lips—the name I'd abandoned when I left the girl he knew behind—ripped away what was left of my defenses, and I heaved a great sob as I covered my mouth with my hand. He inhaled deeply and looked to the ceiling, and then he released the breath with a huff and took a step back.

"This was a bad idea. You need rest. I just wanted to…"

He cut off his words, and I leaned forward, wanting to reach for him but grasping the bedrail instead.

"I'm gonna go," he said as he moved around the edge of the bed, and I cried out in a panic.

"No, please! William, please don't go. Please."

He stopped, but he stood facing the door, not turning back to me.

I ignored the pain in my throat and drew in a ragged breath, taking it in slowly so I didn't send myself into another coughing fit.

"You wanted to what? What were you going to say?"

He swore softly, and then he turned to stand at the foot of my bed. I flinched at the hurt in his eyes, but I squared my shoulders and met his gaze, willing to take whatever punishment his pain gave me.

"I just wanted to see you again. To know that it was really you. To know you were going to be okay."

His kind concern undid me in ways his anger never would have. I deserved his ire. I deserved his venom. I didn't deserve his kindness, and a stabbing pain tore through my chest, making my heart feel like it would cave in on itself.

"I'm sorry," I said again.

"Would you stop saying that?" He spat the words out, and I sensed that the anger I sought lay just beneath the surface.

We both fell silent, but then I couldn't hold the words back. I had to say them.

"I never meant to hurt you, William. I swear I did what I had to do to protect you."

"Oh, for Christ's sake, Catherine. We can't discuss this now. You're barely able to talk. Barely able to breathe. You've just stepped away from death's door. I should go."

"You're right. I was at death's door, and I have no guarantee I won't be back there again. My prognosis is good, but I'm not out of danger. There's too much that needs to be said. Things you need to know. It has to be now. Please."

The words were the most I had spoken since I'd woken from the sedation, and it took everything I had to get them out. I gripped my throat with my hand and swallowed hard, focusing on the physical pain in order to survive the emotional.

"I never wanted to leave you, William. I didn't have a choice. I'm so sorry."

He wouldn't look at me, and I wondered what he was holding back.

"I waited," he finally said. "Just like you asked me to. I waited for years. I worked, I saved, I prepared, and I waited. You never came back."

"I couldn't. When I asked you to wait in that letter, I didn't know … I didn't know everything that was going to happen. So, you got my letter all those years ago, then? Did Charlotte get it to you?"

He shook his head and continued to look down at his hands. I wished he would look at me. I wanted to see his eyes. I needed to know what he was feeling.

"No, I never saw Charlotte. I went to your house that morning, after you called and spoke to my mother."

"I was calling to tell you. To say goodbye."

"I know. I went to find you. I rang the bell, ready to demand to see you, but your maid opened the door, and she stepped out on the porch and pulled the door closed behind her. She told me if I knew what was good for us both, I would get out of there before I was seen. I said I wouldn't leave without talking to you, and she said you weren't there. That he'd taken you away, just like he'd threatened to do. She handed me the letter and went back inside."

The realization that he'd come for me shouldn't have surprised me, but it hit me like a ton of bricks, bringing back feelings I'd suppressed for far too long. My chest heaved with the weight of it, and a coughing fit seized me.

"I'll get the nurse," he said, but I shook my head and motioned toward the water pitcher on the table.

He rushed to fill my cup and held it to my lips as I drank, and then he stepped back as I took it from him. His face was contorted with concern, and I worried he would leave to get a nurse if I couldn't get it under control.

"I'm fine," I croaked out as I held the cup for him to pour more water.

"We don't have to do this now. This is ridiculous. You're ill, and this can wait. Hell, it's waited all this time, hasn't it?"

I shook my head, unwilling to let it go any longer without the truth being revealed.

"There are things you should know."

Someone tapped on the door, and I called, "Come in," without considering who it might be.

Caroline flung the door open with a cheery "Good morning!", and my heart damned near stopped in my chest.

A full-out panic exploded within me, and the dark secrets I'd held so tightly twisted threatened to turn me inside out. Would he see her and know? How would I explain her presence? Or his? It wasn't supposed to happen like this. It wasn't supposed to happen at all!

"Could you give us a minute?" I asked, but my voice sounded clipped and curt, which wasn't my intent. I cleared my throat, intending to speak again in a softer tone, but her stunned expression knocked me for a loop.

Did she know? Did she somehow guess?

I glanced from Caroline to William, alarmed to see the same startled expression on his face.

He couldn't know. How would he? There was no way.

It had to be paranoia. Fear of being exposed.

"Sure," Caroline said before leaving the room.

I watched the door close and turned my gaze back to William, who had gone white.

"She's mine, isn't she?" he asked through clenched teeth, his struggle to stay composed evident in his rigid stance.

My entire body went numb. I couldn't breathe. I couldn't think straight.

How did he know?

How long had he known? Surely, that one chance encounter hadn't given it away. Had my secret not been as carefully concealed as I thought?

"How did you find out?" I whispered when I found my voice.

He sank into the chair next to the bed and rubbed his hands across his face.

"I didn't know for sure," he said as he leaned back in the chair, blowing out a long exhale as he stared out the window. "It was a hunch. A feeling. I met her recently, and there was something there. I couldn't quite put my finger on it. She said she was in town to meet her birth mother, Cat Russo. Who's that, by the way?"

The strangest sensation of relief flooded over me, and I almost laughed at the release of the weight I'd carried.

It was all out. It was in the open. There was nothing more to hide.

For better or worse, the secrets could all be laid bare. I didn't have to hold them anymore.

"Cat Russo is the phoenix who rose from the ashes of Catherine Johnson. The girl I was—the girl you knew—she died, and Cat took her place."

He sat hunched over in the chair with his head in his hands.

I longed to go to him. To hold him. But I'd given up that right long ago.

"You could have told me," he said when he finally looked back up. "I would have been there. We could have faced it together."

I shook my head. "I couldn't. My father would have destroyed you. He would have made your life a living hell. He might have even killed you, for all I knew. I couldn't take that chance."

"But you had our child, Catherine. You carried her, gave birth to her, and never even told me. All this time, all these years, I've had a daughter, and I never knew. I didn't get to see her grow up or be a part of her life."

"Neither did I!"

He jumped to his feet. "But you got to decide that! You had a choice. I didn't!"

"No, you're wrong. I had no choice. If I chose anything, it was to protect you. To keep you safe from the mistake I made."

"The mistake we made!" His voice had grown louder as he towered over my bed, and I shrank back, though I was certain he'd never hurt me. He saw my reaction and backed away from the bed. "I'm sorry," he said, regaining his composure. "We made a child. Not a mistake. And she was our burden to bear, but you chose to bear it alone. You never gave me the option to stand beside you. To do the right thing. By you or by her."

"I couldn't," I whispered, my tears flowing once more. "You don't understand."

"You're right. I don't."

He walked toward the door, and I had no words to stop him.

He stood still for a moment, and then he turned to look back at me, his eyes filled with tears.

"Does she know?" he asked, his voice hoarse with emotion. "Does she know I'm her father?"

I shook my head and wrapped my arms tightly around me. "I don't think so. I don't know how she would. I've never told a soul."

"She deserves to know," he said, pulling the door open. "You need to tell her."

CHAPTER 7
William

It was all I could do to keep my emotions in check as I left Catherine's room. My insides were twisted into knots as I tried to process everything that had come to light in the past few days, and I was all at once angry, hurt, betrayed, bewildered, and sad.

I shouldn't have gone back to see her. I'm not sure what I thought it would accomplish. I'd confirmed on the first visit that Caterina Russo was indeed Catherine Johnson, which meant that Caroline was most likely my daughter.

I suppose I wanted to hear it straight from the source. I wanted her to know that I knew about her deception. That I knew what she'd kept hidden from me. I wanted her to confirm that it was true.

And if I was being honest with myself, I wanted to see her when she wasn't just coming out of a comatose state. I wanted to see her awake and alert.

As pathetic as it seemed, even to me, I couldn't deny that I'd wanted the chance to see Catherine once more.

So much time had passed. So much life had been lived. By both of us.

Had it really been thirty-six years since we pledged our hearts to each other and made plans for a future that would never come to fruition?

True, I'd still achieved some of those goals without her. I had the horse farm I'd always wanted. I'd seen the realization of my rehabilitation facility and added a training center. I was respected among my peers, and I'd achieved a level of wealth that surely rivaled anything Catherine's father could have claimed, along with the power and status that came with it.

But I had to wonder, as I had many times over the years since we parted, how my life might have turned out differently if I had never met Catherine Johnson.

I probably would have gone to college as I had planned. Earned a degree and settled into my career much sooner and with much less blood, sweat, and tears.

Of course, then I never would have met Revae, who taught me how to give my heart over to love again after losing Catherine. Our marriage was one of the things I was most proud of in my life, and our daughter, Piper, was my absolute pride and joy.

Piper. Dammit. How was I going to explain to her that she had a half-sister? She wasn't going to take it well; I was sure of that. We'd always had such a special bond, a close relationship of which even her mother was envious. How could I make Piper understand that this revelation would not in any way affect her standing in my heart?

At the same time, I couldn't just ignore that I had another child. One who was a grown woman with children of her own.

Oh, God. The kids. Ethan and Eva. I was a grandfather, for Christ's sake. That wasn't something to be taken lightly.

I had no idea what Caroline's reaction would be when she discovered I was her father, but I hoped she would allow me to be a part of her life. A part of the kids' lives. We had so much time to make up for. So much lost that we could never get back.

I struggled to grasp what it all meant.

It was too much to think about. Too much to comprehend. I had a child I had neglected through no fault of my own.

Or did I bear at least part of the blame? Perhaps I should have known, somehow.

Maybe I should have tried harder to find Catherine, or to dig into the reason for her absence. Had my child grown up without me because I wasn't strong enough to stand up to Catherine's father? If I had been a better man, would we have raised our daughter together?

I wondered what man had taken my rightful place. Had Caroline's father been good to her? Did they have a relationship similar to the one I had with Piper? Had she been happy? I hoped my child had been loved.

My emotions overwhelmed me once more, and I reached for the handkerchief in my pocket just as I looked up to see the woman who had been that child walking toward me. I wiped at my tears and tried to compose myself, dreading the confrontation she was entitled to.

"You told me you didn't know her," Caroline said, her face flushed with anger and her whole body visibly trembling. "You said the name didn't ring a bell."

"It didn't."

"Then why are you visiting her? Yesterday, and again today. If you don't know her, why are you here?"

I still couldn't believe this was my daughter. My own flesh and blood. I wanted to wrap my arms around her and tell her I was sorry. I wanted to be given back the time we'd lost. I wanted to ask her all the questions that plagued me about her life. But it was not the time or the place. Not yet. She deserved answers first, more answers than I could give her.

"I said I didn't know Caterina Russo. And I didn't. I still don't. I knew Catherine Johnson. And it's not my place to tell you any more than that."

"Who's Catherine Johnson?"

"Again, I'm not the one who needs to explain this to you. I'm still trying to process it all myself. But I didn't lie to you, Caroline. I didn't know."

It was important that she know I was telling the truth. She needed to understand I hadn't misled her, and that I hadn't known of her existence and ignored its importance all these years.

The dam threatened to break, and I didn't know how much longer I could hold tight to the reins of everything raging inside me.

"I have to go," I said, moving to step past her. "We'll talk soon. You need to talk to her first."

And like a coward, I walked away from the child I'd never known before the weight of the situation crushed me.

CHAPTER 8
Caterina

He was right, and I knew it. I had to tell Caroline the truth. She needed to know who her father was. She deserved to know why I'd given her up for adoption and why he never knew about her.

But why did it have to all come to a head so soon?

I needed more time. More time to get to know her. I wanted her to see my heart first. To show her that I wasn't the person I'd once been. To prove that her very existence had made me a better human being.

She'd seemed so happy to find me, but what if that changed when the truth was revealed?

The decisions I'd made—the paths I'd chosen for us all—I'd done what I did to protect William and Caroline.

How could I make them understand that?

William had every right to be angry. He'd been treated unfairly. It was unjust. He didn't deserve what had been done to him.

What if Caroline felt the same way? Once it was all out in the open, would the two of them ever be able to forgive me for what I'd stolen from them?

A light rap sounded on the door, and Caroline peeked in.

I dabbed at my tears with a tissue, hastily pasting on a smile to greet her.

"Caroline, I worried I had dreamed you. I thought I would wake this morning and find you'd never really been here at all."

She walked straight to my bed and sat on the edge of it, her face unsmiling and her arms crossed tightly over her chest.

"Who's Catherine Johnson?" she asked, and I knew I would get

31

no more time to delay the inevitable. There was only one person who could have told her my real name, and that meant they'd already talked. The universe must hate me. How else would the father of my child find her before I did without even knowing about her, and then get to tell her the truth before I could?

"You talked to William." I held my smile in place, trying to lighten the mood to keep from losing it completely. "I can't believe the two of you met already. I've lived here twelve years, and in all that time, I've seen him from afar once. But you come to town and meet him almost immediately. Seems like fate, don't you think?"

"Is William my father?"

Acknowledging that for the first time was even harder than I'd ever imagined it would be. One measly tissue was incapable of handling the flow of my tears, and I grabbed a handful as I prepared to share the secret I'd buried.

"Yes. He is. He didn't know that until today, though."

Her face fell, and her shoulders sank as she wrapped her arms even tighter around herself.

"Why? Why didn't he know?"

It was taking every ounce of resolve I had not to collapse into sobs and beg for forgiveness. I tilted my head back and blinked rapidly, determined to hold it together.

"Because I refused to name him. I thought I could protect him. Keep him from getting hurt. Or worse. But I guess I couldn't protect anyone. All three of us got hurt in some way, didn't we?"

Her eyes held compassion as she reached forward and laid her hand on my arm.

"What do you mean, *name him?* What happened?"

I drew in a deep breath, and my throat contracted as I started coughing. My ribs and abdomen both ached from the frequent fits I'd been having, and my throat burned with every movement.

I took the water Caroline offered, trying to force down swallows between coughs. By the time the fit eased and I could breathe again, I was exhausted. The day had been an emotional rollercoaster so far, and my body cried out for a respite in its compromised and weakened state. I wanted to lay back and close my eyes. I wanted to disappear into the sleep realm and leave the heartache behind.

"What happened, Cat?" Caroline asked, unwilling to give up on her pursuit of the truth. "Who were you trying to protect us from?

Who is Catherine Johnson?"

There would be no sleep just yet.

I'd run from Catherine Johnson as long as possible, but I think I'd always known I couldn't escape her forever. The time had come to face my past.

CHAPTER 9
Caterina

I don't think I was born bad. I didn't come into the world arrogant, pompous, haughty, and vain. It took my parents several years to create the self-important, attention-seeking monster I became.

Not that I blame them entirely. I bear responsibility for the choices I made, especially there towards the end of it all. But I was groomed as a product of my environment, and you can't unlearn what you're taught until you know better.

I believe my mother was overwhelmed by parenting right from the start. She had a difficult pregnancy that kept her violently ill and bedridden for months, followed by a horrific breech delivery that nearly took her life. Once I was released from her body, she refused to have any deep level of involvement with me again.

It wasn't that she didn't love me—she adored me. She just wasn't cut out to be a mother. Not a hands-on one, anyway. She hired the best nannies and tutors, she bought the most expensive clothes, and she filled multiple playrooms with more toys, books, and gadgets than any one child could have possibly played with. Anything I asked for, I received. No price tag too high, no request too extravagant. She parented by purchasing.

As long as all my physical needs were met and I had every material possession my heart could desire, she could tell herself I was well-cared for and she had done her job. As I grew older, her parenting morphed into using financial and material bribery to calm me down, shut me up, or remove me from her to-do list.

I never doubted her love, and I never questioned the way she showed it. It wasn't until years later after much therapy that I realized how deficient her mothering had been, and how that had influenced who I became.

Of course, she wasn't my only parental influence.

My father never made a secret of the fact that he wished he'd had a son. Someone who could carry on his name, his company, and the status he'd worked so hard to achieve.

Unfortunately, my dramatic gestation and life-threatening entry into the world resulted in my mother being told she could never have another baby, so my father was stuck with a daughter as his only child.

I don't think he ever forgave either of us.

I've often wondered why he didn't just leave my mother and find another woman who could bear him a worthy male heir. I suppose he felt some sense of loyalty to her. She'd married him when he had not a penny to his name, and she'd stood beside him on his rise to wealth. And who knows? Perhaps he really loved her—as much as he was capable of loving anyone. Whatever his reasoning, he kept her by his side and punished us both for me not being a boy.

Girls were merely trophy pieces. Pretty things to be dressed up and shown off. Best seen and not heard.

"Catherine, my jewel," he'd call out from the bottom of the stairs during his frequent dinner parties. "Come down and show my guests how well my daughter plays the piano."

Or, "Come here, my jewel, and impress my dinner guests with a recitation of poetry. Choose one of my favorites for them."

And, "Allow my daughter to enthrall you with a soliloquy. You'll see she's inherited her father's gift for oration."

He would beam as they applauded my performances, and then he'd rattle off my latest achievements or accomplishments before dismissing me without another glance.

In the beginning, I basked in those moments, eager to please him and gain his approval. I took his affirmations as confirmation of his love, so I craved his spotlight and did all I could to stand in it. But I soon grew to realize that my only worth in his eyes was tied to the accolades he could receive through me. He'd boast and brag to earn the admiration of his audience, but the swelled chest and flashy smile were for public display only. When no one was around, I was invisible.

It didn't take me long to discover that misbehaving garnered me much more of his time than my futile efforts at being the perfect daughter.

It started with insubordination at school, which always prompted a phone call home followed by a speech from my father on how I was expected to represent the family. It soon progressed to skipping classes with my friends, cheating on exams, and playing pranks on teachers. With every incident, he raged harder and longer, but I had his attention.

I was thirteen the first time I got caught sneaking alcohol from the well-stocked bar in his study, and just shy of fourteen the first time he was called to come get me from a friend's house because I'd had too much to drink.

"Catherine, do you have any idea how embarrassed I am at this moment?" he asked as he stood at the back of the car while I vomited on the side of the road not far from our house. "You have completely humiliated our family. You realize the other parents are probably talking about your mother and me right now, don't you? Can't you see how poorly your behavior reflects on us? How it makes us look?"

He never once expressed concern over my condition or counseled me on the dangers of drinking so heavily, and every time the phone rang in the middle of the night after that, he sent a member of the household staff to bring me home.

By the time the maid found a bag of pills and marijuana in my room when I was fifteen, he had already begun to tell my mother that he was going to wash his hands of me and send me to a boarding school up north, far away from his precious public image.

"Catherine, please," Mother would say. "Why must you act out this way? Your father works hard to ensure we have the best of everything, and this is how you repay him? He'll send you away, darling; don't think he won't. I won't be able to stop him. Think of how devastated I will be if you're off at some boarding school and I can never see you. Why can't you think of my feelings?"

She even resorted to bribery in hopes she could change my ways. She dangled weekend shopping trips to New York if I made it through a week without a call from the principal. Promised Chanel bags if I passed a test. She bought me a convertible the day I got my driver's license in exchange for a promise to stop drinking and focus more on my studies.

None of it mattered.

Her pleas for me to toe the line and act like a well-bred young lady were no match for my dedication to making my father pay for his rejection and dismissal. I was on a collision course with self-destruction, and I didn't care who I damaged along the way.

In the middle of that maelstrom, I met William Ward.

CHAPTER 10
Caterina

We couldn't have been more opposite.

He was shy and quiet, preferring to disappear in the crowd, whereas I was loud and obnoxious, desperate to be the center of attention.

William was a dedicated straight-A student in a public school, while I was failing multiple classes at my exclusive private school and skipping the tutoring appointments my mother scheduled, opting instead to ride around getting high with my friends.

I was an only child, spoiled beyond measure and raised in the lap of luxury with no appreciation for the value of anything I possessed. He was the baby of five, a hard worker in a tight-knit, lower-middle class family struggling to make ends meet.

They say opposites attract, but there were no obvious sparks the first time we met.

He ignored me, in fact, and showed no interest at all. Which, of course, only furthered my determination make him notice me.

I'd known I was beautiful back then. I had no shortage of people telling me so, and I could look in the mirror and see it. I had curves in all the right places. A gorgeous head of black hair that fell in thick waves down the middle of my back. Full lips that could form a perfect pout if things didn't go my way. Brilliant green eyes fringed with black lashes that I batted with great skill when I needed to charm someone. Even though I was only sixteen, I knew the power I wielded, and I used it to my advantage over the teenage boys who panted after me and vied for my affection.

But not William. He seemed unfazed by me, and it drove me mad.

He was working on a crew building fences for the estate next to ours the first time I saw him. I'd gone over to visit my friend, Charlotte, who was the same age as me and probably equally as spoiled, self-serving, and conceited. Her parents always thought I was the bad influence of the two, and they weren't wrong about that, but it was Charlotte's idea to go check out the boys on the fence crew that day.

She'd seen them coming in from the back of the property the evening before, and one particularly tall, dark, and handsome boy had caught her eye. I'm sure her mother, the former debutante from Charleston, would have had a heart attack if she'd known we were primping and preening in front of the mirror to go out and flirt with the hired help, but she didn't ask our destination when Charlotte told her we were going for a horseback ride.

Our arrival at the fence line shut down production, and the irritated foreman called an official water-break when he realized he had no chance of redirecting their focus back to the task at hand. The man had worked for Charlotte's family most of her life, and he'd learned long ago that it was usually less hassle to let her have her way.

The sweat-drenched group of muscular young men practically oozed testosterone as they flirted and bantered with Charlotte and me, and we both played coy sitting atop the horses as we looked down on our wannabe suitors.

They gathered around us like bees to honey. All except one—a slender redhead sitting by himself on a tree stump with his nose buried in a book.

"Who's that?" I asked as I shook my head to refuse the cup of water one of the boys offered me.

"Oh, that one don't talk much," the boy said. "He'd rather read. So, what are you girls doing later?"

I stared at the redhead bent over his pages, seemingly oblivious to our presence and the commotion it had caused.

"What's his name?" I asked as I slid off the horse and pulled off one of my riding gloves.

"Who cares?" another boy said. "Why would you want to waste your time with him? He's obviously not interested, but we're more than happy to talk to you."

"Yeah, he don't talk to anybody," another boy chimed in.

"I bet he'll talk to me." I accepted the challenge with a lifted chin and a swaying saunter as I walked toward the redhead.

He didn't acknowledge my approach, even though my boots had to be clearly in his view as he looked down at the book.

"Ahem," I said with a polite clearing of my throat. "I'm sorry to bother you, but I can't seem to get my glove off. It's too tight, and you look like you might be strong enough to help me."

I smiled in anticipation as I waited for him to look up, eager to see him wear the awestruck, dazzled expression boys got when I turned on the charm.

"Why do you need it off?" he said without glancing my way. "Aren't you just going to put it back on for the ride home?"

The snickers of the boys behind me stung, and I put my hand on my hip and shifted my weight to thrust my breasts forward in an enticing pose.

"What's your name?" I asked in my sweetest voice, choosing to ignore his question for the moment.

He flipped a page and glanced up at me. "William." He turned his attention back to his book before I had a chance to bat an eyelash.

I bent toward him, fully aware the movement would allow my shirt to fall forward and expose my chest in his line of vision when he looked up again. "Aren't you gonna ask my name?"

He shrugged and kept reading. "I wasn't planning to."

Their snickers turned to laughter, and my cheeks flamed hot as my resolve grew stronger. I snatched the book from his hands. "What's this book about?"

He sighed and met my eyes for the first time. His irises were the clearest blue I'd ever seen, but as he looked at me, they clouded with irritation.

"Look, I don't mean you any disrespect, but we only have a few minutes on break, and I'm really into this book. So, if it's all the same to you, I'd like to sit here and read while I can, okay?"

His words were polite and his voice calm, but I felt like he'd thrown a bucket of cold water on me.

I was embarrassed by his rejection, but I was also intrigued. No boy had ever resisted my charms in such a way before. Who was this William, and why didn't my powers of persuasion work on him?

I gave him back his book and walked away without another word, ignoring the stares and comments of the others as I climbed into the saddle. As we rode home, Charlotte babbled on about the boy she was interested in, but I wasn't listening. I was still dumbfounded by the strange redhead who would rather read some stupid old book than talk to me.

CHAPTER 11
Caterina

It hadn't taken much convincing to get Charlotte to go back out to the fence line the next day. Randall, the object of her affection, had mentioned a party when they talked the day before, and she'd been eager to get more details and scheme a way to attend without her parents knowing.

The foreman shook his head in frustration when he saw us coming, and he called out for a water break before we'd even reached the crew.

Any other time, I might have found their excitement at our return gratifying, but the one head I'd hoped to turn didn't even look in our direction as he walked away and settled cross-legged on the grass.

I dismounted and left Charlotte laughing with Randall and the others as I walked toward William.

The book he held had a red cover, but I was certain the one I'd snatched had been blue.

I sat down beside him and stretched my legs in front of me, leaning back on my hands to push my chest up.

"Hi. William, right?"

I knew damned well his name was William, but I was going for nonchalance.

He nodded with a sigh and turned a page.

"That's a different book, huh?" I leaned toward him as though I was interested in seeing what he was reading. "Did you finish the other one?"

He nodded again, still silent.

"Did it end the way you wanted it to?"

He looked at me, and I flashed my brightest smile.

41

"Do you enjoy reading?" he asked, and I sat up, thrilled that I'd finally engaged him in conversation.

"Um, yeah, sure," I lied. "Who doesn't like to read?"

"Then I'm sure you understand what it's like to be immersed in a book and have someone keep trying to talk to you."

I'd never been immersed in a book, so I had no way to relate to his question, but I had been rejected and dismissed, and my angry response to the familiar feeling flared.

"Why are you so rude?"

"I'm not trying to be rude," he said, his blue eyes wide and unblinking. "I don't even know you. I didn't ask you to come over here. I didn't invite you into a conversation. I was sitting here by myself trying to read, and I thought I made it clear yesterday that's what I prefer to do on my breaks. So, it seems to me, you're the one being rude."

My mouth fell open, and hot indignation flooded my cheeks.

"Geez, I was trying to be friendly, but never mind. Go ahead and read your book. You probably don't have anything interesting to say anyway."

I stood and brushed the grass off the back of my jeans as he mumbled, "Nothing that would interest you, I'm sure."

"What?" I spun around and stared down at him with my hands on my hips. "What's that supposed to mean?"

He shrugged. "I don't think you and I would have any interests in common."

"Really? Why would you think that? Like you said, you don't even know me, so you have no idea what my interests are."

He raised an eyebrow and shrugged one shoulder as he looked back down at the book. "You're right."

I never stopped to consider that his words were probably true. It didn't matter. I only knew that he was the most maddening boy I'd ever met. It was bad enough that he resisted my best efforts at charming him and flat-out told me he'd rather read than talk to me. But then for him to insinuate that even if he wasn't reading he wouldn't be interested in me at all was too much.

I marched away from him not even making an effort to saunter or sway. I went straight to the horse and hefted myself into the saddle without so much as a smile in the direction of the other boys, who were all standing around looking dejected as Charlotte and Randall stood off to the side talking in low voices.

"I'm heading back," I called out to her, grabbing the reins and urging the horse forward without waiting for her.

"Catherine! Wait! What are you doing?"

I let the horse walk until she caught up with me, and then I nudged him to a trot.

"What's the matter, Catherine? What happened?"

"Nothing happened. I just don't care to spend my afternoon chatting with a bunch of fence workers. They're hot and sweaty and gross. Why are you wasting your time? It's not like your parents will let Randall show up at your front door and take you out on a date."

"Of course not! My mother would kill me if she knew I was even talking to him. Which is why you can't just take off and leave me down there to come back to the house on your own. What would she say if you came back without me? What would I tell her? Where would I say I'd been? We have to stick together."

I squeezed my knees against the horse's ribs, encouraging him to go faster and put more distance between me and that annoying William boy. I couldn't believe he'd dare speak to me the way he did. He obviously had no idea who I was. Who my father was. He didn't realize how fortunate he was that I'd paid him the least bit of attention. He was right about one thing, though. There was nothing I would possibly have in common with some guy who spent his time pounding fence posts in the ground and reading boring books.

Over the next couple of days, pushing William from my thoughts proved harder than I thought it would be, and when Charlotte begged me to ride out with her one more time, I wasn't nearly as reluctant to go as I should have been.

"I'm going over to Charlotte's to ride horses," I told my mother as she sat at her desk going over seating arrangements for an upcoming dinner party.

"I don't know if that's a good idea, dear. Your father is bringing someone for dinner, and you can't be late to the table. He'll want you on your best behavior."

I stared at the row of bookshelves behind her desk and walked over to peruse the titles, trailing my fingers along their spines.

"Do you have a book with something about a mockingbird in the title?"

"*To Kill A Mockingbird?* Yes, of course." She rose and went straight to the book on a shelf in the corner. "Are you reading it for school?"

"Not exactly." The book she handed me didn't have the red cover like William's. "I don't know if this is it."

"Well, if it's *To Kill A Mockingbird*, that's it. You should read it anyway, even if it's not for school. It's one of my favorite books."

"Really?" I flipped through the pages and tossed it into my purse. "Maybe I will. I'll be back in time for dinner."

She'd already returned to her seating chart with her glasses perched on the end of her nose. "Okay, dear. We're sitting promptly at six. Dressed to impress."

"Of course. Is there any other way to dress for dinner?"

She frowned at my sarcasm as I grinned and slipped out the door. I wished I had time to flip through the book and learn a couple of character names and pick out some key points. I had no problem fooling teachers into thinking I'd read assignments that way, so how hard could it be to fool William?

The crew was a little less enthusiastic than before when we arrived. I suppose they'd decided Charlotte was going to talk to Randall and I was going to annoy William, so there was no need for them to make an effort. Even the foreman seemed less irritated by our interruption as he called for a water-break.

William made eye contact with me as I dismounted, but then he turned and walked away, pulling his book from his back pocket before sitting on the grass.

I followed him and plopped down on the ground next to him, not saying a word as I retrieved the hardcover from my purse and opened it to a random page fairly close to the beginning.

He was silent next to me, and I thought I would self-combust from the effort of not saying anything.

After what felt like an eternity but was probably more like three minutes, I glanced down at the book in his hands, surprised to see it was not the same book he'd held a couple of days earlier.

"What are you reading now?" I blurted out, unable to hide my frustration that he'd ruined my scheme.

He turned the cover so I could see it. It had a grim picture of a hotel on the front.

"*The Shining?* I thought you were reading this." I held up my book.

"I was. I finished it."

"But you just started it a couple of days ago."

44

He shrugged and opened his book once more. "I'm a fast reader."

I closed *To Kill A Mockingbird* and put it back in my purse, no longer interested in keeping up appearances.

"What's this one about?"

He sighed, and I braced for another dressing down, but instead, he flipped the book over to the back cover and handed it to me.

I groaned. "Can't you just tell me?"

"Why? I thought you liked to read." His mouth curved into the closest thing to a grin I'd gotten from him since we'd met.

"Whatever."

The grin almost became a smile. "Okay. It's about a writer who takes his family to a mountain lodge for a job as a caretaker for the winter, and things start to get weird and go sinister."

"Oh. Sounds interesting."

He rolled his eyes and opened the book to continue reading.

I sat and stared at him for a couple of minutes, forcing myself to remain silent.

"Aren't you going to read the book you brought?" he asked as he turned to look at me.

He was handsome when he wasn't scowling and annoyed. His clear blue eyes held the slightest hint of mirth, and without the tight line his mouth had been drawn in when I'd seen him before, his lips were full. A deep ginger stubble peppered his jawline here and there, and a splattering of freckles splashed across his forehead and nose.

"I'll read it later. It's too hot out to read right now."

"How far have you gotten?"

I glanced down at the book sticking out of my purse and wished again that I'd taken the time to flip through it for talking points.

"Um, not far. But it's good. I'm enjoying it. Did you enjoy it?"

"Yeah. I've read it several times."

My eyes widened in disbelief. "The same book? You've read the same book several times? Why?"

He chuckled.

"Because I enjoy the story? I get a lot out of it? I feel like I know the characters, and I find something different in it every time I read it."

"Okay, boys, back to work," the foreman said with a wave of his hand. "Ladies, thank you for the distraction, but Ms. Charlotte's dad will be wondering why we aren't making any more progress with this fence if we keep having these extended breaks."

William stood and shoved his book back into his pocket, and I frowned in disappointment. We'd finally broken through the ice and begun to have a conversation, and it was ending before I wanted it to.

He offered his hand to pull me to standing, and I smiled up at him as I took it.

"Randall told Charlotte about a party this weekend," I said as I brushed off my jeans and pulled my purse strap onto my shoulder. "Will you be there?"

"Not likely. I don't really do parties."

"Me either," I lied. "But I thought maybe if you were there and I was there, I might be farther into the book by then, and we'd be able to talk about it."

He shrugged and looked across the field. "I don't know. Parties aren't really my thing."

I nodded. 'Yeah, I get that. Totally. Well, enjoy your sinister book."

"I'm sure I will. King's a great writer."

"Who?"

He chuckled again, and I liked the way it sounded. I wondered what his laugh would be like.

"Stephen King. Please tell me you've at least heard of Stephen King."

"Oh, yeah, of course," I said with a dismissive wave of my hand. "Who hasn't heard of Stephen King, right?"

Charlotte was already in the saddle, and the other boys were getting back to work on the fence. William looked antsy to join them.

"All right, so maybe I'll see you around," I said, forcing my voice to sound like I didn't care if I did or didn't.

"You'll have to let me know what you think of *To Kill A Mockingbird*."

"Yeah, definitely."

I wondered as we rode back to the barn how he expected me to do that. I didn't know his last name, and he'd never asked for even my first name. I suppose he thought we'd be back out to the fence line, but we were on borrowed time with that. If Charlotte's mother discovered what we were doing, or if the foreman mentioned it to her father, we'd both be in trouble and forbidden to ride until the crew was done.

It wasn't until we'd dismounted and gotten the horses handed off to the stable boy that I looked at the time. It was five-forty. There was no way I could get home, shower, change, and be dressed to impress for dinner in twenty minutes. It seemed that even when I didn't try, I'd become destined to piss my father off.

CHAPTER 12
Caterina

Being tardy to dinner got me grounded for a week. Charlotte was mad I wasn't able to be her alibi or sidekick for Randall's party, which I thought was a bit unfair considering I was the one stuck in my house with nothing to do, and no one to talk to other than the household staff. Luckily, our maid, Isabel, had a great sense of humor and could make me laugh, but after she retreated to her rooms in the evenings, the silence was hard to bear. My parents stuck to their side of the house for the most part, and I stayed upstairs on my side, determined not to run into them and let them see how miserable I was.

William often took over my thoughts as I sulked in my room over the weekend, and at some point in my confinement, I picked up *To Kill A Mockingbird* and started reading. I think it was partly out of boredom and partly out of curiosity for what had interested him enough to make him read it multiple times.

I'd only gotten through a couple of pages in the book when I started fantasizing the conversations we could have. I hoped he would be impressed that I was still reading it, and I figured if we were discussing his favorite book, then he would finally be interested in what I had to say. Perhaps I'd even be witty enough to make his chuckle blossom into a full-blown laugh. Then, when it was time for me to go, he'd be sad for once. Infatuated rather than indifferent.

By the time Tuesday rolled around, I was stir-crazy and ready to get out of the house for something other than school. For once, I didn't mind going to my riding lesson at the equestrian center, even though it meant enduring an hour with my boring instructor.

The lesson prior to mine was running late, so I was told to sit on a bench outside the barn and wait for him to finish.

I'd only been waiting a few minutes when I looked up to see William walking toward me carrying a bucket and a shovel.

I smiled and stood to greet him with a little more enthusiasm than was necessary.

"Hey! What are you doing here?"

He glanced at me but never slowed his stride, unaware of how close we'd become during my imaginary conversations with him.

"I work here," he said as he walked toward the barn.

"Wait! Where are you going?" I followed him inside and watched as he began to shovel horse manure into the bucket. "Since when do you work here? Did you quit working on the fence?"

"Nope. I work there, too."

I took a step back as a whiff of the manure reached my nostrils.

"You work two jobs? Why?"

"To pay for college next year."

"Why? Shouldn't your parents do that?"

He grimaced, and I didn't know if it was due to the smell or my question.

"Not everyone's parents can afford to pay for college."

"Oh, okay." I wasn't sure what else to say to that.

He moved past me with the bucket and went into the next stall to shovel.

I followed him and stepped up onto the bottom rail of the enclosure and leaned over the top one, trying to get a better look at his face as he worked.

"You're a senior, then?"

"Yep."

"So, did you just start working here? I've never seen you here before."

His quiet chuckle was hard to hear above the rattle of the gate as he swung it shut. "I've been working here almost two years."

"What? No way! I've been taking riding lessons here twice a month for a year. I've never seen you."

"I've been here."

"Have you seen me?"

"Yep." He opened a door at the end of the barn and walked toward the next building. I followed close on his heels, but I had to rush to keep up with his long stride.

"But you never said anything."

"Why would I?"

"No, I mean since we've been talking. You never said you'd seen me before."

"You never asked."

"There you are!" my instructor called from behind me. "Sorry for the delay. Ready to get started?"

I swore under my breath, and William must have heard me because he grinned.

Would there ever be a time that I could have a real-life conversation with him without being interrupted or dismissed? Every time we started talking, something got in the way.

"I have to go," I said, hoping he'd show some sign of disappointment.

"All right."

I stopped, but he kept walking without even looking my way. He gave no indication that he wished he could talk longer, and his indifference drove me nuts.

"Would you wait for a minute? I have to go the other way."

He turned and looked back at me, raising his hand to his eyes to block the sun.

"I've been reading the book, the *Mockingbird* book," I said. "And I wanted to talk to you about it."

"Okay, but I have to work, and you have your lesson."

Could he sound any less enthusiastic?

"Right, I know. But maybe we could talk later? I have some questions about the book."

"Ms. Johnson? Could we get started?" My instructor's tone conveyed his irritation.

I forced a polite smile as I waved in his direction.

"Coming, Mr. Wainwright!" I turned back to William. "So, can we?"

William looked away. "I don't know if that's such a good idea."

Mr. Wainwright called out my name again, louder than before, and William turned to go with a lackluster wave of his hand.

I sighed and went back to the barn, exasperated with both of them.

"Sorry," I mumbled to Mr. Wainwright as I neared the barn.

"Everything all right, Ms. Johnson?" He peered over my head in

William's direction.

"Everything's fine," I said, refusing to give him the explanation he wanted. "Ready?"

Thoughts of William distracted me throughout the lesson. I didn't understand why he captivated me the way he did. His ability to ignore me while in my presence infuriated me, and he'd been right when he said we likely had nothing in common. But the less attention he gave me, the more I wanted it from him.

When we returned to the barn, I was disappointed to see a different stable boy cleaning stalls. I took my time preparing to leave, hoping William might walk in or make some effort to tell me goodbye. I waited until my instructor had moved on to his next lesson, and then I approached the stable boy.

"Excuse me. Do you know if William's still here?"

He smiled at me, the type of exuberant smile I wished William would give me.

"Nah. He left already. Is there something I can help you with?"

"No, thanks." My shoulders slumped in disappointment.

"I could get him a message."

"No, that's okay. Thank you anyway."

What was wrong with me? Why was I so hellbent on pursuing someone who obviously wasn't attracted to me? He'd been clear from the moment I met him that he wasn't interested, and yet here I was, making a fool of myself trying to change his mind. And for what? It wasn't like I would actually go out with him. We were from two entirely different worlds. My parents would never allow me to date a stable boy who built fences on the side. Not that I would want to. That wasn't what this was about, anyway. I wasn't attracted to William. I just wanted him to be attracted to me.

I squared my shoulders as I made my way to the lockers that lined the wall outside the staff room, determined to put the whole thing behind me. I had no reason to talk to him or leave him a message. In fact, I never had to speak to him again. I would just forget he'd ever existed and not give him another thought.

But then I opened my locker, and a small, yellow piece of paper had been squeezed through the vent on the front of it. I unfolded it to see a name and a phone number written in neat block letters.

William Ward wanted me to call him.

A slow grin spread across my face, and a smug feeling of

satisfaction filled me.

He *was* interested. He wanted to hear what I had to say.

I decided I'd wait until after dinner to call so I didn't appear eager. My father had a business associate joining us, and it took forever to get through the courses and excuse myself to retreat to my room. I sat on the floor next to my bed and dialed his number, hoping he would answer so I didn't have to ask for him or say who was calling.

"Ward Residence," said a female voice after the third ring.

"Oh, um, hi. Is William there?"

"Just a minute." She yelled his name as she put the phone down, and I twisted the pink phone cord around my fingers and closed my eyes as I waited for his voice on the line.

"Hello," he said, and a rush of excitement coursed through me.

"Hi. It's Catherine."

He didn't say anything at first, and I started to panic thinking maybe it wasn't him who left the note. Finally, he spoke.

"Hey. I wasn't sure that was the right locker, but I figured the pink lock was yours."

"Why would you think that?"

"Because you're always wearing pink."

I grinned at the fact that he knew what color I wore. It meant he had noticed me more than he let on.

"What did you want to ask me about the book?" he asked.

In all my imaginary conversations, I'd had something witty and insightful to say, but I couldn't remember any of those clever things.

"Oh, um, I just wanted to talk about it."

"Did you finish it?"

"No, not yet. I'm not a fast reader like you."

"That's okay. How far are you?"

I cringed, not wanting to admit the truth.

"I don't have, like, a page number to give you."

"Well, what's happening where you are?"

"They met some kid named Dill. What's up with those names? Scout, Atticus, Dill. Why such strange names?"

"I dunno," William said. "I never really thought about it."

"You didn't notice that they're weird?"

"I think I was more interested in the story. So, they just met Dill? That's like the first chapter."

"Yeah? So? I told you I'm not a fast reader. Besides, they started talking about lighting a fire under a turtle, so I quit reading. I really like turtles. They're probably like my favorite animal. I didn't want to read about them being mean to a turtle."

"They're not mean to a turtle," William said. "There is no turtle. It's an analogy."

"Whatever. Where are you going to college?"

"The University of Florida."

"Ugh!" I exclaimed, horrified at the thought of anyone staying so close to home. "Why? It's in Gainesville, which is, like, not even an hour away. Don't you want to get farther from Ocala?"

"Um, not really. I want to work with horses, and Ocala is kind of the best place to do that unless I want to move to Kentucky. Which I don't. My family is here."

"So, you want to buy horses? Like my Dad?"

"No. I want to take care of horses. Help them. I'm planning to be a veterinarian and specialize in equine medicine."

"Oh. My dad says people who are veterinarians just couldn't cut it at medical school."

"I think it's harder in some ways to be a veterinarian than a doctor. Your patients can't tell you what's wrong or where it hurts, and you can't explain to them that you might have to hurt them to make them feel better."

I considered his words as I sipped my lemonade. I hooked the phone cord around my big toe and extended my leg, watching the pink curls of the cord straighten to its full length.

"I guess I see your point. But veterinarians don't make as much money as doctors, do they?"

"They make enough. So, what do you want to be? Career-wise, I mean."

I shifted to lay on my back and stare at the ceiling, wishing I had a more impressive answer.

"I'm still deciding. My dad says I should be an attorney because I have a natural-born talent for arguing, but I'm not sure if he's serious about that. He might be saying it as an insult. I don't know. Do attorneys make a lot of money?"

"I guess. Depends on what kind of attorney, I suppose. Is making a lot of money important to you?"

I sat up and thought about the question. No one had ever asked me that before. I liked having money. It was great having nice clothes and servants to do our housework. I liked having my own car and my own phone line in my room so my father didn't complain when I talked to my friends too much. I loved having a separate section of the house just for me with a mini-kitchen and living area for my friends to hang out when they came over.

I wondered what William's life was like. What kind of house he lived in, and whether he had his own car. He'd said his parents couldn't afford to pay for college, so that must mean they weren't wealthy.

Why would anyone choose being poor over having money?

"Yeah," I said, after reaching my conclusion. "I guess making money is important to me. Isn't it important to everyone, though? Doesn't everyone want to have plenty of money?"

"Everyone's definition of plenty is different. I want to be able to have a roof over my head, pay my bills, and maybe have some left over to do fun stuff without worrying about it. I also want to help animals. If I can do all that on what I make, then I think I'll have plenty of money."

I looked across my room at the wall of closet doors and drawers, all in varying states of open with clothes spilling forth. I couldn't imagine not being able to buy clothes whenever I wanted to.

"Hey, I gotta go," William said. "My sister needs to use the phone."

"Oh. You have a sister?" It struck me as funny that I had no idea whether he had siblings or how many he had. I knew the family make-up of all my friends from school, but since William didn't go to my school, I was clueless about his family.

"Two. Two sisters, two brothers. I'm the youngest."

"Holy crap, that's a lot of kids. No wonder your parents don't have any money." I realized after I said it that it sounded kind of rude, but he didn't give me time to fix it.

"I gotta go, okay? I'll see you around."

"Oh, um, okay. Don't you want my number, so you can call me?"

Someone yelled his name in the background, and then I heard a woman tell him to let his sister have the phone.

"Bye," he said as he hung up.

I stared at the phone, certain he was the most maddening boy on the planet.

CHAPTER 13
Caterina

I'd hoped William would be clever and find a way to call me after our conversation, but days went by and my phone didn't ring. I even checked with Isabel to see if he might have called the main house phone instead of the private line in my room, but no. He either wasn't interested, or he didn't know how to get my number.

After a couple more disappointing days with no word from him, I swallowed any shred of pride I had left and called his number again. He had given it to me, after all, so he obviously wanted me to call.

That didn't work either, though. I tried a couple of times and got no answer. For a family with so many people, they sure didn't stay home much.

When I saw that *To Kill A Mockingbird* would be playing at the old dollar theater on Sunday afternoon, I took that as a sign that I was meant to talk to him. I had to figure out a way to make it happen.

I waited for my mother to leave for her garden club meeting Saturday morning, and then I drove to the equestrian center on the ruse that I might have left something behind when I was there for my lesson.

I wandered into the barn, making a big show of looking at the ground as I walked.

To my dismay, the first person I ran into was Mr. Wainwright.

"Ms. Johnson, do we have a lesson scheduled today?"

"Oh, no! Definitely not. I lost an earring, and I was thinking perhaps it fell off while I was here Tuesday."

He followed my gaze to the ground and then smiled as he rubbed his hand across the back of his neck. "I'm not sure how valuable that earring is, but it could fallen off anywhere along our ride and be lost in the grasses of the pasture or the dirt of the riding ring. If it was here in the barn, well, I'm sure one of the stable boys probably raked it under without realizing it was there."

"I realize it's a long shot, but I thought maybe I'd take a look around. Just in case."

"Suit yourself. Hope you find it. It'd be a miracle."

He continued on his way to the front office, and I ducked inside the barn, scanning the stalls for any sign of the redhead I sought.

The sound of crunching hay carried from the last stall, and I smoothed my hair down as I walked toward it.

William was bent over shoveling, and I leaned against the door of the stall with a grin.

"Hey there," I said, unable to keep my grin nonchalant.

He glanced over his shoulder but continued to work. "Hey."

"I thought I lost an earring Tuesday, so I came to look for it."

"Did you find it?" he asked, not bothering to look my way again as he moved the hay into place.

"Not yet. Probably got buried in the dirt, or it may have even come out while I was in the saddle."

A silent pause hung in the air between us, and I wished he would stop working and turn to face me. Act like he was in any way happy to see me.

"Guess what?" I asked when it became clear I wasn't going to get his undivided attention.

His head stayed bent over the shovel. "What?"

"*To Kill A Mockingbird* is playing at the old Rialto Theater tomorrow."

He stood up straight and crossed his hands on top of the shovel's handle. "Did you finish the book?"

I shifted my weight from one foot to the other and tossed my hair over my shoulder, trying to hold his gaze while I had it.

"Er, no, not yet, but I'm working on it. I thought maybe we could go see the movie. Together. Tomorrow. You know, if you don't have plans." My stilted words betrayed how nervous I was that he would reject my proposal. It was an uncomfortable feeling. I was accustomed to doing the rejecting, not being rejected.

"You should finish the book before you see the movie. I mean, the movie's good, but it changes some things. The book's better."

"You've already seen it? Of course, you have. What am I asking?

You've read the book multiple times. Why wouldn't you have seen the movie?" I sighed and crossed my arms in frustration.

William grinned. "I don't mind seeing the movie again. It's a good movie. I just think you should read the book first."

"Yeah, well, like I said before, I'm not a fast reader like you, so by the time I read the book, the movie won't be playing there anymore."

"They play it about twice a year, so it'll be back."

I rolled my eyes and pouted, a genuine pout of frustration, not the carefully perfected one I typically used.

"Great. So I have six months to finish the book, and then I'll go see it. Perfect. Except you'll be away at college by then."

"I'm not moving to Gainesville. I'm just going to classes there."

"You're going to drive back and forth?" My mouth dropped open. Not only was he going to school close to home, but he wasn't even going to live in the dorm or an apartment near campus? What was wrong with him? I planned to pick a college as far away from my parents as possible and only come home when I had to.

"Yeah. I'm gonna keep working here at the equestrian center if I can fit it around my schedule, and Charlotte's dad hired me on in their stables for weekends. Speaking of work, I need to get back to it, but I hope you find your earring."

"Thanks."

I frowned as he turned his back and returned to shoveling.

It was time to accept the facts. The boy was not interested in me.

I walked back through the stalls, ignoring the curious stares of the horses who hung their heads over their doors to watch me. I was almost to the exit when William called my name.

"Hey, Catherine?"

I turned with a smile. "Yeah?"

"What time is the movie tomorrow?"

My smile widened with the knowledge that he was reconsidering. "There's one at noon and one at four."

"Okay. I could meet you there for the four."

A man walked into the barn and glanced our direction before heading to the stalls on the other end of the building.

"I gotta—" William started, but I interrupted him.

"I know. You gotta get back to work. I'll see you tomorrow, then?"

"Yeah."

I left the barn with a smile, and I woke up Sunday more excited to greet the day than I had been in quite a while.

He stood waiting in front of the theater when I pulled into the parking lot, and as I smiled at how handsome he looked, I realized it was the first time I was seeing him all cleaned up and not working.

"Sorry I'm late," I said as I greeted him. "I told my mother I was going to the movies with Charlotte, and she had stuff to give to Charlotte's mom, so I had to actually drive over there first."

"You lied to your mom? Why?"

"Oh, because they get all weirded out if I'm doing something with a guy. My father insists that he needs to meet everyone ahead of time, and then they ask a bunch of questions about people's parents, and I don't know. It's just easier to always tell them I'm with a friend instead. I mean, not that I go out with a lot of guys. I wasn't saying that."

As we walked to the box office, I wondered if he was going to offer to pay for my ticket, which technically made it a date, or if we were going to each buy our own, which made it more of a friend outing.

"Two tickets, please," he told the girl behind the window, and I grinned as he handed her two dollars.

It was a date.

CHAPTER 14
2018 - William

My confrontations at the hospital with Catherine and Caroline had left me in a foul mood, and I was relieved to find the barn deserted when I arrived. My thoughts and emotions were a jumbled mess, and I didn't care to make small talk with my staff or conduct business as usual, acting as though my whole world hadn't tilted on its axis. My only desire was to get on a horse and retreat into the remote isolation of my property, leaving the world behind.

The memories stayed with me, though, and no matter how hard I pushed the horse or how deep into the woods we ventured, I couldn't escape Catherine Johnson. If anything, the woods brought her back to me.

It had been years since I'd allowed my mind to entertain thoughts of her. Decades, even. Any time there had been the slightest reminder of her or the hint of a memory entering my head, my response was to shove her to the back of my mind and redirect my focus elsewhere.

I would have thought that time and a life fully lived would have dimmed the memories or made them hazy to recall, but scenes of her played out in full-color splendor in my mind, as clear as if they'd happened only yesterday.

She'd been coming in from the field on the back of a horse the first time I saw her, and it was difficult to tell who was the more spirited filly. She was wearing a pair of gray jodhpurs and a pink riding shirt, and her long, black hair flew free in the wind despite being confined at the crown by her helmet. She rode like she'd been born in the saddle, her body synchronized with the horse's gait with such ease that they seemed two parts of the same animal.

I was surprised to see Mr. Wainwright closing in behind her, because her technique seemed farther advanced than those who normally took his lessons.

She laughed as she looked back at him, and then she nudged the horse to go faster as Mr. Wainwright yelled his admonishment.

I couldn't take my eyes off her. She was the most beautiful girl I'd ever seen, and the sight of her galloping across the field with such unabashed delight made my insides feel all funny.

"Hey, you gonna get any of that water in the bucket?" my co-worker Greg had asked, and I had looked down to see the hose I held spilling water all over the dirt and my boots instead of into the bucket.

I moved the water stream to where it should be and looked back up just as Mr. Wainwright caught up with her.

I could tell by his red face and stern expression that he was displeased by something she had done, but she didn't seem to care. She tossed her hair over her shoulder as she pulled the horse to a halt, and then she flashed him the prettiest smile. My insides went all funny again, and I had the strangest hope that someday I would see her smile at me that way.

"Dude," Greg said as he came to stand beside me and follow my gaze. "You're wasting your time even looking at that one. That's Catherine Johnson. Her dad is Phillip Johnson, and he's like a gazillionaire or something. I heard he spent every last penny he had way back when to go in with his college roommate for a piece of equipment the guy had invented, and they sold it for millions. They say Johnson's got the Midas touch, though. Real estate. Stock market. Start-ups. Thoroughbreds. No matter what he touches, it turns to gold."

Greg bent to turn off the hose, but I couldn't stop watching Catherine as she laughed at something Mr. Wainwright said.

"C'mon," Greg said, punching me in the arm. "I'm telling you, you ain't got a chance. She's about as stuck up as they come and richer than God. Now, let's get finished and maybe we can get out of here early. I got a hot date tonight."

I picked up the bucket to follow Greg back inside the barn, but I couldn't help stealing another glance back at her.

She was riding side-by-side with Mr. Wainwright, and though he looked like he was ready to blow a gasket, she looked exhilarated. Her broad smile lit up her whole face, which only served to highlight his dour expression.

Greg and I were in the stalls at the far end of the barn when I heard them come in.

"You pull a stunt like that again, and I will refuse to teach you. I don't care who your father is," Mr. Wainwright said. "And I will call him right now and tell him that myself."

"I was just having a bit of fun," she said, her voice deeper than I expected. Its gravelly sound tickled my ears, and I stepped toward the stall door to try and get another look at her as she continued her plea. "The horse wanted to run, and I let him. We had finished our lesson, so what does it matter?"

"It matters because safety is of the utmost concern," Mr. Wainwright said. His broad back blocked her from my view, and I resisted the urge to walk into the aisle so I could see her. "You must follow my commands and stay within the boundaries I set for you. You can't just take off on your own like that! What if something were to happen to you? What if you'd fallen from the horse and been injured?"

"Then my father would sue the equestrian center, and you'd likely lose your job. But that didn't happen, did it? Besides, wasn't it even a little bit fun to chase me? You have to get bored doing the same old lessons every day. Don't you ever want to just let the horse run free and take you wherever he wants to go?"

"The purpose of lessons is to learn discipline and control. I will not tolerate your insubordination, and I will not put the animals or myself at risk for your pleasure. Is that understood?"

"Of course, Mr. Wainwright." Her tone was pleasant, but the undercurrent of sarcasm was evident.

I'd never heard anyone talk to him even remotely disrespectful, and I have to admit I was in awe of her for having the guts to do it.

After that, I watched for her every Tuesday. It wasn't hard to tell when she arrived since I was not the only stable boy clamoring to get a look. I think she knew what a ruckus she caused, and I think she enjoyed it. She was never outright rude; she just didn't acknowledge the stable staff at all. She'd take her horse's reins or return them without so much as a thank-you, and she never made eye contact or spoke to anyone other than Mr. Wainwright. It didn't take me long to realize Greg was right. Someone like Catherine Johnson would never be interested in someone like me.

By the time she came and talked to me on the fence line that day, I'd grown cynical about her. I wrote her off as a typical rich girl, and no matter how pretty she was or how much she fascinated me, I was determined not to give in to fawning over her like the others did.

I suppose I knew it was a ruse when she showed up the second day with the book in her bag, but I'd be lying if I said it didn't feel good that she'd singled me out of the group and wanted to talk to me. She was even more beautiful close up than she had been from afar, and she smelled so damned good it made me dizzy every time she moved.

"Son, I don't want to stick my nose in your business," the foreman said once Catherine and Charlotte had left that day, "but that's nothing but trouble right there. You need to stay as far away from her as possible, or she'll ruin you. And if she doesn't, her daddy will. You're a nice kid, William. A hard worker. I'd hate to see you throw away your future on some girl who thinks she's better than you."

I tried to heed his warning. To heed my own instincts about her. But every time she talked to me, I got sucked in deeper.

CHAPTER 15
William

A t first, I was sure she was toying with me. Playing some game with an ulterior motive I couldn't see. I was wary but intrigued. And as I got to know her better, that intrigue never ceased. My fascination with her only grew.

She could be haughty at times but also insecure. She could be direct to the point of being rude, but I came to understand that she didn't intend any malice or ill intent. She simply didn't realize the impact of her words. I don't think she'd ever had to care about that.

When her guard was down, she was quite playful. She laughed easily and soaked up joy like a sponge. She had a daring rebellious streak, but at the same time, she harbored a fragility I didn't understand. A sadness that seemed to always be hiding just beneath the surface.

How could someone who had absolutely everything not be happy all the time?

I don't know why I gave her my number at the stables that day, or why I agreed to go to the movies with her. I guess I thought I could handle it. That I could keep a safe distance and not get too involved. I remember thinking that it wouldn't be a big deal to go and see a movie on a Sunday afternoon. It was *To Kill A Mockingbird,* after all; it wasn't like it was a romantic movie. But then she cried on my shoulder, and that completely undid my efforts toward detachment. It was the first time I'd ever seen her look vulnerable. Something within me stirred, and I knew I would do whatever I could to protect her and keep her from being sad again.

"I can't believe you like that movie," she said as we walked from the darkness of the theater into the evening sun. "It was so sad! Why would you let me watch something so sad? Is the book that sad?"

I had shrugged at the time, feeling bad that she didn't like the movie, but also feeling motivated to defend a story that I felt had great value.

"Well, the book's the same basic story, of course, and yes, it's not a comedy, for sure. But you have to look deeper. There's a lot to get from the story that you'll miss if you concentrate only on the sad parts."

"Like what? What on earth do you get from it that would make you want to read it over and over again?"

We had reached her car, and I stopped short, unsure of what would happen next. I had planned to call my brother to come and get me after the show, but I wasn't ready for my time with her to end.

"There's an ice cream parlor about a block over," I said. "You want to get some ice cream and I'll tell you why I like the book?"

"Yes! Ice cream! Maybe I can drown my sorrows in it. Jeez!" She crossed her arms over her chest and started walking as I fell in stride beside her. "So, what is so good about this book?"

"I think it has important messages."

"Like what?"

"That you should always do the right thing."

"Oh, right, because that worked out so well for them. Atticus did the right thing, and Tom still died."

"Well, yes, in the movie, but you're missing the point. Just because you do the right thing doesn't mean everything will work out the way it should. You have to do the right thing anyway."

"Aargh. That's ridiculous. I like movies where good defeats evil and love always wins."

"But good did defeat evil. Atticus did change some people's minds. He gained the respect of those in the community. And he taught his children to stand up for others and do what is right."

"Yes, and his children almost died for it."

I opened the door of the ice cream shop and waited for her to walk inside. "Yes, but, there again, Boo did the right thing."

"Boo, who was locked in the courthouse basement and stays shut up in his house all day with a mean father? Great message there."

"Well, I think the message there is not to judge people based on what you hear from others. Get to know them yourself, and practice compassion and kindness."

"You sound like a walking self-help book." She peered into the ice cream freezer, perusing the flavors. "What are you getting?"

I knew I only had a few dollars in my pocket, and I wasn't sure if I was expected to pay since the ice cream had been my idea. I figured it was best to let her choose first and then make my selection from whatever money was left over.

"I haven't decided yet. What are you getting?"

"Mint chocolate chip. It's the best," she said, her eyes suddenly bright with excitement as her frown curled into a smile.

Something like a tickle spread through me, and I knew that I would do most anything to make her smile like that again.

"Single or double?"

I breathed a sigh of relief when she said single, since that meant I had enough money left to get myself a cone, too.

We settled at a table near the back of the store, and I grinned as I watched her try and lick the dripping cone all the way around. A mint-green smear landed on her nose, and I reached to wipe it with a napkin. She smiled at me with such joy that my heart felt like it would melt right along with the ice cream.

"So, are you smart or something?" she asked between licks.

"I don't know. I guess so. Why?"

"I just never met a boy who reads as much as you do," she said, pursing her lips over the top of the cone. "I definitely never met a boy—or a girl, for that matter—who talks about books and movies the way you do. Most of my friends either get high or drunk before seeing a movie, and they probably couldn't even tell you what it was about half the time. Do you drink?"

I hesitated, wondering if that was going to be the nail in the coffin for me. I should have guessed she'd be a party girl. Most of the rich kids in town were.

Just another thing we didn't have in common.

I didn't have a clue why she was talking to me, or why she'd asked me to go to the movies with her. We didn't have any of the same friends, and I couldn't imagine that our lives intersected in many areas. She was definitely out of my league.

She had taken a huge bite of ice-cream after asking the question, and she gulped to swallow it as I shook my head. She looked at me with her eyes wide and her eyebrows high.

"Really? Not at all? You don't ever get drunk?"

I shook my head again and grinned, more from nervousness than any humor. I had known all along it was too good to be true. Girls like her weren't attracted to guys like me.

"Like, never? Oh, my gosh," she said, her reaction so somber you would have thought I told her I had some rare disease. "We have to get you drunk."

"No, we don't."

"How can you even say that if you have no idea what it's like? I love being drunk. I don't have to care what I do or what I say. I don't care what my parents think or what anyone thinks, really. I can just have fun and not worry about anything."

"You can have fun without being drunk, you know," I said, taking a bite of my chocolate ice cream. "It's not like I don't have fun. I just prefer being in control of what I'm saying. What I'm doing. I like knowing what's going on around me."

"So, what do you do? Like, on the weekends. Other than work all the time?"

"I don't work *all* the time. I'm not working now, am I? I do lots of stuff."

She had momentarily forgotten her ice cream, and it was dripping onto the napkin wrapped around it and then running down her hand.

"Here, your ice cream's melting," I said, grabbing a napkin from the dispenser to wipe her hand and another to wipe the table.

"Thanks." She licked it the whole way around and looked back at me with a puzzled expression pulling her brows close together. "You said the other day you don't go to parties. If you don't party and you don't drink, what do you do for fun?"

I laughed at the ridiculousness of her question before I realized she was sincere.

"I dunno. I like to go for walks in the woods. I love riding horses. I love anything to do with horses, actually. My family plays cards. We play dominoes. Or darts. My brothers and I play football in the field behind my house. I go fishing. I like taking a canoe up the river. I love sitting around a fire and watching the flames dance. And I like to read, of course. You already know that."

"Wow. Other than riding horses, I don't think I've ever done a single thing you mentioned." She crunched a bite of the cone and licked ice cream from her lips.

"Really?" I said as I tilted my cone to keep it from dripping. "You don't know what you're missing."

She sat up tall and leaned forward, her eyes lit up again with excitement. "So, teach me."

"What?"

"Teach me what I'm missing. I'll show you how to party, and you show me how to ... well, do other stuff."

"It's not that I don't know how to party, Catherine. I'm just not interested in it."

"Okay, so no parties. Will you still show me what you do for fun?"

I smiled with the realization that she wanted to spend more time with me.

"Sure."

She tilted her head to the side and squinted like she was in deep concentration.

"Hey, are you good at math?"

"Yeah, I guess so."

"Do you think you could teach me math?"

"I don't know. Don't you have a math teacher at your school?"

"Yeah, but I'm failing his class. I just don't get it, and I hate it, so I don't try very hard. But my mother said if I can bring my grade up by the end of the school year and not fail, then she'll take me to Paris this summer."

"Wow. That's quite the reward."

"Yeah, but I didn't think I was going to be able to do it. Until now. You could teach me. You could help me with math, and then I can pass and go to Paris. What do you say?"

"I mean, I'll try, but I don't know if I'm a good teacher."

"You have to be better than the tutor my mother hired. He is so boring, and I understand him less than I do my teacher. I don't even go most of the time because I hate it so much. Please, William? Will you please try to help me pass? And then maybe we can do some of that other stuff, too. You know, the fun without being drunk stuff."

And so, it began.

CHAPTER 16
William

For the next several weeks, any time I wasn't in school or working, I was helping Catherine with her classes or teaching her the simple joys of life without a bottomless bank account.

It was hard to believe she'd lived her entire life in Florida on the outskirts of the Ocala National Forest but had never stumbled upon an unexpected stream in the woods, paddled a canoe past a gator basking in the sun, or been hypnotized by a camp fire.

At first, I figured she would turn up her nose at anything that involved getting dirty or didn't include shopping, but her adventurous spirit surprised me. Whatever the challenge, she was up for it, and her enthusiasm was contagious. I'd always loved spending time in nature, but somehow seeing it through her eyes made me appreciate it even more.

She'd never seen a frog up close other than the one she'd been forced to dissect in biology, and her reaction when I caught one and placed it in her palm was priceless. She stared at him in wonder before he leapt from her hand to a nearby tree, which startled her but then sent her into a fit of giggles.

The day we saw a deer in the woods, she was beside herself with excitement, and when I took her to a meadow of wildflowers, she danced around like a fairy and put daisies in her hair. With each encounter, I became more enamored of her. Being able to make her smile was intoxicating, and it became my mission in life to find experiences that made her happy, so I could see her light up with joy.

The first time we set out in a canoe, it was one of those perfect Florida days with clear blue skies overhead, the brilliance of the sun on the water, and the tropical breeze swaying through the trees. I had hoped we would have a lot of wildlife sightings, and the river didn't disappoint. Within the first half hour, we passed a fat gator laying on a wide sand bar, a raccoon cleaning his paws in the flowing water, and a family of ducks splashing in a shallow pool along the shore.

When we rounded a bend and saw a row of turtles sunning on a log with their legs outstretched, I thought she was going to flip us over before I could paddle in for a closer look.

"Turtles! William, look at the turtles. Look at their little feet poking out. Oh! Their little faces! They're so adorable! Can we take one home?"

"No. Of course not," I said as I maneuvered onto the narrow sandbar just past the log.

"Why not?"

"Because this is their home. This is where they belong."

I extended my hand to help her as we climbed out of the canoe, and she didn't let go right away as we walked toward the turtles.

"Can I at least hold one? I've never touched a turtle before. Please, William? You know it's my favorite animal on the whole entire planet. Please?"

I waded through the shallow water along the edge of the sandbar, careful to scan the surroundings for any sign of the venomous water moccasins who liked to hang out near embankments or logs. One of the turtles dove to the safety of the water as I approached, and I murmured an apology for interrupting their sun bath as I plucked a small one off the log.

Catherine jumped up and down with a squeal as she clapped her hands, and I smiled at her delight.

She sat cross-legged on the sand as I knelt to set the turtle on the ground in front of her.

"He went inside," she said, clearly disappointed that he hadn't greeted her with equal exuberance.

"Yeah, you probably scared him half to death. He's not sure what's happening."

"Can I touch him?"

"Sure," I said with a shrug, uncertain of why she thought she needed my permission.

She reached to brush her fingertip across his shell before pulling back with a laugh and looking up at me. Her smile was brighter than the sun, and I don't think there's any request I could have refused her when she smiled like that. It made me all funny inside.

She extended her finger again and followed the pattern on his back, giggling the entire time.

Eventually, he ventured his head out for a look around, and she got weepy at the sight of his beady little eyes.

"Oh my gosh, William. He's the cutest. Look at him. I'm going to name him George. Don't you think that's a great name for a turtle?"

"George? Why George?"

"I don't know. He just looks like a George to me. Don't you think he looks like a George?"

"Um, I think he looks like a turtle."

She gave my arm a playful slap and then she bent forward to get a closer look at George, frowning when he retreated back inside his shell.

"I have to take him home with me, William. I have to!"

I grimaced, not wanting to tell her no, but feeling responsible for the turtle I'd put in her reach.

"I think he'd be much happier here, surrounded by his friends and family."

She appeared to consider my answer for only a moment before nodding.

"Okay, you're right. I'll take two, so he'll have company."

I sighed. "C'mon, Catherine. Look around you. What turtle wants to live in an aquarium in someone's bedroom when they have this?"

I motioned to the trees overhead draped in Spanish moss and the gentle flow of the water as it babbled past us.

She put her hands on her hips and stared at me like I was the one being unreasonable. "I wouldn't put them in an aquarium, silly. I'd have an enclosure built. With lots of bushes and greenery. They could have their own stream and a log all to themselves."

I shook my head and rubbed my hand across the back of my neck. It still astounded me that she gave no thought to what something might cost. It was never a question for her. If she wanted it to happen, she knew her mother would pay for it.

But even if she didn't have a respect for the monetary value of something, surely I could make her realize the life value.

"I'm sure you'd build a great home for them. But it's still not the same for the turtles. Why would they want to live their lives confined? Let's leave them here where they can be in their natural environment and at peace. We can visit them again."

"What if they're not here next time?"

The wistful disappointment in her voice tugged at me, and I looked away from her so I wouldn't be swayed to cave in to her request.

"There are plenty of turtles in this river," I said. "Or pretty much any river in Florida. If these particular turtles aren't on this particular log, there'll be others."

She moved across the sand until she knelt knee-to-knee with me, her eyes locked with mine. The sweet, coconut aroma of her suntan oil tickled my senses, and my body began to react to her proximity despite my best efforts to keep it at bay.

I'd been so careful not to blur the lines of friendship since we'd started hanging out. I knew being romantically involved with Catherine was not an option. Not only would her parents never allow it, but I had college looming, and I didn't need the distraction.

But the more time we spent alone together, the harder it was to ignore the natural impulses. Casual touches had begun to linger a little longer than necessary. We seemed to bump into each other or brush up against each other more often. I'd catch her staring at my lips as we talked, and I'd lose my train of thought, unable to come up with words.

She was so damn beautiful, and it was becoming nearly impossible to resist her.

"So, if there's plenty, why should it matter if I take a couple home?" she whispered.

I stood and bent to pick up George and take him back to his friends, anxious to put space between us before I fell completely under her spell.

"It would matter to the turtles you took, and it would matter to their families who were here missing them."

Another turtle left the log as I approached. I put George near the remaining two, hoping they'd hang around and wait for him to come back out of his shell. I didn't want him to get left behind.

"William, can I ask you a question?"

I turned to see her standing on the sandbar in the full sun, and the sight of her took my breath away, as it often did. Her hair, so dark it reminded me of a raven's feathers, was pulled back tightly in a high ponytail, and the sun reflecting off its sheen made it seem to glow.

The cut-off denim shorts she wore put her long legs on full display, and the contrast of her tiny pink bikini top against her tanned skin was enough to drive a boy insane with the wanting.

"Sure," I said, swallowing hard to push down my thirst for her.

She stepped closer as I waded back out of the water, and our eyes locked as she came to stand only a couple of inches in front of me.

I held my breath and silently prayed for strength.

"Do you promise you'll answer it honestly, no matter what the answer is?"

I nodded.

"Say it. Say you promise."

I swallowed again, dreading the unknown.

"I promise. I won't ever lie to you, Catherine. Not ever."

She started to smile, but it faded away before it reached her eyes. She looked to my lips and back up, and her gaze held a vulnerability she rarely revealed. I'd seen it on occasion, but she usually recovered quickly and masked it with a joke or some sarcastic comment. But in those moments when I glimpsed it, I always felt I was seeing a Catherine that no one else knew.

"Do you like me?" she asked, her eyes darting back and forth as she studied my face.

"W-w-what do you mean?" I was certain I knew what she meant, and I was certain of the answer, but I wished I'd been a little less eager to promise her that I'd share it.

"I mean, you know, do you like me? In *that* way. Like boy-attracted-to-girl way. I see you looking at me sometimes, and I think you're gonna kiss me, but you don't. Every time I think the moment's perfect and you're finally going to do it, you look away or you move away or start talking instead. Are you just not attracted to me at all?"

I hesitated, and her eyes narrowed as she crossed her arms over her chest and stepped back.

"No, no, that's not it," I said, reaching to put my arms around her but then catching myself. "I want to kiss you, Catherine. Very much. I just think it's best if we don't, you know, if we don't get involved that way."

She walked past me toward the water, and I cursed under my breath and looked to the sky. What kind of idiot passes up an opportunity like that?

I turned to stare at her back and wished our circumstances could be different.

"Catherine, I…"

"It's okay," she said with a shrug. She moved past me again, pasting on the fake smile I'd seen her flash at others. "Forget I mentioned it. We need to head back anyway."

She wrapped her arms tightly around her waist and walked back to the canoe.

I followed and reached to take her elbow to help her into the boat, but she jerked her arm away from the contact.

"Catherine—"

"It's okay, William. Let's just go. Take me home."

The hurt in her eyes killed me, and I couldn't handle knowing I'd caused it. I threw caution to the wind and took her in my arms, crushing her lips with mine. She reacted immediately, opening up to me as she twisted her hands in my hair and pressed herself against me, her skin warm from the sun.

It was like multiple explosions went off inside me all at once, like nothing I'd ever experienced before. Any thoughts of resistance vanished as I gave myself over to her. The world and all its issues ceased to exist, and all I cared about was the feel of her, the taste of her, and the sensations happening in my body.

A loud splash filled the air behind us, and Catherine jumped back with a shriek as she peered across the water. "What was that?"

"Probably a fish," I said, tugging my T-shirt down to cover the thin material of my swim trunks.

"Are you sure it wasn't an alligator?" she asked, her eyes wide with apprehension. "What if it was that gator we saw back by the other sandbar?"

"It wasn't."

"What if it was?"

I smiled. "It wasn't. Trust me."

"How do you know?"

"Do you see a gator?" I asked, spreading my arms wide toward the water.

"He's probably waiting for us in the water."

I laughed and shook my head. "That gator is probably still in the same exact position he was in when we passed him."

George and his last two buddies left the log with a plop, and Catherine frowned.

"They're all gone. There's no more turtles."

"They'll be back. We'll find them again."

She turned to me and laid her hands on my chest as she stepped back into my embrace. "You promise?"

I nodded and tried to smile, but the reality of what I'd done had started to weigh on me. I'd crossed the line I swore I'd never cross.

Where would we go from there? We couldn't go back, and I knew all too well the many reasons we couldn't go forward.

"Say it," she whispered as she looked up at me, her green eyes sparkling like emeralds in the sun.

"I promise I will find turtles for you."

"Always?" She rose up on her toes and gently pressed her mouth to mine.

"Always," I said against her lips, and I wondered if the pledge I was making went beyond turtles.

Our kisses were more gentle than before. The passion hadn't diminished, but the frantic rush had subsided. In its place was a tender shyness, a timid exploration of each other as we marveled in the newness of it all. The undercurrent of urgency remained, though. It was like being handed something you'd desperately wanted but been denied, and though you enjoyed having it, you were also wary of it being taken away.

A distant rumble of thunder brought us back to reality, and I helped her settle into the canoe as I maneuvered it off the sandbar and back into the current.

She sat between my knees the rest of the way down the river to the pick-up point, reclining against my chest as I tried to paddle and steer without disturbing her.

I tried not to think about the consequences of our actions as I enjoyed her nearness, her laughter, and the happiness that radiated from her as she looked up at me and smiled with her hands rested on my knees.

By the time we pulled the canoe from the river and clambered into my brother's pick-up truck, I had decided to accept my fate. I was in love with Catherine Johnson. She'd become my whole world, and I couldn't go back to pretending she wasn't.

I suppose I was blinded by love and happiness, and though I knew it would be difficult, I thought we could find a way to make it work.

Of course, the sun was still shining then. I had no way of knowing the size of the storm that was building, or that the smell of coconuts would haunt me for years to come.

CHAPTER 17
William

The shift from friendship to romance intensified rapidly, and soon there weren't enough hours in the day. I counted down the minutes I was in school or at work, anxious to be with Catherine. I resented that I'd agreed to work two full-time jobs for the summer, knowing that as soon as graduation passed, we'd have less time to spend together.

As if the time constraints weren't already hard enough to work around, we also had her parents to deal with. She refused to tell them we were dating, and despite my misgivings, I went along with her, unwilling to press the issue if it meant we'd be separated.

It bothered me on many levels that she lied to them every time we were together. It made what we were doing feel like it was wrong, and I worried what would happen if they found out.

"What if you get caught lying, though?" I asked her one afternoon as we sat at the end of the dock, dipping our toes in the lake. "What if someone sees us and tells your parents? Then I won't be allowed to talk to you at all. Wouldn't it be better if I met them, and then if they got to know me, they might say we could date?"

"Ugh. God, no. There's no way my father would let me be alone with a boy. But stop worrying. I won't get caught. Trust me; none of my parents' friends will be in a canoe or hiking in the Ocala National Forest. They're too busy shopping and eating at ritzy restaurants or having cocktails at the golf club. You and I don't ever go anywhere on that side of town to be seen. Besides, as long as I stay out of trouble, my parents don't care where I am."

It didn't bring much comfort to know that we were safe because I couldn't afford to take her to the wealthy side of town where she was accustomed to hanging out. I knew she was trying to protect me by saying her father wouldn't let her date *any* boy. It was more like he wouldn't let her date a boy like me, a boy from a family who didn't measure up.

But if I even hinted at that, she'd get upset, telling me she didn't care what her father thought and that she was determined to make her own choices in life.

I don't know how she kept up with the web of deceit she spun. She lied almost daily, telling them she was going to the movies with Charlotte, hanging out with friends, or studying with classmates. She even convinced her mother to cancel the tutor they hired by telling her someone at school had found one who was better.

When her father was in town, she was held to a stricter schedule, and our contact was limited to late night phone calls when she couldn't leave the house to meet me. But Phillip traveled often, and when he was gone, her mother never inquired much about Catherine's whereabouts. It didn't seem to matter to Miranda where Catherine went or what time she came home as long as her grades were improving and there were no calls from the school or other parents with behavioral issues.

Fortunately, Catherine worked hard on both of those issues. She knew if she got grounded, we couldn't see each other, but she also really looked forward to going to Paris with her mother. Miranda had bought Catherine several guidebooks on the city, and she'd earmark the pages of the landmarks she found interesting and read their descriptions to me, laughing when I insisted she should probably visit a couple of museums while she was there.

Thankfully, my own mother had never been a stickler for curfews or detailed explanations. I suppose by the time I started going out, she'd already been through it with my older brothers and sisters. She'd long ago learned to sleep through the night without waiting for us to arrive home, and as long as I told her where I was going and what time I expected to be back, she didn't ask too many questions.

But as Catherine and I continued to see more of each other, and I started being home less, Ma became more interested.

"You've been on the go an awful lot lately. What's up?" she asked as I yawned over a bowl of cereal.

"I dunno. Trying to make the most of it before the end of high school, I suppose."

She sat at the table across from me and fixed me with her knowing stare. "Hmm. So, who's the girl?"

"What makes you think there's a girl?" I tried to avoid Ma's eye contact and her uncanny ability to read me.

"Oh, I'd say five kids. I've been riding this merry-go-round a long time. I see all the signs. The late-night phone calls. The smell of cologne lingering in the hall bathroom. Coming in all hours of the night. Distracted when you are here. All dead giveaways. It seems to me things are getting pretty serious between the two of you. So, who's the girl, and why haven't you brought her home to meet us?"

I shifted in my seat, not in the mood for an interrogation.

"Um, I don't know. I just haven't gotten around to it, I guess."

"Oh. Does she not want to meet us?"

I stared at the milk in the bowl, dipping my spoon in to fill it up and then tilting it to pour the milk back in the bowl over and over again as I silently prayed she'd just drop the subject. I knew there was no way she would.

"William?" She leaned forward and arched an eyebrow.

"Of course, she wants to meet you. I'll bring her by soon. There just hasn't been a good time, ya know? Between work and school."

"Have you met her parents?" Her tone issued a challenge, and I knew there was no right answer. Either way I was screwed. Either Ma had been slighted, or I'd been without manners.

"Not yet," I said, bracing for the lecture.

"You've been seeing this girl, traipsing all over God knows where with her, and you haven't met her parents or brought her home to meet yours? First impressions are important, William. What are her parents going to think of you not doing things the proper way? I've taught you better. Your brothers have set a better example for you. You need to meet her parents. You need to know what kind of family she comes from and let them know you're a good boy. Her mother might be worried sick not knowing what kind of boy her daughter's out with."

She pushed her chair back and got up, taking the milk from the table and putting it back in the fridge.

I didn't dare tell her that Catherine's parents would likely be more worried if they did know who I was. I didn't want her driving over there to vouch for my credentials or something crazy like that.

"Why hasn't she asked to meet us?" She closed the fridge and turned to face me with crossed arms. "What kind of girl is this that she'd get serious with you but not consider it important to meet your family or have you meet hers? Where did you meet this girl?"

Oh, great. Now my mother was questioning Catherine's pedigree. The conversation was spinning out of control.

"Ma, come on. It's not that she's not interested in meeting you. It's a new thing. It's not that serious yet."

"Not that serious?" Her eyebrow arched so high it almost disappeared beneath her bangs. "Have you not been out with this girl almost every night for weeks? Are you not on the phone with her so much that your sister is begging me to get you your own phone line?"

I made a mental note to thank Patricia for making a stink, and then I scooped up my bowl and headed to the sink with it. "I'll bring her by, okay?"

"When?"

"I don't know. I'll talk to her about it tonight."

"Oh, you have to talk her into coming to meet us? What kind of morals does this girl have? Is this someone you're ashamed to be dating? Because if you don't want to introduce her to your family, that's a red flag, son."

"No, I'm not ashamed of her. Not at all. It's just … complicated."

"How so?" She moved to stand in front of me, and I knew I wasn't leaving the kitchen until she was satisfied with my answers. "Do I know this girl? Do I know her parents?"

"Not likely," I said with a shake of my head, trying not to grin as I pictured my mother sitting down for tea in the fancy parlor of the Johnson house.

"What's her name?"

I chewed on the inside of my lip and considered all the ramifications of telling my mother. It wasn't like I'd been trying to hide it from my parents. They hadn't asked until then who I was going out with, and I hadn't volunteered any names. I certainly wasn't willing to lie to them about it. But the fewer people who knew, the less likely it was for Catherine's parents to find out. Perhaps I could explain to my mom why discretion was so important.

"If I tell you, I need you to promise not to tell anyone."

Her mouth dropped open, and she slapped the counter with her palm. "Not tell anyone? William Joseph Ward, what have you gotten yourself into?"

"Nothing! It's not like that. I just don't want everyone knowing my business, that's all."

"Who is this girl?" She crossed her arms once more, and I regretted ever saying anything. I should have skipped breakfast.

"Catherine Johnson."

A moment's perplexity crossed her features, and then her eyes widened. "Catherine Johnson, like Phillip and Miranda's daughter?"

"Yes, ma'am."

She sat down and clasped her hands in her lap.

"And you haven't met the Johnsons? Do they know y'all are seeing each other?"

I shook my head, and she sighed.

"Did she ask you to hide it? To keep it secret from them?"

"It's not like that."

"Oh? Isn't it? Then what's it like? Is she ashamed to be with you or not?"

"Her parents are just strict, Ma."

"Strict? Her parents are snobs, William. They parade around this town like their last name is Rockefeller," she said with a dramatic wave of her hand. "And it ain't! How do you see this turning out, son? Do you think they're going to welcome you with open arms when they find out you've been seeing their daughter behind their backs?"

"We're just laying low for a while, that's all. Once I'm in college, it won't matter so much. Then she's in college the next year."

She stood and came to stand in front of me once more.

"What won't matter so much? That you're from a working-class family? That you don't have the bank account to keep her in the life she's accustomed to? Don't be naive. This is never going to be okay with her parents, do you hear me? No amount of college classes will change your pedigree in their eyes. You're playing with fire, sweetheart, and you're gonna get burned."

She walked past me and disappeared down the hall, but within seconds she had returned to the doorway. "I want to meet this girl. If you're bound and damned determine to see her, I want to meet her."

"Yes, ma'am."

CHAPTER 18
Caterina

B efore William and I met, I usually skipped the last day of school and spent it in a drunken stupor with my friends. Sometimes, we'd show up for the first couple of classes before sneaking out, but even then, we'd take a little something before first period to start the party early.

I hadn't drunk or done any type of drugs since William and I started hanging out. I was surprised that I didn't miss it. If anyone had told me at the beginning of the school year that I'd be spending my Friday nights sitting around a campfire or my Saturday afternoons walking in the woods, I would have said they were crazy. And if they'd told me I'd be stone cold sober and not using anything to make myself feel better about my life, then I would have laughed in their faces.

My friends had given me a hard time about it at first, especially since no one but Charlotte knew I was seeing someone. But eventually, they forgot about me and went on with their escapades as though I'd never been a part of the circle.

Strangely, it didn't bother me to be so easily forgotten. I was much happier doing absolutely nothing with William than I'd ever been getting into trouble with that group. I also didn't mind studying or doing homework as much when it was William tutoring me, and for the first time in forever, I was actually excited to bring home my report card.

"Catherine, can I see you?" Ms. Frier asked when the bell rang after third period.

In the past, her request would have elicited an eye roll and a groan of irritation, but I returned the warm smile she offered as we waited for the other students to exit the room.

"I wanted to say how proud I am of you," she said once we were alone. "You really stepped up your efforts the past couple of months, and it shows. I've also noticed that you, well, that you seemed to have cut ties with some of the people you'd been associating with. I think it's been a good thing for you. I hope whatever inspired you keeps you motivated for next year. You have so much potential, Catherine, and I know you can achieve great things. I'd love to see you do well your senior year."

I thanked her and made my way into the hall where Charlotte was waiting.

"What did she want?"

"Oh, she just congratulated me on pulling my grades up."

"Wow. I've had straight *As* in her class all year, and she's never congratulated me."

"Yeah, well, I had an *F*, so maybe she recognized that it took a lot more work to pull that up than it did for you to keep an *A*."

"Not true," Charlotte scoffed as she opened her locker. "I work hard for my grades, too. By the way, Coco's parents are still in Canada, so she's throwing a summer kick off tomorrow night. Now that your grades are final, you can party again! Wanna go together? You could spend the night at my house. Like, you know, actually do something with me for real, instead of just telling your parents that you're with me so you can study with nerdy guy?"

"I can't. I'm supposed to go meet William's parents tomorrow night."

"Whoa. You're meeting his parents? Don't you think this is going a little too far? I mean, I'm all for him helping you pull up your grades or whatever, but it sounds like you're starting to think you guys are really dating."

"We are. I told you that."

"Catherine, you can't seriously consider William your boyfriend. He cleans out the horse shit in my stables on the weekend. C'mon. You know your parents are never going to go for that. I noticed you said you're meeting his parents, but you didn't mention him meeting yours."

I frowned, not wanting to discuss it. "Well, no, not yet. But once he's in college, then I can find a way to say we met and introduce them to him that way."

"Right. Because your dad won't ask any questions beyond what he's majoring in and which dorm he lives in."

"He's not going to live in the dorm. He's staying at home."

"Oh, even better. Your dad's going to kill you if he finds out. Or he'll just kill William and punish you for the rest of your life."

The bell for fourth period sounded, and I was relieved to end the conversation.

"Gotta go. I'll see you in sixth period."

"I may skip out at lunch," Charlotte said as she walked backward down the hallway. "Mandy and Tonya want to head over to Pam's and drink fuzzy navels. You're welcome to join us."

"No thanks," I said as I headed into class to get seated before the tardy bell rang.

By the end of the school day, so many people had left early or checked out that my classes were only half full, and I was regretting my decision to stay for the whole day. It was worth it when the report cards got handed out last period, though.

I had brought up both failing grades up to *Cs*. I was so proud of myself and so thankful to William for helping me. This meant I could go to Paris, but more importantly, it meant that my father would finally be proud of me again.

It was all I could do not to whip the card out and show my mother the minute I arrived home, but my father's plane was scheduled to land in time for dinner, so I held onto it until we were all seated around the table and eating the main course.

"I have good news," I said, unable to contain my excitement any longer. "Look!"

I pulled the report card from under my leg and slid it across the table toward my father.

My mother leaned over and clapped her hands as she exclaimed, "Excellent! Oh, dear, I'm so proud of you!"

I smiled and watched my father's face as he picked up the card and stared at it.

"I wouldn't call three *Cs* and three *Bs* excellent, Miranda. I think by definition a *C* is average."

He tossed the card back on the table and continued eating his filet.

My shoulders fell, and I looked to my mother for reassurance.

She looked down at her plate and placed her hands in her lap, so I turned back to him.

"But look at math. And history. I was failing in those classes this semester," I said, trying to keep my voice calm. "I brought those up two letter grades."

"It was never acceptable for you to fail, Catherine. So, for you to actually apply yourself and go beyond failing to achieve average is nothing to be proud of."

A huge lump formed in my throat, and hot anger rose up like bile.

"It took everything I had to pull that math grade up. It would have been impossible to get higher than a *C* with my grade average as low as it was."

"Oh, look, Miranda. Your daughter is now a mathematical genius and can calculate probabilities. An *average* mathematical genius, no less."

"Phillip, please," she said, glancing at me and then back at her hands.

He took a sip of his wine and looked at me over the rim of the glass before setting it on the table.

"Imagine how embarrassing it is for me when someone asks how you're doing in school. Do you think I want to say 'oh, average,' like that's okay? I've given you every luxury in life and every opportunity to succeed, and you repay me by being average? And then you expect your mother and I to somehow applaud that like it's an achievement on your part."

"I don't expect applause, but I thought you'd be proud that I was applying myself and doing better."

He stabbed his fork into the steak and glared at me. "*Better* will not cut it when you start filling out college applications next year. You need the best grades possible to be competitive. My money can't buy your way in everywhere. You have to do some work on your own."

"But I did work! I worked hard! I pulled it up to a *C*."

"Then you didn't work hard enough, or else you'd have an *A*."

I tossed my napkin on the table and blinked back tears, refusing to let him make me cry. "I did work hard. I did my best. I'm just not good at math."

"Nonsense. You didn't turn in assignments. You didn't study. You didn't put in effort."

"Okay, so maybe at the beginning of the year, I didn't. But this last quarter, I've been trying very hard. Math isn't easy for me. I don't understand it. But I worked at it, and I brought the grade up."

He folded his napkin and laid it beside his plate, and I swear he was on the verge of smiling.

"Not far enough. I've talked with your principal, and he's agreed to allow you to enroll in summer school so you can retake those classes with a *C*."

My mother's head shot up, and her bewildered expression told me there was no way he'd discussed this with her.

"Summer school? I have to retake classes all summer? But Mother said we could go to Paris if I pulled the grades up."

He stood and pushed his chair back, and I looked to my mother, who wouldn't meet my eyes.

"Mother, tell him. Tell him what we agreed. You said if I pulled it up to a passing grade, you'd take me to Paris. I did that. A *C* is a passing grade."

She stared at her hands in silence, and I knew she would never stand up to him. There would be no trip to the City of Lights.

"Mother, please. Don't you want us to go to Paris?"

"Your mother *is* going to Paris," he said, and the grin he'd suppressed thus far played at the corners of his mouth. "She shouldn't have to stay at home because of your shortcomings. I have business in Europe for the next six weeks. She'll be accompanying me, and you'll stay here under Isabel's supervision to attend summer school."

She looked at him in astonishment, and her face broke into a smile as she stood and rushed to hug him. I knew then that he had won the battle. She'd begged him for years to do a summer in Europe, and he'd given in to punish me.

CHAPTER 19
Caterina

That night was the first time I sneaked out of the house since meeting William. I had paced my bedroom for hours after dinner, and I felt like if I didn't escape those walls, I would simply go mad.

I had tried to call William several times, but I kept getting a steady busy signal, a sure sign that Patricia would be talking for a while.

I waited until after eleven when I knew my parents would have retreated to their suite. The entire house was dark as I made my way downstairs to the door that led out to the side yard and the garage beyond.

The crunch of the driveway rocks beneath my tires sounded deafening in the silence of the night, but I was careful not to accelerate until I was out on the highway.

I'd dropped William off at his house a few times, but I'd never been inside so I wasn't sure which bedroom window was his. I knew it faced the field behind their house, because he talked about watching sandhill cranes forage for food outside his window in the mornings.

I parked my car along the road not too far from his drive and made my way across his lawn. A large light pole lit most of the yard, and I hoped no one would be awake and looking out the front windows, for they would have surely seen me.

When I reached the back of the house, one room had a light on, and the pink curtains in the window eliminated that one from consideration. I could make out the University of Florida logo on a flag in the window next to the pink one, and I drew in a deep breath as I raised my knuckles to tap on the glass, hoping William's parents weren't such Gator fans that they flew the school's flag in their bedroom window.

I'd tapped a few times when the curtain moved, and I took a couple of steps back, wary of whose face would appear when the curtain and the flag were pulled to the side.

Sleepy eyes squinted at me, and then William managed a half-smile as he raised the window.

"What are you doing?" he asked with a yawn.

"I need to talk to you."

"All right. Meet me around front, and I'll let you in."

"What about your parents? Can't I just come through your window so no one knows I'm here?"

"Oh, hell no. My brother James got caught sneaking a girl in his room years ago, and he still hasn't heard the end of it. It's best if I tell her you're here and meet you in the living room."

"No! Don't tell your mother I showed up outside your window in the middle of the night. What will she think?"

"It's fine. Don't worry. She'll be okay."

I made my way around to the front and waited, blinking against the bright porch light when he turned it on.

"Hey, what's up?" he said when he swung the door open, and after checking to make sure his mom wasn't standing right behind him, I rushed into his arms.

"He's horrible!" I cried as my tears broke free. "I hate him. I want to run away. I want to leave that damned house and never see him again."

"Slow down," William said as he wrapped his arms around me and stroked his hands up and down my back. "What happened?"

I tried to wipe my eyes with my sleeve, and he grabbed a tissue from the box on the end table and handed it to me as he took my hand and led me to the couch.

"C'mere. Sit down and tell me what happened."

He wrapped his arm around my shoulders as I snuggled into his side.

"I showed him my report card, and he told me I was average. He said he's signing me up for summer school on Monday, and I have to retake any class below a *B*."

"Dang."

"Yeah. Dang. I hate him, William. I swear I hate him."

"Don't say that," he said, planting his lips against my hair as he squeezed me closer to him. "He's your dad. You aren't supposed to hate your dad."

"Yeah, well, dads aren't supposed to hate their daughters either, but he does."

"He doesn't hate you. He just has high standards for you. Which means he loves you, in his own way."

"You don't understand," I said, pushing away from him. "I need you to be on my side. Why can't anyone be on my side?"

"I am on your side. Always."

"Then why aren't you agreeing with me?"

"I'm just trying to understand his point of view."

I stood and balled my hands into fists in my frustration.

"I don't want you to understand his point of view! I want you to understand mine. I want you to agree with me."

He stood and tried to hug me, but I pulled away. He refused to let me as he pulled me close.

"I do agree with you, okay? I know how hard you worked to pull that grade up. But I also know that you were failing because you had goofed off at the beginning of the year. You told me that yourself. So, I can kind of see where he's coming from in wanting you to do better."

"Why are you taking his side?" I said, no longer even trying to whisper.

"Is everything okay?"

The voice came from behind me, and I whirled to see a woman tying her robe around her as she shuffled into the living room in her slippers.

"It's fine, Ma."

I turned toward the door, not wanting to meet her eyes. "I'm sorry. I should go."

"No, Catherine, don't," William said, reaching for my hand.

"You okay?" his mother asked. "Do your parents know you're here?"

"She's fine, Ma. Please go back to bed."

"I'm leaving." I tried to pull my hand from his, but he held tight to it, refusing to let go.

"You shouldn't drive if you're upset," she said. "Come. Sit until you can calm down."

"I'm fine. I apologize for showing up like this and waking everyone up," I said, still unable to look at her. "I shouldn't have come."

"Well, you're here now, so you might as well sit down and collect your thoughts. It seems my son has forgotten his manners, so I'll introduce myself. I'm Abigail Ward, but most folks call me Abby."

She extended her hand to me, and I forced myself to look up at her. It surprised me to see no trace of anger in her expression, only concern. She smiled, and I tried to return the gesture as I took her hand and shook it.

"Oh, sorry," William mumbled. "Ma, this is Catherine Johnson."

"Nice to meet you, Catherine," she said as she released my hand. "Would you like a glass of water? Or perhaps some iced tea?"

"No, ma'am. I'm fine. I'm sorry if I woke you."

"I was reading, so I wasn't asleep yet." She sighed and put her hands on her hips. "I'll head back to bed before your father wakes up, William, but if you need anything, let me know." She turned to me and smiled again. "I hope you're still planning to come for dinner tomorrow evening."

I nodded, and so did she.

"All right. Well, I'll leave you two to chat. Don't stay up too late, okay?"

Her reluctance to leave was obvious, and I held my breath until she was out of sight, releasing it with a loud exhale as William took my hand in his and brought it to his lips.

"You okay?" he whispered.

"I don't even know. I can't believe your mom just came out here and offered me a glass of tea and then went back to bed. My parents would have gone ballistic."

"Ma's generally pretty cool. I mean, I'm sure I'll get questioned in the morning, but it's okay."

"I'm sorry."

"Don't be." He pulled me into his arms and kissed the top of my head. "I'm always here for you. You know that. And I *am* on your side. Always."

"I can't wait to be outta that house. I want to get as far away from him as possible."

"Well, hey, he'll be gone all summer now, so that's a good thing, right?"

I looked up at William and groaned. "Yeah. He and my mom will be in Paris seeing all the things I wanted to see with her."

"So, you'll go to Paris another time. Who knows? Maybe you and I will go to Paris someday."

The thought of walking through Paris with William made my heart soar, and I couldn't help smiling.

"Really? Could we?"

"Why not?" He shrugged and settled his arms around my waist as he grinned.

"I didn't know if you'd do something like that."

He tilted his head to one side and grinned. "Don't you know by now that I would do anything for you?"

"You'll go to Paris with me?"

"Sure. I mean, I have to finish college first. And you should probably finish college first. But yeah. I'd go anywhere with you."

He pressed his lips to mine, and I put my arms around his neck.

"At least this means we can see each other without sneaking around all summer," he said, and I frowned.

"A lot of good that does us when you'll have two jobs and I'll have school."

He brushed my hair back behind my ear and smiled. "We've made it work so far, haven't we? We'll find a way."

I nodded just as a girl walked out of the hallway and across the living room.

"Gross! Get a room. Somewhere else!" she exclaimed as she went into the kitchen and turned on the light.

William rolled his eyes and shook his head. "That would be my sister, Patricia."

"I really should go. I feel bad that this is how I'm meeting your family."

"It's fine."

"I just needed to see you. To hear your voice. Somehow, you make everything feel like it's gonna be all right."

He smiled and squeezed me closer to him. "It is going to be all right. You'll see. We're going to have the best summer ever."

Patricia flipped the kitchen light off and made a show of covering her eyes with her hand as she walked back down the hallway with a glass of water.

"Okay, I'm going," I whispered to William. "For real this time."

"Wait a second," he said. "I've got something for you."

He disappeared down the hallway behind his sister, and I took the opportunity to look around the living room. The space was cozy, smaller than my own downstairs den.

The large overstuffed sofa and love seat with their dusty blue and country mauve floral pattern filled the room, and a big brown recliner sat in the corner with a large grandfather clock ticking time behind it. I scanned the myriad of family photos scattered across the walls, trying to pick out William amongst his siblings in the dim light of the table lamp beside me.

"Here," he said as he came back into the room carrying something that looked like a wad of white paper in the palm of his hand. "I was gonna give this to you tomorrow night and have it wrapped and all, but maybe it would better if I give it to you now. Cheer you up a little, perhaps."

"You got me a present? Why?"

"For passing your classes. You worked really hard, and I wanted to give you something to say, um, I don't know, that you did well. I mean, it's nothing big or fancy or anything. It's just something I…well, here. Open it."

He handed me the paper, which felt so light I wasn't sure it held anything at all. I peeled back the edges and nestled inside was a small wooden carving of a sea turtle with a heart in the center of his back.

"It's a turtle!" I flipped the creature over in my hand to see two Ws etched into its belly. "Oh my gosh! Did you *make* this?"

His cheeks flushed red in the soft lamplight as he looked at the turtle and shrugged. "Obviously, I didn't make the wood. God did that, but I carved it into a turtle."

My mouth dropped as I stared at the detailed markings on the shell and the sweet face peeking out from beneath it.

"His head looks kinda funny. I didn't make it stick all the way out because I was worried it might break off, you know?"

I looked up at William, unable to find the words to convey what I was feeling. No one had ever made something for me before. It felt so personal. My closet and my room held countless items with extravagant price tags, but nothing purchased had ever moved me the way William's turtle did.

"I know it's probably silly," he said with a wave of his hand. "You don't have to keep it or anything."

"Are you kidding me?" I asked, clutching the turtle to my chest. "I love it. It's perfect. I can't believe you made this for me." I moved my hand beneath the lampshade, so I could stare at the turtle in the light. "How long did it take you?"

He shrugged. "I started working on it after we saw that carving of the turtle at the wildlife center. You're always saying you want to bring a turtle home with you, so I figured this way you could. I was worried I wouldn't finish it in time for your report card, but luckily, I did."

"How'd you know I would pass?"

His grin returned. "Because I was teaching you! No, seriously, I never doubted you would. I think you could do anything if you set your mind to it."

I stared at him, unsure of how to take his words. I'd been told plenty of times by teachers, both my parents, and Isabel that I could accomplish great things if I'd only apply myself. But somehow, the way William said it didn't sound like he was disappointed in me or angry that I wasn't enough. He made it sound like a positive thing. Like a good quality. Something he admired in me.

Tears filled my eyes, and I threw my arms around his neck, nearly knocking him off balance.

"Thank you," I whispered against his neck before stepping back to wipe my eyes with the back of my hand. "I should go. I don't want your mom or your sister to come back out here and me still be here."

"You don't have to," he said, reaching to wipe away a tear as it fell on my cheek. "Please don't cry. You know I can't bear to see you cry."

"They're happy tears, I swear."

He frowned and laid his palm against my cheek.

"Still, it messes me up inside when you cry."

"Then I'll go so you don't have to see it." I smiled as I turned toward the front door, and he took my hand and walked beside me. He held the door open, his brows scrunching in confusion as he looked out at the driveway.

"Where's your car?"

"Oh, I parked out by the road. I didn't want anyone to know I was here, so I didn't pull into your driveway."

He grinned and released my hand to bend and grab his boots from the mud stand by the door. "Not a lot gets by this household without everyone knowing."

"What are you doing?"

"I'm gonna walk you to your car."

I shook my head. "No, you don't have to do that. That's silly."

"Silly is you thinking I'd let you walk out there by yourself."

I tried to protest, but he made it clear he wasn't going to budge as we walked hand-in-hand down the porch steps and across the lawn.

When we reached my car, he opened the door for me and waited as I bent inside to place my turtle on the dash. Then he wrapped me in his arms and kissed me once more, and I pressed my body against his, not wanting to leave his embrace.

"I hope someday we can wake up in each other's arms," I said when our lips parted, and he gazed into my eyes with such intensity that I was certain he was finally going to utter the words I'd longed to hear him say.

I knew he loved me. I was certain of it. But he'd never said it. Every time I thought he might, he always turned away or said something different instead.

Maybe it was like the first time we kissed. Maybe he just needed a nudge from me. Maybe he was waiting for me to go out on the limb first.

I placed my hands on either side of his face and summoned the courage to speak. My heart pounded so loudly I was sure he could hear it.

"I love you, William."

His eyes widened for a moment, and then he crushed my mouth beneath his, his hands in my hair as he pulled me closer. "I love you, too," he whispered as we paused for a breath, and then we both said it over and over again between kisses until I drove away with a smile.

CHAPTER 20
Caterina

With my parents away in Europe, I was free to see William whenever I wanted. Our time was still limited by his jobs and my summer classes, but without worrying about curfews or explanations, it was easier to work around our busy schedules.

At first, Isabel was a stickler about what time I'd be home and where I was going. I think she was nervous with the responsibility of corralling me for the summer, but when the first couple of weeks went by with no problems, she relaxed a good bit.

She balked the first time I brought William to the house, insisting that my parents would not be okay with a gentleman caller coming over while they were away. I told her he was a friend from school who was helping me pass my classes, and though she kept a wary eye on us as we studied, she didn't make him leave.

The more he visited and the more I showed her the high grades on my tests and assignments, the more comfortable she grew with his presence. Soon, she didn't feel the need to stay in the room the entire time he was there. I think she knew there was more to it than math and history, but she'd always had a soft spot for me, so she let things slide as long as my behavior wasn't a problem and my grades were good. I think she also felt sorry for me that I'd been left behind while my mother mailed postcards from all the sites I'd dreamed of us seeing together.

Plus, with William able to hang out at the house with me, I stayed home more often, and that meant Isabel knew where I was and who I was with.

On Sundays, William only had to work the first half of the day, so Sunday afternoons and evenings became our adventure time. It was the only day of the week we had enough daylight to get out of town and explore beyond the nearby woods and rivers.

"Let's go to the beach," I said one evening as we sat on my sofa discussing plans for the upcoming Sunday.

"Look at my skin," he said with a grin. "Do you want me to have even more freckles? Redheads don't do the beach."

"That's what sunscreen is for, silly. We've never been to the beach together."

"That's because I don't go to the beach."

"I thought you loved nature! Do you know how much nature there is at the beach?" I moved the textbook from his lap and straddled his hips as I wrapped my arms around his neck, pressing my forehead to his. "C'mon. I love the beach, and I haven't been all summer. I want to play in the waves with you."

He started to protest again, but I kissed him into submission, and when Sunday arrived, we set out for the Atlantic coast with me wearing a brand-new yellow bikini, William slathered in sunscreen with an extra bottle in the beach bag, and a gigantic umbrella filling the back seat of my convertible.

My friends and I usually went to Daytona Beach, famous for its raucous fun, but William and I opted for a lesser-known area north of Daytona where the chances were slim that we'd see anyone I knew from school.

After we'd frolicked in the waves for a bit, we decided to take a walk down the shore. We'd gone quite a ways from our beach blanket and were just talking about turning around when William spotted a large sea turtle up ahead. It lay motionless in the wet sand just out of reach of the crashing waves, and at first, my heart was broken with the thought that it might be dead.

I held my breath as we got closer, but then a slow blink assured me it was alive.

I jumped up and down and clung to William's arm as I squealed. "It's alive! It's alive, William!"

William squatted beside the turtle, tilting his head to get a closer look. "Yeah, but he's in distress. He needs to be back in the water."

"So, what do we do? Do we pick him up and put him back in?"

"No. We shouldn't touch him." He stood and shaded his eyes to look up and down the shoreline. "We have to find a lifeguard. Someone who can call a wildlife rescue."

"Is he gonna die?"

"I don't know. Here, cup your hands together and pour some water over him. Try to keep him wet, and I'll run to find a lifeguard."

While he was gone, a family came by, and they used their plastic beach bucket to help me keep the turtle as wet as possible in the relentless heat of the sun.

I know William ran as fast as he could, but it seemed to take forever for him to return with a man wearing a collared shirt with the county name embroidered on it.

A wildlife rescue crew had been called, and by the time they arrived almost an hour later, there was a crowd circled around us, and a relay team of people with a constant flow of water streaming over the turtle.

"Will he make it?" I asked one of the wildlife crew. "Will he be okay?"

"We're going to do all we can for him."

I was crushed to watch them take him away, knowing that I would likely never know his fate.

We walked back to our beach umbrella, and it was only then that I turned to look at William. He was burnt to a crisp.

"Oh no!" I said, covering my mouth with my hand. "You're red as a lobster!"

"Yeah, I can feel it. I'm gonna be hating life for a few days."

"I'm so sorry! We got all caught up in saving the turtle and forgot to keep putting sunscreen on you. Oh, William!"

"It's okay. It's not your fault. I should have grabbed the sunscreen when I ran to get the lifeguard."

"Let's go. Let's get you out of the sun."

We packed up and went to the car, and I put the top back in place to give him shade on the way home.

"So much for our day on the beach, huh? Sorry we didn't get to stay and watch the sunset like you wanted," he said as I drove.

"Are you kidding me? This is like the best day at the beach ever! I mean, other than you getting fried, of course. But I got to see a sea turtle up close, and we might have saved his life."

"I hope so. He could have been stranded on the beach for a reason. There might have been something wrong."

"Don't tell me that. Let me believe that he just got too tired to swim and couldn't find his way back into the water. Let me go on with my life believing that we saved him, and they're going to put him back out to sea where he can reunite with his family."

"If you say so."

"I do. I say so."

William dozed most of the way home, which was good since it kept him from knowing he was in pain.

He winced as he got out of my car in his driveway, but his smile had returned when he came around to my door to say goodbye.

I frowned at the sight of his bright red skin.

"I hate that you got burned. I hope it doesn't hurt too bad. You might want to take something. Like, I don't know, an aspirin or something."

"I'm sure my mom has some aloe vera gel somewhere. Once she's done lecturing me about the sun, I'll douse myself in it."

"Hey, I thought a lot about it on the drive home, and I think maybe that's what I want to do."

"Douse me in gel?" he asked with a raised eyebrow.

"No, silly. Turtle rescue. I mean, that's like a career, right? Can I major in that?"

He shrugged. "You could probably major in marine biology or some type of environmental science. I don't really know exactly what qualifications you would need, but we can research it."

I grinned, pleased to have the seed of an idea for my future.

"Cool. I think I'd like that."

He leaned forward, bracing his hands on the car door. "You know, animal rescue doesn't typically pay a lot of money."

"I figured. But how cool would that be if my job every day was to help turtles?"

"Pretty cool," he said with a grin. He leaned through the open window to kiss me, and I reached up and put my hands on his shoulders, forgetting about his sunburn.

"Yeow," he howled. "Watch the skin, babe."

"Oh, sorry."

He grimaced and took a step back from the car. "It's okay. I'll call you later. Love you."

"Love you, too. Thanks for going to the beach with me and helping me rescue the turtle."

"I told you I'd always find you turtles, didn't I?"

I laughed as he walked backwards toward the house. "Yes, you did."

CHAPTER 21
Caterina

We went to the beach several more times in the weeks that followed, but always later in the afternoon or early evening so that William wouldn't get burned again. One night, we even got lucky and witnessed the full moon breaking the horizon as it journeyed high above the waves, illuminating the entire beach in an eerie glow.

The weekend before my parents were due to return, William told me he'd arranged to have Saturday off and had planned a surprise adventure.

I'd been in a funk knowing our free time with minimal supervision was coming to an end, but the thought of spending the entire day together cheered me up, and I couldn't wait to see what he had in mind.

He drove my car toward the east coast, but instead of going to our normal beach spot north of Daytona, he headed south down the Atlantic coast. No amount of guessing and pleading could get him to tell me our destination, and I had no idea where we were going until we pulled into the parking lot of a sea life rehabilitation center.

"Are we going to see turtles?" I asked, clapping my hands together in excitement.

"Not just any turtle," William said with a grin as he took the keys from the ignition and handed them back to me.

"What?"

He waited for me to join me at the front of the car. "Our turtle."

I shook my head in confusion. "What do you mean? Are we getting a turtle? I thought you said—"

"No, we're not getting a turtle!" He laughed and slapped his palm against his forehead. "Good grief! The turtle we helped on the beach that day. I was thinking about him, and I called the wildlife group that came and got him. They told me he'd been moved to this rehab center, and when I called here and explained the situation, they said we could come and visit him."

"Oh, wow! William! Are you kidding me?"

He laughed as I wrapped my arms around him and planted kisses all over his face.

Once we'd checked in on our turtle, whom I'd taken the liberty of naming Albert, we spent the better part of the day exploring the center with our guide, Nikole. We fed stingrays and manatees, and we learned so much about marine life that my head was swimming by the time we left.

"What a cool job! Can you imagine working there every day?" I asked William as we ate a late lunch in a burger joint near Melbourne Beach. "That would be awesome. Nikole was so cool, wasn't she?"

"Yeah. That was nice of her to talk to you about her degree and her career path. Helpful info!"

"Yeah. Did you see her tattoo?"

He shook his head as he took a long draw on his soda straw.

"She had a turtle on the back of her right calf. You didn't see it?"

"No, I didn't notice it. Why?"

"It was really cool." I crumbled my napkin over the remnants of my burger and fries and pushed my plate away. "I think I want one."

"A tattoo? Really?"

"Yeah. Why? Why do you say it like that?"

He paused as he finished chewing and swallowed. "I'm just surprised, I guess."

"Why? You think tattoos are bad?"

"I don't think they're bad or not bad. For me, it's just too permanent. What if it's something you like when you get it, something you feel strongly about, but then you change your mind later? You're stuck with it painted on your skin for the rest of your life."

"So, you wouldn't ever get one?"

"I don't think so. I can't imagine anything I'd feel strongly enough about that I would need it displayed on my body. Permanently."

I waited for the waitress to take away my plate and nodded when she asked if I wanted a refill on my soda.

"I'm going to do it," I said, my mind made up. "I'm getting a tattoo of a sea turtle."

"Okay," William said with a one-shoulder shrug. "But I think you have to be eighteen to get one. Unless you have your parent go with you or something."

"Ha! Like that would happen." I chuckled at the thought. "My father would die if I got a tattoo. Actually, he'd probably kill me first, and then he'd die."

"Is that why you're getting one? To piss your dad off?"

"No. I'm getting it because I want it. I love turtles, and I'm never going to *not* love turtles, so as soon as I turn eighteen, I'm getting a sea turtle tattoo."

I grinned, pleased with my decision and already picturing what it would like and where I would put it.

I looked up to see William smiling at me.

"What?" I asked, suddenly self-conscious. "Do I have something on my face?" I grabbed a napkin from the dispenser and wiped my face with it as he laughed.

"No, not at all."

"Then what? Why were you smiling at me like that? What were you thinking?"

He reached across the table and took my hand in his, stroking the back of my hand with his thumb. "I was thinking how beautiful you are when you're smiling. I love your smile. I love you, Catherine."

Warmth spread throughout me, and I smiled even bigger. "I love you, too. Thanks for taking me to see Albert."

He laughed again, and it made me feel giddy inside.

"Albert, huh. What kind of name is that for a turtle?"

"He didn't seem to mind it." I pulled my hand from his and shifted to tuck my feet beneath me.

"It's not like he could tell you if he did."

"Nikole said they communicate. She said even the fish have ways of communicating with her. You just have to be around them long enough to get to know them." I picked at the paper fibers of the napkin as I thought about Nikole's job and what we'd seen that day. "Do you think I could ever get a job there?"

William shrugged. "I don't see why not. You'd have to get your degree first, of course."

"Well, yeah. I know that. But that would be like the coolest job ever."

His grin faded, and he looked away.

"What?" I asked, leaning across the table in concern. "Why do you look sad all of a sudden?"

"Nothing."

His mood had changed, and I needed to know why.

"What? William, tell me."

"It's nothing. It's just that it's an awful long way from Ocala."

I chewed on my bottom lip as I considered his words and what they meant.

"True. But I'm sure there's places like that closer, right?"

He arched an eyebrow and stared at me. "To Ocala? We're practically in the middle of the state, Catherine. If you're gonna work with marine life, you have to be on the coast."

"And if you're gonna work with horses, you need to be near Ocala."

He nodded and then looked away as he drained the remainder of his soda.

"So, we build our own place," I said. "We build one big huge rehab center, and you work with horses, and I work with turtles."

He scoffed with a grunt.

"Do you have any idea how much money that would take?"

"I have money! Lots of it. We don't have to worry about that. We can build whatever we want."

I reached across the table for his hand, but he pulled it away. His eyes narrowed, and his jaw grew tight, something I'd rarely seen.

"I don't want your father's money, Catherine."

I opened my mouth to respond, but just then the waitress came to take his plate and lay the check on the table.

William thanked her, and then he reached to take his wallet from his pocket as she walked away.

I grabbed my purse to pay my half as we'd agreed at the start of the summer, but William held up his hand and shook his head.

"I got it today. It was my surprise adventure, so I'll pay."

"But what about your college fund? You need your money. We said if we were going to do things that cost—"

"I know what we said, but I can buy my girlfriend lunch. I've worked and saved all summer for college. Just let me pay for your meal."

"You don't have to—"

"I want to. Let's just go," he said, laying the cash on the table as he stood and cleared his throat.

We walked to the car in silence, and he went to the passenger side without offering to drive or bothering to open my door for me.

I stared at the road ahead and did a mental replay of the conversation, wondering what had gone wrong. We'd never had an actual argument, and I was normally the one to get sulky and act like a jerk, so I wasn't sure what to do with his foul mood or what had caused it. I suspected it had to do with money.

I knew he was sensitive about us splitting the cost of everything, but we'd discussed at the beginning of the summer that it only made sense for me to pay my own way since he needed money for school. He'd gotten a couple of academic scholarships, but they weren't enough to cover his tuition, fees, and textbooks, plus he'd need money for fuel and food.

He still had to buy a vehicle of some kind before school started. He'd relied on his family to give him rides during the summer, but that wouldn't be an option for going back and forth to Gainesville. His brother James drove a semi-truck cross-country and was often gone for long stretches, so it had been easy for William to borrow his pick-up, but he wouldn't be able to depend on that for classes and work daily.

Still, I didn't understand why my statement about our future had upset him. We talked about the future all the time, and our conversations often included random references to the time beyond college when we could be together out in the open. We'd talked about getting married after college many times. It had to be my mention of money that bothered him, but surely he knew we wouldn't have money problems once were together.

"William, you do realize that I'm my father's only heir, right?"

He sat with his head leaned against the passenger side window as I drove, and he glanced at me and looked back at the highway with a frown. "What?"

"You said you didn't want my father's money. But it's going to be *my* money. I'll inherit it someday. I have a trust fund that kicks in when I turn twenty-one, and then I'll get more increments of my inheritance as I reach ages designated by my father's lawyer. That money will be our money. We'll be able to do whatever we want with it."

His scowl darkened. "You don't get it. I don't want us to depend on your father's money. I don't want us to need his approval or his permission to live our lives. I want us to make our own way. To pay our own bills. Build our own life. That way we don't have to answer to anyone but us."

"But that's ridiculous. Why would we go without when I have the means for us to never worry about things like that? I get that you grew up poor, but I didn't."

His back straightened, and he turned to face me. "Poor? You think I'm poor?"

"No, that's not what I meant."

"That's what you said."

"I didn't mean it like a bad thing. C'mon. You have to admit we've grown up very differently."

"Yes, we did. But just because I wasn't handed everything I wanted on a silver platter doesn't mean my family is poor. My family works hard, and my parents taught us to appreciate everything we have and to work for what we want."

My mouth dropped open in indignation. "I appreciate what I have, too. I appreciate that my father built up a whole bunch of money so that I don't have to work two jobs to pay for college. I appreciate that I have this car, and that I have an allowance that lets me buy what I need and what I want. Don't think for a minute that I don't appreciate what it means to have money. But I'm telling you that you can have this life, too. When we get married, my money is your money. You won't have to struggle. You don't have to worry about that. I'll have enough money for us to do whatever we want."

He shook his head and looked out the window.

"You don't get it."

"You're right. I don't. This should be a good thing, and you're acting like it's some sort of insult."

"It is! I want to be able to provide for you. I want to be able to take care of what we need without having to get it from your father."

"Is this about ego? Is that what this is? Some sort of male rooster crowing thing?"

He scoffed, but I knew I'd hit a nerve.

"It is, isn't it? If this whole situation was turned around and you were the wealthy one, and I was the one working two jobs, you wouldn't have a problem at all with the money becoming ours someday, would you? You wouldn't think twice about sharing it with me and using it to build our future."

"It's not the same," he said, his tone more dejected than angry. He continued to stare out the window, his arms crossed tightly over his ribs.

"It shouldn't be any different, though. Why should I give up my inheritance, give up the life I've known and enjoy, just so you can feel some sense of manliness by struggling?"

"You shouldn't," he said. "You shouldn't have to give anything up. I'm going to sleep."

He leaned the seat back and closed his eyes, and I knew the conversation was over.

Hot tears stung my eyelids, and I blinked them back, determined not to let them fall. I wasn't going to apologize for who I was or what I had. And I wasn't going to become poor and stress out about money if I didn't need to. William would come around. He'd have to. He'd fallen in love with a rich girl, and there were worse problems in life to have.

CHAPTER 22
Caterina

Whether from guilt or genuinely missing me, I don't know, but my mother was more clingy when she and my father returned. She didn't want me out of her sight, and if I asked to go anywhere, she'd moan and remind me that she'd been gone all summer and wanted me all to herself.

William and I could still talk on the phone at night after my parents had gone to bed, but we hadn't seen each other in over a week since they'd returned, and summertime was running out. I missed him terribly, and the more insistent my mother was that I not leave her side, the more sullen and irritable I became.

"Why don't you come to the Women's Club with me?" she asked as she stared at the clothes flung across my bedroom floor with disdain. "I'm going to be sharing a slideshow of photos from my trip."

As if one viewing of all the sights I'd missed hadn't already been enough.

"No thanks," I mumbled, keeping my focus on the fashion magazine spread on the floor beside my bed as I lay on my stomach and flipped the pages.

"We could go shopping afterwards. Anywhere you'd like. We can get started on new school clothes."

There was a time when that offer might have made it worth it to sit through a luncheon of matronly socialites gossiping about the whole town, but this was my first opportunity to escape her clutches and see William, and nothing was going to stop me.

"I don't really feel like shopping today."

"Oh, dear heart, are you all right? You're not ill, are you? I'm gonna have Isabel come and take your temperature."

She left without any further questions, as I knew she would if she thought I would need care beyond her wallet.

As soon as her car had left the garage, I was already on my way downstairs.

"Where are you off to?" Isabel said as I passed her on the landing.

"I'm going to the stables to try and catch William before his shift ends."

"Oh, no you are not! Come here. Don't you walk away from me. Turn back around here."

I groaned, but I stopped.

"I mean it," she said. "Turn around."

I did as she requested, and she came and stood in front of me.

"You had your fun this summer, but now your mother and father are home, and it's time to straighten up and remember who you are."

I glared at her and turned to go, but when she growled my name, I stopped, unwilling to push her.

"You know you can't keep hanging around that boy. I shouldn't have let it progress like I did, but I'd never seen you so happy, and I couldn't bear to make you miserable. But enough is enough. It ends now."

I spun to face her. "It isn't going to end, Isabel. Not ever. I love him, and he loves me. We're going to finish college, and then we'll be married. And no one will be able to keep us apart."

She closed the space between us, her eyes wide as she placed her hands on my shoulders. "You listen to me, and you listen good. I know you weren't completely honest with me about who he was. He doesn't go to your school. He's not someone your parents would approve of for a suitor. He was a summer fling, young lady, not marriage material. Your father would be livid if he found out about this, and you know it."

"He's not going to find out, though, is he? I'm not going to tell him, and you're not going to tell him because he'd fire you for letting us be together all summer. William goes away to school in three weeks. Then we just have to get through this year, and I can join him at the university. Then when Father meets him, he'll be a college student, just like any other college student I might meet."

She suddenly wrapped her arms around me and squeezed me so tightly that I couldn't breathe.

"Oh dear Lord, what have I done?" she wailed. "This can't be. It can't."

I wriggled free of her grasp and was surprised to see tears in her eyes.

She swiped at them and shook her head. "I never should have let him in here. I never should have let this go on. I wanted you to be happy."

I reached to place my hand on her arm, wanting to give her comfort as she'd so often given me.

"I am happy. He makes me happy. Don't worry, okay? It's not your fault, Isabel. I would have found a way to be with him, one way or another. I love him. I don't care what my father says."

"What he *says?*" Her face contorted with fear and worry. "It's not what he says, Catherine. It's what he'll do! He'll destroy that boy and his entire family. You have to end this. It was a summer fling. A crush. You've had your fun. Now be done and tell the boy goodbye."

My chin trembled even as I jutted it forward in rebellious resolve and clenched my teeth together.

"No. I love him, and no one is going to stop me."

I spun on my heel and ran from the house, ignoring her cries behind me. I punched the gas as I pulled my car from the garage, the tires squealing as I floored it and headed down the driveway.

By the time I reached the stables, my need to see William had reached a fevered pitch. I was frantic to be in his arms. To feel the security of his love. To know that it was all going to turn out all right.

"Have you seen William?" I asked the first stable boy I encountered.

"I think he's over in the second barn," the boy said, and I ran across the mulch-covered courtyard, searching for any sight of the redhead I loved.

He was shoveling hay when I burst into the stall behind him, and the smile that lit up his face quickly faded when he saw how upset I was.

"What's wrong?"

I ran into his arms, and he tossed aside the pitchfork he held as he wrapped me in his embrace.

"What's going on?" he asked. "What's happened?"

I shook my head, aware of the danger that I was putting us in but unwilling to let go of him just yet.

VIOLET HOWE

He pulled my arms from around him and stepped back just enough to look into my eyes.

"Babe, what's wrong? What happened?"

"Tell me we'll be together," I whispered.

"What?"

"Tell me. Tell me that nothing can come between us, and we'll be together. Always."

"What's this about?"

"Tell me!"

The sound of footsteps in the corridor drew his attention, and he stepped back from me and picked up the pitchfork as another stable hand entered the stall.

"Oh, sorry!" the boy said. "I didn't realize you had a visitor. I'll, just, uh—"

"Can you give us a minute?" William asked.

"Sure thing," the boy said with a grin as he looked me up and down. "I'll go get the water buckets, but don't think you're getting out of shoveling shit just because she's here. If your days are numbered, I'm making sure you shovel every day before you leave so you won't forget us."

William waved the boy away and looked back down at me. "What are you doing here? What happened?"

"What did he mean?" I said, replaying the boy's words in my head.

"Did something happen with your parents? You have to tell me quickly. I don't have much time."

"You're still working here when you go to college, so why would he say you're leaving? Why would you forget them?"

William ran his hand through his hair and looked out the window of the stall.

"I was waiting until I saw you to tell you. I didn't want to tell you over the phone."

A sick heaviness settled in the pit of my stomach, and I laid my hand over it in an effort to calm my fears.

"Tell me what?"

"It's good news, actually." A smile formed in one corner of his mouth, but it didn't carry to his eyes. "I got a grant. All my expenses are paid. Tuition, room, meals, books. Everything. Four years."

His eyes darted back and forth watching mine as he waited for my reaction.

The smell of horse manure in the air coupled with the sweet stench of the hay and the sour aroma of animal bodies in the humid heat of August made me put my hand over my nose and mouth to keep from gagging.

The world around me had slowed to a crawl, and there was no sound other than my own heartbeat and the distant stamping of horse hooves and the exhaling of their breaths.

"What does that mean?" I asked, though I knew fully well.

He swallowed hard and put his hand on his hip, propping his boot on the bottom rung of the stall gate as he looked out the window again.

"I'm moving to Gainesville."

I took a step back and bumped into the wooden post that held the gate. I couldn't breathe. I couldn't swallow. I couldn't think beyond the response that was playing over and over again in my head.

"You're leaving me," I finally managed to say out loud.

"No," he said, grasping both my hands in his. "That's not it at all. You know that. This is a great opportunity—"

"You're leaving me," I said again, pulling my hands away.

"No, I'm not. This doesn't change anything. I'll still be less than an hour away. We can talk on the phone every night. We can still—"

"You're leaving me." My voice shook, and tears filled my eyes and refused to be held back.

"Oh, God. Catherine, don't do this. Not now. Not here." He glanced over my head and lowered his voice, which had already been just above a whisper. "You know we can't be seen together. You know I can't talk right now. I—"

"You're leaving me," I said one more time, and then I turned and ran. I ran all the way to my car, not looking back to see if he followed, and not caring who saw me on my way out.

CHAPTER 23
Caterina

Much of what happened after I left William at the stables is a blur. I know I went to Charlotte's to try and score something that would take the edge off, but her mom said she was staying at Pam's for the weekend. That pretty much guaranteed that Pam's parents were out of town, so I headed there determined to find a way to stop my world from spinning out of control.

That's the funny thing about substance abuse, though. It only makes everything spin faster. That might seem like more fun in the beginning, but it can leave you passed out and choking on your vomit until you wake up in an emergency room surrounded by doctors.

The memory of my father's face when he arrived at the hospital is one thing from that night that is not blurry. His face was bright red with anger, and his cheeks puffed out with each exhale as he paced at the foot of my bed and listened to my mother cry.

He didn't speak to me. He didn't even look at me.

He nodded as the doctor explained that I'd aspirated and was lucky to be alive. He gave no response when they told him they'd pumped my stomach or that they'd found a near-lethal cocktail of alcohol and amphetamines in my blood. He ignored my mother's wails when the doctor mentioned cocaine, and then he left the room as she bent over my bed and cried.

He didn't come back in when the police questioned me about where I'd gotten the drugs and alcohol. He wasn't there when they asked who had left my car outside the emergency room with me passed out in the back seat or if I had any idea who might have called from a nearby pay phone to alert hospital staff to my predicament.

In fact, I didn't see my father again for the rest of my two-night stay at the hospital.

My mother left that first night once Isabel arrived to stay with me, and she returned alone the next day at midday. She stayed by my side while Isabel went home to shower and eat, but when my faithful maid returned, my mother stood with a sigh. She drew her purse onto her shoulder and leaned over me to smooth her hand over my hair.

"I need to go home and rest, dear. Hospitals give me such anxiety. Isabel will be here if you need anything, though."

I think if Isabel had been able to sign my discharge papers, my mother would have stayed at home, but the hospital required a parent for the procedural part.

"Are you hungry?" Isabel asked as we entered the house. "Do you want something to eat?"

"No, thanks. I just want to sleep. I just want to be in my own bed in my own room."

I also wanted to be alone, so I could call William. I hadn't talked to him since I ran away from the stables on Saturday, and I was sure he'd been worried sick.

"Where's my phone?" I asked my mother as Isabel turned back the covers on my bed.

"Oh, it wouldn't stop ringing, so I unplugged it," she said as she stared out my window. "Someone kept calling over and over again. Probably those good-for-nothing friends of yours who abandoned you at the hospital."

"At least they took her to the hospital," Isabel said. "She's lucky they did."

My mother let out a whimper and covered her mouth with her hand, and I climbed into bed and closed my eyes, not wanting to go through it with her all over again.

She sat on the side of my bed and smoothed back my hair.

"Are you sure you don't remember anything, dear? Is anything coming back to you? Where you were or who you were with?"

I shook my head without opening my eyes. "No, Mother. I've told you, and I've told the police. I don't remember anything after leaving our house that morning."

That was only partially true. I remembered going to the stables, which I didn't dare tell anyone since I had no reasonable explanation for being there. I remembered stopping by Charlotte's and then driving to Pam's. I remembered everyone there giving me a hard time for not hanging out with them all summer and teasing me that I wouldn't be able to handle my liquor after not drinking for so long.

My memory held glimpses of the evening after that, but none that I cared to reveal to my mother or the police. I truly had no idea who had loaded me into the back seat of my car and driven me to the hospital, or which friend was the caller who'd probably saved my life.

But given the situation, it was best to just say I had no memories of what had happened the whole day. There was no way I was going to sell out my friends or send anyone to jail. My condition was all my own doing, and no matter who had supplied me, it wasn't their fault. I had to stand firm in my lie.

My eyes were heavy with exhaustion as my mother sat and cried, and though I desperately wanted to talk to William, I couldn't fight off sleep long enough for her to leave the room so I could search for my phone.

When I awoke later that afternoon, my father was seated at the foot of my bed staring at me.

My head pounded, and my throat was sore. I needed to pee, and the residue of the charcoal they'd put in my stomach made me want to throw up again, but I didn't dare move under his gaze.

When he spoke, his voice was so quiet I had to strain to hear him.

"Do you know when I was your age, I had to get up every morning before dawn so I could get my farm chores done before school?" He shifted to cross his right ankle over his left knee, dangling his hand over his knee as the light from the window reflected off his Rolex. "I had no time for friends, and if my father so much as thought that I did have a free moment, he would find a way to fill it with work."

I really had to pee, but I was certain he didn't want to be interrupted.

"Back then, I only dreamed of not having blisters on my hands or not wearing plastic bags inside my boots to keep my feet dry. But I made myself a promise that one day I wouldn't have to do manual labor to put food on the table. I also made myself a promise that when I had children, I would never treat them like cheap labor who existed to do my bidding."

He stood and went to my window, putting his hands in his

pockets with a deep sigh as he looked down at the pool and courtyard.

"I fear that I've done wrong by you. I thought if I gave you the best education, the best opportunities, and all the comforts of wealth, that you'd be better off than I was. That you'd have a better upbringing. An easier time. Less bitterness, perhaps. But now, I'm not so sure. Maybe it was that bitterness that drove me to succeed. Maybe it was that pain, that discomfort, that made me successful. Have I slighted you by not having you earn what you have? Have I ruined your chance at excelling by making life too easy for you?"

I cleared my throat, more as a distraction for my bladder than anything else, but it seemed to startle him, almost like he'd forgotten I was in the room.

He turned, his eyebrows raised, and then he came to the side of the bed and stood staring down at me, his hands clasped behind his back.

"You could have died, Catherine."

I stared back at him, uncertain of what I could possibly say in response, but he continued without waiting for me to speak.

"You've gotten a second chance at life, and I'm hoping that means it's not too late for me to turn this around. I've spoken to the headmaster at the Clover Edon School for Girls School in New York, and although they typically require an application process that begins in the early spring, they've agreed to take you. With a hefty late fee, of course."

All thoughts of my bladder or my headache dissipated as I processed his words. Panic exploded inside me, and I sat up, my heart gripped by fear as I realized he finally meant to make good on the threat he'd used for years.

"No!" The word escaped my lips with no sound as I struggled to breathe.

"We leave in two weeks to get you settled in the dormitory and get your uniforms fitted."

"No!" I repeated, and it came out as a ragged groan. My thoughts were a jumble of chaos as the full weight of his decision sunk in. I had to stop this. I had to change his mind. I didn't want to be banished to New York for my senior year for many reasons, but the thought of leaving William behind and not seeing him for months was unbearable.

My hands shook as I pulled the covers back and stood to face my father.

"Please, no! I'll be better, I promise. No more trouble. No more drinking. I'll make good grades. I'll make *A*s, I swear. Please don't do this."

The steely glint in his eye stoked my panic to near hysteria. This was no empty threat. His mind was made up. He was going to send me away.

"No! Please! You can't do this. Don't make me go. Please! I'm begging you."

I rushed forward and wrapped my arms around him, clinging to him as I pleaded. I'd never begged him for anything before. I'd always stood in defiance—challenging him, arguing with him, matching his stubborn temper stride for stride. But this time, I was desperate, and I was willing to humiliate myself.

He untangled himself from my embrace and stepped to the side.

"Save your tears. It's too late."

"No, it can't be. I only have one year of school left. I'll do better. I will. I swear, I will." I reached for his arm, but he pulled away. "Please, please don't send me away. I screwed up. I know I did. And I'm sorry for that. But I know I can do better. I know I can make you proud. Please. Give me one more chance."

"I've given you every opportunity. Every chance. And you've blown them all," he said through clenched teeth. "I'm doing this for your own good, Catherine. I've failed you in your upbringing, and this is my final effort at making things right."

"No!" I screamed, anger overtaking my fear as I clenched my fists. "It won't make things right for you to kick me out. You're banishing me. It's my senior year, and you want me to go to some new school where I know no one and where I'll never see" —I stopped short of saying William's name and hastened to replace it with something else— "my friends."

Anger flashed in his eyes, and his calm resolve disappeared. "Your friends? Do you mean the friends who left you to die outside the hospital? Do you mean the friends who doped you up and got you drunk and dropped you off alone? Tell me who you were with Saturday night. Tell me who supplied the drugs and alcohol."

I stepped back and shook my head. "I don't remember."

He moved to stand toe-to-toe with me, his breath hot on my face.

"Tell me who drove you to the hospital. Who were you with?"

I tried to take another step back, but my legs were against the bed. I could go no farther.

"I don't remember."

"I don't believe you. I'm going to find out, you know. I will ask everyone in this town, and I won't stop until I know the truth. Until I know whose house you were at and who allowed you to get that messed up. I will not allow this act of humiliating our family to go unpunished. Someone saw you Saturday. Someone knows something. Someone will talk. And when I find out who you were with, I won't give up until they're in jail and their parents don't have a penny left to their name. You don't want to tell me? Fine. You'll be gone soon, and I'll find out what I want to know anyway."

While I feared him finding out who I'd been hanging out with Saturday night, I feared more that his questioning might reveal my relationship with William. I had no way of knowing who might have seen us at the stables Saturday or at some point over the summer. What if he uncovered my secret?

My situation was getting worse by the minute. It was as though the entire world was falling down around me, and I had nowhere to turn.

"Why do you hate me so much?" I whispered.

"Hate you?" His mouth curled in a sneering grin, and my stomach roiled. "I don't hate you, Catherine. You're my flesh and blood. My heir. Everything I've done has been for this family. Everything I do, every sacrifice I make, is for this family. But you? You seem hellbent on destroying it. On destroying my good name, my reputation, and my hopes for the future. So, no, I don't hate you. But right now, I can't stand the sight of you, and I want you gone. I want you out of my house. I want you far away from here under lock and key where you can't do anything else to embarrass me or your mother."

He had leaned so far forward that I fell backwards on the bed retreating from him. He towered over me with that twisted grin, and then he turned and left, slamming the door behind him to leave me alone in a shattered heap.

CHAPTER 24
William

I'd just pulled back the shower curtain when Patricia pounded on the bathroom door.

"William! It's Catherine! She's on the phone!"

I wrapped a towel around my hips and sprinted to the living room, not caring that I was dripping water all over the floor.

"Hello? Catherine?"

"William! I have to see you. Please! Can you come over?"

Relief washed over me at the sound of her voice, but the tension and worry I'd been consumed with for the past two days couldn't subside until I knew what had happened.

"Are you okay? I kept trying to call you after you left the stables, but no one answered, and then Patricia said you overdosed. Is that true?"

"How does she know that?"

Damn. She didn't deny it. I'd hoped somehow that my sister had been mistaken or had misunderstood what she'd heard.

"She's a nursing student, and she interns at the hospital. She was there when they brought you in. So it's true? You overdosed?"

"No, not exactly," Catherine said, her voice quiet. "I got a little too drunk and passed out, and then I got really sick."

I closed my eyes to try and calm the myriad of emotions twisting my insides. Worry. Concern. Fear. Anger. Disbelief.

"Why, Catherine? I thought you quit drinking."

"And I thought you weren't moving to Gainesville."

A pang of guilt wrenched my stomach. She'd left the stables so upset, and when I couldn't reach her, I figured she just didn't want to talk to me. Was I the reason she'd done this? Had she ended up in the hospital because of me?

"Why didn't you call me, Catherine? I've been worried sick."

"I couldn't! My mother took my phone away at home, and I was never alone in the hospital. If it wasn't doctors and nurses, it was my mom or Isabel. Or the police."

"The police? Why? Why were the police there?"

"It's kind of a long story. I need to see you. Can you come over?"

I looked up to see my mother standing at the edge of the hallway, her arms crossed, and her eyes filled with concern. I waved to her to go back to bed and turned toward the wall to try and get some privacy.

"I can't come over right now. Aren't your parents home? It's almost midnight."

"I'll sneak you in. I'll find a way. Please! I have to see you!"

My mother had grabbed a towel and was swishing it around my feet to dry up the water I'd been dripping.

"Hold on," I said to Catherine, grimacing at Ma as I picked up the phone base to carry it down the hall to my room. I was careless with the cord and it knocked over the lamp on the end table, but my mother sighed and told me she'd pick it up.

"All right, I'm back," I said when I'd gotten the cord under the bedroom door, so I could close it.

"I need to see you, William. Please come over!"

"Maybe I can try and meet you somewhere tomorrow."

"No, I have to see you tonight."

"I want to see you, too. Believe me, I do, but I can't come tonight, Catherine."

"He's sending me away, William. He's sending me to New York for my senior year."

I slid my back down the bedroom wall and sat on the floor as the words sunk in.

"When? How long do we have?"

"Two weeks. But he's taken my car keys. I don't know if I'll be allowed to leave the house. I need to see you. Please come. You said you would always be here for me."

I pounded my fist onto the carpeted floor and cursed under my breath.

It was a damned near impossible request. I had no vehicle without asking to borrow one. Patricia was at work, James wasn't home, and there was no way my mother would let me take hers. She wasn't too keen on Catherine in the first place, and now that my sister had blabbed about the overdose, Ma was even less enthusiastic about me seeing her.

Of course, even if she did like Catherine, she wouldn't let me go over there without Phillip and Miranda's knowledge. It wasn't just that it was inappropriate or impolite. I had to consider what would happen if Phillip caught us. If he was angry enough to send his daughter away, I couldn't imagine he'd be okay with finding a teenage boy alone with her inside his house. Especially on the heels of his daughter coming home from the hospital.

"Please? I need you, William." Her voice broke with emotion as she whispered my name, and I decided none of the rest of it mattered. She was hurting. She needed me. I had to get to her, no matter what the cost or consequence.

"Give me a few minutes to find a vehicle. Can you come outside?"

"Yeah. Park in that little dirt road between my house and Charlotte's, and then cross the field to come up behind my garage. I'll meet you by the swing and let you inside."

I couldn't tell which was making me more nauseous as I hung up—the fear of getting caught or the pain in her voice.

My mother was sitting in the recliner when I brought the phone back into the living room. She took in the fact that I was fully dressed and immediately stood.

"No. You cannot go over there, William. This is a bad situation, and you need to keep your distance."

"Ma, she needs me."

"She needs help, son, but there's nothing you can do to help her. This girl has been lying to her parents about seeing you, William. How do you know she hasn't been lying to you? She obviously has a drug and alcohol problem. Were you aware of that?"

"She was upset, and she—"

"Don't make excuses for her. This girl will get you in trouble, do you hear me? What do you think her parents are going to say if you show up there at this hour of the night? They don't even know about you. You could get shot! Or arrested." She crossed her arms and set her jaw in what I knew was a non-negotiable stance. "No, William. Absolutely not. You call her back and tell her you can meet her somewhere tomorrow if you feel you must, but you cannot go there tonight."

"He's sending her away, Ma. He's sending her to New York to school, okay? So, she'll be gone. There—does that make you happy? Are you happy now? Because I'm not. I love her, Ma. I love that girl like nothing I've ever felt before for anyone. And she got sick because of me. That was my fault. I haven't been there for her the last couple of days, but I can be there for her now."

"Wait just a minute," she said, holding up her hand. "What do you mean she got sick because of you? How on earth is this your fault?"

"I told her I was moving to Gainesville. That's why she went out and got drunk. She wouldn't have been in the hospital if it wasn't for me."

She grabbed both of my arms and shook them once. "Now you listen to me, William Joseph. You are not responsible for that girl. You are not married to her. You are not her parent. You have to make decisions for what is best for your life. You don't have to consider her in those decisions, do you hear me? She makes her own decisions. Bad ones, from what I can tell. She's lied to her parents and hidden things from them. God only knows what she's lied to you about or hidden from you. But whatever she did that landed her in that hospital, she did because of her issues and her choices. That has nothing to do with you."

I pulled my arms from her grasp and drew in a deep breath.

"I'm going, Ma. Can I borrow your car, or do I have to walk? Because either way, I'm going."

"What has gotten into you? Does she have you bewitched? This is not like you, William."

"I have to get going. She's waiting for me. Am I walking, or can I borrow your car?"

She gave me the keys, but her reluctance and her disapproval weighed heavily on me. I understood her concern. From her viewpoint, it did look pretty bad. But she didn't know Catherine like I did. She didn't know what Catherine had been through with her dad. Ma didn't understand how we felt about each other. What we meant to each other. She didn't understand how much I loved Catherine.

The thought of her going away to New York made me sick to my stomach, and I gripped the steering wheel tighter and tried not to think about it. It had been hard enough when it was going to be me in Gainesville with Catherine at home, but it was a relatively short drive, and we would have been able to see each other every few weeks as long as she stayed out of trouble. New York might as well be the other side of the planet. I wouldn't see her for months. And there would be no way we could call each other without incurring long distance charges.

I pulled into the narrow dirt road and cut the lights on the car, staring into the dark woods that surrounded me. I didn't dare use a flashlight to call attention to myself as I walked to her property line and scaled the fence. I stayed low to the ground as I crossed the field, my eyes darting back and forth between the uneven ground beneath me and the dark windows of the house looming ahead of me.

I feared that at any minute the floodlights would come on, and I'd be caught in the cross-hairs of her father's rifle. I hoped he'd give me an opportunity to explain before a shot rang out. But what explanation could I possibly give?

CHAPTER 25
William

S he was sitting in the swing underneath the huge oak tree, and the eerie glow of her white gown was like a beacon in the night.

She stood as I walked closer, and then she ran to me, throwing her arms around my neck and nearly knocking me over.

"William!" she cried, squeezing me tightly as I lifted her off the ground.

"Are you okay?" I set her back down and held her face in my hands to examine her. I don't know what I thought would be different, but I was relieved that she looked the same.

Her ebony hair was dark as the night, and her green eyes were filled with tears that spilled onto her soft cheeks.

"Christ, Catherine! You scared the hell out of me. I couldn't reach you Saturday night, and then Patricia came home and said you were at the hospital. That you'd overdosed. I was freaking out. I called in at work Sunday morning and went to the hospital, but no matter how many times I walked past your room, it never was safe to go inside."

"You came to the hospital?" Her eyes were wide with surprise.

"Yeah. I mostly hung out in the waiting room waiting for you to be alone, but there was always someone in your room. I was sick with worry all day yesterday. Then Patricia told me this morning that you got discharged, and I've been on pins and needles all day hoping you'd call. Are you all right? What happened?"

"I'm fine. I'm okay now that you're here."

I pulled her to me again, holding her as close as possible as I kissed the top of her head. She lifted her face to look at me, and I claimed her mouth with mine as I sought to ease the panic in my heart.

"C'mon," she said in a whisper, taking my hand and leading me to the door on the side of the house.

My heart was already pounding from the exhilarating trip across the field and the surge of passion that always came when she was in my arms, but it went into overdrive when she opened the door and led me inside Phillip Johnson's house. I'd been there plenty of times during the summer, but even then, it was hard to relax knowing I wasn't welcome and shouldn't be there. This was the first time I'd ever set foot inside with her father home, and it was unnerving to say the least.

"Are you sure your dad won't wake up?" I whispered against her hair, my voice barely making a sound in the silence of the laundry room.

She nodded and placed her finger over her lips, and then she led me up the back stairs to the second floor and into her bedroom. She closed the door carefully and flipped the lock, and then she turned and wrapped her arms around my neck and proceeded to kiss me like the apocalypse had come and we were the last ones alive.

Somehow, we ended up across her bed, and before I knew what was happening, her gown was off, and her breasts were exposed in the light coming through the window.

It wasn't like I hadn't seen them before. We'd fooled around a bit here and there. We'd done some heavy petting and timid explorations of each other's bodies as our relationship had progressed. But this was different.

Something in her mood, in her manner, conveyed a sense of urgency, almost a desperation, and she seemed determined to take us farther than we'd gone before.

It took every ounce of resolve I had to pull back and take a deep breath. She lay on the bed beside me with her black hair fanned out across the sheets, her flat stomach quivering with each breath, and the curve of her hips accented by the white lace panties she wore. Her breasts were full, and her nipples stood firm and high, almost impossible to resist. I flicked my tongue across my lips, thirsting for the taste of her, but unable to ignore the feeling that something wasn't right.

"Catherine, I—"

"Shh!" She placed her finger on my lips, and then she took my hand and laid it over her breast, arching her back to press the soft mound into my palm.

My entire body responded, and a moan escaped my lips as my fingers kneaded and caressed her despite my mental reservations.

"Make love to me," she whispered, and I had to adjust my jeans and swallow before I could speak.

"Catherine, God knows I want to, but—"

"No buts," she said, rolling to press her body against mine as she moved my hand to her crotch. "We always said we'd wait until we were both in college, but now that I'm leaving, everything has changed. I want us to share this before I go. Make love to me, William."

She opened her lips against mine, her tongue searching for me as I wavered in my resolve.

A door closing somewhere in the house set off an alarm in my head, and I jerked my hand away from her warmth to sit up and listen more closely.

"It's okay," she said as she stroked my back. "It's probably Isabel. My parents are on the other side of the house. We can't hear them from here, so they can't hear us."

She gripped my shoulder, and I turned to look back at her, my breath catching in my throat.

I'd never seen anything so beautiful in all my life, and I couldn't believe I was about to turn down the incredible gift that was being offered.

I exhaled with a swear, and then I stood and adjusted myself again.

She sat up with a frown and pulled her hair over her shoulders to cover her breasts.

I picked up her gown and handed it to her, and she shook her head.

"No." She took my hand and pulled me back to the bed, but I sat and refused to lay down.

She moved to kneel beside me, her eyes wide as she stared into mine. "Don't you want me?"

"Are you kidding me? Yes," I said with a half-chuckle, half-groan. "God, yes. Of course, I do. But this is not the way I want this to happen, Catherine. Not with both of us half-listening for any sound of your mom and dad, and you just out of the hospital, and me having to escape back across a field and go home."

I laid my palm against her cheek, caressing her soft skin with my thumb as she laid her hand over mine.

"When we do this, I want us to take our time, babe. I want us to enjoy every single detail. And I want to hold you in my arms all night long and wake up to your beautiful face. I don't want this to be some rushed, frantic, panicked thing."

"But we don't have much time," she said.

"We have all the time in the world," I whispered. "Whether you're here or in New York, it doesn't change how I feel about you. It doesn't change our plans for the future. Our future. It will make it harder for the next year, that's for sure. But we'll get through it. Then you'll graduate, and we'll be together. We'll have plenty of time then."

She dropped her hand from mine and drew in a ragged breath as she looked up at the ceiling.

I tucked my thumb beneath her chin and made her look at me.

"I don't want to rush this. I want our first time to be special. I don't want us to do this because we're scared. I want us to do this when it feels right."

"But it does feel right," she protested. "I love you."

"And I love you, too. More than anything. But this is not how I want it to be for us. Not like something that's dirty and wrong, and in fear of being caught."

I kissed her, and she wrapped her arms around my neck and pressed herself against me, which made it even harder to forget she was still only wearing a pair of panties.

I chose to bring up the many questions I still had so I could try and keep my lustful inclinations from taking over.

"You never did tell me what happened. Why were you drinking? How did you end up in the hospital?"

She reached to grab her gown and pull it over her head, jerking her arms through it as though she was irritated.

"I don't really want to talk about that."

"Patricia said she heard the nurses saying you overdosed. That you had drugs in your system. Like, cocaine. Not just drinking. Is that true?"

"Let's not waste what time we do have by talking about bad stuff. Kiss me."

"No, Catherine, I need to know what happened. Patricia said it was serious. That you could have died. What were you thinking?"

"What was I thinking? I was thinking that I didn't want you to go away. That I didn't want you to leave me behind. I was thinking that I didn't want my dad to be a total asshole who hates me. That I didn't want my mother to be someone who says she loves me but then does whatever he wants her to and won't stick up for me. I just wanted to escape it all. I wanted to not think for a little while. To not feel anything."

"How'd that work out for you?"

She glared at me and laid on her back across the bed.

"I'm sorry," I said, laying my hand on her thigh. "That was a crappy thing to say. I just can't believe this happened. I don't understand why you would do something like that." I hesitated, unsure if I should ask the question that had been gnawing at me. It seemed petty and trivial in light of what she'd been through, but I knew it wouldn't stop bugging me until I knew the answer. "Who were you with?"

"What?"

"Who were you with? I mean, you were partying with other people, right? You weren't alone. Patricia said someone dropped you off in your car at the entrance of the ER and then called to let the hospital know you were out there. So, who was it?"

"The cops have been asking that for days, and I told them I don't remember."

"But do you? Do you remember?"

She stared at me, and I could see that she was weighing whether or not to tell me the truth. My mother's warnings replayed in my head, and I wondered how I could be sure that Catherine was as honest with me as I was with her. Lying did seem to come easily for her, and it would be stupid to think I was the only one she didn't lie to.

"No, I don't remember who dropped me off. I remember whose house I was at, and I remember most of the people who were there, even though I told everyone I don't. I don't want to get anyone in trouble, so I have to say I don't remember. But I really don't know how I got to the hospital or who took me. I passed out at the party, I guess, and then I must have started vomiting after that."

I closed my eyes and pushed away the thoughts of what could have happened if her friends hadn't taken her to the ER. It was easier to focus on jealousy than to consider that she might have died.

"At this party, were you, you know, *with* anyone?"

Her mouth dropped open and her eyes narrowed. "God, no. Why would you think that? You think I'd just run off and be with someone else?"

"I don't know. Obviously, you weren't thinking very straight that night. I mean, you were doing drugs and drinking, quite a lot evidently. So yeah, it does make me wonder what other crazy shit you did. I keep thinking that if you were that drunk, maybe you—"

"I wouldn't cheat on you, William. Not ever."

"Okay, okay. I'm sorry. I shouldn't have even thought that, but I just … I just can't believe after the summer we had and all the time we spent together that you took off and got wasted with your old friends. Like, wasted enough to OD. I thought you were past all that."

She ran her hands through her hair and squeezed them into fists as she closed her eyes. "I told you, I needed to escape everything I was feeling. I'd been caged in this house for a week, and I felt like I was suffocating. Then I found out your news, and it seemed like everything was spinning out of control. It seemed like everything was going wrong."

"Look, it's not a bad thing that I got the grant. Now, I won't have school loans to pay, and I don't have to buy a vehicle right away. This means that the money I saved up will still be there. In the long run, this is good for us. It means we start out our life together with less bills, and I won't have to work as much while I'm at school, so who knows? I could probably even buy a plane ticket and come visit you in New York sometime."

She got up and paced the floor. "I have to find a way to change his mind. I can't go to New York for my senior year. I just can't. I have to make him see."

"Did you try talking to him?"

"Of course, I did!"

"Well, maybe he was just worried because of, you know, what you did."

"That's what my mother said. She's hoping he'll change his mind once he calms down, but you didn't see him when he told me. He was actually happy about it. It was like he was relieved I had done something to make it easy for him."

"Just lay low for a few days. Give him time to think about it."

"I have no choice but to lay low! He has my car keys, and I don't think I'm getting those back any time soon." She flounced down on the bed beside me and propped her weight on her elbow. "Promise me you'll keep coming to see me. If we only have two weeks, I don't want to miss a day. Promise me you'll find a way to come here if I can't escape."

"I'll try, but it's hard to get a vehicle right now. James is working locally, so he needs his truck when he gets done with his shift every day."

"So, wait until he goes to sleep at night. He won't need his truck then."

"Don't you think it's a little risky for me to keep coming here? I mean, if your dad catches us, he's definitely not going to change his mind about New York, and God only knows what he'll do to you. Or me."

"He won't catch us. Once he goes behind those doors on his side of the house, he doesn't come back out until morning. And my mother takes so many sleeping pills every night that it's a wonder she even wakes up at all. The night can be ours if you can find a vehicle. We don't have to stay here if it makes you nervous. I can meet you out by the road and we can go somewhere else. As long as I'm back before morning, we're good."

"No, that's just playing with fire. Why would you risk that?"

"I've done it plenty of times. Before I met you, I would sneak out and go places every time I got grounded." She grinned, and her eyes narrowed with a mischievous gleam. "Trust me. I'm like a ninja getting in and out of this house. No one knows when I come or go."

"Speaking of going, I probably should," I said with a sigh. "Ma wasn't too happy about me coming here, so I'm sure she's sitting up waiting for me to get back."

"You told her? Why?"

"I had to borrow her car. Plus, she was awake and heard part of our conversation, so she knew I was planning to come. Oh, and she knows, um, about the hospital and everything. Patricia told her."

"Oh, great. I can only imagine what she thinks of me now. I'm surprised she let you come see me at all."

I didn't think it would help the situation to tell her how strongly my mother had opposed the idea.

"We just have to get through the next year, okay?" I took her hand and kissed it before wrapping it in mine. "We get through the next year, and we'll be together in Gainesville. Then it won't matter what anyone thinks, right?"

"Yeah." She looked down at our hands and frowned. "If you don't meet someone else before then."

"I'm not looking for anyone else," I said as I leaned in to kiss her. "I have my girl. She's the one for me, and no one is going to change that. Besides, what about you, up in New York?"

She smiled. "Hopefully, I can find a way not to go, but if I do, it's an all-girls school, so you have nothing to worry about there. Not that you need to be worried anyway."

We kissed goodbye, and she led me down the stairs to the side door, where we kissed again. Then, I ran across the field, trying not to stumble and break my neck in the darkness.

The light in the front window of my house when I pulled in the driveway confirmed what I already knew. My mother had waited up for me. But to my surprise, she had no lecture prepared.

"Is Catherine all right?" she asked as I walked through the door.

"Yes, ma'am. She's upset, but she's fine."

"No trouble for you at her house?"

I shook my head. "No, ma'am."

She sighed, and I could see her shoulders drop with relief.

"Get some sleep, so you're not exhausted at work tomorrow," she said with a yawn. "I'll be glad when you're safely tucked away in Gainesville and can get on with your life. G'night, son."

"Night, Ma."

CHAPTER 26
Caterina

Despite his reservations, William borrowed his brother's truck every night that week to pick me up at midnight at the end of our driveway. At first, he insisted he should walk me to and from the house in the dark, but I disagreed since it slowed the whole process down and meant he would have to make four trips back and forth each night. If I was somehow found alone in my yard, it would be one thing. But if William was found, it would be an entirely different dilemma. He reluctantly agreed.

Most of our time was spent talking and laughing as we rode the winding country roads, but we'd usually find a secluded spot to park and make out. Sometimes we went to the lake and sat on the dock, and one night, we went to a park in town to ride the swings and the seesaw. It didn't matter to me what we did or where we went. I just wanted to be with him every minute I could.

I don't know how William got by working two shifts a day with as little sleep as he was getting, but he never complained. I was lucky since I got to sleep however late I wanted, which not only made up for the hours I was missing at night but also meant I didn't have to see my father at breakfast.

The two of us had avoided each other since the afternoon he'd told me he wanted me gone. I didn't emerge from my room until after he'd left every morning, and he worked late and had dinner somewhere other than home each night. By the time he returned late in the evening, I had already retreated back to my side of the house, where I counted down the hours until it was time to shower and get ready to meet William outside.

My mother was a basket case. She wandered the house in tears with a gin and tonic as her ever-present pacifier, and every time she saw me, she'd cover her mouth with her hand and start crying again. I stayed in my room or in my den most of the day, but she insisted that the two of us have dinner together each night. It was a shit show of slurred speech and erratic fits of tears, and by the third night, Isabel and I both were worn thin on patience and not knowing what to do.

"I can't believe you won't be here for dinner after next week," Mother cried as Isabel set our plates on the table. "Oh, Catherine, I can't imagine how lonely it's going to be."

Isabel stood behind her and glared at me, using hand gestures to indicate that I should go to my mother.

I heeded the request, pushing my chair back with a sigh to go and put my arms around Mother in a futile attempt to comfort her.

She clung to my hands and looked up at me, her eyes bleary and glassed over with inebriation and tears.

"I'll be sitting here all by myself while your father's out entertaining his clients and God only knows who else. I'll be all alone. What will I do?"

"Drink yourself into a stupor, by the looks of it, Mother."

Isabel frowned at me and rolled her eyes.

"Come on, now," I said as I patted my mother's back. "You have to pull it together. I'd be going off to college next year, and you'd have the same issue. It's inevitable, you know."

It seemed rather unfair to me that I had to console my mother about my banishment when there was no one to console me, but if I was ever going to enlist her help in convincing my father to change his mind, I needed her sober and coherent.

She pushed my hands from her shoulders as her mood shifted to anger without warning.

"Why did you have to provoke him? He warned you. How many times did he tell you he'd send you away? But you never listen. You don't think about me and how this will affect me. Neither of you do. You don't even care."

I plopped back down in my chair and picked up my fork to push the mashed potatoes across my plate.

"I do care, Mother. I promise you I did not choke on my own vomit and get my stomach pumped out just to make you live alone while father works late or goes out of town."

"Don't you make light of this!" She hiccupped and rubbed the back of her hand across her nose as her anger faded in favor of imagined grief. "You could have died! I could be planning your funeral right now. Oh, God, what would I have done? How would I have coped?" She laid her palm on her forehead and rattled the ice cubes in her glass as she looked around for a refill. "Isabel?"

Isabel stepped forward and took the empty glass. "Why don't you eat something, Mrs. Miranda?"

She looked over Mother's head at me and frowned, and I shrugged, not sure what she expected me to do. I couldn't force my mother to eat, and I certainly couldn't make her stop drinking.

"I can't eat," Mother said, pushing the untouched plate away. "I can't even think about food. He's taking my baby away from me, and I can't bear it. I'm going to sit by the pool for some fresh air. Will you bring me another gin and tonic, Isabel?"

She pushed her chair back and stood, grabbing onto the table's edge to steady herself.

"Are you sure you want another one, Mrs. Miranda? You're gonna have a terrible headache in the morning."

"I'll have a headache either way, Isabel. Sorrow brings pain. My heart is shattered. My daughter and my husband have busted it all to pieces, and no one cares."

She stumbled from the room, and I pushed my plate toward the center to the table and sat back with a groan. "This family is so messed up."

Isabel frowned again as she gathered Mother's silverware and plate. "I'm worried about your mother, Catherine. She's always loved her evening cocktail, but I've never seen her go days on end like this. I worry what she's going to do when you leave."

"Maybe you should tell my father that."

I was worried about her, too, but I was also pissed that she couldn't stay sober long enough for us to have a conversation. I needed her to talk to my father. I needed her to intervene and stand up for me for once. But her drunkenness didn't allow for any reasonable arguments, and the clock was ticking.

It seemed my father was unaware of the extent of her drinking since he left early in the morning and didn't return until late at night. She was asleep when he came and when he went. But he stayed home on Saturday, and by early afternoon, he had no choice but to see there was a problem.

I was in my room when things came to a head down by the pool, so I could clearly hear the entire exchange outside my window.

"Isabel! Stop refilling my wife's glass. Can't you see she's had enough? It's the middle of the day, for God's sake, and she's already three sheets to the wind."

"Don't you dare tell her I've had enough! If I've had enough of anything, it's the fact that no one in this house cares about my feelings. No one asks what I think about anything. I will not sit here alone day in and day out with no one to love. I will not!"

I went to the window to watch her performance.

Father turned to face her, his expression one of genuine bewilderment. "What are you talking about?"

Mother burst into tears, so he turned to Isabel.

"What is she talking about? Do you know what's going on?"

"Mrs. Miranda is having a hard time with Miss Catherine going away for school."

My mother wailed louder, and my father threw down his newspaper and glared at her.

"Oh, for heaven's sake, Miranda!"

"It's all your fault!" she screamed. "I can't believe you're doing this to me. I've stood by you from the very beginning. I've supported you and done all I could to be a good wife. I've let you make all the decisions, and I've turned a blind eye and swallowed my pride more times than I care to count. But I will not stand by and let you do this to me. You're making her abandon me. I can't live in this house alone, Phillip. I won't. I can't bear it. You have to do something!" She stood and leaned over him, and then she balled her hands into fists and shrieked right into his face. "Fix it!"

She ran inside the house, careening to the left and right as she went and grasping the door frame to keep from falling.

Isabel stood wide-eyed, holding my mother's empty glass while my father stared after his wife with his mouth gaping.

I'd never seen my mother yell at him before, and based on his stunned expression, he was as surprised as I was.

"How long has this been going on?" he asked Isabel when he'd recovered his composure. "The drinking."

"Pretty much all week, sir. I noticed it seemed heavier than usual over the weekend, when Miss Catherine was in the hospital. But then she really started hitting it heavy once you, well, once the school decision had been made. She's been going through a bottle, bottle and a half each day. She's upped her sleeping pills, too, and she's having a hard time waking in the morning. Quite disoriented at first, but then when her head starts to clear, she starts the crying again, and she's ready for a drink."

He stood and bent to pick up the newspaper from the ground and fold it, and then he slapped it against the palm of his hand.

"I trust you've been discreet while shopping for the gin," he said.

"Why, yes, sir. Of course. I often buy in large quantities, so we have it on hand for dinner parties, sir. I'm sure no one thought anything was amiss."

"Please call the club and cancel our dinner reservations. We'll be eating in tonight."

Isabel nodded, and my father went inside in search of his wife.

CHAPTER 27
Caterina

My parents had dinner in their room that night, which was fine by me. I wasn't hungry anyway, and I had no desire to sit and stare at either one of them.

Unfortunately, being Saturday night, James had plans and didn't intend to be home until late, so William had no vehicle. I suggested I could try and find where my car keys were hidden and come to him, but he wouldn't hear of it.

Too risky, he said.

We talked on the phone until the wee hours instead, and neither of us wanted to hang up. We'd doze and wake off and on, each of us saying the other's name to ensure we were both still on the line.

The phone was off its cradle beside me in the bed when Isabel knocked on my door the next morning, but when I said William's name, I got no response. I didn't know if he'd hung up at some point or if someone woke at his house and retrieved the phone, so they didn't trip over the wire trailing down the hallway.

"Catherine?" Isabel called as she tapped a second time. "Your father has requested that you join them for breakfast. You have twenty minutes."

I rolled to my back and stared at the ceiling, my mind still groggy and not fully awake.

"Catherine?" she called again.

"I hear you!" I moaned, rubbing the sleep from my eyes. "I'll be down with bells on."

"Hmmph. Not likely."

When I came to the table, my mother looked more alert than she had all week. Not a hair was out of place, and her make-up was perfectly done. She was dressed in a pair of white capris and a blue button-down shirt with a scarf, and I hoped it meant they had an outing planned which would leave me on my own for the day.

"Good morning, sleepyhead," Mother said with a big smile. "I had Isabel make blueberry French toast for you, dear. Your favorite!"

I forced a smile in return, but I couldn't maintain it when my father entered the room.

He went immediately to my mother and patted her shoulder as he planted a kiss on her cheek, and then he greeted Isabel as she came into the dining room. "Something smells delightful!"

"Thank you, sir." She poured his coffee and put two dollops of sugar in it, and then she returned to the kitchen.

Everyone seemed abnormally cheerful and polite, and I wondered if I'd somehow stepped into *The Twilight Zone*. Were these the same people who had been swirling in a vortex of dysfunction the day before?

We ate in silence broken only by my mother's occasional spouting of random facts.

"Did you know that a giraffe's tongue is over a foot long? Can you imagine?"

No one responded, but that didn't deter her.

"It wouldn't take a giraffe long to eat an ice cream cone, would it?"

"May I be excused?" I asked.

"No," Father said curtly.

My mother's eyes met mine, and her smile faltered for a brief moment before she plastered it back in place and gave us the average weight of a baby rhino at birth.

"I was listening to a show about animals on the television while getting ready," she offered as some sort of justification for her bizarre conversation. "Simply fascinating."

I sat and stared at my plate, wondering how long he would keep me there before releasing me.

When Isabel cleared the dishes, I moved to stand, but my father tapped the table and waved me back down.

"Sit. Your mother and I have something to tell you."

Mother gave me what I'm sure she thought was a reassuring smile, but my French toast felt heavy in my stomach as I waited to hear his announcement.

"After a lengthy discussion about what would be best for the family, your mother and I have decided that you can start school here for your senior year."

I gasped and sat up straight, eager to hear more.

He held up one finger and twisted his lips as though he was considering what his next words should be.

"The key word there is *start*. That may not mean you finish the year here. You're out of strikes. You're out of chances. If at any point in time this year there is any infraction at all, you can be sent to New York with a day's notice. Your tuition there will remain fully paid, and they will be holding your spot pending your ability to abide by our new rules."

"You get to stay home with me," my mother cooed. "Isn't that marvelous, dear?"

I nodded, excited that I wouldn't have to leave William, but nervous about what rules would be put in place. Father wasted no time in laying them out for me.

"Your car? Gone. Not only are they unable to effectively clean the remnants of your disastrous evening from the back seat, but you have demonstrated that you are not responsible enough to have your own vehicle. You will be driven by your mother, Isabel, or I to whatever is deemed necessary."

I frowned. Losing my car took away my independence, and along with it, any chance of driving to Gainesville to see William.

"Horse riding lessons are not necessary," he continued. "Football games are not necessary. Social outings with your friends are not necessary. We will not be providing transportation for anything other than school."

I struggled to stay optimistic. Anything was better than being sent to New York, but how would I see William if I could never leave the house?

"You will submit to random drug and alcohol testing whenever I request it. If there is ever any sign that you have used any substance, you're on a flight to New York. I will be corresponding with your teachers and principal on a regular basis. Any report of belligerence, misbehavior, or less than excellent grades, and you will be on a flight to New York. If you miss turning in one assignment in even one class, you will be on a flight to New York."

He was so smug, so satisfied with himself and his plan.

I was trapped. I could either be shipped off to New York to live under some headmaster's thumb, or I could be imprisoned here in my own home with my father watching me like a hawk and waiting for me to screw up. Hoping I would, knowing him.

"Lastly, you will be required to gain employment. Starting today, your allowance is cut off, and any expenses you have going forth will need to be paid from your own pocket. It's time you earned what you have so that maybe you will appreciate it more."

"Oh, but we'll drive you to and from whatever job you get, dear. Don't worry about that." My mother pitched in that helpful fact with a smile so big that it seemed she thought it was the greatest news ever.

My father glanced in her direction then back to me before continuing.

"If you can prove you deserve a spot at this table and in this family, you can remain here. But make no mistake in understanding what I am telling you." He leaned forward and pointed his finger at me, and then he used it to poke the table and emphasize each of his next words. "I am done giving you chances. You screw up one time, just one time, and you will be on a plane so fast your head will spin. Do you understand?"

I nodded, certain that I had descended into the very depths of hell.

CHAPTER 28
Caterina

My excitement at not being banished to New York was stymied by the new restrictions I'd been put under.

"A lot of good it does me to be here if I'm imprisoned in this house and can't escape! I might as well be in New York," I said to William as we talked on the phone that evening.

"Maybe if you have a month or so of good behavior, he'll relax a bit. Why don't you let things settle down and see what happens? He does travel an awful lot, and your mother isn't usually as strict when he's gone. I'm sure she'll let you do more when he's not home."

"I don't know. I think he'll be watching her more closely now. She thwarted his plans. I'm telling you the only reason he's letting me stay is because she had such a meltdown over it. It's not like he changed his mind about me. I bet he's going to be looking for a reason to go back to Plan A, and he'd probably like nothing more than for it to be because of her. Then he could punish us both in one move."

"At least she stood up for you. That's got to make you feel good, huh?"

"She didn't stand up for me. She was standing up for herself, which is progress, for sure, but it had very little to do with me. She just didn't want to be alone. But enough about them. Where are we going tonight? What do we want to do? I can't wait to get out of here."

"Are you sure you want to keep sneaking out? Like you said, he's looking for any reason at all. Why give him one? Why don't you just lay low and stay on the straight and narrow for a while?"

His words stung me with rejection, even though I'm sure he thought he was looking out for my best interests.

"If you don't want to see me, don't come. I'll find something else to do."

"That's not it, and you know it. Of course, I want to see you. But I don't want to be the reason you get sent away."

"You're leaving in two weeks. What are you saying? We shouldn't see each other at all before you go? Seriously?"

There was silence at the other end of the line, and I silently prayed that wasn't where he was headed.

"I have to see you, William. I'll go crazy if I can't. I'm not letting you leave without spending all the time I can with you."

I fell back onto my bed and closed my eyes, wishing he would tell me he wanted to spend every moment with me too. I didn't want it to be okay with him for us to be separated.

His silence was maddening, and I was about to yell at him to say something when he finally spoke again.

"Well, then maybe we just need to be more cautious. Like not seeing each other every night. Not taking too many chances. And maybe we don't leave your house. We'll just, um, uh, oh hell, I don't know, Catherine. I don't know what to do. I don't want to go without seeing you, but I don't want to make things worse for you, either."

"Things can't get much worse! He's taken everything away from me already. I won't let him take you away, too."

"No one is going to take me away, babe. I just think it would be worth it to wait until he goes out of town again, and then figure out a way to see each other."

"But by then you'll be gone!"

"Catherine, I'm not going that far. I'm sure I'll be able to come home in a few weeks. Let's do what we can to keep you out of trouble until your dad calms down. Or until he goes out of town. It won't be that long."

I grabbed a pillow and threw it against the wall in frustration. "No! No, dammit! You're the only thing in my life that makes me happy, and I am not giving up the time I have left with you. I want to see you. I want to be with you."

He ended up giving in to me, but he didn't stop worrying. He insisted on picking me up later every night and dropping me off earlier every morning to try and minimize the chance of being caught. I hated that it gave us less time together, but as the days kept getting closer to his move date, I was thankful for every minute I could get.

When I first broached the idea of going to the beach for our last night together, William refused.

"No way. That's like three hours round-trip. Do you know what all could go wrong? C'mon, babe. We've made it this far. Let's not push our luck and have a problem the last night. We're almost in the clear."

"But think how awesome it would be! There's a full moon Friday night, and the weather is supposed to be clear. We haven't been to the beach since my parents got back, and it's a perfect night to go. Let's go out with a bang. End the summer on a high note."

I kept begging him all week, and he kept saying no, right up until Friday night when he picked me up.

He was standing outside the truck when I came walking through the field down to the road, the full moon high in the sky and providing enough light that I could see his grin long before I reached him.

I ran to him and wrapped my arms around his neck. He picked me up and twirled me around, then he kissed me and set me down as he held the truck door open.

"Where we gonna go?" I asked once he'd gotten in the truck.

"Well, I guess if my girl wants to go to the beach, I'll take her to the beach."

"Really?" I threw my arms around him again, kissing him so hard that he pulled back laughing.

"James has to leave for work at six in the morning, but he said as long as I have the truck back by then, he doesn't care where I take it. So, if you're sure that's what you want to do, we'll do it, but we gotta leave now if we're gonna have any kind of time to spend at the beach."

"Yes! Let's go!"

We rolled the windows down and turned the radio up, and we laughed and talked the whole way to the east coast. It was a gorgeous night for a drive, and when we arrived at the beach, the view of the moon's reflection on the water dancing like diamonds on the waves was breathtaking.

William spread out the blanket he'd brought, and we noshed on the snacks we'd picked up at a twenty-four-hour convenience store near the beach.

When we'd finished the last of the chips, I stood and held my hand out to him.

"Let's go in the water."

"We don't have our suits."

I grinned and reached for the hem of my sundress to pull it over my head.

"What are you doing?" he said with a grin as he looked around as though he thought someone was going to see us on the empty beach.

"Let's go skinny-dipping." I tucked my thumbs into my panties and teased them down over my hips.

"What? You're crazy. No. No way. What if someone comes?"

"It's two in the morning. Who else would be nuts enough to be out here?"

"I don't know, but I'm not too keen on meeting whoever it might be in my birthday suit.

"Then let's swim in our underwear."

He stared past me toward the water, and then he looked at his watch.

I bent and took his hands, pulling him up to standing. "Come on. Stop being a worry wart."

"I just want to make sure we have plenty of time to get back. You never know if you're gonna have a flat or if there's gonna be traffic."

"Yeah, because traffic jams happen at this time of night all the time. C'mon, silly."

I led him into the surf, and I squealed in exhilaration at the cold water and its dark unknown mysteries.

We made our way past the crashing waves and out deep enough that we could stand comfortably with the water at our shoulders.

"I can't believe it doesn't scare you to come in the ocean at night," he said with a grin.

"Why would it? I've been in the water plenty of times in the day, and I've never seen anything scary. It's not like there's some night creature that stalks the shoreline looking for teenagers to gobble up."

He suddenly dropped his grin and opened his eyes wide. "What was that?" He turned left and right scanning the water, and I threw my arms around his neck and jumped to put my legs around his waist and lift myself as high as possible.

"What?" I shrieked. "What did you see?"

His laughter rang out, and I put both hands on top of his

shoulders and shoved him under the water as I realized I'd been pranked. He pulled me under with him, grinning as we both resurfaced.

"Oh, babe! The look on your face was priceless!"

"You jerk! Why did you do that?" I splashed his face as I wiped water from my own. "You scared the crap out of me."

He laughed again and pulled me into his arms, placing his hands under my legs as I lifted them back around his hips.

"I'm sorry. I couldn't resist. I'm telling you, the look on your face was worth it!"

I draped my arms over his shoulders and tucked my ankles together behind his back to hold on as the waves bobbed us.

He kissed me, his lips wet with the water that surrounded us. Our tongues tangled in the most delightful way, and he tightened his grip on my hips, pulling me even closer as the ocean's rhythm made all the right places rub together. I twisted my fingers in his hair as the kiss deepened, and the world disappeared as we rocked back and forth with the constant ebb and flow of the tide. We didn't realize we were being pulled back toward shore until a wave crashed over us, rolling us beneath it as it churned the sand.

William grabbed my hand and pulled me up just as another wave hit, and I laughed as we clung to each other and struggled to exit the water upright.

CHAPTER 29
Caterina

William led me back to the blanket and reached to hand me a towel.
I dried my face and wrung some of the salty water from my hair, and then I grinned down at him as he lay on his back staring up at the stars.

I tossed the towel aside and knelt on either side of his legs, straddling him as I crawled up his body. I licked the salt from his belly and trailed my tongue up to tease his taut nipple, and he grabbed my hips with his hands and groaned.

I sat up and unhooked my bra, flinging it aside as I arched my back, aware of the effect the moonlight would have on the white peaks of my breasts.

He reached to cup his hands beneath them, lifting and caressing as I leaned back to brace myself on the blanket.

His thumb grazed across my nipple, and I quivered in response. I leaned forward over him, my hair dripping as it fell across his chest and shoulders. He sank his hands into the wet strands and pulled me closer, and then his mouth was on mine, wet and hot and seeking.

Our hands explored as we writhed with wet skin upon skin, and soon we were both breathless with need.

"We need to slow down," he cautioned as he stared into my eyes. "Give me a minute."

I moved my hips against him, ignoring his request, and he closed his eyes with a sharp intake of air.

"You're so bad. You're driving me crazy," he whispered.

"Look at me."

Our eyes locked, and I knew I would never be more certain of anyone than I was of William Ward. It had to be him. And it had to be that night.

I bent to brush my lips against his, and then I whispered in his ear.

"I don't want to wait. I want you to be the one."

"The one?"

I sat up and placed my hands on his chest. "You know, *the one*. I want you to be my first.*"

He frowned, and I rushed to convince him before he could refuse me like he had every other time I'd brought it up.

"You said the other night that you want it to be special and magical and all that stuff. Well, look around you! It doesn't get much more special than this. Who needs candlelight when we have that huge moon up there? And we don't need any romantic music because we have waves crashing behind us for a soundtrack. This is perfect!"

He half-smiled as he threaded his fingers through mine.

"C'mon, babe," he said as he brought my hands to his lips. "We've been through this before, and we decided it would be best to wait."

"You decided that. What I decided is that I want you to be my first."

He sat up and planted a gentle kiss on my lips as he wrapped his arms around me. "And I want to be. I plan to be."

"So, why wait? If you're so sure that nothing is going to change when you leave, then it shouldn't matter whether we sleep together now or a year from now or two years from now. If we're going to stay together, then there's no reason to wait."

He sighed and looked past me toward the water.

"You want to know what I think, William Ward? I think you know just as well as I do that neither one of us knows for sure what's going to happen. That's why you want to wait. It doesn't have anything to do with it being special or being the right time. It's because deep down, you know that when you leave here, things may never be the same."

"No, that's not it. We may not know what's going to happen, but I know nothing will change my feelings for you. But this is a big step in any relationship, and I don't want us to have any regrets."

I rolled off of him and sat cross-legged on the blanket. "Why would we have regrets if we stay together? The only reason either of us would regret having sex now is if we break up and get with someone else."

He stood and grabbed a towel to wrap around his waist.

"Look, Catherine. I love you. You're the first girl I ever said that to, okay? You're the first girl I ever loved. The only girl I've ever loved. I've told you I want to spend the rest of my life with you and that I want to marry you someday. And of course I want to make love to you. Geez, how could I not?" He turned and looked out at the water. "But I just think it's best if we don't make things even harder than they're going to be. I'm already going to miss you something terrible. I can't even think about it without getting all messed up inside. Sex would just add another layer to that."

I rose and went to him, wrapping my arms around his waist and laying my cheek against his chest.

He enveloped me in his strong embrace, and I closed my eyes and breathed in the smell of his skin with its slight musk of sweat and salt. His heartbeat in my ear was like the clock counting down the minutes we had left, and I squeezed him even harder, dreading the moment I'd have to let go.

I didn't want to spend our last couple of hours at odds with each other, but I wasn't willing to back down. It was too important to me.

I understood what he was saying. But for me, what I was asking for went beyond just having sex. I'd had boys chasing my cherry for a long time, and while I'd dangled it like a carrot to get them to do my bidding, I'd known that if I ever actually gave in, it would cease to be powerful.

But with William, none of that mattered. It was different with him. It wasn't about power or control. I loved him, and I wanted to give myself to him. I wanted to be his in a way no one else would ever be able to claim me.

It was different in another way, too. I was certain William loved me, and I knew that if I gave my virginity to him, it would never be viewed as a trophy he'd won. I'd never have to wonder if that was all he was after or if he'd used me for bragging rights. I would always know that it had been given and received in love.

I had to convince him before he left. Despite what he had promised, there were no guarantees that he wouldn't meet someone else on campus or that the strains of distance and time on our relationship wouldn't be our undoing.

I pulled back to look up at him.

"You're right. It would add another layer to our relationship. It would add a bond between us that no one could ever break." I took his hand and placed it over my chest. "You already have my heart, and now, I want to offer you a part of me that I've never given anyone else. Once I give it to you, I can never give it to anyone the same way again." He moved his hand to my cheek, and I laid mine over his, turning my head to kiss the inside of his palm. "William, please. Be my first experience, and let me be yours. Then, no matter what happens after tomorrow—whether we grow old and gray together or end up going our separate ways—you and I will share something special that no one else will ever get from either one of us."

"Dammit, Catherine."

A guttural moan tore from his throat as he closed his mouth over mine, and I could tell by the intensity of his kiss that he'd surrendered. He lifted me off my feet and stumbled us both back to the blanket. We pretty much fell onto it together, our lips never parting as our hands tugged at the remaining barriers of clothing.

Suddenly, he froze. "Wait, what about protection? Are you still on the pill?"

"Yeah, we're good."

I'd been insulted when my mother insisted on putting me on birth control a year earlier, and though she'd insisted she was doing it to help with my irregular periods and heavy cramping, I knew it was because she feared I was sexually active and just not telling her. I didn't think at the time that I'd be thankful for her paranoia, but it was a relief that we didn't have to stop when we'd finally started.

I wish I could say what followed was a romantic, soft-focus moment pulled straight from the pages of a romance novel, but it was exactly what might be expected from two awkward, inexperienced teenagers trying to fumble their way through the act on a moonlit beach in the middle of the night.

We got sand in places sand should never go, and the whole thing was over pretty quickly.

But looking back on it over the years, it couldn't have been more perfect. It was filled with love. It was tender and passionate. And it was more special than anything I'd experienced in my life before that moment.

CHAPTER 30
Caterina

A fterward, we lay wrapped together in the beach towels as we stared up at the stars, marveling at the wonder of what we'd just shared.

"I swear the moon is moving across the sky faster every time I look up," William said with a sigh as he hugged me to him and kissed the top of my head. "We should get on the road soon."

"Not yet! We still have plenty of time."

"Yeah, but I'd feel better if we were a few minutes away from your house instead of an hour and a half. Let's get back to our neck of the woods, get local, and then we'll park somewhere for whatever time we have left."

He stood and pulled me up with him, handing me my sundress before grabbing his shorts.

He had just pulled his shirt over his head when he spotted the mama sea turtle emerging from the surf, and I have wondered so many times over the years how differently our lives would have turned out if he hadn't seen her. If he hadn't glanced toward the water, or if she had made her way onto the sand a little farther down the beach in either direction, we never would have been delayed by watching her. We wouldn't have fallen asleep, and I would have been home on time.

William did the best he could to save us once we woke, driving like a bat out of hell to get back as soon as possible. It was a miracle we didn't have an accident or get a traffic ticket on the harrowing ride.

When we reached the edge of my property, he slowed to a stop, and I jumped out without a kiss goodbye or any acknowledgment of what had transpired between us the night before.

"Catherine," he called, and I stopped to turn and look back at him. "I love you. I'll call you as soon as I get home to make sure you make it inside, okay?"

"I love you, too," I said, and then I broke into a run, desperate to get to my room before the household was up and about.

My father had coffee in his study every morning at half past six, and then he would go to the breakfast room at seven when Isabel had his eggs and bacon prepared.

It was almost eight when I got out of the truck, but I was still hopeful that I could get inside without anyone knowing.

I might have made it. He might have lingered over the newspaper after finishing his eggs. He might have gone back to his study to plan out his day. But about halfway to the house, my foot went in a hole, and my ankle gave way, pitching me forward to slam against the ground.

The contact peeled back skin from my knee, my elbow, and the palm of my hand, but it was my ankle that was most painful. I managed to stand, but any weight on the foot took my breath away with a stabbing pain.

I hobbled forward as best I could, fully aware of what the delay would cost me. I toyed with the idea of hiding out somewhere on the property until I could come up with a good excuse for not being inside, but I knew no flimsy story would hold up to my father's scrutiny.

If only it hadn't been a Saturday. I could have just stayed out of sight until he left for work and then snuck in before Isabel came looking for me.

Of course, given my mother's recent penchant for breakfasts as a family on the weekends, for all I knew I'd already been discovered missing and they were already searching the house for me.

It turned out to be another weird circumstance of that disastrous day that just happened to derail my life further.

I never found out why they had breakfast without me that morning, but I know that somehow, my father got grape jelly on his shirt. For reasons I will never understand, he chose to take it to the laundry room himself rather than have my mother or Isabel do it.

I can't imagine what he must have thought when he passed the window and looked out to see me hobbling up the drive.

He came out the front door just as I fell again, and instead of showing any concern, he roared in fury.

"Where the hell have you been? Look at you! You're a complete mess. Have you been out partying all night?" He came and stood over me and watched me struggle to get to my feet as he yelled. "It wasn't enough that I took away your car. You're so determined to defy me that you would walk out of this house and spend the night cavorting with your friends. Are you drunk? Are you high?"

"No. I promise. I wasn't drinking. I wasn't doing anything. I was just—"

"Don't even bother. I don't want to hear your excuses, Catherine. We're done here. Game over. You screwed up, just like I knew you would."

I tried to take another step and stumbled, and he stepped back rather than catch me. I hit the ground but caught myself with my elbow, and then I yowled in pain as the raw wound hit the driveway.

"Who were you with this time? Was it the same friends as before?" he yelled. "Where were you and who you were with?"

I closed my eyes and gritted my teeth against the pain, refusing to look at him.

"You know what? It doesn't even matter. Drag yourself inside and pack a bag. I want you out of my house *now*. You're getting on the first plane to New York and by sunset, you'll be the newest resident at Clover Edon."

My tears sprang forth as I forced myself to stand.

"No! No, please. I swear, I wasn't partying. I'll do whatever you ask. I'll never sneak out again. Please, just don't send me away. Please."

He turned and walked back inside, and I limped as best as I could after him.

He yelled for Isabel and instructed her to help me pack my bags to leave, and then he went to find my mother.

Isabel came out the front door and put her arm around me, helping me to walk.

"Oh, honey, why?" she cried. "Why did you push him? Why?"

"I didn't mean to. William and I fell asleep."

She stopped short and grabbed both my shoulders. "Shh. I should have known! I told you to leave that boy alone. If your father finds out you were with him, there's no telling what he will do. You have to keep your mouth shut. You can't let anything slip. You may not be able to protect yourself at this point, but if you care about that boy like you say you do, you can still keep him safe."

I nodded, and we continued inside the house just as my mother ran down the stairs, her robe flying behind her as she cried out my name between sobs.

"No! No! No! Oh, Catherine, what have you done? What have you done?"

She and Isabel took me up the stairs to my room, and then Isabel left us alone to go and get bandages for my scrapes.

"What will I do?" Mother cried. "No, no, no. Why? Why, Catherine? Why did you do this to me?"

"I didn't mean to!"

We both were sobbing, and I clung to my mother and begged her to try and change the outcome.

She left me to go and plead with my father, and I took the moment alone to try and call William.

His mother answered on the first ring, and I was crying so hard I could barely talk.

"I need to speak to William, please."

"Catherine?"

"Yes. Can I please talk to William?"

"He can't come to the phone right now. I'll tell him you called."

"No! Please! It's an emergency! I have to talk to William?"

As his mom protested, Isabel came in to tell me that my father was not far behind her. I was out of time.

"Please, just tell him that I'm sorry," I whispered into the phone. "Tell him that I love him, and that I'll find a way to come back as soon as I can. Ask him to wait for me, please? Be sure to tell him I love him."

I slammed the phone into the receiver as my father's footsteps got closer in the hall.

"Do you have your bags packed?" he asked, stopping just inside the doorway with his hands on his hips. "I have a very busy day, and I'm not rearranging my schedule to accommodate you."

"Father, please. I'm begging you. Please don't send me away. I swear—"

"You swear. You promise. Do you have any idea how many chances you've had to do the right thing? And yet, every time you always screw up again. You push the envelope. You step across the boundaries. You disregard the rules. No more. I told you I'm done. It's time you learned that your choices have consequences. I should have sent you away a long time ago, and maybe you would have turned out differently."

His demeanor was eerily calm, as though he had no emotions tied to the decision he'd made.

My mother was in the hallway behind him, crying. Isabel was crying. I was crying so hard that I could barely see him through my tears.

But my father had the strangest look on his face. Almost like he was joyful. Validated. Triumphant.

"Phillip, please," my mother begged, her hand on his arm.

He looked down at her and then back at me.

"You want to stay? Tell me who were you with and where you were."

I swallowed hard and squared my shoulders, accepting my fate. There was no way I would sell William out, and I doubted Father would let me stay even if I did.

"I'm going to pull the car around," he said to Isabel. "Have her outside the front door as soon as you get her bag packed. Be quick about it. Don't make me come back up here and haul her down the stairs myself."

Father left without even looking at me again, and Mother followed him with a constant barrage of pleas.

I grabbed a notebook that was lying on the floor and frantically penned a letter to William as Isabel opened the suitcase and began to pack my clothes.

"I don't even know what to put in here," she said, her voice breaking with emotion. "I don't know what you'll need. What the weather might be. How long you'll be gone."

"Here," I said, shoving the letter in her hands as I glanced over my shoulder at the door. "Get this to Charlotte and tell her to give it to William. Promise me, Isabel. Swear to me that you'll make sure she gets it. It's very important."

She nodded and tucked the letter inside her shirt. "We have to hurry. What should I pack?"

I hobbled to my closet and started grabbing clothes and throwing them to her. "I don't need much, because I'm not staying there. The first chance I get, I'm finding a way to escape. But I promise you, I'll never come back here again."

Moments later, I said goodbye to my mother on the front steps, still wearing the sundress I'd slept in on the beach, my bra and panties still damp with ocean water.

Within an hour, my father and I were seated on a private jet, headed to New York to a place I'd never been and a group of people I'd never met.

He didn't speak to me the entire flight, and he barely even looked at me through the process of getting to the school and completing the paperwork needed to register me for the new reality of my life.

At some point, I became numb. I couldn't think. I couldn't feel. I couldn't hurt. I could only breathe because my body managed that on its own.

It wasn't until later that night, as I lay in a narrow bed in a dorm across the room from a girl who seemed none too pleased to suddenly have a roommate, that I allowed myself to cry again.

If only we hadn't fallen asleep. If only we'd woken before the sun rose. If only I hadn't twisted my ankle and slowed my progress. There were so many things I wished had happened differently.

And oh, how I wished I'd taken the time to kiss William goodbye.

CHAPTER 31
Caterina

Though I relived every vivid detail in my mind, I'd tried to condense the story as much as possible as I recounted it to Caroline, only hitting the highlights and key events while skipping the parts that might embarrass her—or me—and leaving out the abundance of teenage angst. I'd just gotten to that dark point of our story when Patsy burst through the door like a ray of sunshine.

"Good morning!" she called out as she entered with shopping bags on each arm. "How are you feeling this morning?"

She planted a kiss on my cheek and did the same to Caroline, and then she pulled the items from the bags with a grin.

She'd brought several things from my home to cheer me up, and while I appreciated her efforts to make my hospital space more homey, what I appreciated most was the break in reliving my past. As much as I wanted to answer Caroline's questions and give her the truth, it was also heart-rending to open doors and walk through rooms that had been long sealed shut.

"Thank you, love," I said to Patsy. "You've brightened the whole space with your presence and your thoughtfulness, and I can't thank you enough for all you do for me."

"Oh, hush. You'll make me weepy. Caroline, how are you this morning? You feeling okay?"

"Um, yeah," Caroline said.

She seemed unsettled, and I knew she wanted to get back to the story. My story. Her story.

"How did your dinner go?" Patsy asked, and I realized I hadn't even thought to ask.

"Good." Caroline paused. "Well, not so good. Brad showed up

after dinner and threatened to take my kids from me, but other than that, it went well."

"Oh my!" Patsy exclaimed.

"You should have said something!" I said, reaching forward to grab her hand as I admonished myself for being so self-absorbed. "Here I've been rattling on about myself, and you've been sitting here needing to talk. I'm so sorry."

"No, no. I wanted to hear what you have to say. I still want to hear. I can't do anything about Brad. I'm hoping it will blow over, and he'll calm down without going through with his threat."

"Why would he say he wants to take your kids?" Patsy asked.

Caroline shrugged. "He was upset that I was with Levi."

"How did he even know where you were?" I asked.

"He had some kind of tracker thing set up so he could see where my phone was."

This guy sounded like a real piece of work. I was glad she was no longer married to him but concerned about what he might do now that she'd found a new love interest.

I squeezed her hand and grimaced at the thought of her being in danger. "He's tracking you without your permission?"

"I don't think that's legal," Patsy said.

"The phones are all on his account," Caroline said, pulling her hand from mine as she paced the floor beside my bed. "So, evidently he had something set up where he can see where they are. I just need to go and get my own phone. I need to not have anything be tied to him financially anymore."

I nodded. "Very important."

"But he's an attorney, so he's got plenty of friends who are attorneys. He said he can tie me up in court for years. He knows I don't have the money to fight him."

I was liking this guy less by the minute.

"That's total bullshit," I said, reaching for my water before I worked myself into a coughing fit. "You need to get a job. You need to get some independence from him. Quickly."

"I know, but I have no idea what to do about the move, and I can't really find a job until I know what's going on with that."

Caroline's phone rang, and she excused herself to the hall to take the call.

"What an asshole!" I said to Patsy when she'd gone. "Thank God she's not married to him anymore."

"Yes, but she still has to deal with him because of the kids. Plus, from what I gather, she doesn't work outside the home, and he pays her bills. Which he uses to control her decisions."

I shook my head as I swallowed the cool water and returned the cup to the bedside table. "That's gotta change. She needs to get a job and have her finances under her own control. There's no way in hell I would ever give someone that much power over me."

"Keep in mind that not every marriage functions that way, dear. George has never once said a word about anything I've spent, and we've made all our major financial decisions together."

"I realize it's not always like that, and you know I think George is a saint, but this situation with Caroline is just wrong. I can't believe he was tracking her. That sounds stalkerish. Kind of scary, actually."

Patsy nodded in agreement and stared out the window. "I wish there was something we could do."

"You and I both know that no one else can make a woman stand on her own two feet. That's something she has to decide to do for herself."

"I know," she said with a frown. "But sometimes, all someone needs is a plan."

"And I can tell by that look of concentration that you're formulating one right now. So, you gonna let me in on it?"

She glanced back at me and then returned to staring out the window without answering.

"Well? C'mon, Patsy. You gonna keep me in the dark?"

She sighed and sat on the foot of my bed as I moved my feet out of her way.

"We both know the accounting aspect of running a non-profit foundation is not your strong suit, and it certainly isn't mine. I told you I asked Caroline to take a look at the books. Well, she took right to that. She said that was what she had intended for her career to be, but that got cut short with baby-making and that husband of hers insisting she give it up. We've talked about hiring someone before. Why not hire her?"

The idea had merit, but it wasn't without its challenges. I could certainly admit I needed help. Math had never come easy for me, and meticulous organization of all things finance wasn't my forte. When I'd started the foundation, I had simply wanted an easier way to help prospective adoptive parents and the children trapped in the system. As an official organization, I had more opportunities to cut through the red tape and bureaucracy and help in a legal capacity. But as the foundation's reach had expanded and its needs had gotten more complicated, I'd come to the realization that I was in over my head with the behind-the-scenes inner workings. I'd hired Patsy to help me organize the office and manage my calendar and email, but I hadn't yet broken down and turned the books over to someone else. It was definitely something I needed to consider doing.

Caroline and I had just met, though. Aside from the obvious shared DNA, we knew nothing about each other. Just because we wanted to get to know each other better didn't mean that working together would be the best way to achieve that. What if our work styles were completely opposite? What if working together proved too difficult and that affected our ability to develop a relationship outside the office?

I also didn't want her to feel like she was a charity case. Like I was hiring her just because she was my daughter and I wanted to make up for lost time.

On the other hand, she might have pursued accounting when she was in college, but judging by Eva's age, that had been about fifteen years ago. Was she qualified to run the books for me? Because nothing would be more awkward than me offering her a job and then needing to let her go if it didn't work out.

"Is it my turn in the dark now?" Patsy said. "You want to tell me what you're thinking? I swear I see smoke coming out of your ears the wheels are turning so fast up there."

"Hiring Caroline is an idea worth considering, for sure, but that could backfire and go south real quick."

Patsy plopped down in the recliner by the bed and sighed. "I think it can be a short-term fix for both of you. You can't jump right back in. You need to slow down, and you need to recover. So getting some help, even for a little while, could be beneficial for you. Caroline could easily work from home, so it gives her a job right away without her having to wait until she moves to Orlando. If it works out for both of you, it could turn into a long-term prospect. Based on what I've seen, I think she'd be good at it."

"I have to admit, I feel a little jealous that you got to know her without me, and now I'm playing catch-up."

"Oh, honey. It might seem like that, but we were both spending all our time wishing you'd open your eyes! It's not like the two of us were going shopping and having lunch dates."

"I know. I'm being silly. I realize that. But I feel like you had all this time with Caroline, and now she and William have already spent time together, too."

Patsy looked up in surprise. "William? I knew there was something to him being here."

I sighed and flipped the sheet off my legs, suddenly hot and feeling confined. "I guess the cat's out of the bag now, so it doesn't matter who knows now. William Ward is Caroline's dad."

Patsy whistled low, her eyes wide. "I can't say that I'm surprised. Caroline had been thinking he might be, and then when we saw that he'd visited you yesterday—"

"And again today."

"Really? You know, he's been a widower for a while."

"Oh, Patsy! It's not like that. At all. The poor man had no idea he had a daughter. He never knew I was pregnant, so he's understandably upset that I made the decision to give her up without consulting him."

"Did you talk to him? Did you explain what happened? That your dad made you give Caroline up?"

"I didn't really get to explain anything. He got upset and left. I still can't believe he and Caroline met out of the blue while I was in the hospital. It's like the universe brought us all back together at the same time."

"It's a second chance for all of you."

I shook my head and stared down at the sea turtle tattoo on my foot.

"No. Some stories never have a second chance."

Patsy wagged her finger and raised her eyebrows. "Never say never, my dear."

"Oh, believe me. I'm certain of this one."

"He did come and visit. Twice."

"Yes, because he wanted answers."

She leaned forward and rested her elbows on her knees.

"You told me before that you didn't want to talk about Caroline's father, but if you need to get it out, I'm here."

"Thanks, Patsy. I do appreciate that. There's nothing really to say." I stretched with a yawn and laid the sheet back over my legs. "He was the love of my life. My first love. I would go so far as to say probably my only love. And I thought I was going to spend the rest of my life with him. But things didn't work out that way. I had to leave him without even saying goodbye." I laid my head back on the pillow and took a deep, slow breath. The exertion and the emotion of the day were taking their toll, and I closed my eyes. "It was like someone died, ya know? One day he was there, and he was my everything, and the next he was gone. But then when I was pregnant, it was like with the baby, he was still with me. Still a part of me. But then suddenly she was gone, too, and I slid into darkness."

"I can't even imagine what you went through."

I opened my eyes again and stared at the ceiling, assaulted by the memories that wouldn't stop coming. "I've buried it all for so long, and now it's back at the forefront of my mind and I can't stop thinking about it."

"Pain has a way of festering when we bury it. Sometimes it's best to get it out in the open so you can start to heal and move forward."

"My first response when this all happened was to numb it. To try and escape it. I abused a lot of substances in the months after Caroline was born. I was drinking myself to death and taking pretty much anything I could get my hands on. Staying out all hours for days at a time. Belligerent. Angry. I was still living with my poor grandmother at that time, and she was beside herself. She didn't know what to do with me. I got arrested just before my eighteenth birthday. Drunken and disorderly conduct and possession of alcohol by a minor. I was lucky I didn't have anything stronger on me, and I was very fortunate they didn't charge me as an adult."

"Cat! I had no idea!"

"Yep. My life nearly took a very different path. Nonna came and got me from the jail, and she pulled over on the side of the road and gave me a strong dose of honesty right there in her Cadillac. She told me that one day that baby I'd had taken from me would be an adult, and that adult might come looking for me. Nonna said that I needed to decide who I wanted her to find. I still remember her exact words. She said, 'You have the opportunity to be someone this baby could be proud of and someone she would want in her life, or you can prove your father right and continue to screw up past the point of no return.' Somehow, that got through to me, and I've been sober ever since."

"Well, I think you've lived your life in a way that your grandmother and your daughter can be proud of. I certainly am."

"Thanks, Patsy. I just wish I'd had time to get to know Caroline longer before this whole thing with William blew up."

"It is what it is, my dear. There's no turning it back, only moving forward with what you're given. I'm sure you made the best decision you could at the time you made it, so you just have to explain that to them. You can't control what Caroline or William will decide to do, but you can forgive yourself, which I think is long overdue."

I rubbed my hands over my face and sighed, longing for sleep. "Easier said than done. I've caused so much pain, Patsy. I can't imagine what William must be feeling right now. He was so angry when he left this morning. So hurt. Part of me wants to contact him, to try and explain. And yet, at the same time, I know there's no explanation that will make any of this right. He probably wouldn't be willing to listen anyway."

"Oh, I wouldn't be so sure of that. I don't think you've seen the last of William Ward. Give him some time to get over the jolt of it all, and I bet he's going to want to hear what you have to say."

CHAPTER 32
William

I'd spent a couple hours on horseback deep in the woods to process Catherine's return and Caroline's existence, but eventually, revisiting the past became too painful. I turned the horse back toward the barn, no longer able to be alone with my thoughts. I called Patricia as soon as I was back in cell range and asked if she'd meet me to talk. My sister and I had always been close, and she was the only person I'd confided in when the facts revealed by Caroline became too coincidental to ignore.

I hadn't thought anything of it when Levi first introduced Caroline, but as she and I talked more, I became curious about her birth mother and the similarities between her and Piper. When I met the kids, my curiosity grew, but as I asked more questions about her mother, none of the answers fit, and I convinced myself that my imagination was running wild.

Still, with the timing of Caroline's birth and adoption, I hadn't been able to shake the gnawing suspicion that somehow Catherine Johnson and Cat Russo were connected.

When Caroline told me the adoption foundation her mother ran was called Turtle Crossing, my suspicion was confirmed. There was no way the name was a coincidence. When we'd made our plans as lovestruck teenagers, Catherine and I had been certain that one day we'd own a farm together. She'd care for injured sea turtles, and I'd care for injured horses. She'd insisted that we would call it Turtle Crossing, and she wouldn't entertain any of my protests about the name.

So, against her better judgment, Patricia had agreed to use her status at the hospital to circumvent hospital procedures and let me see Cat Russo. I assured her I only want to see her sleeping face. That I would know the truth if I could see her, and I'd be able to put my mind at ease.

But it hadn't been as simple as that.

I drummed my fingers on the table in the coffee shop near the hospital while I waited for Patricia to join me.

"Well, did you get any answers?" she asked as she slid into the chair across from me. "Is she yours?"

I glanced around the cafe, fairly certain no one could hear us in the spot I'd chosen near the back. The news would get out soon enough that I had another daughter, and that was fine. I'd accept the responsibility and all that came with it. But until my head stopped spinning and I could wrap my mind around the news, I didn't care to discuss it with just anyone.

"Thanks for coming," I said to my sister, thankful I had someone I could trust so implicitly.

"Any time, you know that. What did Catherine say?"

"That she was sorry."

My eyes grew wet again and a thick knot formed in my throat as the waitress came to take Patricia's order for coffee and a piece of pie. I looked out the window and avoided eye contact while she refilled my tea.

"You look like hell, baby brother," Patricia whispered when the waitress had gone. "You holding up all right?"

"Yeah. I'm fine. Just so many thoughts swirling around in my head. What might have been. What could have been. What I didn't know about. Or rather, who. Patty, I have a kid I never met. She's a full-grown woman with kids of her own. I've missed her whole life."

She reached across the table to take my hand. "I'm sorry, Will. I can't imagine what you're feeling. I don't even know what to say."

I lifted my eyebrows in mock surprise. "You? Speechless? Damn. This is one for the record books."

She released my hand and slapped at it. "All right. Now I feel better. You're still being a smartass and teasing me, so you're going to be fine."

"Oh, I'll be fine. I'm sure we all will. But this is a mess. How do I even begin to unpack it?"

"Have you told Piper?" The expression on Patricia's face mirrored the anxiety in my heart.

I shook my head, the knot in my throat too large for me to speak. I took a swig of the iced tea, hoping to dislodge it. "No. She left for Denver this morning."

"What's she doing out there?"

"Looking for a job."

Patricia's brows came together as she frowned. "Doesn't she have a job? Doesn't she work for you?"

"She feels like no one takes her seriously because she's my daughter. She says they hire her as a trainer based on my reputation or they view her as a less capable stand-in for me. Which isn't true. Piper is damned capable. She's a fine horsewoman in her own right. It's her attitude that gets her in trouble, and she doesn't see that."

"You just think she has attitude now. Wait until Piper discovers she's not the only apple vying for Daddy's eye."

I sat back and exhaled with a swear. "It's not like that. No one is going to take Piper's place. It's not a competition."

"I know that, and you know that. But that niece of mine is a fireball. And she's rather protective of her daddy and her place as Daddy's little girl. This might be a bigger explosion than you think."

"Oh, I'm not underestimating how difficult this is going to be. She's gone for a least a week, though, and that gives me a little time to process this and figure out how to tell her."

"You're gonna wait until she gets back, then?"

I shrugged. "I don't think it's the kind of news I should share over the phone. Do you?"

"She's gonna be upset either way. She might be more pissed if you wait. But then again, if she's trying to get a job, it may mess her up if she finds out now."

The waitress set down Patricia's slice of pie and her coffee, and then she asked for the third time if I was sure I didn't want something to eat. I told her no, again, and picked up the straw wrapper from the table and begin to twist it.

"Have you eaten anything?" Patricia asked.

I shook my head.

"I've never understood how you do that. Since you were a little kid, if you were upset about anything, you couldn't eat. When I'm upset, I can't stuff my face enough."

"I need to talk to Caroline," I blurted out. "She tried to talk to me this morning, and I couldn't. I was angry. I was upset. I was reeling. I don't want her to think I'm unhappy about this. Or that I don't want her in my life. I need to call her."

Patricia stopped chewing and stared at me. She covered her mouth with her hand and mumbled around the pie she hadn't swallowed. "So, she knows you're her father?"

The headache I'd been fighting all day had intensified, and the muscles in my neck and shoulders were so tight that it hurt to turn my head. I reached up to rub my neck in an effort to relieve the tension, though I knew it wouldn't help. The stress I was under couldn't be cured with any massage techniques.

"I didn't tell her. I didn't think it was my place to. I told Catherine that she needed to tell her.

"So what's up with the name?" Patricia said as she scraped her fork across the graham cracker crumbs scattered across the plate. "Why is Catherine going by Caterina Russo?"

"I don't know."

She looked up from the crumbs wide-eyed. "You didn't ask her?"

"I did, but she said something vague about being a phoenix rising from the ashes."

"Hmmph. Catherine always did have a flair for the dramatic. And that's it? Was that all she said?"

"I don't know. It's all a blur. We didn't really have a whole lot of conversation, you know? I wasn't intending to get into anything at all. When I was in her room yesterday, she looked like death. Like she wasn't going to make it. When you called last night to say she was doing better and they were moving her to a regular room, I wanted to see her. I wanted to see that she was okay."

"And you wanted to know what the hell happened. Why she never told you she had your child."

"Well, yeah, that too, but I knew she was ill. I didn't want to press it. Not yet. I was willing to wait."

"Oh, please. You were more than willing to wait for Catherine. For years, you waited. Without a word, remember? Because I remember."

"Don't start, Patty. Please?"

She rolled her eyes and sipped her coffee.

"So what *did* the two of you discuss? What did she have to say?"

Catherine's voice replayed in my head and her face flashed through my thoughts as I heard her say she was sorry over and over again.

"She kept apologizing—"

"As she should have."

"—and she said she didn't tell me to protect me. That she worried what her father would do to me."

"Which," Patricia paused to swallow the last bite of pie, "is a valid concern. Her dad was batshit crazy, and it's very likely he would have made your life a living hell. Not that Catherine leaving didn't do that anyway, but she may have a point."

"She could have told me," I said, my anger rising again. "I should have had the choice to be involved."

"What would you have done? At the time she left, you were planning to head off to college. Did you tell her you didn't go because of her?"

I shook my head, but she didn't wait for a response.

"How would you have supported a baby? Look, you know I've never been a fan of Catherine Johnson. I still remember the first time you brought her home after Mom insisted she needed to meet her. That girl was snooty and stuck-up and full of herself, but I know, I know." She waved her hand and rolled her eyes. "You somehow saw a side of her none of us ever saw. Whatever!" She shook her head as she smirked. "But playing devil's advocate for a moment, she was, what? Sixteen? You were seventeen. She's right. Her dad would have come after you with a vengeance. You know what an asshole he was. You really think he would have ever let the two of y'all raise that baby in peace? What were you going to do? Marry her? Like she would have been content to live in some rundown apartment somewhere after growing up in a palace!"

I glared at my sister, who had never shied away from laying the truth bare.

"I don't know what I would have done, but I should have had a choice in the matter. Caroline deserved to know her father."

Patricia sighed and crossed her hands in her lap with a frown.

"So, how did you and Catherine leave it off? Is she going to let you know once she tells Caroline, so you can call and address the elephant in the room?"

"We didn't get that far. My emotions got the best of me, and after I demanded to know if Caroline was mine, it didn't go well from there. I stormed out."

"Nice. So how are you going to know if Catherine has talked to her?"

"I think I told you that Caroline's been seeing Levi, my farm manager. I figured I'd call him and just check on her. See how she's doing. Maybe ask for her number."

"And then say what? I'm your father; let's get some ice cream?"

I glared at her again, and she held up her hands in protest.

"Look, Will, this is going to be awkward no matter what. You realize that, I'm sure. I think you should know what Catherine's told her first. Why don't you call Catherine?"

I rubbed my hand across my forehead and groaned.

"I can't. I can't keep it together right now. My chest is so tight with emotion that I feel like I'm going to explode. One minute I'm angry and want to punch something. The next, I feel this overwhelming sensation of loss, and it's all I can do not to cry, for Christ's sake. I didn't sleep at all last night, and since I saw Catherine this morning, I can't focus on a damned thing. I can't concentrate to work. I've avoided seeing anybody at the farm by staying out in the woods on a horse or in my truck all day. I can't think straight. Hell, the last thing I need to do is talk to that woman again."

"But you think it's a good idea to talk to Caroline in this condition?"

"I don't have a choice, Patty!" I snapped much louder than I should have. I ignored the casual glances from across the cafe and leaned across the table, lowering my voice so as not to be heard. "She's my daughter. I need her to know that I didn't abandon her. That I didn't know about her. That I would have done everything in my power to be with her if I had known."

My voice broke, and the tears that had been threatening to appear came forth. I closed my eyes and rested my forehead in my hands.

Patricia reached across the table and rubbed my arm.

"Okay, this sucks. I know it does. And my heart breaks for you, little brother. But the truth is, you were better off not knowing about that baby. Sure, your heart got busted up, but you got over it. You met Revae. You built your farm. You had Piper. None of that would have happened if you'd had to support a baby at seventeen. It just wouldn't have! I think in some screwed up way, Catherine did protect you. She carried your child and brought her into the world, and then she carried the secret for all these years. You got to go on with your life."

I waved her hand away and grabbed the handkerchief from my pocket. It was still damp from the tears I'd shed throughout the day. Patricia sat back and crossed her arms.

"Will, if you're ever gonna have any kind of closure and move on from this and be healthy with it, you've got to find a way to forgive Catherine. Maybe not today, or tomorrow, next week, or even next month. But you have to forgive her. I think to do that, you need to listen to her side of the story. You need to know what she went through, and why she made the choices she did. When the dust settles, the two of you share a daughter. And if you're both going to be in Caroline's life—as you should be—then you're going to need to be okay with seeing Catherine and being around her."

I put the handkerchief back in my pocket and nodded, more to end the frustrating conversation than out of any real agreement.

"I gotta get back to the hospital," Patricia said as she dug out her wallet and laid the money for her pie on the table before standing. "Let me know how it goes with Caroline. And with Catherine."

She squeezed my shoulder and planted a kiss on my cheek, and then she left me to stew in my own mess.

I refused to consider her words about Catherine just yet. I wasn't ready. I didn't want to forgive her. Didn't want to consider her side. I was still consumed by betrayal and the sense of being wronged.

One thing I knew for certain, though. I wasn't going to let another minute pass without acknowledging my daughter and making sure she knew I wanted her in my life.

CHAPTER 33
Caterina

I don't know how long I'd been sleeping when Caroline returned. I opened my eyes when I heard the door, catching a glimpse of her red hair as she turned to go.

"Caroline?" I called, not wanting her to leave.

"Sorry, didn't mean to wake you."

"I doze and wake off and on." I tried to push myself up to a sitting position, but the hospital pillow had little substance to support me. I spied an extra one in the recliner and motioned to it. "Could you put that pillow behind my back?"

"Sure." She fluffed it as best she could and put it behind me, but it was about as flat as the first one. I sighed, wishing hospital beds weren't so damned uncomfortable and that I wasn't confined to one.

Caroline seemed uncomfortable too, like she didn't know what to do with herself, and I knew she was anxious to hear the rest of the story. Our story.

"So, I'm assuming you want to know how you got here if I left town and never saw William Ward again?"

Relief played out across her face, and she smiled as she took a seat.

"The question had crossed my mind."

I took a deep breath and prepared to go back to that dark place in my mind I had long avoided visiting.

"I had been at the boarding school a little over a month when I realized something was wrong. I hadn't had a period since I'd arrived, and my breasts were so sensitive that I couldn't stand to wear a bra. I kept it to myself as long as I could, but eventually one of the headmistresses started questioning why I missed the morning classes but seemed to make the afternoon without a problem. I begged them not to call my parents, but, of course, they had to."

The memories brought with them an anxiety that increased my physical discomfort, and I tugged at the lumpy pillows in agitation.

"I refused to name William, and my father was beyond livid. He threatened me with everything he could think of, and I think he would have forced me to have an abortion had I not been at a Catholic boarding school. I couldn't stay at the school, though, and I couldn't go home. Not that I wanted to!"

My father had been dead and gone for years, but he was still able to get me all worked up. I lay back and exhaled, reminding myself that it served no purpose to give him power over my emotions or my blood pressure.

"He ended up disowning me. Formally. Drew it up in the courts and everything. He forbade me to ever set foot in his home again and told my mother she wasn't allowed to speak to me anymore. She was never one to stand up to my father, but she arranged for me to go to her mother's house, my grandmother in New Jersey, who took me in and loved me in spite of myself."

It would be my mother's greatest act of courage, and the only time she ever outright defied him. She may not have had the strength to leave him or to openly go against his wishes and associate with me, but in giving me over to her own mother, she had ensured I was well taken care of and thoroughly loved.

Mother secretly stayed in contact when she could, even daring to visit me at Nonna's on a couple of occasions when Father was conducting business out of the country. She somehow managed to pay for all my medical expenses throughout the pregnancy and delivery without his knowledge.

I chose to see her actions as proof of her love for me, and by extension, the child I brought into the world. With the help of a great therapist, I even forgave her for not doing more, which allowed us to become closer in the years after Father died.

As hard as that time of pregnancy and post-delivery was, at least I wasn't thrown on the streets as my father had intended. I don't think I would have survived the experience to become a respectable adult if it hadn't been for Nonna's influence and the knowledge that Mother hadn't given up on me completely.

The anger from before gave way to tears as I thought about my beloved grandmother and my mother, both long gone.

"My grandmother, Nonna, loved me unconditionally. She took care of me. She even offered to keep the baby. *You.* To keep you. But my mother was scared of what my father would do if he found out, so she arranged a private adoption."

It wasn't until after Mother's death that I learned she had personally overseen the arrangements, hiring her own attorney behind Father's back and poring over each potential couple's profile before making the final choice all on her own. She kept in touch with Caroline's adoptive mother, Lorna, through that attorney, always ready to step in if there was ever an issue with the child's well-being. In her personal papers, I found a meticulously maintained file that had Caroline's school records, medical records, pictures, and notes about her family situation and her life. When the couple divorced and Caroline's adoptive father left them to fend for themselves, Mother had even paid off the family's house and arranged employment for Lorna.

My tears fell faster as I considered how much Mother's efforts meant, especially in light of the beautiful woman beside me who stood and squeezed my hand in hers. I looked up at Caroline, still unable to fully comprehend that the tiny babe taken from my arms all those years ago was back in my life.

"The day you were born, I got to hold you for a total of twenty minutes. You had this fiery tuft of red hair on the top of your head, which I loved, because it was William. It was like having a piece of him there with me that day. I loved you so much, Caroline."

My throat constricted as my voice faltered with emotion, and I tensed, not wanting to descend into a coughing fit. Caroline was quick to hand me water, but neither of us broke our hand hold. I think the physical contact gave us both comfort.

She smiled at me, and my heart tightened at the sight of her tears.

"Thank you, Caterina. Thank you for carrying me. For giving me life. For welcoming me into the world as someone who was loved."

"Oh, how I loved you! I was so in love with you, and when they took you, I thought I would die. I wanted to die. But Nonna held me. She held tight to me, and she didn't let go. She gave me the strength to go on. She'd say, 'Caterina, head up, chin up, you must live.' And in that strong Italian accent of hers, you couldn't deny her, you know? I had no choice but to soldier on."

"Is she why you changed your name to Caterina?"

I nodded, remembering clearly the day I made the decision to leave Catherine Johnson behind. I wanted a fresh start. I wanted to begin a new life unencumbered with Catherine's mistakes and her heartache. It turned out a legal name change couldn't erase the past, but it gave me enough of a barrier to move forward without constantly looking back. Caterina hadn't screwed up or been tossed aside like Catherine had. She could be whoever I chose for her to be.

"Catherine died that day. Caterina survived."

"What about the Russo? Was that your grandmother's last name?"

"No. I didn't want to be that easy to find. I chose Russo because it had Sicilian ties, which was for Nonna. It's also associated with red, so with it, I could carry you and William both with me. I changed my name on my eighteenth birthday and began to reclaim my life and my dignity. My sense of worth."

To my surprise, Caroline sat next to me on the bed and wrapped me in a huge hug. The solace and healing we found in our embrace moved us both to cry harder, but eventually, we made our way to laughter.

"So, what am I going to say to William?" Caroline asked once we'd calmed ourselves and she had moved to sit at the foot of my bed. "When I saw him this morning, he said I needed to talk to you first. What now?"

I was the last person to advise her on what to do about William. I had no idea what he was thinking or feeling other than the hurt and anger I'd seen on display that morning. All of which was justified, of course. It was impossible to know how he'd react to Caroline, but I had to think that no matter what his feelings might be toward me, he would be open to connecting with her. Undoubtedly, he wouldn't turn his back on her now that he knew.

I shook my head, wishing I could offer more insight. "I don't know. As you can imagine, he's pretty upset with me. I think it was a shock to find out about you, even though I'm fairly certain he had figured it out before we talked. The last thing I ever wanted to do was hurt him."

"But you never thought about contacting him? All these years? Did you ever look him up on-line? Try to find him?"

"No."

In truth, I hadn't dared look for him, not knowing what I would want to find. Part of me hoped that he'd moved on and been happy, but the selfish part of me wanted to think I'd been hard to forget. Besides that, I couldn't be sure if it would be more torturous to never know where he was or to know but be unable to ever contact him. Then fate intervened, and I found him without trying.

"I didn't even know he lived in Cedar Creek until after I'd moved here to be near my mother. I saw an article in the paper about him and his wife about a month after I bought my house. How's that for bad luck? Out of all the cities and all the towns in the central Florida area, I pick the one place I should have avoided at all costs."

The sleepy little town had seemed a safe choice, close enough to Ocala to be near my mother's assisted-living facility, but far enough away that I wasn't immersed in the scenery of my past life every day. Of course, I'd assumed William would have stayed in Ocala like he planned, so I was shocked to discover he and his wife were local celebrities in my new hometown.

"She died, you know," Caroline said. "Revae. His wife."

"Yes, I sent flowers, anonymously, of course. I was heartbroken for him when I heard. What I wanted most of all was for William to be happy, and it seemed he was when she was alive."

"So, you never tried to contact him? Even after she died?"

"No. And say what? Hello? Here I am after disappearing thirty-six years ago? And oh, by the way, you have a daughter? But I have no idea where she is? No. Even if he'd been single all that time, I still wouldn't have chosen to drop this bombshell on him."

Caroline paused, chewing on her bottom lip. "But don't you think he had a right to know?"

"Of course, he did! But once the wheels had been put in motion to rob him of that, there was no way I could make it right. I didn't dare try to reach him and tell him in those first few years because I knew he would try to find you. I knew he wouldn't stop searching until he did. I couldn't risk my father finding out it was William. I couldn't risk what my father might do to him. Even years later. Then, by the time my father had passed, you were an adult. I'd already cheated him out of your entire life at that point. What could I have possibly said?"

"What did you say this morning?"

"I said I was sorry. What else could I say?"

CHAPTER 34
William

Levi didn't ask any questions when I dialed him requesting Caroline's number. I didn't know if Catherine had told her I was her father yet, or what she may have confided in Levi if she knew, but I wasn't willing to wait any longer for us to connect.

Once I'd contacted her and arranged to meet for coffee, the frantic sense of urgency was replaced by uncertainty about what to say.

Few things in my life had made me as nervous as I was walking into that coffee shop to meet with her. I kept telling myself that I was being silly. I already knew Caroline. We'd developed somewhat of a friendship since she started visiting the farm, and I even knew the kids.

But it was much different to sit down across from her and know that she was mine.

We exchanged pleasantries, and I could tell by her changed demeanor that she knew. She seemed nervous and suddenly shy with me, and I couldn't help but notice as she stirred the creamer in her coffee that her hands were trembling. I figured we were both having similar feelings, and the best thing to do would be to acknowledge it. I just didn't know how to start.

I knew I should meet her eyes, but I feared getting emotional, so I kept my gaze on my hands.

"I have no idea what to say," I blurted out, wishing I could figure out how to put my thoughts into a coherent sentence.

"Me, neither," she said.

"If I'd known," I started, and as my voice broke, I made myself look up and face her with the strength she deserved from me. "I would have fought for you. I would have found you, and I would have raised you. I don't know how, but I would have."

Tears filled my eyes, and I silently cursed my emotions. She was going to think I was a weepy mess. I'd never been one for crying or outward expressions of my feelings. Why in the hell couldn't I hold it together when it mattered so much? I needed to explain to her. I needed her to know my truth. I swiped at my eyes and forced the words out.

"Catherine was my first love. I waited for years for her to come back. I amassed what wealth I could so that when she returned, I could take care of her. But then time went by without a word, without a visit. No call. No letter. Nothing. I gave up. I moved on. I met Revae, and I knew a love so strong and so passionate that it healed all the cracks in my heart. It kills me to know that all that time, you were out there somewhere." My voice broke again, and I cleared my throat as I worked to maintain my composure.

"I had a happy life," she said with a sweet smile. "I was loved. I am loved. My life is good."

I nodded at her attempt to comfort me and wished she didn't feel like she had to. I was grateful for her words, but while both of us had experienced love without each other, it didn't make up for what we should have shared.

I swallowed hard against that damned knot in my throat and blinked at the tears that kept filling my eyes no matter how hard I tried to hold them back. "You should have had your family. *My* family. You should have had your aunts, uncles. Grandparents. You should have known your father."

She reached across the table and grasped my hands, much like my sister had done not long before.

"It's not too late for me to know my father, William. I would love to get to know you. In the short amount of time that I've known you, I've grown fond of you. I would hope we could build on that."

I smiled and opened my hands to hers.

"I'd like that. I've grown fond of you, too. And the kids." The flood of emotions swept over me again as I thought about being a grandfather and how much I'd missed with them. "I can't believe I have grandchildren."

"I don't expect anything from you, William. I know this is all a shock for you, and I know you have your own life. Your own daughter."

"Oh, Christ. Piper. I have no idea how I'm going to tell her. She left for Denver this morning. She'll be gone at least a week, seeing if she's a good fit for a job out there. I can't tell her something like this over the phone. I wanted to tell her last night before she left, but I needed to hear it from Catherine first. To be sure."

Caroline pulled her hand from mine and sat back in her chair, and I wondered if I'd said something to upset her. I hoped she didn't think that Piper's reaction would in any way prevent me from including them in my life.

"I want you to know, that if you or the kids need anything at all, anything, I'll do whatever I can to help you."

She gave a brief nod and a smile. "Thank you, but we're fine. We have everything we need."

"I'd like to spend more time with them. With Eva and Ethan. Do they know?"

"No," she said, her gaze darting away as she shook her head. It was a difficult topic for her. "I only found out myself today. I mean, I thought there were some coincidences that were hard to explain."

"Likewise," I said, remembering the instances that had spurred us to this discovery—among them, Ethan's uncanny resemblance to William's childhood photo and my similarities to William's daughter, Piper.

"But I guess I have to figure out how to tell them."

"Are you still bringing Eva to work with the horses tomorrow?"

"I don't know. I had planned for my mom, Lorna, to bring them down and meet Cat, but that was before, well, this."

"Bring them. It's not going to get any easier. Best to get it out of the way, and then we can all move forward with this new norm."

I didn't want to rush her, but I also didn't want to waste any more time.

CHAPTER 35
Caterina

Patsy was catching me up on calls I'd missed and foundation business that needed my attention when Caroline returned from her meeting with William.

"How did it go?" I asked, relieved to see her relaxed demeanor and her easy smile. I'd been on pins and needles waiting to hear what had happened.

"Good, I think. He wants to get to know me better. He wants to spend time with the kids."

It didn't surprise me that William would welcome our daughter and her children into his family once he knew about them. What surprised me was my reaction to it. As happy as I was for Caroline and for William, a piece of my heart grieved for what could never be. Their relationship could progress and grow closer. I no longer had a relationship with him, nor would I ever again. I would never be a part of his family as I'd once hoped to be.

It was silly and selfish of me to feel sad when I had so much to be happy about, and I clapped my hands together to refocus my thoughts onto the positive. I had my daughter back, and we had a future together!

"So, Patsy told me last night that you've been working the books for the foundation. She said you suggested doing it online or with something on the computer."

Caroline nodded. "Yes, I think that would be your best bet. I know she said you have some, um, *challenges,* with technology, though."

Patsy and I immediately burst into laughter at the thought of my technological challenges.

"That's an understatement, if there ever was one. I can't do the computer thing, and as I'm sure you saw, I suck at keeping up with receipts and bank entries. It's simply not in my skill set. In fact, there are several things about running a foundation that I have discovered are not in my skill set." I leaned forward and dove into Patsy's suggestion with both feet. "Let me hire you, Caroline. You need a job, and I need help. I can't keep working at the pace I have been without ending up back in this hospital. I'm behind on everything after being out so long, and you've seen how messy it was already."

She didn't respond at first. I wasn't sure how to take her hesitation, but I held my hands up and continued before she could turn me down.

"Look, I realize it may not be something you'd want to do long-term, but it would get you some income and some independence, and it would help me greatly. I'm assuming if you're doing something online it could be done from anywhere, right?"

"Um, in theory?"

"Okay, so then no matter where you choose to live, this would work. At least until you found something else, right?"

Another long pause hung over the room, and I realized Patsy and I were both staring at Caroline with eager expressions. She obviously needed time to consider what she wanted without feeling pressured.

"You can think about it," I said. "You don't have to answer now."

A huge grin spread across Caroline's face. "Yes."

"Yes?" I asked, just to be sure.

"Yes."

"Woohoo!" Patsy cried. "Thank you, Lord! This is cause for a celebration."

Ever prepared for any circumstance, Patsy dug into her shopping bag and broke out a bottle of sparkling grape juice and three clear, plastic cups.

"I had thought we might celebrate the two of you being reunited, but I think we could manage a toast for this as well."

We did have much to celebrate, and the festivities continued that evening when Levi joined us. My heart swelled to see how happy Caroline was in his presence, and it made me all warm and fuzzy inside to see their new love blossoming.

"You've had a busy day," Patsy said when the lovebirds had gone.

"Are you kidding me? I've never been on any roller coaster that

176

had as many twists and turns and drops and build-ups as today."

"How are you feeling?"

"Good," I said with a nod. "I'm tired, of course, and I'm ready to be out of this bed, this place. But wow, huh? How mind-blowing have the past couple of days been?"

"You meet the kids tomorrow. You ready to be a grandmother?"

"I'm excited to meet them, but I don't know that they'll view me as a *grandmother*. I mean, they don't even know me. And they already have a grandmother."

"Yes, they do. Children can have lots of grandmothers, though. Their hearts have quite large capacities to love and be loved, and they don't usually worry about the complexities of titles or relations as much as we adults do."

I nodded, seeing the pictures of Eva and Ethan in my head and wondering how they would receive me.

"Speaking of their grandmother, how are you feeling about meeting Lorna?" Patsy asked.

I grimaced and then chuckled. "Nervous! I mean, I'm thrilled that she wants to meet me and that she's okay with Caroline and I connecting, but I can't imagine that it's easy for her. I don't know what to expect."

Patsy smiled and put her hand over mine with a light squeeze.

"I would imagine Lorna is just as nervous and uncertain as you are."

"What if she's angry with me?"

"Why would she be?" Patsy asked, her eyes narrowing in confusion. "Caroline has already said Lorna is fine with everything."

"No, not about Caroline and I talking. What if she's angry with me that I gave my baby away? The file my mother kept on Caroline's family said that Lorna was unable to have children of her own. I worry she might not think too highly of me."

"Oh, honey. I don't think Lorna will be angry that you gave her a beautiful baby girl to raise and love as her own. You have to forgive yourself for this."

I smiled and tried to force a nod, but she was asking something of me that I had no idea how to do. What I had done to Caroline and William, to my mother and even to my grandmother, was unforgivable. Not even my therapist had been able to change my thinking on that point.

"I wish I wasn't trapped in this hospital room to meet everyone. Not a great first impression, is it?"

"Cat, you carry yourself with grace and elegance no matter where you are. I'm sure they're all gonna love you!"

While I appreciated her supportive words, they didn't keep me from being a bundle of nerves from the moment I woke the next morning until Caroline arrived. I was surprised to see her enter my room alone, but then she explained that she and Lorna had thought it might be overwhelming for me to have the entire group standing around my hospital bed, so they'd decided to have everyone meet me one-on-one.

Eva was the first in, and I was captivated immediately by her beauty and her confidence. She was striking, with dark brown hair and dark green eyes, her complexion much deeper than Caroline's. I assumed she must look like her father, but I could see her mother in Eva's slender build and in her smile.

Ethan was next, and it was obvious that visiting a hospital to meet some stranger was not his first choice of fun activities. He stayed close by Caroline's side, his wide blue eyes staring at the medical equipment and the hospital bed as though they were torture devices. I think he was quite relieved when his mom tousled his red hair and said it was time to go.

As I waited for Caroline to return with Lorna, I checked my appearance in the mirror. I even adjusted my gown and smoothed the covers on the bed, doing whatever I could to make a good impression.

Caroline and Lorna both seemed nervous as they entered my room, and I realized I wasn't the only one feeling a little tense given the circumstances.

Caroline's eyes were on Lorna as she introduced us, and she seemed as caught off guard as I did when her mom asked for a moment alone with me after the general niceties had been exchanged.

A wave of nausea hit me, and my anxiety grew as Caroline exited. Was Lorna going to tell me what a terrible person I was? Was she going to tell me how callous and uncaring I had to be to give away my own child?

"May I?" Lorna asked, indicating the chair next to the bed.

"Of course, please make yourself comfortable."

"I won't keep you long," she said as she sat. "Caroline said you tire easily, and I don't want to wear you out. I just wanted to say thank you."

Her words were not what I expected, and I tilted my head as I stared at her and tried to understand her meaning.

"My body couldn't conceive and carry a child, but I was able to have one because you were willing to give me that opportunity," she said, her eyes suddenly glassy. "I cannot imagine what that cost you, what it must have taken for you to let her go. I'm sorry for whatever it was in your life that led to that decision, but I am so grateful to you."

A huge lump lodged in my throat and I swallowed hard, hoping I wouldn't have a coughing fit in the middle of such a poignant moment. I opened my mouth to speak, but no words would come, so I reached for her hand and squeezed it tightly.

"I didn't mean to make you cry," she said, and I shook my head.

"No, please. I appreciate your words more than you know, and I appreciate you loving Caroline and being her mother. She's incredible, and I know that's a direct reflection of your love."

"She's been a blessing; that's for sure. I'll go now. I just wanted a moment to say thank you and to welcome you to our family."

She stood and bent to hug me, and we both cried and laughed together as we said goodbye.

Once she'd gone, I wiped my eyes and marveled at how much my circle had expanded in such a short period of time.

"Hey! I think that's everybody," Caroline said when she entered the room again. "You okay? Mom didn't tell me she was going to do that. Sorry if it was awkward."

"She's lovely, Caroline. They all are. You have beautiful children and a mother who adores you. My heart is full having met them all."

"I'm going to take Eva to the farm," she said. "Mom is going to drive Ethan back to Gainesville because he has a soccer tournament tomorrow. But I'm going to stay, and hopefully, they'll spring you from this joint, and I can help get you settled at home."

As much as I wanted more time with her, I also didn't want to be a burden or to keep her from her own responsibilities.

"You don't have to stay if you need to be with Ethan," I said.

Caroline smiled and put her hands on her hips.

"I've been to every game and every tournament so far until today. I think he knows at this point that I love him and I support him, but this weekend, I have somewhere I need to be."

"Have you told the kids? About William, I mean?"

She shook her head. "I have to tell Eva today. I think I'll hold off for a bit with Ethan. Wait until I'm back home to discuss it. He doesn't have to know right away, and I think Eva needs some time alone with me. She's had her first break-up. She's discovered boys are jerks."

"Oh, God bless her, are they ever!"

I bent my legs to sit cross-legged on the bed, and Caroline pointed to the sea turtle tattoo on my foot.

"I like your turtle," she said.

I traced him with my finger, as I had done countless times over the years since I'd first had him drawn on my skin.

"William and I had a turtle connection," I said, allowing the flashes of memory to play in my head without the admonishment that normally accompanied them. "They were always special to us, and I got this to remember him with."

It felt incredibly liberating to say that. To be able to be honest about the tattoo's meaning seemed such a small thing but was so powerful. If asked about it, I had always said I was fond of the creatures, which was true. But that tattoo went much deeper than a love for turtles.

I'd always envied people who could casually discuss past relationships or memories from their teenage years. It was something I had avoided out of fear that someone would learn my secrets and possibly destroy the lives of those I cared most about.

But the shroud of secrets had been thrown off my back now that both William and Caroline knew the truth.

I had nothing left to fear and nothing left to hide. My past couldn't hurt me any more than it already had. William might never forgive me, but it seemed like Caroline had, and she and the kids were good reason for me to look with optimism toward the future.

CHAPTER 36
William

L evi was just finishing a phone call when I walked into his office and sat down, pulling the door shut behind me.

"Haven't seen you around the past couple days," he said as he hung up and came around the front of his desk to sit on the corner. "You okay?"

"As well as can be expected, I suppose. I'm assuming you know what's going on."

He nodded and rubbed his hand across the back of his neck. "Yeah. I wanted to come and talk to you, but I wasn't sure what I should say or how involved I should get. Damnedest thing, ain't it?"

"It was unexpected, for sure."

"Have you told Piper yet?"

I shook my head, and he let out a low whistle.

"I figured I'd wait until she gets home from Denver," I said as I glanced at my watch. "At this point, what's a few more days going to matter? Better to manage that powder keg face to face."

"How do you think she's gonna take it?"

"Hmmph. How do *you* think she's gonna take it?"

He chuckled and crossed his arms.

"Let's just say I don't envy you."

"Things seem to be going well with you and Caroline," I said, eager to shift the conversation away from the inevitable blow-up with Piper.

His expression softened, and his smile grew wide. "Yeah. They're good. Things are going good."

"Is this getting serious? I've never known you to be one to rush in."

His smile grew even more, and his eyes held something I'd never seen before in the fifteen years I'd known him. He had it bad.

"I don't know, man." He shook his head with that goofy grin plastered on his face. "There's something about her. I've never met anyone who affected me the way Caroline has."

"Well, I'm happy for you. Both of you. But keep in mind she has kids involved, okay?"

His grin faded, and he sat up straighter in the chair. "Yeah, definitely. I mean, we're both making sure we take it slow. I don't, that is, *we* don't, well, I mean, we're careful with how we act in front of them, you know?"

I'd never seen Levi stutter or stammer. He was one of the most confident men I'd ever met, and he was, without exception, calm and cool as a cucumber even in the most stressful of circumstances. It seemed he really had fallen hard.

He was my righthand man on the farm, and I had long viewed him as a member of my family. I loved him like the son I'd never had. But now as I wrapped my head around my new family members getting involved with him, it was hard not to look at him through a different lens.

He'd always been trustworthy and hardworking, and the man had a heart of pure gold. He'd do anything for anybody in need. But he also had a bit of a playboy reputation with the guys on the farm, and though I wasn't sure how warranted the title was, it did give me pause to think of him and Caroline getting serious so soon.

It wasn't like Caroline was a teenager. She didn't need me playing the role of protective papa, for sure. But I hated to see the two of them chase a spark and end up with a crash and burn that would make it difficult for all of us moving forward, especially the kids.

"Look, Levi. I'm not ever gonna be one to stick my nose in your personal business. I think you know that by now. Caroline is an adult who's fully capable of making her own decisions. But this situation is still new for everybody. Just make sure you're thinking with the right head here, okay? Take your time. Don't move too fast. And always keep those kids in the forefront of your mind as the top priority."

He nodded, his expression somber. "Yes, sir. I will. I do. I hear you."

"Well, speaking of those kids, Eva should be arriving any minute for a riding lesson. I swear that girl is a natural. She moves with the horse like they're two parts of the same animal. I'm really looking forward to seeing what she can do with a little training."

I stood and extended my hand across the desk, and he stood as he accepted the handshake offer. I turned to go, but as I opened the door I remembered the other reason I'd stopped by his office.

"Did you get that fiasco with Kentucky settled? Is the horse cleared to fly this afternoon?"

He nodded just as his phone rang. "I'm on it. In fact, that's probably what this call is about now."

I nodded and made my way out of the office building just as Caroline and Eva were pulling into the parking area. I smiled and gave a wave as they parked, relieved to see that Eva had still wanted to come.

Caroline had said she was going to tell the girl that I was her grandfather before they arrived, and I had no way of knowing how Eva might react. I hoped she wouldn't feel uncomfortable around me or suddenly become shy. It was going to be an adjustment for all of us, getting used to the new reality.

"So you came back for more?" I asked Eva as they got out of Caroline's Tahoe.

"Yes, sir. I'm ready to ride."

"All right. That's what I like to hear. Let's get to it. Caroline, Levi's on a call, but I'm sure he wouldn't want to miss saying hello. Why don't you wait for him in the office, and I'll take Eva up to the barn? You can join us when he's done."

Caroline looked hesitant for a moment, but Eva climbed in the truck, ready to get to work.

We were both silent for the first part of our ride to the barn, and I knew I needed to broach the subject and get it out in the open.

"So, did your mom tell you what we discussed yesterday?"

"Yeah," Eva said, and then she twisted in her seat to face me with her leg tucked beneath her. "This means you're my grandfather now. Isn't that wild?"

Her huge smile conveyed her excitement about the revelation, and I chuckled with relief.

"Yeah, it's *wild* all right. I've never been a grandfather before, so I'm in new territory here," I teased.

"It's okay. Trust me, the bar has been set pretty low by the grandfathers I've had up until this point, so pretty much anything you do will be fine." She rolled her eyes, and though her voice was still light-hearted and happy, it made me sad.

I hadn't been able to discuss much with Caroline about her adoptive parents yet, but she had said at the coffee shop that she'd been happy. That she'd been loved. I couldn't shake my curiosity about the man who had taken my place in her life, and it seemed that Eva didn't have too high of an opinion of him.

"Oh? Do you not have a good relationship with your mom's dad?"

"I've never met him. He took off when my mom was little. I think she was like three or four? I don't remember."

Pain and anger pierced my heart. I should have been there for Caroline. I certainly never would have left her. It had been hard enough accepting that I'd missed out on her life when I thought she'd been raised by a loving man who adopted her because he wanted to be a father. To think that my daughter had grown up without a father in her life made it even worse.

"What about your dad's dad? Are you close with him?"

"I wouldn't say we're *close*," Eva said with a tilt of her head. "I mean, Grandfather's okay. We just don't see him and Mitzi very often. They travel a lot. We see them around Christmas time, and before the divorce, Ethan and I would go and stay with them at their condo at the beach for a week every summer."

I'd never given much thought to what kind of grandfather I would be. I admired the relationships my own father had with my siblings' children, and my older brother and sister both had grandchildren of their own they were close to. Piper had never even been in a serious relationship, so the concept of me as a grandfather hadn't been on my radar yet.

As I listened to Eva's views of her grandparents, I made up my mind that I would make sure she and Ethan both knew they were important to me. I may have missed their childhood up until this point, but going forward, I would make every effort to be involved and engaged in their lives.

Of course, that wouldn't be easy with them two hours away in Gainesville, but once Caroline moved to Orlando, I could work my schedule to try and make soccer matches or school functions. And if Eva continued to pursue her interests in horses, that would be a way for us to bond and spend time together.

I'd need to figure out a way to connect with Ethan, but I knew I couldn't expect it to happen overnight with either one of them. I was still a virtual stranger, after all.

CHAPTER 37
William

Eva and I kept our conversation to horses and the business at hand as we saddled up and went through the steps of her lesson. When we were finished, she asked if we could go out into the open pasture to ride without the constraints of the ring's fencing.

"Looks like your mom is waiting at the barn. Let's go let her know that's what we want to do and make sure she's okay with us taking longer."

"Okay. I'm sure she'll say yes if it means she gets to spend more time with Levi."

Perhaps they hadn't been as careful with their behavior as Levi had thought.

"There's a show coming up next month," I said as we were headed back to the barn. "I'd like you to come and see the horses and the riders if you could. And if you're interested."

"Sure! I'll have to see whose weekend it is, but it shouldn't be a problem. Even if it's my dad's weekend, I can probably still come."

"Is that hard? Going back and forth on the weekends?"

She paused for a moment and then shrugged. "It's fine, I guess. I like my room better at Mom's, and Mom's is, I don't know, *home?* Dad's only got two bathrooms at the apartment, so I have to share with Ethan, which sucks. And he usually has some girlfriend staying over at his place, which means we have to do whatever she wants to do and eat wherever she wants to eat. Which is cool if she's cool, but once he dated some girl who only ate fish and salad. Ew."

"You don't like fish?"

"It's okay every now and then. But not like every meal of the weekend except breakfast. I was glad when he broke up with her."

"Are you and your dad close?"

"No. I mean, I love my dad, but he's been a real jerk the last couple of years, and I'm just over it. He cheated on my mom, and then he left us. Half the time he doesn't show up or just cancels when it's his weekend. Mom tries to make excuses for him or tries to make it okay, but it's not okay. If he didn't want to be a dad, then he shouldn't have had kids. You don't get to just decide you're not going to be responsible anymore, you know?"

"I would imagine that's been tough to deal with. I'm sorry you guys have been going through that. Maybe your father needs some time to adjust and figure out who he's supposed to be."

"He's supposed to be our dad. How hard is that to figure out?"

I could see Caroline pacing by the fence as we arrived at the barn. She was on the phone, and by the sound of her voice carrying on the wind, she was upset.

As we got closer, her words became clearer. Her back was to us, but we could hear her end of the conversation. It was obvious she was talking to Eva and Ethan's dad.

"Take me to court," she said, her voice bitter with anger. "I would love to explain to a judge that you put our house on the market without knowing where we will go when it sells. That you couldn't wait the five weeks until school is out to do that. That you purposely changed your transfer location to make it farther from my parents and therefore, harder for the kids to see them. Not to mention your parents, too. As crappy as they are as grandparents, they still deserve to be in the kids' lives."

She ran her hand through her hair and then flung her arm out to her side as though exasperated, still facing away from us.

I motioned to Eva to slow down, wondering if I should turn her back toward the pasture. Caroline hadn't seen us yet, and I was fairly certain she probably wouldn't want Eva to listen to the exchange.

"I'm done with this conversation, Brad. If you're going to take me to court, take me. If it leaves me broke and destitute, so be it. But I will no longer let you dictate how I live my life."

She ended the call and turned, her eyes widening and her mouth falling open when she saw us.

"Daddy's taking you to court?" Eva asked. "Why?"

"Oh, God, Eva. I didn't intend for you to hear that."

"But why's he taking you to court?" Eva asked as the horse shifted under her.

"I don't know that he will. He's threatening to."

"Is this because you want us to move to Cedar Creek?" Eva asked.

I turned to look at Eva, unsure if I'd understood her correctly, and then I focused my gaze on Caroline.

"You're moving to Cedar Creek?"

"Yeah," she said with a sigh. "I plan to. When the kids are out of school."

"Is that why?" Eva asked again.

Caroline groaned and laid her hand against her forehead. "That's part of it, Eva. He wants us to move to Miami with him."

"Miami? No way! I don't want to move to Miami!"

"You don't have to." Caroline put her hands on her hips and squared her shoulders. "We're moving to Cedar Creek, so don't get yourself all worked up about that."

"I thought he was moving to Orlando," I said.

"He changed his plans."

"Why?" Eva said. "Was it because of Levi?"

Caroline squinted as she stepped closer to the fence. "Why would you say that?"

Eva shrugged. "He's been asking all sorts of questions. About Levi. About Cedar Creek. How often we've come here. How long you stay here. Where you sleep when you're here. He's been texting me for the last couple of days. It's actually, I think, the first time he's ever texted me."

"I'm sorry," Caroline said. "I didn't mean for you to get caught in the middle of this."

She suddenly looked very tired, and my heart went out to her. I hated that she was dealing with so much. There had to be some emotional upheaval to suddenly finding both your birth parents, especially when one of them was on the brink of death in a hospital bed and the other didn't know you were born. At the same time, she was juggling both the kids' schedules and their needs and trying to coordinate moving the family. Add to that her ex-husband being a jerk, and it was bound to take its toll. I wished I could do something to help her, to bring relief in some way.

"Mom, you need to do what you think is best," Eva said, sounding wiser than her years. "Daddy doesn't think about anyone but himself. You can't keep trying to make him happy. If he wasn't happy when y'all were together, he's not going to be happy now. At least if you're happy, one of you will be."

I nodded. "I agree with Eva. We were coming to let you know we're going out in the open field. I'm sorry if we caught you at an inopportune time."

"Oh, it's okay," Caroline said. Then she closed her eyes and gave a brief shake of the head before opening them again. "So wait, you're what? Oh, going in the field. Yeah, as long as you're with her, and you think it's safe, I guess it's fine."

Eva thanked her mother and turned her horse, but I nudged mine to take me closer to the fence, unable to walk away without extending what assistance I could to Caroline.

"I told you yesterday if you need anything at all, just ask. My legal team might not be well-versed in family law, but I guarantee they know someone who is. You don't have to fight your battles alone any more, Caroline. You're part of this family, and we stand together in a fight."

Her astonished expression tugged at my heart, and I turned to catch up with Eva, not trusting myself not to go all weepy again. Something about Caroline made an emotional mess of me. *Like mother, like daughter,* I thought with a frown.

CHAPTER 38
William

Catherine, Caroline, and the kids had consumed my thoughts all day, and I went to bed restless and unsettled. Sleep eluded me, and some time after midnight, I got up and went down to the pool to swim some laps. I hoped the physical exertion would help my body relax for slumber, but if anything, the cool water refreshed me and left me wide awake.

I stood in the shallow end of the pool and stared up at the house Revae and I had built.

Patricia's words rang in my ears, and I couldn't dismiss them completely.

Life had been relatively good to me. I'd achieved great success in my career, and I was happy and fulfilled with what I did on a daily basis to help horses and their owners.

The farm was home to a group of hard-working and loyal staff, and together, we'd cultivated a family environment. I also had my own siblings and parents close by, and I knew how blessed I was to have that tight-knit circle supporting me and loving me without question.

Though Revae had been taken from me much too soon, I cherished every day we'd spent together. Our marriage had been the accomplishment I was most proud of, and I remained forever grateful for the love we'd shared, the home and business we'd built, and the daughter we'd raised. A beautiful, intelligent, strong, and confident daughter who was determined to carve out her own path on her own terms.

So, other than the loss of Revae, I couldn't say with any measure of honesty that I regretted the way my life had played out. I wasn't sure I agreed with Patricia's conclusion that Catherine had done me any favors by leaving me the way she did, but all in all, I had to admit it had turned out okay in the end.

Now, I had a new set of blessings to consider.

It was still hard to wrap my head around having another daughter and a couple of grandchildren. I couldn't think of Caroline, Eva, or Ethan without thinking of the time we'd lost.

But what would my life have been like—what would Caroline's life have been like—if I'd known about her back then? Was there any narrative that would have included Catherine and I being married and raising our daughter together? It was hard to imagine how I would have supported the three of us working as a stable boy. I likely never would have attained my career goals. After I dropped out of college, it was only the freedom my schedule allowed me for endless hours in the barns that had paved the path for me to work my way up and take advantage of opportunities along the way. If I'd had a baby and a wife, I would have been needed at home. My time would not have been my own.

Catherine would have surely been on the outs with her family. She would have needed to finish high school, but she would have probably had to work too, and what job would she have done? She was only sixteen when she left. She had no work experience, and her pregnancy and then tending to a baby at home would have limited her options. She'd grown up accustomed to having whatever she desired simply by asking for it. Would she have been happy living on the limited income we would have had, or would the financial stress and family strain eventually split us and have Caroline bounced back and forth as a product of a broken home?

I slapped at the water with open palms and climbed the steps to exit the pool.

There would never be an answer to those questions because I'd never had the chance to have input into Caroline's fate. I didn't have that chance because Catherine didn't give it to me.

How could she give away our child? How could she just let Caroline go like that? Did she fight for her at all or was she relieved to be out from under the obligation? Had she wanted to tell me? How could she not have even tried to reach me, even if not at first, then at some point in all these years?

She said she'd stayed silent to protect me. I guess on some level I understood that. I knew how vindictive and scornful Phillip Johnson could be. He wouldn't have taken the news well that his sixteen-year-old daughter and only child was unwed and pregnant with a stable boy's baby.

Neither of us were adults yet or capable of being self-sufficient. What options would we realistically have had?

I stepped inside the air-conditioned house and shivered at the cool air hitting my damp skin after the balmy humidity of the outdoors. I lifted the towel to rub my head and absorb any remaining drops of water, and the truth sat heavy on my shoulders.

As much as I would like to think that I would have done something—that I would have intervened to save my child—I couldn't avoid the facts. Catherine's father was a very wealthy and powerful man, and I'd be kidding myself to pretend I or my family would have had the resources or the ability to go up against him back then. Simply being the baby's father wouldn't have guaranteed me any rights against someone so ruthless.

What hell would I have lived if I had known of Caroline's existence but been helpless to prevent her being taken from me?

As the thought lingered in my mind, I stopped in my tracks, the realization of what Catherine had been through hitting me like a ton of bricks.

Whatever hell I could conceive it might have been to know about my child and not be able to keep her, Catherine had already lived through.

Her tearful apologies at the hospital came back to me, and for the first time since I'd had any suspicion that the girl Levi brought home might be mine, I began to consider what Catherine had endured.

My own pain had been so strong that I'd been blinded to the agony on her face when I visited her, but it came back to me in sharp recollection as I thought about things through her point of view.

My anger had been directed at the wrong person.

Though we'd both created the situation, she'd been the only one trapped by it, and she'd been the one to face her father's wrath alone.

Phillip Johnson had pulled the strings to control the outcome for all of us, and Catherine would have been helpless to stop what was happening. She would not have had a choice, any more than I would have, and if anything, even less.

And yet, she had chosen to protect me. I was certain he must have punished her handily for keeping my identity a secret from him. I had no way of knowing what he might have done, but whatever it was, she had stood strong through it for my sake. Even beyond that, she had known all along that our daughter was out there somewhere, and she had borne that sorrow alone while I went on with my life, unscathed by my actions until now.

I wondered what it had cost her to carry a child she knew she could not keep. What had it been like for her to deliver our baby and have Caroline taken from her arms without a choice?

That part of my heart that had loved her so fully contracted in pain as I considered how lonely she must have been.

I thought back to my heartbreak when Catherine left, and the difficulties I had experienced moving on. As time had stretched on with no word from her, I'd convinced myself that she hadn't really cared for me. That I'd been a summer fling and nothing more. That she'd returned to her life of luxury and never given me a second thought.

Now, I realized Catherine had likely gone through that same heartbreak of separation when we parted without warning but with the added agony I'd known nothing of.

I owed her an apology. I owed her more compassion than I had shown her.

Patricia had told me that Catherine's condition had improved, and she would likely be discharged the next day. I had to get back to the hospital. I had to see her and let her know I'd been wrong to jump so quickly to anger and judgment. I needed to tell her that while I didn't know what she had been through since that last fateful night so many years ago, I believed she deserved to be heard.

CHAPTER 39
William

Making the decision to hear Catherine's side of the story gave me the first peace I'd had in days, and I slept soundly through the remainder of the night.

When I arrived at the hospital the next morning, I knocked on her door, hoping she didn't have Caroline or another friend or family member staying with her. I had a pretty good idea of what I wanted to say, but I didn't want an audience when I said it.

Catherine looked surprised to see me, and she sat up straighter in the bed, her hand going to her hair where it was loosely piled on her head. She was sitting cross-legged on top of the blanket, and I was happy to see that she looked much healthier than she had on my previous two visits. The tube was gone from her nose, and color had returned to her cheeks.

She was still a strikingly beautiful woman. Time had left fine lines around her eyes, but they were the same emerald green that had haunted me for years after she disappeared. Faint smile lines framed her full lips, but otherwise, her skin was smooth. She had the same delicate cheekbones and slender nose that I remembered from her youth, along with the same heart-shaped face and pointed chin. Her hair was still as thick and full as ever, though its ebony darkness was heavily streaked with white and gray. The dramatic effect only added to her allure.

"I hear you're going home today," I said as I made my way to the foot of her bed and stood with my hands in my pockets.

"That's the rumor." She smiled and stacked the playing cards that were spread on the bed in front of her before putting them back in their box. "I'm about ready to climb the walls if they don't let me out."

I cleared my throat and wondered why the words I'd rehearsed since waking had suddenly left me.

"Um, I wanted to come by and apologize for leaving angry the other day."

Her smile faded, and a pained look settled over her face.

"You don't have to apologize for that, William. You have every right to be angry."

I swallowed hard and clenched my fists in my pockets, hoping my emotions wouldn't get the best of me again.

"Maybe so, but I didn't come up here that day with the intention of upsetting you or getting into everything. It wasn't the time or the place."

"I understood," she said. "I understand. I know this has all been a bombshell. I can't imagine what you're going through. What you're feeling."

I picked up the newspaper from the chair beside the bed and placed it on the table next to her so I could take a seat.

"Hell, Catherine, I don't even know what I'm thinking or feeling." I looked down at my hands and tried to take my time to make sure my words came out the way I wanted them to. "I guess I came here today because I don't want this conversation to be over. I need to fill in the missing pieces of the puzzle to get any kind of peace with this." I took a deep breath and met her eyes. "Look, you were right when you said the other day that I don't understand. But I want to. I want to understand. I want to know what you went through and why you made the choices you did. It's not fair of me to be angry and hold you responsible without knowing the facts. I have so many questions."

She exhaled with her hand on her chest, and I realized she must have been holding her breath to hear what I would say.

"Sure. Of course. I will answer whatever I can." She licked her lips, and her eyes grew wide with anxiety as she waited.

"Not now," I said, rushing to reassure her. "I meant maybe we could talk more later. You know, when you're recovered. When you're up to it."

Her shoulders relaxed, and the tight line of her mouth softened into a smile. "Oh. Yeah. Definitely."

"I just didn't know how to reach you after you left here, and I didn't want you to leave the hospital and then disappear again."

She tilted her head and studied me with her brilliant green eyes.

"I'm not going anywhere. Cedar Creek is my home. But I tell you what…" She reached to open the drawer of the bedside table and pulled out her purse to hand me a business card. "There's my number. Now you can contact me any time."

She had uncrossed her legs in the process of getting the card, and my eyes were drawn to the large sea turtle tattooed on the top of her foot.

Warm memories flooded my mind, and I nodded toward the turtle as I stuck her business card in my shirt pocket.

"So, you got the tattoo. Just like you said you would. You still have a fascination with sea turtles?"

She looked down at the artwork and then slid her foot under the sheet as her cheeks flushed pink.

"Oh, I got that thing years ago."

I rolled my sleeve over my bicep and up to my shoulder, turning so she could see the almost identical turtle on my arm.

Her eyes softened as she reached out as though she might touch it, but then she quickly pulled her hand back.

"Wow. I can't believe you got a tattoo. You always said you never would. Do you have any others?"

"Nope. Just that one. I can't believe you named your foundation Turtle Crossing. When Caroline told me that, I had no doubt at all that it was you."

She smiled, but she kept her head down and didn't meet my eyes.

"I guess I ended up saving kids instead of turtles, but the sentiment was the same, so I kept the name."

"Do you remember the first time we went to the beach to try and see the turtle hatchlings, and you got so upset that people were walking around with their flashlights searching for them? We were there to see them, too, but you were irate that people might disturb the turtles and confuse them with the lights. You said they should make signs on the beach that said *Turtle Crossing* so people could avoid their nests."

Her smile widened as she glanced up at the window, then back to her hands. "I still think it was a good plan."

"And when I pointed out to you that the turtles couldn't read and wouldn't know where to cross, you got so mad at me."

I laughed at the memory, and she chuckled with me.

"The signs would have been better than doing nothing!"

"Yeah, but the turtles come ashore for almost the entire Atlantic coast in Florida and a good portion of the western coastline. How would anyone know where to put the signs?"

She looked at me, and I was happy to see the anxiety gone from her eyes as she spoke.

"I told you, they could watch for the turtle tracks and put the signs up once the nests were in place."

We both laughed, and it felt good to allow myself to remember something of our time together without heartache or bitterness attached to it.

A knock sounded on the door, and our walk down memory lane ended as Caroline entered with an elderly lady I'd seen with her before.

Part of me wanted to stay and visit with Caroline, but the three of us together in one room was awkward, and the easy banter from moments before was gone.

I stood to say goodbye, and Catherine looked up at me with such warmth that I leaned forward and kissed her forehead, hoping the gesture might convey that I was sorry for her pain.

I left the hospital feeling like some part of the weight that had plagued me for days had been lifted. I would still need to deal with the changes in my life and what they would bring, especially once Piper returned home. It hadn't erased what had happened, but releasing the anger toward Catherine had given me some measure of calm, and I was finally able to focus on work and attend to business without feeling like I might go to pieces at any moment.

CHAPTER 40
Caterina

I'd been home from the hospital for a few days when William called and asked if he could come by. I gave him the address and changed clothes at least three times before he arrived.

He showed up with a bouquet of Gerbera daisies in a bright array of colors, and I took them from him with a smile.

"Can I get you something to drink?" I asked as I walked to the kitchen to put the flowers in a vase. "I have iced tea. I can make coffee."

"No, thanks. I can't stay long."

It seemed surreal to walk back into my living room and see William Ward standing there. It was something I'd only thought could happen in my dreams.

He turned and smiled, and a wave of nostalgic memories hit me. I'd known that smile so well.

"I just wanted to check on you," he said. "How are you doing?"

"I'm good. Still weak, which is to be expected, I suppose. Haven't gotten rid of the cough completely, but so far so good. The home health nurse says she's happy with my progress."

He nodded toward a large framed photo on the wall behind the couch. It was a picture of the back of my head in a big floppy hat as I stared out over the blue waters of Santorini.

"Is that Greece?" he asked.

"Yes. One of my favorite places. Have you been?"

"No. Horses don't allow for many vacations. They require constant attention."

"I would imagine so. Travel is my vice. The only addiction I still allow myself to indulge in."

It was impossible not to notice the raised eyebrow and the question in his eyes, but I chose to ignore it.

"You sure I can't get you something? I'm going to pour myself a glass of iced tea."

"I guess I could drink a glass. If you're sure it's no trouble."

"No trouble at all. Here, have a seat."

I waved my hand toward the couch and returned to the kitchen. When I came back with our beverages, he was looking at the framed photos on the end table.

I handed him his tea and smiled at the grinning faces looking back at me from the pictures.

"Those are some of my Turtle Crossing kids. A few were just with me for a short period of time while their lives got sorted. Others stayed until we found them their forever homes."

"I think it's good that you, well, that you've done something so positive."

His voice held a sadness, and I turned away and went to curl my feet beneath me in the papasan chair in the corner.

"I read about your place in the paper a while back. The article said it's the largest equine training and rehabilitation facility east of Kentucky. That's impressive."

He nodded as a faint blush crept into his cheeks. "Thank you. I'm proud of my team and what we've been able to accomplish."

"You achieved your dreams. You always wanted to help horses, and you've done that. So you got your veterinary degree, then?"

He shook his head and took a swig of his tea.

"No. That wasn't in the cards."

"Oh, I'm sorry. I didn't realize. What happened? Did you change your mind and major in something else?"

He set the tea on the end table and sat back against the sofa cushions, looking down at his hands.

"I didn't attend college."

"What? But you had—" I stopped and stared at him, unable to believe what I was hearing. "Why? What happened?"

His gaze met mine, and I flinched at the pain I saw in his clear, blue eyes. He cleared his throat and looked away.

"You know what happened."

I shook my head, confused as to what he meant. "No, I'm sorry. I don't. You were supposed to move into the dorm that weekend. You had a full scholarship. What do you mean you didn't attend college?"

"You said in your letter in that you meant to escape. That you'd be back as soon as you could. I thought that you meant within weeks. Months, maybe. I thought I needed to be ready to take care of you. To take care of us. I went full-time at the equestrian center and kept the weekend work at Charlotte's. I socked away every penny I could so that when you came, I'd be ready. I knew we'd need enough to get a place on our own, and I didn't want you to have to live in a dump."

I sank my head into my hands, my mind reeling from the knowledge that the opportunity I'd worked so hard to protect had been lost anyway.

"Oh, God, William. Here I thought all this time that I kept your life on track. That you were able to go on and achieve your dreams because I didn't name you. And you gave it up anyway because of me?"

"I still lived my life, and I achieved a good many of my dreams. College just didn't pan out."

My chest clenched in sorrow, and I started to cough. I bent to pick up my tea glass from the floor beside my chair, bringing it to my lips with shaking hands.

William stood as the coughing intensified, but I waved him away.

"I'm fine," I whispered when it had passed. I lay back against the suede cushion and inhaled as slowly as possible to keep from triggering another bout of coughs.

"I should go. These conversations can wait. You need to recover."

"No, I'm fine. William, I'm sorry. Again. I feel like I keep saying that, but there's no way I can ever say I'm sorry enough."

He came and squatted next to my chair and took my hand in his.

"Stop. Stop saying you're sorry. You've already said it, and I believe you mean it. It is what it is. Our lives are what they are. I didn't come here to make you feel bad or make you feel like you need to keep apologizing. I want to understand what you went through, and I guess I need you to understand what I went through, too. But if we're going to share the truth with each other, you can't keep apologizing every time we discuss the past."

I stared into his eyes, nearly undone by the compassion and kindness I saw there.

"I know you want answers," I whispered.

"I do, but I don't have to have them today. Rest. Recover. We'll talk again."

He stood and kissed the top of my head, and then he was gone.

CHAPTER 41
Caterina

After William left, I wasn't sure how long it would be before I heard from him again, but I certainly didn't think he would call the next day.

"How are you feeling?" he asked after we exchanged hellos.

"Good. Each day seems to get better. Stronger. I had a visit from the home health nurse this morning, and I passed with flying colors. I'm still on the inhalers for a while, but she was pleased with my progress."

"That's good to hear." He paused, and then he cleared his throat and continued. "I was wondering if you had any plans tomorrow night. I have something I'd like to show you, so I thought perhaps you could come over and have some dinner."

A dinner invitation was the last thing I'd expected, and it stunned me into silence for a moment.

"I mean, I understand if you're not up to leaving the house yet," he stammered when I still hadn't answered. "Or if you're not interested in dinner. It's fine."

Curiosity outweighed my astonishment as I wondered what on earth he could possibly want to show me. I was also fascinated by the thought of seeing his house and being able to gaze into a window of his life.

"No, I'm up for it. I was just trying to think of what's going on tomorrow. I'm pretty sure I'm free. It seems my social calendar has been rather forcibly cleared recently. What time should I be there?"

"I can pick you up at six-thirty if that works for you."

"Oh, you don't have to do that. I'm not on any driving restrictions."

"It can be a little confusing to find the house on the property, so I thought it might be easier if I came to get you."

Confusing to find his house? Good Lord, how big was his property? Did he really think that little of my navigational skills?

It didn't matter, because I wasn't about to get myself stranded without a way to leave when I wanted to. Without knowing what he wanted to show me or what painful direction the dinner conversation could take, I preferred to have my own vehicle.

"Hmm, how about you give me directions, and we'll see how well I can follow them?"

He chuckled and gave me the address for the farm, and then I took notes as he talked me through the twists and turns after I entered his gate.

For the rest of the evening and much of the next day, all I could think about was the impending dinner. Why did he want me to come to his house? What did he want to show me? What would we talk about? I knew it was inevitable that our conversation would return to the past. I'd promised him answers, and I would honor that commitment, but I didn't look forward to dredging up more emotions and memories that I'd suppressed.

I wondered what it would be like to see the home he'd shared with his wife. Even after all the years that had passed and everything that had transpired, it was still difficult for me to think of him being married to someone else. While I was certainly glad he'd found love and been happy in my absence, I couldn't help feeling a twinge of envy for this unknown woman who'd taken my place by his side.

She'd held no blame in our situation. They'd married long after I had deserted him. He'd had every right to move on with his life, and it was tragic that he'd lost the woman he loved.

How selfish of me to be jealous of the dead.

By the time the clock struck six and it was time to head over to William's place, I was consumed by jittery apprehension. I had changed my outfit so many times that Patsy finally threatened to bar the closet door and refuse to let me in for more options.

"I declare, Cat, you'd think you were going on a first date with your high school crush."

Her sarcastic tone was teasing, but it struck too close to home to be funny. William *was* my high school crush. My first love. But though we were about to share a meal together, it was about as far from romance as you could get.

"It's not a date, Patsy. I have to explain to him why I abandoned him, betrayed him, and hid his daughter's very existence from him. Not exactly pleasant dinner conversation."

"How do you figure you betrayed him?"

I shrugged as I surveyed my reflection in the mirror and frowned at the way my hospital stay had made the jeans hang loose across my rump.

"One day I was there, and the next I was gone. We'd made promises. Commitments. We had plans. I didn't hold up my part of the deal."

"Yeah, because you were pregnant and forced into decisions out of your control by your parents. The way I see it, you protected him and shouldered all the blame alone. That's not a betrayal by any means."

"You sound like my grandmother," I said as I shimmied out of the jeans and pulled on a skirt.

"I'll take that as a compliment based on all you've told me about her. So why would you disagree with me and Nonna?"

The skirt landed on top of the jeans as I flipped through hangers for an alternative.

"Because, like I told her when she was trying to convince me to give up his name and make it easier on myself, it wasn't his fault."

"Excuse me, honey, but it takes two to tango."

I pulled on a pair of brown jeans and turned to face her.

"Patsy, William didn't want to date me. I pursued him relentlessly until he gave in. I pushed him to get more serious. I pushed him to have sex with me."

"I think you're giving yourself way too much power over him. You can't make other people do anything. They do what they choose to do. You have to let William carry some of the responsibility in this."

I shook my head as I walked back into the closet. "None of this was his fault."

Patsy groaned. "Bull malarkey. There were two of you involved in every decision that led up to Caroline's existence. Now, your parents may have strong-handed what happened beyond that, but you are absolutely putting too much on yourself to take sole responsibility. It's like you see you through a magnifying glass where as you see him through rose-colored lenses. It's not fair to you."

I slid my arms into a cream silk shirt and began to button it.

"I swear you and Nonna would have gotten along fabulously, Patsy. It's like hearing her harping on me all over again."

"Harumph. Harping? More like trying to reason with you. Might as well reason with a fence post. Don't do the scarf. You have such a lovely neck, and the scarf hides it. What do you think he would say?"

"Who? William? About the scarf?"

"Yes, William. About you shouldering all the blame. Do you think he would feel like it's all your fault?"

"Oh, I'm pretty certain of that based on what's he's said so far."

"I still find it interesting that he wants you to come to his house. I mean, one would think he'd choose a nice, neutral location. That is, unless, he wants a more private, intimate setting."

"Trust me, Patsy, this has nothing to do with intimacy. The man wants answers. That's all."

"The man got all the answers that matter while you were at the hospital. He knows Caroline is his and that you gave her up for adoption because you had to and that you didn't tell him because you were trying to protect him. What more does he need to know? The only reason for him to contact you now is that he wants to see you again. He wants to talk to you. To reconnect."

I caught her eyes in the mirror as I put my earring in, and then I turned to face her with a sigh.

"Please don't do this. Don't make this into something it's not. I know you're a hopeless romantic, and you want to see rainbows and butterflies, but this is not a romantic dinner. That bridge washed away in a catastrophic flood a long time ago, and it won't ever be rebuilt. You wanting it to be otherwise doesn't change reality, and it certainly doesn't make me feel any less nervous. All right, so how's this one?" I asked as I turned around in the newest ensemble.

"Perfect. Just like the last ten outfits. There's nothing you're going to put on that won't look beautiful, Cat. You're gorgeous in everything you wear. Now, tell me one thing, and I'll zip my lips about tonight."

"You don't zip your lips about anything, and we both know it."

"True. Answer me this. If you believe his request has nothing to do with romance, and you don't think anything will come beyond this conversation tonight, why are you so concerned with how you look?"

She crossed her arms and raised an eyebrow with a knowing grin, and I rolled my eyes and turned away from her to inspect my appearance in the mirror.

No matter what I wore, I couldn't erase thirty-six years. The lines on my face, the gray in my hair, and the faint spots on the backs of my hands didn't fade away with a nice pair of boots or a fashionable scarf.

"I'm not any more concerned than I would be going to dinner with anyone else," I said as I turned my back on my reflection and pulled the scarf from my neck to toss it on the bed. "I just don't want to look like someone who spent the last two weeks in a coma, that's all."

"If you say so. I need to get George's dinner on the table, but you call me when you get in tonight, okay? I won't be able to sleep until I hear from you."

"Yes, Mother," I teased. "Do I have a curfew?"

"No, but don't overdo it, either. You *are* someone who just got out of a coma, after all." She walked toward the bedroom door but turned back as she stepped into the hallway. "And Cat? Answer his questions if you must, but don't let him make you feel any worse about yourself than you already do. You did the best you could under the circumstances at that time, and you have more than made up for it with how you chose to live your life since then. You have nothing to be ashamed of, love."

CHAPTER 42
Caterina

I hadn't driven too far past the arched entryway for Ward Farms when I realized what William meant about it being confusing. Despite my scribbled shorthand on which way the road would twist and where I was to turn, I quickly found myself lost, just as he'd warned.

It seemed every time I turned off the main drive, I ended up at another barn. I'd underestimated the size of his farm. It was massive. Far bigger than the property where I'd grown up or Charlotte's estate next door.

I turned on the map light in the car and re-read my notes, realizing I'd deciphered one turn incorrectly. Once I'd made my way back toward the highway and retraced my path, I was able to find the turn-off he'd described.

After a few more winding curves, the road opened up into a circle drive with a huge fountain in the center that had life-sized horses standing on their hind legs as water danced at their feet. In the distance behind them was his house. The stately home had an antebellum feel with tall white columns all across the wide porch. It had so many windows reflecting the lights that shone upon it that the whole house sparkled like diamonds.

I slowed at the fountain to take it in. It was gorgeous, without a doubt. Quite impressive by anyone's standards. William had obviously done well for himself.

Once I'd exited the circle drive and parked, I noticed several men standing near a two-story building on the left. William wasn't among them, but they nodded in greeting when I got out of the car. I lifted my hand in a polite wave and then walked across the gravel to the sidewalk that led to the front door, smoothing down my hair before I rang the bell.

William swung the door open almost immediately, and I wondered if he'd been waiting on the other side of it.

"Hi. Sorry I'm late," I said as I entered a wide foyer with staircases on either side and a glittering chandelier hanging overhead.

"Did you find the place okay? I was worried that you might have gotten turned around and had no cell signal to call."

"I did take a few extra twists and turns, but I would have driven around all night before I called and let you know that you were right."

He laughed, and a little of the tension in my body eased at the familiar sound.

I followed him down a hallway lined on either side with family photographs, resisting the urge to stop and scan each one for his wife or daughter.

We passed a room with a massive dining table, and then we entered the kitchen, where the smell of roasted chicken and herbs wafted through the room and made my stomach growl. If he heard it, he didn't let on.

"Can I get you a glass of wine? We have an extensive wine cellar."

"No, thanks. But please, feel free to have a glass yourself."

William smiled. "I don't touch the stuff."

"Then why do you have an extensive wine cellar?"

"Well, we have guests. Business associates. Revae loved throwing dinner parties and holiday gatherings. She was a wine connoisseur, so the bulk of the cellar is left from her collection." He waved toward the patio bar visible through the window. "We have rum, vodka, whiskey. Gin, too. There might be some tequila if that's more your speed."

"Actually, I'd love some ice water if you have it."

"Sure."

I looked around the room as he got me a glass and filled it with ice and water.

The ceilings were high, at least twelve feet, and the white cabinets that lined the wall on my left stretched all the way to the top, their glass doors revealing perfectly organized dishes and kitchen gadgets. At the back of the room was a built-in desk nestled among floor-to-ceiling white book shelves filled with cookbooks, photos, candles, and horse-themed decor. An expansive island with dark brown granite countertops sat in the center of the room with a lower section on one end that looked to be a prep station with a small sink. To my right was a double set of French doors that opened onto a patio overlooking the pool.

It was hard not to think about it being Revae's kitchen. Revae's house. Revae's husband. I wondered how many happy memories they had shared in this very room. My heart ached for his loss, but the empty space inside it where our memories might have been hurt worse.

I bit down on my lip, hoping the sharp burst of pain would stop my thought process. I had no right to be jealous of anyone. Especially not a ghost.

"Thanks," I said as he handed me the glass.

"Dinner's ready if you are."

I nodded, and he led me through the kitchen to a family room dominated by a U-shaped leather sectional. There were more bookshelves, and another set of double French doors leading out to the patio and pool. On the back wall, a round table was beautifully set for two in front of the windows.

"I thought we'd eat in here since it's just the two of us. The dining room seems a bit formal unless it's filled with people."

"This is fine," I said, sitting in the chair he pulled out for me.

He disappeared into the kitchen and returned with a plate for each of us.

"These plates are hot," he said as he set them down. He laid the pot holders he'd carried them with on the table and then pulled his chair out and sat. "Gaynelle, the farm's cook, prepared this for me and put the plates in the warmer before she left. She was only gone a couple of minutes when you arrived, so it should be plenty warm."

"I'm sure it's fine," I said. "It smells delicious."

"She's a helluva cook. We're lucky to have her around here, and I hope she never decides to leave. I think my guys would block the driveway and beg her to stay."

He pulled back the napkin on the basket of rolls and offered me one, and then we both began to eat.

"You have a beautiful home," I said after a few bites.

"Thank you, but I can't take any credit for it. It was my wife's pet project, and pretty much everything you see is a reflection of her."

"She had beautiful taste. That actually makes more sense."

"What do you mean?"

"Oh, um, it doesn't look like you. I mean, granted, I can't say what your style would be at this point in your life. I haven't known you in many years, and you didn't have your own place then. I don't know. It just doesn't feel like you. If I'd walked in here without knowing who owned it, I never would have guessed it was yours."

He glanced around the room and smiled.

"I still can't bring myself to move anything or have anything out of place. I don't want to change the way Revae had things."

His smiled faded, and he looked down at his plate as he cut his asparagus.

"You must miss her very much," I said. "I'm happy you found a love like that."

He nodded and took a drink of water.

"What about you? Caroline said you'd never married. Any great loves?"

"No. None to speak of. I've dated here and there, but nothing that developed into anything serious. I think perhaps I value my independence too much to endanger it."

"So, is Turtle Crossing your full-time job?"

"Yes, it is now. I still do some lobbying work in DC when there's a bill or policy affecting adoption. And I have some speaking engagements on the calendar for a few organizations I'm affiliated with. But when I moved here to be closer to my mother and got involved with foster care in the state, I saw pretty quickly that I could do more to help families and children if I could assist in an official capacity."

"How is your mother?" he asked.

"She passed away. Six years ago now."

"I'm sorry to hear that."

"She suffered with dementia, so she was gone long before her body gave up the fight. The last two years of her life, she was mentally still in her twenties, and she'd tell me all about her little girl who was the model of perfect behavior."

"That must have been hard," William said, his eyes filled with compassion.

"It was. I had only just gotten her back. So, to have her with me, but not really be there, was like a cruel joke."

His eyes narrowed in confusion, and he did a slight shake of his head. "What do you mean by *only just gotten her back*?"

We were delving into the territory I normally never discussed with anyone, and my body tensed in self-defense. I'd come prepared to share the details of my life. To answer whatever questions he had and fill in whatever blanks were necessary. But being willing to do it didn't mean it was going to be pleasant.

"My mother was not allowed to be a part of my life until my father died. We reconnected after his death, and I moved here to Cedar Creek to be closer to her."

His brows scrunched together, and he wiped his mouth with the napkin and placed it on the table as he sat back in his chair. "She wasn't allowed to be part of your life? Why?"

I picked at the remainder of the chicken breast with the tip of my fork and took a deep breath.

"My father disowned me. He had papers drawn up to sever our relationship legally, and he insisted that my mother cut all ties as well. She didn't. She still wrote letters from time to time. Occasionally, she'd call. And when he died, she reached out and begged for my forgiveness, which I gave with no small amount of difficulty."

"When did this happen?"

I stared at my plate to avoid his eyes. My skin flushed hot and grew prickly with the uncomfortable tension that held my body rigid. This was a conversation I'd had with less than a handful of people over the course of my life, and I'd never thought I would be having it with William. Somehow, it seemed even harder to tell him than it had been to tell my closest friends and my therapist. I suppose it was because they were never involved. They didn't know my father. It wasn't them I was disowned to protect.

"It happened pretty soon after I left—when he found out I was pregnant with Caroline and I wouldn't tell him who the father was."

William swore under his breath and stood. He walked to the window and gazed out into the night.

"All that time, all those years, he never changed his mind?"

"No. I never saw my father again after he left me in New York. It was the last conversation we ever had."

William turned, his jaw tight and his mouth a grim line. "I'm sorry, Catherine. I'm sorry that I wasn't there for you. I'm sorry I put you in that situation."

"You didn't. I put myself in that situation."

"We made a decision together that had far-reaching consequences. You bore those consequences alone, and I'm sorry that I didn't help you in any way. If I had known…"

I stood and walked toward him, but I stopped myself from getting too close.

"It was my fault. I'm the one to blame. You wanted to wait, and I talked you into it. I insisted. I wouldn't take no for an answer."

"You make it sound like I had no choice in the matter. I don't think you're remembering things clearly. We both wanted what happened that night, Catherine."

"Okay, but even so, I screwed up the pills. I missed two the nights I was in the hospital, and I took them once I got home. Then that whole week that we were staying out all night and I was sleeping off and on during the day, I think I missed another and doubled up one day. Maybe two. I was taking them sometimes at morning, and sometimes at night. I didn't know it would matter. I was stupid. Naive. I thought as long as I took them all, we couldn't get pregnant. I was wrong. I didn't realize it compromised the pill every time I missed a day. That's on me. You asked if we were protected, and I told you yes. I thought we were."

He looked out the window again, and I wanted to go to him. To put my arms around him. To have him turn and wrap me in his embrace. God, it had been so long. Why was it that I could forget so many things that happened in my life over the years, but the memory of his arms around me was still so strong?

I looked up to see him gazing at me, his expression hard to read. His eyes were sad, but his jaw was tight like he was angry, and a muscle twitched near his ear.

"Where did you go? What did you do?"

"My mother arranged for me to stay with my grandmother in New Jersey."

He swallowed hard and looked back out the window.

"Why didn't you contact me?"

"I couldn't. He had threatened to do all sorts of things if he found out who the baby's father was. Hell, I couldn't be sure he wouldn't kill you, he was so angry. That he wouldn't kill us both."

"But you said he disowned you. That you never talked after he left New York. If you went to your grandmother's, why didn't you contact me then?"

"I couldn't!" I said, my voice rising as my defenses kicked in. "I couldn't risk someone else finding out it was you. I did think for a while that maybe I could keep her at Nonna's, and then at some point with my father out of the picture, I could find you again. That maybe the three of us could be a family."

"But that didn't happen."

I shook my head even though he faced away from me. "No. My mother insisted there was no way I could keep her. She said my father would eventually look for me, and if he found the baby with me, it wouldn't be safe for any of us. She arranged for Caroline to be adopted. I had to go along with her. I didn't know what else to do. I had nowhere to go. I had no money. I had no other options." Tears stung my eyes, and I dug my fingernails into my palms and willed them not to fall. "I wanted to call you, William, but I was terrified of him. I was scared of what would happen to you if he ever found out. Of what would happen to me. I was scared for our baby. And then, once she was gone, I knew you would never forgive me."

He turned to look at me, and his eyes were filled with tears.

"I'm sorry, Catherine," he said, his voice barely above a whisper. "I'm sorry I got you pregnant and couldn't stand by you through it. I'm sorry you went through all that by yourself. You never should have been alone."

Somehow, his remorse and guilt made me feel even worse, and I tried to force a smile, but it didn't work well.

"Hey, no, look. You told me that it is what it is. Our lives are what they are. You said if we were going to share the truth—"

"I didn't know!" he said, his voice much louder as his eyes flashed. "I didn't know the truth. I felt horrible that we came back late. I felt like it was my fault you got sent away. I beat myself up for driving us to the beach. For falling asleep. I felt responsible for you being gone. But God, I had no idea what I was responsible for! I didn't know what you were going through all that time. Here I was thinking you'd decided I was a summer fling and you just weren't interested in me anymore."

"Oh, William. It was never—"

"Daddy?" an angry voice rang out as a door slammed elsewhere in the house. "Daddy, where are you? We have to talk!"

CHAPTER 43
Caterina

"Oh, Christ! That's Piper," William said, wiping his eyes on his shirt sleeve as he moved past me toward the kitchen. "She's not supposed to be home yet. I'll be right back."

"Daddy? Where are you?" She had already made her way to the kitchen to confront him. "There you are!"

I shrank back out of sight against the wall of the family room, wishing I could disappear.

"I thought you were flying back tomorrow." His voice was calm despite her angry tone.

"I can't believe you! How could you do this to me?"

Caroline had mentioned that William's daughter was away on a business trip and that he planned to tell her about the new developments when she returned. I wondered if she'd found out somehow and perhaps that was why she was upset. If so, it wasn't a conversation I wished to be a part of. I glanced at the French doors, but there was no way I could make an exit without being seen from the kitchen since its doors led out onto the same patio.

"Piper, calm down and tell me what's wrong," William said.

"I don't want to calm down! Why didn't you tell me you talked to Warren Clarke?"

"Why didn't you tell me you were coming back early? I would have picked you up at the airport."

"Answer my question, please. Why didn't you let me know you talked to him?"

"I don't ever discuss a reference with an employee."

"A *reference*? Oh, my God, Dad. I thought this was a job I got on my own merit. I thought he knew of me through A&M, and that was why he was interested in hiring me. But no. It was you. It's always you. No matter what I do, no matter where I go, I am just William Ward's daughter. I'm trying to stand on my own two feet here. I want to make my own way. But everyone connected to horses knows you. You're the miracle worker, and they think that somehow if they hire me, they'll have access to you."

"You earned that job on your own. He did find you through A&M, and he got all his initial information from the university. He called me for a job reference, Piper. Nothing more. He would have called me for anyone working on this farm. And I gave him a fair and just reference, the same as I would have for anyone else. You didn't get that job because of me."

"Oh, please. Spare me the bullshit."

"No bullshit here. You got that job because you're the most qualified candidate. You're an excellent horsewoman, and one of the most capable trainers I've ever seen. That's why people want to work with you, but you don't believe that, so you come across with this chip on your shoulder and an attitude that most people find abrasive."

"Half the questions in the interview were about you, Dad. He came right out and asked me if you would be available for me to consult. He said he knew you weren't taking on any new clients, but he figured hiring William Ward's daughter was the next best thing. He spent more time talking about how highly you spoke of me than any of my qualifications. This is so damned frustrating. I can't escape your shadow no matter what I do."

She moved across the kitchen and then turned back around to face him, and when she did, she saw me. Her eyes widened, and for a moment she looked frightened to see someone standing in the shadows of her family room.

I stepped forward and lifted my hand in a weak attempt at a wave just as William moved into the doorway.

"Who are you?" Piper asked, her expression still bewildered.

William came to my side. "Uh, this is Catherine—"

"Caterina," I corrected.

"Right. This is Caterina Russo. Caterina, this is my daughter, Piper Ward."

"I've heard that name," Piper said as she walked toward me, her forehead furrowed in confusion. "Have we met?"

I shook my head and extended my hand.

"No, we haven't, but it's nice to meet you."

Her grip was firm, and as she tilted her head and stared at me, I was struck by her resemblance to Caroline. The eyes were different. Whereas Caroline had a grayish-blue that was light like William's, Piper's were a deep brown with a stunning blue fleck in each iris. Both women had hair in shades of deep red like their father, but Piper's held lighter streaks. They had a similar build, but something in the way Piper carried herself was much different from Caroline. She was more direct in her movements. Outwardly confident.

She looked past me to the table where our plates still sat unfinished, and then she looked back at William.

"Um, we were just having dinner," he said, his discomfort obvious in his shifting stance and the hesitation in his voice. "Are you hungry?"

"No." Piper crossed her arms as she stared at her father.

The whole situation was beyond awkward, and I felt it was best if I excused myself before she asked for further explanations.

"I'm going to head home," I said. "Thank you for a lovely dinner. Your house is beautiful. Piper, it was a pleasure meeting you."

"I'll walk you out." William gave me a relieved half-smile and extended his arm toward the kitchen as he waited for me to pass.

He didn't speak again until we were outside. "I'm so sorry about that. She's been in Denver for a job interview, and she wasn't supposed to be home until tomorrow. She's gotten into her head that she needs to work somewhere else to validate her resume, and as you heard, she's quite determined to find someone who has nothing to do with me."

"I would imagine that would be hard to do if you're running the largest facility east of Kentucky."

"Yes, hence her interest in a farm farther west. It's not that big of a community, though, so any major players in the thoroughbred industry have likely crossed paths somehow with Ward Farms."

"Well, I hope the two of you work things out. Thanks for dinner," I said as we reached my Jeep.

"I'm sorry it got interrupted. I wasn't sure what to say. She doesn't know yet, um, about, you know."

I nodded. "Caroline mentioned you were going to wait until Piper returned to tell her."

"I guess I get to go and do that now. I'm sure she'll want an explanation as to why you were here."

"Speaking of which, you never did tell me what you wanted to show me."

He leaned back against my Jeep and looked up at his house with his hands in his pockets. "It seems silly now."

"What? What was it?"

"I wanted to show you this." He swept his arm toward the house and then toward the two-story building near it. "You felt so bad about me not finishing college, and I guess I wanted to show you that I'd done okay."

"Yeah, I'd say you've done okay, all right. It still seems odd to see you in a place like this."

He pushed off from the Jeep and stood upright with his hands on his hips.

"Why? You didn't think I'd be able to afford something like this?"

"No, no. That's not what I'm saying at all. It had nothing to do with what level of success you'd achieve. I always knew you'd achieve great things. Even then, you were such a hard worker. Dedicated and motivated. Driven. But this isn't you. Not the you I knew. You weren't caught up in the trappings of wealth."

"I wouldn't say I'm caught up in the trappings now. But I have the ability to live comfortably, and I do."

"I'm sorry. I didn't mean it as any kind of criticism. It's just unexpected, that's all. You were the person who taught me that life wasn't all about bank accounts. That I didn't need money to have happiness. I've held onto that lesson long after we parted, and I'm just surprised to see that you might have let it go."

He looked down as he kicked at the gravel with the toe of his boot, and for a moment, the years disappeared, and he was a shy and awkward teenager again.

"I guess for a long time I thought I had something to prove. It started with wanting to be able to provide for you. To be ready when you came back. I knew I couldn't come close to giving you what you'd had, but I was determined to make sure I had enough to get us started. Then somewhere along the way, after I realized you weren't coming back, it turned into a desire to be as successful as possible so that if you ever did return, you'd see that I wasn't just a stable boy anymore." He looked up and toward the two-story building with a sigh. "At some point, I realized I had achieved most of the goals I'd set, I was enjoying what I was doing with my life, and it wasn't about proving anything anymore. But by then, I'd met Revae, and she had expensive tastes." He smiled as he stared into the night. "So we lived the lifestyle that made her happy. As long as she was happy, I was happy."

"You didn't have to prove anything to me, William. You were much more than just a stable boy. Even when you were just a stable boy."

He looked up and our eyes locked. My heart caught in my throat as the cricket chorus surrounding us seemed to grow louder, and I opened the door to the Jeep, eager to make an escape.

"I should go so you can talk to Piper. Thanks again for dinner."

He stood and watched me back away, and I knew I'd been kidding myself to think that I'd gotten over my feelings for William Ward. When you give your heart to someone so completely, do you ever really get it back? Or does part of it always belong to them no matter how much time passes?

CHAPTER 44
William

Piper was making herself a turkey sandwich when I came back into the kitchen.

"What was that?" she asked as she laid the bread on the plate.

The moment I'd been dreading was upon me, and I still couldn't figure how to tell Piper what I'd discovered while she was gone.

"That was Caroline's mother."

She stopped spreading the mustard on the bread and looked at me in surprise. "That's why I recognized the name! I thought she was in the hospital. Like, in a coma."

"She was. Her condition improved. She was discharged on Sunday."

She plucked out a few pieces of lettuce from the crisper and put them on her sandwich.

"That's good, but why were you having dinner with her?"

"It's a long story," I said, rubbing my eyes as I prepared to throw a grenade in the middle of my life.

She turned to face me with her hand on her hip.

"Really? How long could the story possibly be? I've only been gone a week, and the woman was in a coma when I left. So how did you even meet her, much less end up having dinner here alone?"

"I think we should sit down."

"Why?" She grabbed the sandwich and took a bite.

"Because I'm not sure how to tell you this, and I think I'd like to sit down."

She looked up at me with wide eyes and swallowed hard.

"Tell me what?"

I leaned back against the counter and looked down at my feet, wishing I'd been able to broach this subject under different circumstances.

"What is this? What's going on?" Her eyes narrowed. "Wait a minute. Was this a *date*?"

"Piper, listen—"

"You were on a *date* with Caroline's mother? Are you kidding me? You don't date! And you don't even know her! When did you meet her? For God's sake, it's been less than a week! What kind of pheromones do these women have that first Levi and now you just go nuts as soon as you meet them?"

"It's not like that. If you'd give me a chance to explain—"

"Oh, please. By all means. Explain why you brought some woman you haven't even known a week into my mother's kitchen and shared dinner with her at my mother's antique table. You know how much Mom loved that table. She fell in love with it at that antique store in Tennessee, and you worked like hell to get it to fit in the back of the truck. And now you're entertaining some stranger at Mom's table?"

"I wasn't entertaining her, and I'm fully aware of your mother's affinity for the table."

"So, then why was she here? Where's Caroline? Why were you alone with her mother?"

"I'll explain if you'll let me."

She opened her mouth but then clamped it shut and waved her hand in a dramatic flourish as she glared at me.

"Go ahead."

"You know how much I loved your mother."

"Okay, if this is going to be some long, drawn-out explanation of how you're ready to date, all right. I get it. It's been four years. And no, I'm not ready to think about you dating someone other than Mom, but I get that at some point you may want to. But why Caroline's mother? Why is it this Caroline chick seems to be invading every aspect of this farm? First, Levi's losing his shit over her, then you're offering riding lessons to the daughter and giving the son free rein of the barns, and now her mother's going to be your initiation back into single life when you don't even know the woman? Hell, for that matter, you don't know either one of these women. Please explain to me what is happening."

I'd known this was going to be difficult, but it was even harder than I'd thought.

"No one is invading anything. And I do know Catherine. Uh, Caterina. I knew her a long time ago. Dated her, in fact. Years before I met your mother."

Shock registered on her face, and she blinked a couple of times before shaking her head and holding up her hand. "Wait a minute. You've got to be kidding me. Did Caroline know this? Did she know you knew her mother?"

I shook my head. "No. We're all just trying to figure everything out now."

"Figure what out?"

I took a deep breath and waited for a moment to see if the dots would connect themselves and save me having to make the connection for her, but it wasn't happening.

"Piper, I didn't know about this, but Cather—uh, damn, *Caterina* and I conceived a child together when I was seventeen years old."

The color drained from her face, and I could see that the truth was beginning to dawn.

"Are you telling me that you're Caroline's father?"

I gazed at the ceiling and asked the heavens for strength before meeting her eyes. "Yes. That's what I'm telling you."

She took a step back, and I waited, wary of how she was going to react. Piper's tendency had always been to blow loud and hard when her emotions were too much for her and based on the tremble of her hands and her lower lip, I knew it was coming.

"No. This can't be. You can't be her father. You can't be!"

I stepped forward to grab her hands, trying to hold her together, willing her to be all right.

"Sweetheart—"

She pulled away. "No. No, Daddy. I'm your daughter. I'm your only daughter. You loved Mom. You adored her. How could you have a child with another woman?"

"I didn't even know your mother then. It was years before we met."

"I don't understand. This is not like you. How could you just have a baby with some random girl you didn't even care about it?"

"Make no mistake in thinking I didn't care about Catherine Johnson, which is the name I knew her as. I loved her. She was my first love."

Piper shook her head. "No, Mom was your first love. Mom was the love of your life."

"Piper, the feelings I had for Catherine in no way diminish what your mother and I shared. I loved your mother deeply, you know that. But before I found her, I loved another. A child was conceived of that love. If I had known, I would have married her."

"Why didn't you know? Why didn't she tell you? How could you not know that you had a baby together?"

"That's another long story, and I'm still trying to wrap my head around that myself. But just suffice to say that she thought she was doing the right thing."

She bent over the kitchen island and propped herself on her elbows, dropping her head forward to sink her hands into her hair.

"I can't believe this. First, Caroline takes Levi, who was basically the only brother I've ever had, and now she's taking you. What the hell?"

"No. Absolutely not. Nothing and no one will ever take me from you. You and I are the same as we have always been. Nothing will change that."

She stood up straight and flung both hands out to her sides.

"This changes that, Daddy! I'm not your only daughter anymore. I'm not your only child." Her expression changed as despair morphed into suspicion. "Is that why Caroline came here? Is that why she suddenly appeared out of nowhere?"

"No. She didn't know."

"Really? Are you sure? Because that's one helluva coincidence. You don't think it's strange that she happens to show up at our farm? How do you know the two of them didn't plan this? How do you know they're not working together, like some kind of scam? You're a very wealthy man. They could be preying on you to try and get money or something."

I shook my head, certain that neither of them had ulterior motives. "That's not the case."

"You don't know that. We need to look into this. How can you be sure she's your daughter? Have you seen a DNA test? How do you know they're telling the truth? Does Levi know about this? Does he know what she's trying to pull?"

"Stop. No one is trying to pull anything, okay? Caroline is my daughter. I'm certain."

"Okay, maybe she is. But that doesn't mean they're not working together to cheat you. Daddy, things like this happen all the time. They're using you. They're using Levi. Both of you may be blind to it, but I see what's going on. I'm not going to stand by and do nothing while they take advantage of you."

I pinched the bridge of my nose with my thumb and forefinger, trying to think of some way to calm her concerns and keep her from going after Caroline or Caterina in her defensiveness of me. Piper had always been like a rabid bulldog when it came to protecting her family, and I needed to make clear that I didn't want her unleashed on them.

"Piper, I need you to listen to me. I realize this is a shock, and I knew this wouldn't be easy for you. It's not easy for any of us. But I am telling you there's no scam. There's no ruse. I'm asking you to treat Caroline and Caterina with the respect I would expect my daughter to give to any other family member."

Her mouth dropped open.

"Family member? They're already elevated to being family members? Both of them? I can't believe this. My mother must be rolling over in her grave right now."

She stormed from the room, and I walked to the windows and looked out into the night. I understood her anger. Her suspicion. Her pain. But the truth wasn't going to change. Caroline was a part of our family, whether Piper liked it or not.

And Caterina, well, I didn't know how Caterina fit into the grand scheme moving forward, but something within me knew that having found her again, I wasn't going to be willing to lose her once more.

CHAPTER 45
Piper

I left my father's house and drove straight to Levi's, using my fists on the door to release some of the rage I felt.

"What the hell?" he said from the other side before pulling the door open like he was ready for a fight. "Piper? I thought you were—"

"How long have you known?"

"What?"

"How long have you known about Caroline and my dad? You probably knew before anyone else, didn't you? And yet, you never said a word."

He sighed and scratched his head. "Why don't you come in and sit down?"

I clenched my fists at my sides and stood my ground. His betrayal cut deep, and I wasn't going to pretend everything was fine.

"I don't want to sit down. I want you to answer me."

"Well, will you at least come inside?"

"No. Answer me."

"I'm sorry, Piper. I couldn't say anything. Caroline had her suspicions, but she wasn't certain. Then, when everything got confirmed, you were out of town, and your dad wanted to wait until you got back. Which I thought was tomorrow. Why are you back early?"

So, he had known. A part of me had hoped that when I confronted him, he'd be taken by surprise. That he'd be just as taken aback and wary as I was, and that he'd be on my side, as he pretty much always had been since we'd met.

"How could you keep that a secret from me? Since I was ten years old, I've trusted you implicitly. I've confided in you, I've come to you for advice, and I've told you stuff that I never told anyone else.

You've been my older brother for all intents and purposes. I thought you had my back no matter what. I thought I could count on you."

"You can! I do! I just told you, I didn't know for sure until you'd already gone for your job interview. How'd that go, by the way?"

"Would you stop trying to change the subject? Why didn't you tell me when you first found out it was a possibility? I thought we were close."

"We are! Damn, Piper! What was I supposed to do? Caroline told me her suspicions in confidence."

"And that meant more than your loyalty to me? You barely know her, Levi! We have almost fifteen years of history together. Why should her feelings suddenly be so much more important than mine? I get that some chicks ditch their friends when a new guy comes in the picture, but I never saw you as being a pansy-ass chick."

"C'mon, that's not fair. Nobody's ditching anybody. It wasn't like she came to me with some kind of proof. She just thought there were odd coincidences."

I crossed my arms and shifted my weight. "I would agree. Several odd coincidences, in fact. Don't you think it's bizarre that you randomly meet her at the diner, and then lo and behold, out of all the people on all the planet, she happens to be my dad's long-lost..." I clamped my mouth shut, unable to bring myself to say the word *daughter*. "You don't see anything strange about that?"

He braced his arm against the door frame and sighed again. "I don't know what you're getting at. Of course, it's strange. The whole thing is strange. It's been an unexpected turn of events, that's for sure."

"Is it? Is it *for sure*? How do you know Caroline and Caterina didn't plan this whole thing? How do you know this isn't some elaborate scheme to take my advantage of my dad, and you've played right into it?"

He laughed, and it took every ounce of resolve I had not to punch him in the gut.

"Oh, damn, you're serious? C'mon, Piper. You can't honestly think Caroline or Cat would do that."

"I don't know them. How well do you know them? *Really* know them?"

"Pretty well, I think." He turned and walked inside, and I had no choice but to follow him if I wanted to continue the conversation.

"I've gotten to know Caroline on many levels," he said as he opened the fridge. "I have absolutely no doubt that she's being genuine. I've met her mother—both her adoptive mother and Cat—and I've met her kids. Her ex." He rolled his eyes and scowled with that admission. "I've heard quite a bit of the story of how Cat and William met, how they parted, and I don't have any issue at all believing either one of them. You want something to drink?"

I shook my head and watched him pour himself a glass of milk.

"Have you talked to your dad about this? I'm sure if William felt at all uncomfortable, he'd look into it. You know he doesn't make rash decisions, and he does his research and asks his questions. He seems confident that it's on the up-and-up."

"Yeah, well, he's not thinking clearly right now. I think he went down memory lane and got stuck there."

"What do you mean?"

"I came home tonight to find him having dinner with this Caterina person."

Levi's lifted eyebrows and widened eyes conveyed that this was news to him.

"Really?"

"Yes, really. I'm glad I finally got your attention. Now, do you think it's suspicious?"

He chugged down about half the glass of milk.

"Suspicious? No. Interesting? Yes."

"You don't find it suspicious that this woman my father barely knows and who was supposedly in a coma only a week ago is having an intimate dinner alone with my dad?"

"First of all, from what I understand, he actually knows her pretty well. Or he did, once upon a time. Second, she wasn't *supposedly* in a coma, okay? I was at the hospital. She was *definitely* in a coma. And third, no, I don't find it suspicious that your dad would invite a woman he hasn't seen in years over to his house to discuss what happened in the time since they last saw each other. That plus, I don't know, maybe the fact that they had a daughter together that he never knew about?"

He was obviously blinded by his feelings for Caroline. His view of the situation was filtered through the hazy lens of infatuation.

"This is a waste of my time. I gotta go. But watch your back, *brother*. Because this new flame you've got might just get us all burned."

I walked back to the front door but paused and turned when I got there.

"And hey, thanks for letting me know who I can count on. The circle just keeps getting smaller and smaller."

I slammed his door and left the farm in search of one person I knew I could trust no matter what. Someone who wouldn't likely be compromised yet.

CHAPTER 46
Piper

My cousin Lauryn and I had been born three months apart, and we'd pretty much been inseparable since then. If anyone was going to be on my side in this matter, it would be Lauryn.

She'd been the one to pick me up from the airport when I called her to explain that Denver hadn't gone well and I just wanted to get out of there.

Since I'd planned to confront Daddy about his conversations with Warren Clarke regarding the job, I'd told Lauryn not to bother coming inside. But now, I wished she'd been there to hear the conversation so I didn't have to recount the whole thing.

I'd had a key to her apartment since the day she moved in, but I opted to knock since she wasn't expecting me. I knew I should have called to let her know I was coming, but my thoughts had been consumed with the situation at hand.

She opened the door with a surprised smile.

"What are you doing here? Did you forget something in my car?"

I walked past her and plopped down on her couch.

"No. Can I crash here tonight?"

"Of course," she said, sitting cross-legged on the opposite end of the couch from me. "Didn't go well, huh? What did Uncle William say?"

"That he only gave Warren a reference, the same as he would any other employee. But that's not why I'm here."

"It's not? Okay, why are you here? I mean, you know you don't need a reason. This is practically your second home already, but what's up?"

"When was the last time you talked to your mom?"

I wondered who else in the family knew, and if my father had gone to anyone, it would have been Aunt Patricia. I didn't think Lauryn would keep secrets from me, but after what had happened with Levi, I needed to know who could be trusted.

"I talked to her this afternoon. Why?"

"Did she say anything about my dad? Anything strange?"

She twisted her lips and scrunched her brows. "No. She didn't mention him at all. Why? Is Uncle William okay? Would you just tell me what's going on already? Why are you being so weird?"

"There was a woman at the house when I went inside."

Her eyebrows shot up and her mouth dropped open as she leaned forward and playfully slapped my hand. "No! You're kidding! Uncle William has a girlfriend?"

I shook my head, not even wanting to consider that. "No, but get this. Evidently, this woman dated my father when they were teens, before he even met Mom."

Lauryn bent her elbow and propped her head in her hand, her eyes bright. "Whoa, get out! How did they find each other again?"

Her excitement annoyed me. This wasn't good news.

"That's where this gets so freaking bizarre that I can't believe it's happening. You remember I told you that Levi is dating this girl, Caroline?"

"Yeah. The one he went head-over-heels for after trying to steal her car thinking it was yours?"

"Yeah, that one. Well, it turns out this woman is Caroline's mother."

Her mouth dropped open again. "What? Are you kidding me?"

"I wish I was. And it gets even more bizarre."

I took a deep breath and prepared to say out loud what I didn't want to accept.

"This woman says that my father is ... that Caroline is ... well, that she and my dad ... had Caroline."

Finally, someone looked as blown away by the news as I had been.

Lauryn's eyes were wide, and her hand went to her open mouth as she stared at me.

"I know," I said as she sat stunned. "Pretty wild, right?"

"Is it true? I mean, what did Uncle William say? Does he think Caroline might be his?"

"Oh, he says he's certain of it. I tried to bring up a DNA test, and he wouldn't hear of it. He shut me right down."

"You think my mom knows about this?"

I shrugged. "I don't know, but if my dad told anyone, it would be Aunt Patricia. You sure she didn't say anything?"

"No. Not at all. So did Uncle William know that he had another daughter?"

I flinched at her calling Caroline that. "No. This woman hid it from him. She never told him."

"Oh my God! Who does that? That's foul!"

"Right? And yet, my dad seems calm as can be. He had her over for dinner, for Christ's sake! The two of them had been sitting at the table in the family room—at my mother's table—having a meal together like it's the most normal thing in the world. He doesn't even seem angry about it. Hell, he seemed to be more angry with me because I was questioning their motives. We don't know these women. We don't know what they're after."

"Well, yeah. I'd be wary. You see all the time on the news where people take advantage. This could be some kind of snow job. Uncle William needs to be careful."

"Yes! Thank you! Finally, someone has some common sense. Levi and Dad both think I'm the crazy one!"

"Man, Piper, I don't even know what to say. This is nuts. Are you okay?"

"I don't know. I feel numb. But I also feel angry. It's like my entire life was a lie. I thought I was my dad's only kid. I'm not. I thought my mom was his first love. She wasn't. I thought it was just gonna be me and him. The two of us, you know? Me taking care of him when he got older. Him walking me down the aisle. Well, if I ever do that. Grandkids—that's the other thing! Caroline has those two kids. My dad is a grandfather already."

Lauryn did a slow exhale. "Whoa. I can't believe this. But you can't say your whole life was a lie! You're still his daughter just as much as you ever were. You and Uncle William still have the same relationship you had before. That's no different."

"But it is, Lauryn. I'm an only child. I've always been a Daddy's girl. You know how much I've struggled with feeling like I wasn't fair to my mom when she was alive. I always preferred my dad. You know I always made Mom feel like she was second. And now, I find out I'm second. He had another child before me."

"Not one that he knew, though. He's been with you since the beginning. He's raised you. He doesn't even know Caroline."

I wrapped my arms around a throw pillow and hugged it to me. "I feel like this changes my entire identity. I don't know who I am anymore."

Lauryn chewed on her lip and tucked her feet beneath her. "I'm sorry, Piper. I can't even imagine. I'm trying to think of something profound, but I don't know what to say." She scrunched her nose and gave me a tiny smile. "I don't think Uncle William is going to treat you any differently, though. He adores you, Piper. You're his whole world."

"Not anymore." I closed my eyes and leaned back against her sofa cushions. "That woman and her daughter have taken over his world."

"You keep calling her *that woman* or *this woman*. Does she have a name?"

"Hmmph. Yeah, but even that's bizarre. I guess when they dated she was named Catherine Johnson, but now her name is Caterina Russo."

"She has a different name? Why?"

I shrugged. "Who knows? Probably because she goes around scamming wealthy men and has to change it to keep from going to jail."

"Let's Google her."

Lauryn went to get her laptop, and we sat side by side as she typed in Catherine's name.

Nothing came up. It was like she had never existed.

Caterina Russo was a different story. She'd been a lobbyist in DC, and there were numerous articles covering her clashes with Congress over adoption issues or speeches she gave on behalf of foster children and potential adoptees.

"I don't know, Piper. She seems pretty legit. I don't think she'd be scamming people with her name so well-known."

"But why did she change her name? There had to be a reason. There's got to be some kind of dirt here. She's hiding something, and I'm going to figure out what it is."

"If they dated when they were teenagers, my mom probably remembers her. I could call her and ask. What time is it?"

"It's late. I don't want you to wake her up. And I don't know if I want to be the one making announcements to the family, you know? I don't mind telling you, but I think Dad should be the one to tell everyone else. If he hasn't already."

Lauryn closed the laptop and reached to put it on the coffee table.

"Wow. This a lot to unpack. I can't believe you have a sister."

"She's not my sister."

"Well, half-sister."

I stood and went to the kitchen. "Whatever. It's a technicality."

"I can't believe Levi is dating your half-sister. That's kind of gross, actually. It's like your siblings are having sex with each other."

"Yeah, well, he's not actually my sibling." I got a glass and opened the fridge to get out the orange juice.

"I know, but you've always considered—"

"Not anymore. He showed me his true colors. He knew about this, and he didn't tell me. Didn't bother to give me a heads-up or anything. He let me walk back into an implosion with no warning. So, screw him. I'm done."

"You're sure he knew?"

I had just turned up my glass to drink, and I gulped it down to swallow and answer her.

"Yes! I went there before I came here, and he admitted it! He said Caroline didn't have proof, only suspicions, and that she'd told him in confidence. So, it's official. We just thought he'd lost his mind over her before. Now, we know for sure. He kicked me to the curb in favor of some woman he's dating. I never thought he'd do that to me. Can you imagine Eric turning his back on you for some girl?"

"No, but my brother doesn't get serious enough about anyone for it to be an issue. You know that."

"That's what I thought about Levi. And yet, here we are."

I finished off the orange juice and rinsed the glass under the faucet before setting it in the sink.

Lauryn yawned and stood with a stretch.

"It's past your bedtime, lightweight," I said with a grin. "Thanks for letting me stay. I just couldn't be in that house. It didn't feel like home anymore. It was hard enough to be there after Mom died. And now, I don't even know who my dad is."

"Well, you know you can stay here as long as you like. You know that. You have your key right?"

"Yeah. I didn't want to pop in unannounced tonight and you bash me over the head with a lamp or something."

"You gonna be all right?" she asked as she tilted her head to the side. "I can stay up with you if you want."

"No, I'll be okay. I just don't know how to get to there from here yet. It's funny. I've been banging my head against a brick wall trying to escape being who I am, and now I don't even know who that is."

"I know who you are. You're my cousin. You're my best friend. And you'll get through this, because you're the toughest person I know. You're the tougher half of me."

"And you're the sweeter half of me."

We bumped our fists together and smiled, though nothing in me felt like smiling.

My life as I had known it had changed again. And just the same as when my mother died, I didn't want the change and felt helpless to stop it. If there was anything in life I truly hated, it was feeling helpless.

CHAPTER 47
William

Patricia pulled the lid off the plastic container and grabbed a chocolate chip cookie from inside it.

"You sure you don't want one?"

I shook my head, and she held the cookie between her teeth as she closed the lid, pausing to grab another at the last moment before pushing the container to the back of the counter. I swear my sister had consumed more sugar in her lifetime than an entire candy factory could produce, and yet she was reed-thin and as healthy as a thoroughbred horse.

She pulled a paper towel from the dispenser and sat back down across from me at her kitchen table. "So, how did Ma and Dad take the news?"

"Exactly like I thought they would. Ma cried, and Dad got up and went out on the front porch without saying anything."

My father had always been a man of few words, and he'd been known to go silent for days if he was angry or upset. He only raised his voice in the direst of circumstances. I'd seen it happen a very few times in my life, and I'd been the cause of it on three occasions.

The first was when I was seven and shoved Patricia off a curb in town while goofing around. She'd nearly been hit by a car, and I don't know what scared us most—the car's horn blaring as the driver swerved to miss her or the unfamiliar roar of my father's voice as he swooped her into his arms and yelled at me for being careless.

The second was the morning after Catherine and I fell asleep on the beach when I brought my brother's truck home hours after I was expected. My mother had been certain I was lying in a ditch somewhere needing help, and my father's fear for my safety coupled with dealing with his wife's panic pushed him over the edge when he saw that I was not injured, just irresponsible.

The third time was only a couple of weeks later when I told my parents I was quitting college and giving up the full-ride grant in order to work and save for Catherine's return.

"Have you lost your damned mind?" he had thundered, his face white with rage. "This is insanity! You're throwing away your future. You've been handed an education, and you're tossing it aside, for what? For some girl who's got her nose so high in the sky it's a wonder she doesn't drown when it rains."

"I love her," I'd said, standing with my shoulders squared and my fists clenched, trying to hide the fact that I was trembling in the face of his wrath.

"Love? You have no idea what love is. What you have is called lust and stupidity. You're thinking with the wrong head, son! You got a little taste of something that's made you go all crazy and you can't even think straight. Didn't you learn anything from your brother Henry?"

Henry had married his pregnant girlfriend a month after they graduated from high school, and he'd been working to support her and their four kids ever since, barely keeping his head above water at any given time. My father's disappointment in my oldest brother had been funneled into never-ending lectures for James and me. Since before we were old enough to even think about having a girlfriend, Dad had drilled into us both that we should avoid being distracted by girls and focus instead on building our future.

It was probably his words ringing in my ears that had kept me from consummating the relationship with Catherine any sooner than I had. But his warnings hadn't kept me from distraction, and luckily, his predictions of my ruin had been short-lived. He'd never acknowledged my successes, and I knew that despite my career achievements and firm financial footing, he'd never forgiven me for forgoing college.

"Well, at least you didn't get grounded," Patricia said with a grin. "I suppose there's some advantage to being fifty-three."

"It's been a long time since I sat at that table and worried about how they were going to react to something I'd done."

"What are you talking about? You never did anything to get in trouble. You were always the good kid. I think the only time I remember you actually being in hot water was that morning you brought James's truck home so late. James waited until well after daylight to tell Ma, and then Ma called Dad at work and said you'd been out all night and never made it home. They were going nuts thinking you'd been in a wreck or something, and you came driving up all nonchalant."

"I wasn't nonchalant."

Patricia laughed at the memory of that morning, but I found nothing funny about it. That had been the last time I'd seen Catherine, and she had called the house while my father was giving me hell. My mother had answered the phone and refused to interrupt Dad to let me talk to Catherine. I had a hard time forgiving Ma for that, though she'd had no idea how serious the situation was at the time.

Patricia picked up a chocolate chip that had fallen to the table and popped it in her mouth. "You didn't tell Ma I knew about Caroline before her, did you?"

"No."

"Whew! Thank you! You're lucky Piper didn't get to her this morning before you did. Can you imagine how that would have gone down?"

I shook my head, not even willing to consider how mad my mother would have been if she'd heard the news from anyone other than me.

Patricia finished the cookie and crumpled the paper towel in her hand. "I guess Piper went to Lauryn's when she left your house last night."

"They've always been the closest of the cousins. I'm glad she had somebody to talk to. I knew this was going to be tough for her."

"Definitely. Lauryn called me this morning and asked if I already knew what was going on. I didn't want to lie to my own daughter, so I just said I wasn't at liberty to discuss anything you'd told me. I guess now that Mom knows, the cat can be let out of the bag and everyone will know, huh?"

She got up and opened the container to grab another cookie, her fourth since I'd arrived. She took a bite of it as she sat cross-legged in the chair.

"Let's go back to the part where you invited Catherine—"

"Caterina."

"Whatever! You knew who I meant. You said you two were having dinner at your house when Piper came home?"

"Yeah. I thought Piper was flying in today, but I guess she caught an earlier flight."

"Right. You're missing the question. *Why* were you having dinner with whatever-her-name-is-these-days?"

"Oh. Um, well, we had things to discuss. I wanted some answers about why she'd made the choices she did. You're the one who told me to do it."

"Me? I told you to call her. I didn't tell you to invite her to dinner."

"It seemed like something best discussed in person. What's the difference?"

"Um, it's a pretty big difference. And you not only felt you needed to discuss it in person, you invited her to your house. That makes it more intimate, don't you think?"

"It wasn't like that. I asked her over so we could talk with some measure of privacy. I swear, between you and Piper, you would have thought we were skinny-dipping in the pool or something. It was baked chicken. In the family room. Nothing that even hinted at inappropriate."

Patricia nodded and sat back in her chair to cross her arms over her chest. "This is me you're talking to."

"I know that."

"Okay. So, then let's not pretend. You're one of the least confrontational people I know. You don't like anything uncomfortable, and you'll avoid conflict whenever possible. But you expect me to believe that you preferred to have this difficult topic discussed face-to-face when a phone conversation would have sufficed? I'm not buying it."

"All right, Dr. Patricia. I somehow missed you getting your therapist degree. Tell me why I invited her to dinner, other than it was the polite thing to do."

"Polite! Hmmph. This had nothing to do with manners. This is Catherine Johnson we're talking about. The one who got away. The one you pined over for *years* like the saddest sap on the planet. You know as well as I do why you invited her to dinner."

I stood and put my cap back on my head. "You're being ridiculous."

"Am I?"

"I did what you told me to do. I listened to her side of things. And you were right. It was very beneficial in getting some closure and in understanding what happened. While I'm not sure there's any way to be okay with all of this, I feel much better after talking to her."

"I told you to forgive her. Not wine and dine her."

"We didn't have wine, thank you very much."

"Probably a good thing. I recall her being quite the drunkard back in the day."

"Don't call her that. Why do you insist on being petty? I know you never liked her, but she's been through quite a bit. How about you cut her some slack?"

Patricia's eyebrows raised, and I turned to go.

"Tell me this, little brother," she called out as she followed me to the front door. "If that's all it was—just you being polite and getting her side of the story—then you're done now, right? You've gotten your answers, and you heard what you needed to hear. So, you won't be seeing her again, right?"

I stopped on her front porch steps and gazed up at the sky. "You yourself said that she and I may need to see each other from time to time if we're going to be involved in Caroline's life. I'm not sure what you're getting at, but I think your brain's working too hard. You might want to give it a rest."

"If you say so," she said as she stood in the doorway and watched me walk to my truck. "But be careful, Will. Protect your heart. This one broke it before. I'd hate to see her do it again."

CHAPTER 48
Caterina

My phone rang a few minutes after eight in the morning, and I was surprised to see William's number flash across the screen. I hadn't heard from him since the morning after his daughter came home and interrupted dinner. He said when he called then that he was just checking to make sure I'd made it home okay, but he'd seemed reluctant to hang up, like there was something else he wanted to say.

When almost a week had gone by without any further word from him, I wondered if perhaps all his questions had been answered and our conversations had come to an end.

The thought made me sad, even though I knew it was to be expected. But now here he was, calling again, and I answered with both excitement and trepidation.

"I was wondering if you might want to grab breakfast," he said after I assured him he hadn't woken me. "I drove into town this morning for a meeting but got a call that the guy had to cancel at the last minute. I could swing by and pick you up if you haven't already eaten."

The offer caught me off guard, but before I even took the time to consider what it might mean, I was already accepting the invitation.

"Sure. How long do I have to get ready?"

I'd been sitting at my desk in my robe, and I got up and went toward my bedroom to throw open the closet door and stare at the options.

"The town's not that big," he said with a chuckle. "I'm probably ten minutes from your house. How long do you need?"

"Um, can you give me twenty?"

"See you in twenty."

I told myself it was ridiculous to be excited. It wasn't like it was a social invitation. He probably had thought of something else he wanted to clarify about the past. But that didn't stop me from obsessing over which outfit would be appropriate for a casual breakfast that meant nothing at all.

I'd just finished braiding my hair and spritzing on a light perfume when the phone rang again, and I thought it might be William again.

Instead, it was one of the foster parents I'd been working with in the process of getting approval for a placement in their home. They'd been going through the necessary procedure for a few months, and they'd finally been cleared for the teenage girl to move in with them.

"Oh, Cat, thank goodness you answered," Kim said, her voice panicked. "They're saying they didn't get the paperwork with the judge's signature in Jacksonville. It had to be to them by noon today."

"But I thought the clerk here sent it overnight earlier this week?"

"She says she did, and she said she has a signature receipt. But they're saying they don't have it in the file, and without it, I can't pick Natalie up and bring her home today. She's been having so many problems with one of other girls at the juvenile holding center, and I promised her she wouldn't have to stay there any longer. I don't know what to do. The lady said she could send it by the courier, but they don't pick up soon enough to get it there by noon. I can't take off work to drive to Jacksonville today and then take off again Monday to get Natalie's physical and get her registered in school here. What should I do?"

I answered without hesitation. "I'll go to the courthouse and get a certified copy of the paperwork, and then I'll drive it to Jacksonville."

"Oh my goodness, you'd do that for us?"

"Kim, I told you we're here to help you every step of the way. The reason I created this organization was because I know how tough it is to jump through all the hoops when you're trying to foster or adopt. You focus on your job and looking forward to picking up Natalie after you get off tonight. I'm happy to drive up there to make this happen. Call the clerk at the courthouse, though, and let her know I'm on my way. See if she can get any kind of extension in Jacksonville to buy me extra travel time. I'll be cutting it close to get there by noon."

My doorbell rang as we were finishing our call, and I felt a pang of regret that I had to cancel my breakfast with William.

"Good morning," he said when I opened the door. He wore a dark navy shirt that made the clear blue of his eyes sparkle, and my heart did a little flutter in my chest at the sight of him standing there smiling on my doorstep. Why couldn't things have worked out differently for us? Why couldn't I see him without remembering his touch?

"Mornin'. I'm so sorry, but I have to cancel. I just found out I have to drive to Jacksonville. Like, now."

The disappointment on his face mirrored my feelings.

"Oh, okay."

"You're welcome to come in," I said as I backed up to make room for him to enter. "We can chat for a minute while I get my stuff together, and then I've got to get on the road pronto. One of my foster parents needs some paperwork delivered by noon, and if it doesn't make it there, then a young lady will have to spend another weekend in a very unpleasant environment."

He followed me down the hallway toward my office at the back of the house, pausing as we passed the bookshelves.

"Whose books are these?"

"What?" I asked, peeking out the office door to see him standing there with a grin as he pointed toward the shelves.

"I can't believe these would be yours, so whose are they?"

"Very funny," I said as I went back into the office and scooped up my planner to put it in my bag. "I'll have you know I've become a reader in my adult life. Not as avid of a reader as you are, I'm sure, but I read."

He chuckled at his own joke and stood looking around the office as I gathered my purse and shut down my computer.

As I reached to turn off the desk lamp, he picked up the small wooden turtle that sat on the shelf by the door leading out to the patio.

"Wow. I can't believe you still have this."

A warm flush crept across my cheeks, and I took the turtle from him and opened the desk drawer to toss it inside.

"Yeah, well, I like turtles. What can I say?" I refused to meet his eyes as I brushed off the significance of the carving he'd made for me all those years ago.

I'd left our relationship with no pictures, no love notes, and no mementos at all other than that turtle. It was my sole souvenir of our love.

"You say you gotta be in Jacksonville at noon?" he asked as we walked back toward the living room.

"Yeah, and I have to go to Orlando to pick up the paperwork first."

He gave a low whistle. "You're going to be hard-pressed to make it by noon."

"Yes, I know. Which is why I have to get going."

I grabbed a travel cup from the cabinet and filled it with ice and water as he leaned against the kitchen door frame and watched me.

"You want some company on the ride?"

I turned in surprise, not sure I'd heard him correctly. The water overflowed, and I jerked the cup out from under the refrigerator dispenser, spilling water all over my hand and the floor.

He stepped forward to help as I grabbed a paper towel, but I waved him away.

"I got it," I said as I bent to wipe the floor. I tossed the wet towel in the trash and then turned to look at William. "I'm literally just driving up there and driving back. It's at least six hours round-trip, and it's all interstate, so it's pretty boring."

He shrugged. "Sounds like an adventure that would be better with company."

The offer intrigued me, but I paused, uncertain of why he was asking and wary to be trapped in a vehicle together for hours in case the conversation grew heated or turned emotional.

"It was just an idea," he said, his smile fading. He seemed disappointed that I'd not taken him up on the offer yet. "Probably not a good one."

"I mean, if you want to ride with me, you're more than welcome to. I just don't know how interesting it will be, that's all."

"I've never known a road trip with you to not be interesting."

He grinned, and my heart betrayed me by racing in reaction.

Something told me that I was treading on dangerous ground. A little voice somewhere in my head whispered that I needed to keep my distance, and that it would be oh-so-easy to fall for William Ward all over again. But I'd never been one to heed warnings at any point of my life.

"Then, let's hit the road. The clock's running."

CHAPTER 49
Caterina

Being on a road trip with William felt eerily familiar, despite the decades that had passed since we'd last been in a vehicle together.

The first few minutes were awkward as we both tried to act as though it was the most normal thing in the world for us to be setting out to spend the day together. We were overly polite and largely silent at the start of the journey, but it didn't take long for us to settle into an easy rhythm of conversation much like the many we'd had when we'd spent hours riding around together in our youth.

He answered my questions about his farm facility and what types of cases they typically handled, and I answered his about my lobbyist career in DC and my work with various adoption agencies and organizations before starting Turtle Crossing.

Talk about adoption inevitably turned to Caroline, and the easy flow of the conversation became more stilted. It was still new for both of us to have her be part of our lives, but to casually discuss *our* daughter together was even more strange. Almost surreal.

"So, Caroline is going to be working with you, eh? Handling the books?"

"Yes. I've never been great at math—which you, of course, know—and organization of all things financial is not my strong suit. It may be temporary, just until she gets settled and gets some distance between her and this Brad character."

"How much do you know about him?"

"Just what she's told me. He seems like a real piece of work."

"Yeah. He threatened to make legal troubles for her if she moves the kids to Cedar Creek, but I don't know that he has grounds to do so. He's moving to Miami, so it's not like she's taking Eva and Ethan away from him. He's the one leaving them behind."

I shrugged. "I don't think it's about them at all. I think it's a power grab. He wants to stay in control of her life, and she's starting to stand up to him. He'll use the kids to get to her. I just hope she's strong enough to do what she needs to do for her sake and for theirs. If not, he'll continue to manipulate all of them, just like my father always did."

"Did you know Caroline's father left the family when she was a small girl?"

I nodded. "Yes. My mother kept tabs on her and her family as she was growing up, which I didn't know at the time. After Mother died, I found a file of Caroline's school records, notes about milestones, photographs. It mentioned in there that her father had left, and her parents had divorced soon after."

"I'd like to see that file if you don't mind. Well, and if Caroline doesn't mind. It would be nice to see some of what I missed."

The bitterness in his voice was unmistakable, but I couldn't give him back the time he'd lost with her, no matter how badly I wanted to.

We rode in silence for a few miles, each of us lost in our thoughts, until William cleared his throat.

"Eva sure does remind me of you. The way she moves on a horse. Her fearlessness. Her ability to communicate with the animal just with slight adjustments of her body. She's a natural rider, just like you were. Do you still ride?"

"No," I said, shaking my head. "I haven't ridden in years. I think the last time was on a jungle trek through the rainforest in Costa Rica with a group of twelve people in a single-file line. Definitely not the same as galloping across an open field with the wind whipping my hair and the horse's hooves pounding the earth."

I could feel his eyes upon me, and I glanced in his direction, surprised to see that he was smiling.

"You're welcome to come and ride any time. I have plenty of open fields, and I have a horse in mind that I think you'd be well-suited for."

An image of the two of us riding side-by-side flashed through my mind, but my joy at the thought was quickly squashed by the idea of possibly having another encounter with his daughter.

"How are things going with Piper?" I asked. "Did you explain everything to her?"

He shifted his weight in his seat and looked out the window, and I got the idea it was a sensitive subject he'd probably rather not discuss.

"Things are going, um, pretty much like I thought they would. My daughter's a bit of a firebrand. Her mother and I probably should have set stronger boundaries for her when she was younger, but we both tended to be free with the reins. Piper's a hothead. She's got a mouth on her, that's for sure, and she's not afraid to use it if she doesn't agree with what's going on."

"And I take it she doesn't agree with what's going on?"

"She doesn't have much of a choice in the matter. It is what it is. She can buck all she wants, but it won't change the outcome. Life as she knew it will be different now. Not just for her. All of us, I suppose."

"I'm sorry," I said, wishing I could spare him and his family the conflicts that my choices had brought them to.

"I thought we'd agreed you weren't going to say that again."

I smiled despite the melancholy sadness that had come over me. "That was about things I'd already apologized for. This is something new. I haven't apologized for Piper yet."

"Why do you feel like you need to?"

I shrugged and turned on the blinker to change into the passing lane. "Because it's my fault? Because I got us all into this mess and now everyone is affected by it? Caroline, Eva, Ethan. You. Your family. Your daughter."

"I still don't figure how you see this as your fault alone. You and I both created the situation, and then your parents didn't help matters much with the way they handled it."

"I shouldn't have pushed you into doing things, William. I should have listened to you when you tried to reason with me—when you tried to do the right thing. You warned me that we shouldn't sneak out. That we should lay low and let things blow over with my dad. You wanted to wait until we were older and farther along in life before we got involved in … in … *that way*. I didn't listen. I dragged you into my rebellion."

"We could just as easily say that I shouldn't have driven to your house and picked you up every night. I shouldn't have taken us to the beach. I shouldn't have fallen asleep. Hell, we could go on with this all damned day with what we should have done differently or shouldn't have done the way we did. But what good does that do all these years later? It doesn't change anything. We're still where we're at."

"I know, but we're where we're at because of me. Everything Caroline went through. Everything you went through. Everything you're both going through now. What Piper's going through. I could have prevented all of that if I'd just not been so damned hardheaded and selfish."

"You were a teenager, Catherine, er, Caterina. We both were. We made some stupid choices, but that's what teenagers do. They do dumb things. They don't think about the consequences. If you'd known this was how it was all going to turn out, I'm sure you would have done things differently. It's not like you maliciously and purposely caused all this to happen."

He turned in the seat to face me as I swallowed hard and gripped the steering wheel tighter, trying not to cry.

"Look, Cat, I'm not going to lie and say that I'm okay with everything that's happened. I'm not. I'm frustrated. I'm pissed off. I'm hurt. I hate feeling helpless because I can't go back and change any of it. I'm angry for all that's been lost that I can't get back. But my anger is no longer directed at you. I don't blame you. I don't think this is all your fault."

"But I didn't tell you about Caroline."

He nodded.

"Yes, and I was angry with you for that, for sure, and I'd been angry with you for years for not contacting me, even before I knew about Caroline. It hurt that you left and never came back. That you seemed to disappear and go on with your life without giving me a second thought. But now I know why. So, as much as I wish that you could have and would have gotten in touch with me and told me what was going on, I understand why you didn't. I'm not angry at you anymore. I'd say I forgive you if I thought it would help what you're feeling, but I don't know that there's really anything I have to forgive."

"How can you say that? After all I've put you through, how can you say that?"

My voice broke off at the end of the question, and I gulped in air and held it to try and keep my emotions at bay.

"Okay, what about what I put you through?" he asked. "We both made the choice to sneak you out of the house that night. We both decided to take it all the way on that beach, and we both fell asleep afterward. But you're the one who got shipped off to another state because of it. You got disowned by your family. You had to drop out of high school. You carried my child and gave birth to her, only to have her ripped away from you. It sounds like you suffered a larger portion of the consequences for actions we chose together. Can *you* forgive *me*?"

His voice was calm and steady, the same way I remembered it being when I'd be upset and he'd talk me off the ledge and make me feel like it would all be okay somehow. But this could never be okay.

I turned off the highway into a rest area, unable to maintain my focus in the traffic any longer as my tears fell. I pulled into a parking space and turned to face him, prepared to take responsibility for the hard truth.

"I appreciate what you're trying to do, William. I really do. But it goes back farther than that night. From the very beginning, you didn't want anything to do with me, and I refused to respect that. I pushed and pushed. I insisted that you pay attention to me, chasing and pursuing you relentlessly. And even once you'd given in, I kept pushing. You wanted to be honest with my parents. I pushed you to hide with me. You needed to work and save for school, but I pushed you to go out all the time. You needed sleep—you were working two jobs, for Christ's sake—but I insisted that you stay out with me all hours of the night. You didn't want us to have sex, but I—"

"Whoa, whoa, whoa." He held up his hands and shook his head. "Is this really how you remember our relationship? If this is how you see our story, you're quite the unreliable narrator. I fell in love with you the first time I saw you, and I couldn't believe I was lucky enough to have you pay attention to me. What makes you think I wanted nothing to do with you?"

"At the fence line, you didn't even want to talk to me. You told me that you didn't want to talk to me."

"I figured you were yanking my chain to make the guys laugh at me. I didn't think there was any way you were actually interested in me. But then when you kept coming around, I thought maybe I'd been wrong about that. It was never that I wasn't attracted to you or that I didn't want to talk to you. I wanted nothing more than to talk to you. And yes, I did wish we didn't have to sneak around all the time, but it was worth it just to be with you. I didn't need sleep. I didn't need anything but you. Don't you know that? How can you say that what we had wasn't real?"

"I didn't say it wasn't real. I said—"

"You said that you pushed me every step of the way. You basically said I was dating you because I didn't have a choice. Because you made me somehow. That's bullshit. You're saying that my feelings for you weren't real. That what we experienced together wasn't real. It was all something you forced to happen. I can't believe that's how you remember it."

The clock on the dashboard caught my eye, and I panicked.

"We're running out of time. We have to go." I looked in the rearview mirror and wiped at my tears, trying not to completely destroy my make-up.

I eased back into traffic, and we rode the rest of the way in silence with William staring out the window and me replaying his words over and over, wishing I could believe that things were the way he said.

CHAPTER 50
William

It became apparent there was no way we would make it to our destination by noon, but luckily, the court clerk in Orlando called Cat and said she'd bought us a little time since her signature receipt proved the office in Jacksonville had the paperwork on time but had misplaced it. They said they closed at noon for an hour lunch and would be happy to accept our delivery when they returned.

It was welcome news, not only because of the extra travel time but also because Caterina and I were both starving, having not had breakfast or even a snack to hold us over.

We found a cafe downtown whose proximity to the office would make it easy for us to eat and still be at their door by one.

Cat's entire demeanor had relaxed when she learned the trip wouldn't be a waste, and we'd had a nice lunch. Then once we'd dropped off the paperwork and gotten assurances that Natalie could be picked up by Kim that evening, Cat became downright jubilant. Her happiness was contagious, and I wanted to prolong the day and soak up as much of it as possible.

"Let's take a walk around St. Augustine," I said as we got back on the interstate to head south.

"Yeah? You sure you don't need to get back to anything right away?"

"I'm sure. I called Levi this morning and told him to handle anything in my absence. I don't take a day off too often, so I figure I've got one coming to me."

Her grin in response lit her up her face and lit up my heart, the same way it had all those years ago.

For the next couple of hours, the outside world ceased to exist.

The seemingly insurmountable tasks of juggling Caroline's entry into my family and Piper's pain in response to it, was pushed to the back of my mind.

The skies were a gorgeous blue without a cloud in sight, and a gentle breeze rolled through the narrow cobblestone streets of St. Augustine's Historic District as we meandered in and out of shops.

In many ways, it felt like no time had passed since I'd last walked by Cat's side. Despite the faint lines that framed it, her smile was the same. Her sense of humor still meshed with mine seamlessly the way it always had, and we drifted in and out of topics of conversation with the same ease we'd always experienced in sharing our thoughts with each other.

Of course, time *had* passed, quite a lot of it. We'd lived nearly our entire lives apart, and the life experiences we'd had during those decades had shaped our world views, our philosophies, our musical tastes, clothing preferences, and much more. We found common ground in many areas and engaged in friendly debate in others.

Perhaps the biggest difference was one of which I was keenly aware. We were walking around in public together, and it didn't matter. There was no reason to hide. No fear of being seen. Nothing to be ashamed of. For the first time since I'd met Catherine, we could walk side-by-side without a care in the world.

"Oh, listen to that bass guitar!" she said as we approached a shaded courtyard of picnic tables where a band was playing on stage. "Let's stop and listen a while!"

We found an empty table beneath a massive oak tree, its limbs laden with old-fashioned lanterns whose bulbs glowed despite the brightness of the spring day.

"You want something to drink?" I asked, indicating a bar near the stage.

"Just a bottle of water, thanks."

I paid for two waters and joined her at the table as she snapped her fingers and bopped her head to the music.

She downed about half the bottle at once and then grinned at me as she set it on the table. "Whew! I didn't realize how thirsty I was!"

"So, this may be none of my business—"

"Uh-oh," she chuckled. "Any time someone starts a sentence that way, more often than not, it's definitely none of their business."

I took a swig of the cold water and reconsidered my question and its intrusiveness.

"Oh, go ahead," she said. "You already started it now, and curiosity will kill me wondering what you were going to say. Besides, I already told you I'm an open book. I'll answer whatever you want to know."

"You've made a couple of statements that made me wonder … I mean, like, you mentioned travel being the only addiction you allow yourself to have, and you said something earlier today about not needing wine glasses in your house. So, I was just wondering if there's a reason you don't drink anymore."

She finished off her water and screwed the cap back on the empty bottle.

"There's definitely a reason, and I'm pretty sure you already know what it is. I had a problem with using alcohol, as well as a few other substances, to numb myself when life seemed unbearable. It was a problem before I met you, and it became an unmanageable problem after everything that happened. I had gone down a dark path that held no light at the end of the tunnel, but my grandmother reminded me that I might have someone to answer to someday, so I found healthier ways to cope." The band started a new song, and she turned with her mouth open and her eyes bright. "Oh, I love this one!"

She stood and put both hands in the air, her hips swaying back and forth as she sang the lyrics along with the lead singer. She was so relaxed and at ease. It made me happy just watching her, but she had other ideas.

"Dance with me!"

"Oh, I don't dance," I said, waving my hand as I shook my head.

"Come on," she pleaded, coming around to my side of the picnic table and extending her hands in invitation. "You're not going to make me go up there and dance all by myself, are you?"

I glanced toward the dance area in front of the stage where several other couples were already dancing. Cat's smile enticed, but the thought of making a fool of myself in front of a group of strangers was daunting, so I shook my head again.

"No, I don't dance, Cat."

"Well, you should! You don't know what you're missing. Life's too short not to dance!"

I watched her sashay away, her hips moving and her fingers snapping as the other dancers made room for her.

It didn't take long until she was the center of attention, though perhaps it was just me who could see no one else on the floor. Her face conveyed pure joy, and her comfort in moving her body in front of the crowd was alluring. The lead singer asked everyone to sing louder, and Cat tossed her head back and belted out the chorus with a smile. She turned then and made eye contact with me, and my entire body responded to her in much the same way it had all those years ago. She was an attractive lady, and I'd have to be a dead man not to admire her sensuality.

Before I thought too much about what I was doing, I found myself beside her on the floor, and her excitement when she turned and saw me bolstered my confidence as I tried to keep time with the music. It was way out of my comfort zone to be up there, but I couldn't remember the last time I'd felt so free and so alive.

It was as though I'd been seeing life through a gray filter since Revae had died, and suddenly, the world was awash with color again. The blue of the sky was electric. The vivid green of the leaf canopy above us was only matched in intensity by the green of Cat's eyes as she laughed and twirled in front of me, her bright pink skirt swirling around her as she lifted her hair off her neck and sang along with the crowd.

My heart pounded and raced, and I couldn't be sure if it was from embarrassment, unusual activity, or just an organ coming back to life after being dormant for far too long.

By the time the song ended, I'd relaxed into my left-and-right sway a bit, and I actually sang along with the last chorus, having picked up the words from everyone around me.

"Whew! I get winded so easily," Cat said as we left the dance floor. "I forget I'm supposed to be recuperating. I need to get some more water, and then I need to take a few hits on my inhaler." She turned and walked backwards for a few steps, pointing at me as she grinned. "You were killing it out there! And you said you don't dance!"

"I don't!"

"Yeah, well, I beg to differ. Just because you don't dance doesn't mean you're not a dancer. Admit it—you had fun out there."

I laughed as she ordered two waters, and then my phone vibrated on my hip.

It was Piper, and I grimaced as the real world intruded into the bubble I'd spent the day in.

"I need to find a place I can hear," I said to Cat.

"Okay, I'll meet you just outside the entrance."

I nodded as I slid my finger across the screen and turned back toward the courtyard exit.

"Hey, sweetheart," I said into the phone as the band's next song kicked into high gear. "It's really loud, so hold on and let me get somewhere that I can hear." I reached the street and scanned the area for a more secluded spot, ducking down a narrow alleyway to a table and chairs behind an ice cream shop. "That's better. Can you hear me?"

"Where are you?" Piper asked.

I braced for conflict, knowing there was no way my answer would go over well.

"Um, St. Augustine."

"Okay. Do I even want to know why you're in St. Augustine? You're supposed to be here. We have a meeting in fifteen minutes with the salesman for the new fencing material."

"Oh, I'm sorry. I talked to Levi earlier, and he's going to handle it for me. I didn't realize you'd planned to be in that meeting or I would have let you know."

Her silence made me wonder if we'd been disconnected, and I put my finger in my ear to shut out the strains of the band carried on the breeze.

"You still there?"

"Yep. Why is Levi handling that without you?"

"Because he's the farm manager, and he's in charge of the structures on the property, which includes fencing. He's perfectly capable of making those decisions."

"What's in St. Augustine that's so important?"

"Nothing important," I gazed up at the sky and smiled at a bird flying overhead. "Just a beautiful afternoon, and I decided to take the day off and enjoy the sunshine."

"I see. And who are you with?"

"What's with the interrogation?"

"No interrogation. I just don't remember you ever taking the day off and driving across the state for sunshine before. It's a little out of character, and I was wondering if the reason might be the company you're keeping."

I sighed and closed my eyes. If I answered the question, it was just going to make her more upset. And if I didn't answer it, she wouldn't be any less upset.

"Piper, I don't pry into your life. I don't ask where you're going every time you leave or who you're going to spend time with. I trust that you're an adult and that you are smart enough to make your own decisions about your life. I would appreciate that same measure of respect from you."

"You're with that woman, aren't you?"

The pain in her voice was sharp, and it cut me to the core. The last thing I wanted to do was hurt Piper or upset her. She was still resistant to considering Caroline or the kids as members of our family, and she saw their importance to me as some sort of betrayal to her and her mother.

I wasn't inclined to pour salt into that wound by telling her I was spending time with Caterina. Why did a day that had brought me such joy have to be something that caused my daughter pain? Was it wrong of me to want to spend time with Cat? Was it a bad thing that I was intrigued by her and wanted to be in her company?

Having her back in my life had been like switching on a light. I wasn't too eager to go back into the darkness so soon. How could I make Piper understand that?

"I rode up here with Cat, yes. She was coming to Jacksonville on an errand, and I offered to ride with her. Then on the way home, we decided to take advantage of the weather and spend some time in St. Augustine."

"You know Mom loved St. Augustine."

I frowned at the reminder, though it wasn't anything I'd forgotten.

"Yes, I'm aware of that."

"Well, enjoy your day, Dad." Her sarcastic tone conveyed insincerity, but I chose not to be drawn into the argument.

"Thanks, sweetheart. I'll see you later."

"Will you be home for dinner?"

I looked at my watch and grimaced again.

"Probably not."

"Great. I'll let Gaynelle know not to cook for you. Unless you've already called her too."

"Er, no. I haven't."

When our call had ended, I stepped back out into the throng of tourists on St. George Street. I spotted Cat right away, sitting on a bench and licking a mint chocolate chip ice cream cone.

Her smile filled her face when she saw me, and a warmth flooded my heart. Perhaps there would be hell to pay when I got back home, but for rest of the day, I could choose to be happy.

CHAPTER 51
Piper

"**P**iper, you want a brownie? I just took them out of the oven."

I pulled out a chair at Aunt Patricia's kitchen table and plopped down in it.

"No, thanks, Aunt Patty. I'm not hungry."

"I'm not either, but I can't pass up a warm brownie."

She came to the table with a mouthful, moaning in pleasure as she set her plate on the table and sat down across from me.

"That's just so damned good. You know Uncle Paul swears he married me for my brownies. I don't blame him. I'd marry myself for them if I wasn't already married. You sure you don't want one? It might turn that frown upside down. How are you holding up, honey? You okay?"

"I'm fine, but I'm worried about Dad, and I'm hoping you can talk some sense into him."

"Girl, you know nobody can talk sense into your daddy. He's the one that talks sense into all of us."

"I think he's lost his damned mind over all this!"

"It is a lot to process, that's for sure. But when I've talked with him, I thought he was handling everything pretty well, all things considered. Why do you think he's not?"

"He's just blindly accepting all this without question. There's been no DNA test. No proof. But he just says *okay, she's my daughter,* and everybody has to be fine with it."

She raised an eyebrow and cocked her head to the side.

"Piper, have you looked at the girl? I saw her at the hospital from a distance, and you can't help but notice the resemblance between the two of you. And she has your daddy's eyes."

I shook my head, not wanting to hear yet another person compare me with Caroline. There was more at stake here than whether or not we had passing similarities. Did no one else see the cause for alarm?

"Okay, so maybe we're related, but does that mean we have to suddenly throw open the doors and welcome her in? Don't you think it's bizarre that she just showed up at the farm? Supposedly a random encounter, but how weird is that? And this woman, this Caterina or Catherine or whatever name she goes by, she just happens to be in Cedar Creek but never contacted Dad before? Did you know he invited her over? I came home to find him sitting there having dinner with her."

"Oh, sugar. I know this is tough. I can't even imagine what you're feeling right now, but this has been tough on your daddy, too. He didn't know about Caroline, and he's been blindsided by this as much as anyone. He's trying to get answers."

"Which is exactly what I mean! Why would Caterina keep it secret that she had a baby? Who does that and doesn't tell the other person?"

Aunt Patricia wrinkled up her nose and frowned.

"There's a lot you may not know yet, and it's not my place to tell you. I think you need to talk to your dad to get these answers."

"Well, I'd love to, but he's not around. He took off to St. Augustine for the day with Caterina."

I crossed my arms and watched her surprised expression with great satisfaction.

"Really? Are you sure?"

I nodded. "Yep. He told me himself when I called to find out why he wouldn't be at an important meeting that had been on the books for over a month. Now, you tell me, what reason would he have to be in St. Augustine with her? And when have you known Daddy to take a day off for anything? She's bewitched him somehow, I swear."

Patricia pushed the plate with the unfinished brownie to the side and let out a deep sigh.

"Piper, there's so much you don't understand. Once upon a time, this woman was very special to your daddy, and it hurt him deeply when they split up."

"But then he met Mama, and she was the love of his life. She never would have kept such a big secret from him. She never would have hidden a child from him."

"You may be right, but none of us know what we would do in someone else's shoes. I think you need to cut your daddy some slack as he tries to come to terms with all that's happened. As hard as it for you, imagine what he's going through. He just found out he had a daughter all this time that he knew nothing about. And on top of that, he found out that something he'd believed for most of his life wasn't true. This great pain he suffered was for totally different reasons than what he thought. Can you understand how that would shake a man?"

"All the more reason for him to stay away from this Caterina woman. She can't be trusted. She already proved that. I think she's up to something. I went to Tristan Rogers and tried to get the sheriff's office to open an investigation to see if I'm right, but he refused. Said they don't have probable cause to investigate."

Patty's eyes widened. "Piper! You didn't!"

"I most certainly did! I'm not going to stand by and let someone come in and take advantage of my dad."

"Your daddy's a grown man. He can take care of himself."

I shook my head, determined to convince her. "No, I'm telling you, these two have him under some kind of spell. He's not acting normal. Did you not hear me? *He took the day off.* He's been with *her* all day in St. Augustine. Does that not mean anything to you?"

"I think it means he wanted to spend time with her, which is not exactly a surprise to me. This was someone he spent a great deal of time with who suddenly disappeared from his life, and now she's back. I think it's natural that he would be curious about her."

"So, you're fine with him dating this woman who completely screwed him over and hid a kid from him?"

Patricia shrugged. "I don't think they're *dating*. But even if they were, it's not my decision, and truthfully, it's not yours either. Your dad doesn't need us to give our approval to how he spends his time. Would you want him telling you who you could hang out with now that you're an adult? Or whether or not you could go out on a date?"

"That's not the same. I'd be fine with him dating someone, but not this woman."

Patricia leaned across the table, and her eyes narrowed. "Would you be? Are you sure about that? I know you're concerned about your dad, but I wonder how much of this is about you. It can't feel good to suddenly have this other daughter appear out of nowhere, and then to have your dad paying attention to another woman on top of that has to be hard. Especially since there hasn't been anyone in the picture since your mom passed. Are you sure you're not a teensy bit jealous of the attention they're getting from your dad?"

There was enough truth in her question for it to sting, but I shook my head in denial. "That's ridiculous."

She reached across the table like she was going to take my hand, but I put it in my lap out of her reach.

"Piper, you and your dad have such a special relationship, and nothing is going to change how he feels about you. *Nothing*. But you have to try and see this from his point of view. And from Caroline's! She's gone her entire life without knowing her father. She didn't get the time with him that you did. She deserves to have a relationship with him, and he deserves to know her and have her and those kids be in his life."

Classic Aunt Patty. Turn it around so that I felt like an ass when I'd done nothing wrong. I don't know why I even came to talk to her. I guess I thought out of all the family, she might be the one who could help me with my dad.

"He can have a relationship with Caroline," I said. "Her kids, too. But that doesn't mean he needs to have a relationship with that woman."

"He already did have a relationship with her, and it was a close one."

I groaned and reached across the table to pinch off a bite of her brownie. "How much do you remember about Caterina? Or Catherine, I guess she was then."

She shrugged, and a faint grin played at the corners of her mouth.

"I didn't know her well. She came over to our house for dinner once, maybe twice, and I saw her a few other times with your dad, but it's not like we all hung out together. I was in nursing school at the time, so I was pretty preoccupied. And he was never home. If he wasn't working, they were always off somewhere together."

"What did you think of her?"

"It doesn't matter what I thought of her or what I think of her. It matters what your daddy thinks of her. And if he wants to spend time with her, he has a right to."

I sighed and crossed my arms, wishing she would understand how dire the situation was.

She leaned forward, and though her expression held compassion, her tone conveyed that her point of view wasn't going change.

"Piper, this is all new. It's been quite a revelation for everyone involved, and I think once the dust settles, it will all calm down a bit. But if your dad decides he wants Caterina in his life, then you have to find a way to be okay with that."

I looked away from her but she leaned to the side and forced herself into my line of vision.

"Do you remember when your aunt Diana died, and after a while, your mom kept trying to find someone for your uncle Dax to date? I mean, this was her sister's husband, and she'd lost her sister, but she was bound and determined to find someone for Dax. Do you remember that?"

I nodded, uncertain of where she was going, but sure I wasn't going to like where she went.

"Do you know why your mama did that?"

"Not a clue."

"Because she didn't want Dax to be alone. She didn't want him to be lonely. She didn't want him to live the rest of his life without love. Now, this was her sister's husband, and she was willing to put aside her feelings of loss about Diana to try and do what was best for Dax. Don't you think she would want the same for your dad? Revae wouldn't want your dad to live the rest of his life lonely. Or without love."

"My dad is loved!" I crossed my arms even more tightly to keep from pounding my fists on the table. "I love him. His family loves him. His crew loves him."

"Yes, but that's the not the same as the love of a companion. You're going to fall in love someday, and you'll be focused on a life of your own. Do you really want your dad wandering around that big ole house all by himself? Wouldn't you rather him be happy? Wouldn't you rather he have someone who makes him happy? It doesn't change what he shared with your mom. It doesn't make it mean any less. Look at Dax now! He's with Maggie, and he's happier than I've seen him in years. You've seen the two of them together. You know what a difference she's made in his life. That doesn't make what he shared with your aunt Diana any less powerful. But she's gone. Why should he live in solitude when that won't bring her back?"

The conversation hadn't gone at all the way I'd hoped it would, and it had taken a turn I'd never expected.

"Great. So, you're saying I should be happy that this lying, conniving woman has come back into my father's life so that he won't be lonely when and if I ever find a guy to love. Awesome. Except what if she breaks his heart again? Have you thought about that?"

She nodded. "I have. I've thought a lot about that. And that concerns me much more than her being some kind of criminal who's trying to scam him or pull the wool over his eyes. But again, I don't think this is something that's going to be long-term. I think he's getting the closure he needed, nothing more. If I'm wrong, if he does want to pursue an interest in her, then that's his decision. I have to allow him to make his choices and deal with his own consequences for those choices. The same as we all have to do."

I couldn't listen to her any longer. I stood to go, so frustrated that I wanted to scream.

"Well, you may be fine with all this, but I'm not. I'm going to keep my eyes open, and if either of these women makes one wrong move, just one, then I'm going to be there to catch them."

CHAPTER 52
Caterina

We shopped and walked St. Augustine most of the afternoon, and we were almost back to where we had parked when I spotted a second-hand book store.

"Wanna take a look?" I asked William.

"That's a dangerous place for me," he said with a chuckle. "Do you have any idea how many books I already own?"

"What's a couple more? It's a big house. You have room." I held the door open, and he laughed as he stepped inside.

His enthusiasm as he perused the titles was charming, and it interested me more to watch him than to look for a book.

At the back of the shop, the owner had created a cozy reading area with a large overstuffed chair beneath a lamp. I'd just walked past it when I saw the locked glass display of special editions. A familiar title caught my eye on the bottom shelf, and I squatted to see it more clearly.

"Hey, William. Look at this. Do you own a first edition signed copy of *To Kill A Mockingbird?*"

He glanced back over his shoulder. "No. I can't say that I do."

"Well, they have one!"

"Nice! I bet that'll fetch a pretty penny."

His attention returned to the book in his hands, and I frowned. I'd expected a bit more excitement.

"Is it not still your favorite book? You used to read it over and over again."

"Oh, I still like it, for sure, but I haven't read it in forever."

I went to stand beside him as I considered his words. I'd always thought of him any time I saw a mention of the book or the movie, and I was curious as to why his passion for it had waned.

"Is there a reason you stopped reading it? Did you just get tired of it?"

He closed the book he held and slid it back into place on the shelf. Then he turned to face me, his clear blue eyes clouded with emotion.

"I guess you could say I moved on from it. It held certain … attachments … for me that were painful. So, I chose not to read it anymore."

He moved past me to grab another novel from the shelf and flip it over to read the back.

"I'm sorry to hear that," I said as I watched him. "I know you enjoyed it, and if it had anything to do with me leaving, then I hate that I messed that up for you."

He replaced that book and gave me a weak smile. "Let's get out of here."

"Okay. You want to head home?"

He sighed, and he didn't look any more eager to leave than I felt.

"Are you hungry?" he asked. "I know a great seafood place over on the coast. I don't know if you still like to put your toes in the sand, but you could do it at this place."

I grinned, relieved that he wasn't ready to call it a day yet. It had been almost magical, like something from a dream. I'd never thought I would spend a whole day with William again, and I couldn't remember the last time I'd laughed so much or had such fun. I didn't want it to end. I didn't want to go back to our real lives with all their complications and scars.

"I would love to put my toes in the sand, and I'm always up for seafood!"

We removed the top from the Jeep before heading to the restaurant, and I felt like I'd stepped back in time—driving to the beach with William, the wind whipping my hair in my face, the radio blasting out tunes, and the sun sinking low in the sky.

The restaurant he'd picked had a casual vibe, but it was much nicer than anywhere we'd eaten together before,

"Is this all right?" William asked as we walked toward the doors.

"Of course! You can't beat the location."

After a short wait, we were seated at an outside table where we could see and hear the waves crashing in the distance. It was the perfect setting to end a perfect day.

"I highly recommend the pecan-crusted grouper," William said as the waitress handed us the menus. "I've tried several things here, and that's the one I keep coming back for."

"Sold!" I told the waitress without even looking at the menu. "Bring me whatever he says."

"I merely suggested it," William said. "You are more than welcome to peruse the offerings and make your own decision."

"I trust you. You've never led me wrong before."

I'd been speaking about food choices, but as his expression softened into something more tender, and I realized the statement could have a deeper meaning. It didn't change anything. It was true no matter how it was interpreted.

The grouper turned out to be an excellent suggestion, and when he insisted we share a slice of Key Lime pie afterward, I didn't bother to resist, despite being full already.It was another great recommendation and worth the discomfort of a full belly, but I had to stop after two bites.

"I'm stuffed. I don't think I'll be able to eat anything else for days." I set my fork on the edge of the plate and leaned back in my chair.

William grinned as he finished off the slice. "I may have to let out my belt for the ride home, but I can't leave Key Lime pie uneaten."

He refused my offer to split the bill, and when we rose from the table, he nodded toward the water.

"How about we get your toes in the sand? A walk along the beach might help settle our dinner and make the long ride ahead more bearable."

The moon was just rising over the water on the horizon, so bright against the clear night sky that the whole world seemed to glow with its brilliance.

We sat on a beach towel I'd found in the back of the Jeep and watched the waves roll in, each of us lost in our own thoughts for the longest period of silence we'd had all day. I wondered what he was thinking and if he felt as mixed up inside as I did.

I didn't know how I was going to walk away from my feelings at the end of the day. As much as I had enjoyed being with him, I knew not to read more into it than what it was. We'd both been curious. We'd wanted to reconnect after all that time apart, but too much water had passed under the bridge for there to be anything else. We couldn't possibly keep seeing each other. Could we? It had been so long. We were different people than we had been before. And there were, oh, so many complications.

Common sense said that if we were both going to live in the same town with Caroline and the kids and interact with them, our paths would certainly cross from time to time. We could be friends, I suppose. But would I be able to do that? Could I be a casual acquaintance of William's and pretend that the very sight of him didn't make my heart race? Could I ignore the way his voice sent tremors down my spine and made me feel things in places that weren't at all casual?

I'd caught him looking at me a few times throughout the day, and it seemed I wasn't the only one struggling with desire. His eyes smoldered with it, which only added fuel to my own fire.

This was crazy. I'd known it was dangerous to be around him, and I'd ignored the caution flags. But I didn't regret it. I couldn't. For one day—one blissful day—he'd been mine again, and it was worth whatever withdrawal I had to go through when we returned home.

"I went to check on Albert when I moved back to Florida," I said, hoping to change the subject in my head.

"Who?" William's forehead crinkled in confusion.

"Albert! Our turtle!"

"Oh! I forgot you named the damned thing. Wow. Is he still alive?"

"He was the last time I visited. Sea turtles in captivity can live, like, fifty years or something. He was a youngster when we helped him get rescued. He's still at the rehabilitation center. Nicole's long gone to another job—she was the girl we talked to on the tour. The one who inspired my sea turtle career that never happened."

So much had never happened. So much never would.

I had to get myself under control. I had to remember it wasn't just about me anymore. I couldn't chance making things awkward for Caroline, or Eva and Ethan. I had to distance myself. Keep my heart in check and not let it fall into trouble.

I stood and walked to the water's edge, staring out across the moonlit waves as they pounded the shore, one after another.

"You okay?" William asked as he came to stand beside me.

I nodded and hugged myself in the cool evening breeze.

"I'm sorry I didn't remember Albert's name," he said.

"Oh, that's all right. Seriously. It was ridiculous of me to name him, and even more ridiculous for me to think you'd remember that."

A wave broke close in, and the water rushed over my feet as William stepped back and bent to roll up his jeans.

"It's funny," I said as I stared into the blackness of the water. "I feel like I spent my whole life trying to remember you—to remember every little detail, every moment. To keep you alive and with me somehow. It seems like you spent your whole life trying to forget me. To erase me and everything connected to me. Everything we shared."

He was silent, and after a moment, I turned to see if perhaps he'd walked back to the towel, offended by my words. But he was still there, off to the side behind me, just out of reach of the water.

I looked toward the moon, wishing I'd kept my mouth shut. I didn't want to end such a spectacular day on an awkward note.

"It was different for me," he said, his voice so quiet I could barely hear him over the roar of the waves. "You knew why we were apart. I didn't. I thought I'd been left behind. That hurt. When I realized you weren't coming back right away, I thought maybe you'd wait until the school year ended and you'd graduated. I worked like hell to be ready for you, but summer came and went with no word from you. Then, I thought maybe you were waiting to turn eighteen. That way you'd be an adult, and your father wouldn't have any say in your life."

He'd picked up a shell as he talked, and he tossed it into the surf with a heavy sigh.

"But when your birthday passed and there was still no contact, I had to accept that you weren't coming back. So yes, I tried to erase you. Tried to erase us. Tried to forget. I had to. I needed to move on with my life, and I couldn't do that and hold on to you, too. I avoided anything that made me think of you. The beach. The river. The woods. That book. Then, when I met Revae and we married, it seemed like a betrayal of her to remember you. I pushed you even farther from my mind and refused to allow the memory of us to have any space in my head."

He closed the distance between us, and my heart felt like it would hammer itself out of my chest.

"But I never forgot you, Cat. I tried, but I never could. I never stopped looking for your face in a crowd. I never stopped wondering where you might be or what you were doing with your life. Now, here you are." He reached to cup my cheek in his hand, the light stroke of his thumb on my skin taking my breath away. He moved even closer, and the anticipation of his kiss made me so dizzy that I swayed into him before our lips even touched.

It was gentle at the start—a chaste and polite kiss more timid than our first one had been all those years ago—but then a tiny moan escaped me, and it was like a match thrown into gasoline.

I threw my arms around his neck as his encircled my waist, each of us pulling the other closer though we were pressed tightly together already. Our mouths were relentless as we plundered and explored like we'd found a source of water after years of dying in thirst of it.

Perhaps inspired by our passion, the ocean sent a rambunctious wave crashing at our feet, its currents swirling around our shins as the foam clung to our skin. We broke contact momentarily to move to higher ground, but the interruption only served to heighten our sense of urgency when we came back together.

The clear night and the splendor of the moon illuminating it had brought out many beachgoers to walk the shore. When a stranger yelled for us to get a room, William pulled back from our kiss and looked toward the man with contempt.

"Ignore him," I whispered, and he looked back at me. Two small kids ran past us, one chasing the other as they giggled, and I sighed. "I guess we are kind of making a spectacle of ourselves, huh?"

The desire in William's eyes stoked the fire in me to an almost unbearable intensity. If we'd been on a deserted stretch of beach, I'm pretty sure we would have repeated our history right then and there, but the intrusion of those around us had broken the spell.

He drew in a deep breath and kissed my forehead as he wrapped me tighter in his arms. I laid my head against his chest, his heartbeat loud against my ear.

I'd only dreamed of being back in his embrace, and the reality was both dizzying and disconcerting. What were we doing? What line were we crossing, and what would be the consequences for all the innocent people it could affect? We'd spent the day swept up in nostalgia, but we had to take care. It was too soon, and everything was too raw. We weren't thinking clearly.

I needed to put the brakes on whatever this was before it went past a salvageable point. I had to think about Caroline and the kids, and what would be best for occasions when we all needed to be in the same room. I also had to protect myself. We didn't have a future together for many reasons, and I knew I couldn't do a one-night fling for old times' sake. My heart was too invested in William Ward to pull that off. It always had been.

"What are we doing?" I blurted out as I pulled back and looked up at him, unable to contain my anxiety. His eyes searched mine, but his hold on me didn't loosen. If anything, his arms tightened ever so slightly.

"I don't know," he whispered after a long pause. "But I don't want to stop."

I smiled and spread my hands across his shoulders.

"I don't either. But we need to consider how complicated this might make things. Everyone's still trying to adjust—Caroline, the kids, Piper, us. I don't know if it's a good idea if we blur the lines."

He bent to rest his forehead on mine, and he swallowed hard, so hard that I could hear the effort.

"I know you're right. But Christ, I want you. I don't want to let go."

I closed my eyes, breathing in the scent of him, savoring his proximity and the way my body reacted to it. I certainly didn't want to let go. I didn't want to move past that moment. I wanted to freeze time and have him all to myself without having to think about anyone else's needs. But that was a Catherine way of thinking. Selfish. Self-absorbed. Not caring who got hurt.

I'd worked hard to put those patterns behind me and to always try and put others first.

The most important people in the world to me could be hurt by my actions, and I had to protect them, even if it meant denying myself what felt so damned good.

So, I held his face in my hands and pressed my lips against his, and then before he could react, I pulled away from his embrace and walked back toward the spot where we'd been sitting.

"Let's get on the road," I said as I scooped up the towel and shook it out. "We've still got a couple of hours to drive, and I'm sure you've got people wondering where you are."

CHAPTER 53
Caterina

The early morning doorbell didn't surprise me. I'd been surprised the night before when Patsy didn't traipse across the space between our houses as soon as William left.

"Good morning, neighbor," I said as I pulled the door open and walked toward the kitchen, leaving her to close it and follow close on my heels.

"Good morning, indeed. When you texted me yesterday that you were driving Natalie's paperwork to Jacksonville, you didn't mention that you had a passenger."

"Oh, did I fail to mention that?" I smiled as I handed her a cup of coffee and slid the sugar bowl across the counter to her.

She arched an eyebrow and gave me a playful glare as she spooned sugar into her coffee.

"I nearly fell out in the floor when I looked out the window yesterday mid-morning and saw William Ward's truck in your driveway. I thought at first he'd stopped by without realizing you weren't home, but that truck was still there every time I looked. And I kept looking until nearly ten last night."

"I would have told you, but it wasn't a planned development. It just sort of … happened."

"Hmmm," Patsy said as she stirred her coffee. "And what else just sort of happened? Last I checked, Jacksonville wasn't an all-day-and-half-the-night excursion."

A warmth crept into my cheeks, and I busied myself putting the creamer back in the fridge so she didn't notice me blushing and call me on it.

I wasn't sure how to explain what had happened between William and me. I didn't understand it myself.

I thought we'd established on the beach that for the sake of everyone around us, it was best if we drew some strong boundaries and honored them.

It had made our ride home much less talkative than the ride there, and I'd been thankful for the constant din of the radio and the roar of the wind with the top off the Jeep.

He'd offered to walk me to the door when we got back to my place, and we both stood on my porch and stared at each other, not ready to end the day and sever the connection we'd shared.

"I guess I should go," he finally said, though he didn't sound enthused.

My heart clenched at the thought of him walking away. Once he got in that truck, we'd never be back in the same place again. The next time we saw each other, it would be in the company of others, and we'd be back to the business of protecting everyone else.

"Did you want to come inside?" I asked, mentally cursing myself even as the words escaped my lips. "I could make us a cup of coffee."

"I can't drink coffee this late or I'll be up all night," he said, and I nodded, wishing I felt more relief than disappointment that he was choosing to do the right thing. "But ... a glass of iced water would be nice."

He grinned, and I grinned back as I unlocked the door and led him inside to wait in the living room while I fixed our glasses of water.

"Here ya go. It's such a lovely night tonight without the humidity. Let's sit out on the back porch."

He took the glass and gave me a nod. "I'll follow you."

Once outside, I turned on the string lights that lined the screened enclosure over the pool, and then I fluffed the pillow in a chair before motioning for him to sit in it.

The evening breeze made the wind chimes surrounding us tinkle and ping, and he smiled at the melody they played.

"I take it you like wind chimes," he said. "Your neighbors must love you."

I chuckled and sank into the solo hammock swing, figuring it was a far safer choice to keep me in check than the lounge chair beside his. "My closest neighbor is Patsy next door, a dear friend. She works here with me during the day, and she loves the sound of the chimes in the background. The people on that side have a barrier wall, and since their pool is on the opposite side of the house, I don't know if they even hear them."

He settled into the chair and took a long swig of water before setting the glass on the table next to him.

"So, tell me more about this foundation, Turtle Crossing. Where do you see it headed? What else would you like to accomplish with it? With you bringing Caroline on to do the books, it seems like you're expecting growth."

I nodded and began to explain my ideas for ways the organization could be of more help to adoptive families and foster children.

As was usually the case when I talked about the future of my passion project, I grew animated and overly talkative, but he listened intently. He even asked several questions that conveyed he was engaged in the conversation and not just making small talk to be polite.

"Do you need investors?" he asked when I'd laid out a few of the projects I hoped to get off the ground, including a transition house for teenagers who aged out of the state's system at eighteen but had nowhere to go.

"Well, I don't know of any nonprofit that turns away donations, do you? But I wasn't doing a fundraising pitch. I hope it didn't come across that way."

"Not at all," he said. "I'm interested in what you're trying to achieve, and I've learned quite a bit from you today and tonight that I didn't know was happening in my own state. My own community. I'd like to help if you'll tell me what you need."

"I appreciate that. Right now, I'm busy catching up from this hospital stay and trying to get a system in place with Caroline for the accounting. Then, maybe I can focus on the larger fish to fry."

"When you get ready to talk to builders, let me know. I've got a guy I've used for years out at the farm. I'm sure he'd be willing to give you a fair rate for a good cause."

"I'll keep that in mind. Thanks." I got up and moved to sit on the side of the pool, dipping my feet into the cool water and swinging them back and forth as I watched the ripples the movement created. "We're fortunate to have started in a pretty comfortable place, funding-wise. When my mother put her affairs in order before moving into the assisted-living facility, she told me she wanted to leave the bulk of her estate to me. That, of course, included what she had gotten from my father's estate, which he didn't want me to have and had taken legal steps to keep me from having, though I didn't want it anyway."

"It was your birthright." He came to sit on the other side of the corner from me with his jeans rolled up so that he could put his feet in the water. Our knees were almost touching, and I had to take care not to tangle our toes underwater as they dangled so close together. "Whether he liked it or not, you were his sole heir, Cat."

"It was tainted money. I didn't want what it stood for. My mother's attorney found a loophole that would have allowed me to have it, but I refused. When she begged me to take it in order to allow her to die in peace, I agreed, but only if it went to the foundation instead of me. So, that's how Turtle Crossing got its start and how it's been funded since its inception."

I laid back on the pool deck and stared up at the stars.

"I find it rather humorous, actually."

"What do you mean?" he asked.

"My father's fortune was the most important thing in his life. The thing he protected at all costs and loved more than anything or anyone. And I'm giving it all away. I'm handing it over to people who don't have the necessary money or social status to navigate adoptions on their own. People he wouldn't have given the time of day to when he was alive. He shunned his own child and grandchild, but I'm going to spend every last penny he had making it easier for people to be a family. Helping children who were left behind or who got lost in the system somehow." I let out a little chuckle. "I like to think it makes Father's blood boil in the afterlife to consider that his fortune is all going toward those less fortunate, and that I'm the one in control of that."

I sat up, careful not meet William's eyes though I could feel his stare.

"I suppose that makes me a little like him, doesn't it? That little sadistic seed of wanting him to suffer in some way. I'm sure my therapist would have plenty to say about it."

William's knee pressed against mine as he leaned over to brush back a strand of hair that the breeze had lifted across my face. His hand lingered, and then he tucked his knuckle under my chin and turned my face to look at him.

"He can't ever hurt you again," William whispered. "You've taken the worst of him and turned it into something good, and I don't begrudge you enjoying the irony of that."

Damn, I wanted him to kiss me. I wanted him to hold me. I wanted to fall asleep in his arms and wake up without panicking at the sight of the sun.

Instead, I pulled away from his touch and stood to gather our glasses and make my way back inside the house.

"Come ride with me Sunday," William said as he joined me in the kitchen.

"What?"

He pulled a chair out from the table and sat to roll down his jeans and put on his socks and shoes.

"The weather's supposed to be beautiful all weekend. Tomorrow's busy. Caroline's bringing Eva for a riding lesson, and I plan to see if I can coax Ethan into getting onto a horse, but Sunday's a pretty slow day for me. Come out, and let's take a ride. I'd love to show you the property and spend some time out in the woods."

I leaned back against the counter and crossed my arms—confused, conflicted, and intrigued.

"I thought we decided—"

"Look, you said you haven't been on a horse in a while, and I remember you loving to ride. I don't get out into nature nearly as much as I'd like to, so it would do me good to spend an afternoon enjoying it. I heard what you said about the complications and the consequences and all that. I don't see what it can hurt to just take a ride together."

We'd taken a ride to Jacksonville together, and that had caused all sorts of feelings and sensations. It had caused a lot of doubts and questions, too. But, God, it had been fun!

I hesitated for a moment longer but then nodded, sure I was going to chastise myself for the decision after he'd left, but certain I'd be miserable if I said no.

His eyes lit up, and his smile widened. "Yeah? You'll go?"

I nodded again, and he stood.

"Well, all right! I'll see you Sunday! Meet me at the house at, let's say, one-thirty?"

He was nothing but a gentleman on his way out. He didn't try to kiss me again. His hand didn't reach for mine. His gaze wasn't smoldering in the least or even the tiniest bit naughty.

He just thanked me for a lovely day and walked to his truck. Though he did look back with a grin about halfway across the yard, which I was watching for and hoping for, of course.

But how could I tell Patsy all that? How could I explain everything that had transpired? Especially when I knew it couldn't go anywhere. It couldn't mean anything. There was no reason to relive events that would only cause me sorrow if I delved too far into them. For the time being, I would keep them to myself and smile with their memory.

CHAPTER 54
Caterina

"Y ou're holding out on me," Patsy said with a suspicious grin when I told her we'd discussed mostly work.

"Okay, so we talked about religion, politics, music, art. There were a couple of times when the past came up and things got all weird, but we moved beyond it. All in all, it was a nice day."

"And night."

"He didn't stay all night. He left a little after ten," I said with a grin. "Can we get back to work please? Caroline is going to be here soon, and I want to have all those receipts organized and ready to go for her. Plus, did you see that email from the family in Leesburg? I need to respond to them right away. Being out all day yesterday put me even further behind."

"Look, I'm not one to pry—"

I laughed and gave her a look that said I knew that was a lie. "Who? *You*? Oh, no! Of course not!"

"I'm just worried, that's all. You've been through a lot lately, what with the illness, and Caroline, and everything happening all at once. I don't want to see you get hurt, love."

"Neither do I! And I don't plan on it. C'mon. Let's get back to work."

We dug into the pile of receipts on my desk and began to sort them, and just when I thought perhaps she'd decided to drop the subject, she spoke up again.

"I've never seen you act like this about somebody. You light up when you talk about him. You blush when you say his name. Your eyes are sparkling. I swear it's like someone's shot you full of Red Bull or something. You're buzzing around here all chipper, which you have *never* been in the morning. If you'd just met any other man and started acting like this, I'd be over the moon excited about it. I'd be crossing my fingers and down on my knees thanking the good Lord above."

"Why do I feel like that whole thing was a set-up for the *but* that's about to come out of your mouth?"

"Because this isn't just any man, Cat."

"Oh, believe me, I'm well aware of that."

"So, while I'm cautiously optimistic, I'm also a tad bit concerned. I think beneath that chipper giddiness, you are, too."

I exhaled in frustration and pulled my feet up into my chair, wrapping my arms around my knees.

"Of course, I'm concerned, Patsy. Who the hell wouldn't be? This whole thing has been a whirlwind. I feel like I'm in some alternative dimension and any minute I'm going to wake up from the coma again and be back in my life but this time without Caroline and William in it. I don't have the answers to how this is all going to turn out. Right now, I'm just taking things one day at a time. One moment at a time, really."

"Just be kind to yourself, Cat. You're always so focused on everyone around you. I want to make sure you're considering what you need, too."

What if what I wanted and what I needed weren't necessarily the same thing? Because I sure did want to see William Ward again, and I was counting down the hours until that was possible.

I also wanted to see my daughter and grandchildren again, and it made me antsy when the time had passed for their arrival with no word from Caroline.

When the doorbell finally rang, I sprang out of my chair and down the hallway, flinging the door open with a bit more gusto than was necessary.

"Hey, sorry I'm late," Caroline said as she came in and set her purse in the closest chair. "I would have called, but I guess one of the kids took my car charger inside, and now my phone is dead. Do you have a wall charger I could borrow?"

"Sure. Where are the kids?" I asked, looking out toward her Tahoe for any sign of them.

"That's why I'm late, actually. William offered to take Ethan for a horseback ride, and he refused, as he has done every time we've been out there. Then, when we were saying our goodbyes and ready to go, Ethan piped up and said he was ready to ride." She rolled her eyes and shook her head. "I told him he'd missed his opportunity, but William wanted to take him. And of course, then Eva wanted to stay and ride with them."

I closed the door, disappointed that the kids weren't there but happy to hear that Ethan was facing his fears. I handed her the charger cord, and she dug her phone from her purse and plugged it in.

"I hung around talking with Levi for about twenty minutes or so, just in case Ethan changed his mind and they had to come right back. But I guess he stayed in the saddle with William longer than I thought he would. Levi's said he'd call when they get back, and then he'll bring them over here for me."

"All right. Well, I think we've got everything sorted and ready to go for back here."

We walked to the office, and after a round of hugs and greetings, Patsy excused herself to run errands.

Caroline and I settled into work mode rather quickly, and her mind amazed me. The numbers and the technology came so naturally for her, and she navigated the computer systems she'd chosen with ease, though she had to slow down multiple times to explain what was happening for me, the non-techie.

She had inherited William's brain, for sure.

It still weirded me out sometimes to look at her and realize that she was my daughter. *Our* daughter.

I could catch glimmers of both of us in little movements and physical traits, and yet, she was all her own person, and a fascinating one, at that.

She noticed me staring a few times, and she'd smile when I apologized, but I caught her looking at me a couple of times, too.

"You think we'll ever get used to this?" I asked her. "That it will ever be just normal life, and we won't think twice about it?"

Her grin was wide as she nodded. "I think so. It's still new. I still feel like I have to pinch myself to make sure I'm not dreaming, you know?"

I nodded. "Oh, yeah. I know."

"Like earlier today, when William was riding away with the kids, I kept thinking, *Holy Cow! That's my father. That's their grandfather.* It still hasn't sunk in all the way. For most of my life, I knew I had parents out there somewhere, and I concocted all sorts of scenarios in my head. But now, the reality is so different than what I'd imagined."

"I hope it's not disappointing," I said, and she laughed.

"Oh, God, no. Not at all! You and William have both been so open and welcoming, and that's been awesome. I worried that if I ever found my parents, they might not want to be found."

I smiled and reached to squeeze her hand. "I'm thrilled that you reached out, Caroline."

"Me, too! I'm glad we were both looking for each other so it could work out. And then William! I still can't believe how that all came to be. I mean, it was such a random circumstance that I was driving Brad's car, and then the blow-out, and then Levi stealing the car, and then you being in the hospital. Man! It's just crazy. But without all that happening exactly as it did, I never would have crossed paths with William."

As she talked, I couldn't help but wonder if my path and William's would have crossed again if I hadn't moved back to Cedar Creek. I liked to think Caroline and I would have eventually found each other no matter where I lived. Once reunited, I would have answered her inevitable questions about her father, but after that, she probably would have sought him out on her own without me involved. If I hadn't been living minutes from him, would I have ever seen him again?

Caroline sighed and sat back in the chair. "Now, I've got this whole other family who wants to meet me, and that's a little scary, but exciting, too."

"William's family? They're good people. They're nice. Have you met his mom yet?"

"No. He told me today that she wants him to throw a party at his house to introduce me and the kids to the family."

"Wow. A party, huh? You okay with that?"

She shrugged. "William asked me the same thing. He said he wouldn't agree to it if I wasn't comfortable with it or if I thought it would be too much for the kids."

"And how do you feel about it?"

"I don't know. It kind of freaks me out to think about meeting all these people at once. But William said he didn't want anyone in his family or his circle of friends to hear hushed rumors and think he was ashamed of us in any way. He wants to claim us loudly and proudly, he said. He wants to make sure everyone knows that we're part of his family now and should be welcomed as such. Which is great, I mean, I thank him for that. I really do. But I don't know if everyone in his family will feel that same way."

She frowned and looked down at her hands.

I leaned forward and laid my hand on her arm.

"Has someone said something or done something that made you feel unwelcome?"

She shrugged and gave a weak attempt at shaking her head.

"Not really."

"What does that mean?"

"I haven't seen or talked to Piper since all this came to light. She was out of town when everything happened, and I know William's told her. I know she knows. But it's like she's avoided me any time I'm at the ranch. She hasn't talked to Levi again either, which is unusual since they're so close."

I didn't have any trouble imagining Piper upset about the new developments. My heart went out to her for the big changes in her life, but a mama bear instinct I'd never experienced came over me, and I was ready to fight for Caroline and the kids to be treated fairly.

"What does Levi say about this?"

"He said for me not to worry about it. He said Piper's a hothead, and she takes time to accept change. He also said it's not like she can do anything about the situation, so she has to get over it eventually. But that's not how I want it to be. I mean, I just found out I have a sister. A half-sister, but still. I've always wanted a sibling, and now I have one, but she doesn't want to speak to me or talk to me. It's kind of a bummer."

"What about William? Has he addressed this issue?"

"I asked him where Piper was and told him I'd love to talk to her. He said she's been staying with her cousin, Lauryn. He said she's having a hard time with things, but she'll come around, and he asked me not to worry about it. But I can't help worrying about it. I don't think Piper liked me much to start with, and this certainly hasn't helped. But Eva was very taken with her, and I hope she doesn't treat the kids differently now." She ran her fingers through her hair and sighed. "Which is also why I'm not sure about this family party. It's one thing if someone in his family snubs me or looks down their nose at me. I can handle it. And despite William's efforts to make a positive statement, the truth is that technically I'm his illegitimate kid showing up thirty-five years later to say: *Hey, guess what? I want to be part of the family.* So, I can understand if there's hesitation or judgment. I don't want the kids subjected to that, though."

I flinched at the word *illegitimate.* Anger rose up in me at the thought of Eva or Ethan being looked down upon. They were innocent in all this, as was Caroline. If William's family needed to be angry with someone or look at someone with scorn, it should be me. I was the one responsible for Caroline and the kids not being a part of his family from the beginning. No one should blame them for that or think less of them because of it.

"Why don't you tell William you don't want this party? Tell him you'd rather meet his family one by one, or in small group settings. He needs to make sure whoever you're meeting is going to be welcoming."

She smiled and reached to pat my hand. "I'm sure they will be. I can't imagine that anyone would come to his house at his invitation to meet us and then be ugly about it. I guess I'm just nervous. I shouldn't have said anything. I'm sorry. Now, I've got you all worried, too."

"No, please, Caroline. Don't ever apologize for telling me your concerns. I would hope that we could discuss any topic. I realize we don't know each other all that well yet, but I would like for us to. You can tell me anything. I promise to hear it with open ears and an open heart." I held up two fingers. "Scout's honor. Though, to be honest, I never was a scout. I'm not even sure that's the right finger formation."

We laughed together and shifted the focus back to work until the kids arrived, sweaty and rambunctious and ready to go in the pool. Patsy and George had offered to grill hamburgers and hot dogs for everyone, and so after they'd gotten their fill of swimming and had thoroughly tired Levi and Caroline out with pool basketball and several rounds of Marco Polo, we all headed next door to eat.

It was a lovely afternoon, but my thoughts kept returning to Caroline's fears. I wished I could protect her and the kids from any negativity. It also bothered me that William's daughter was having such a hard time with the situation. I hated that my actions had caused her pain, but I didn't want her pain to make her lash out at

Caroline, William, or the kids.

As much as I wanted to see him, it didn't make sense for me to go to the farm and ride with William. I couldn't imagine that Piper would be happy to see me there, and it would probably only cause more problems for everyone involved.

I texted him once Caroline had gone and I was back home alone.

I'm not sure riding tomorrow is such a good idea. Maybe another time.

He called within minutes.

"What's up? You getting cold feet about getting on a horse again? It's like riding a bicycle, I swear. You'll be right back in the groove before you know it."

"No, it's not that. I'm just not sure I should be out there."

"What do you mean? Oh, because of your lungs? You think it's going to be too much exertion?"

"No, I'd be fine, I think. The home health nurse said I'm actually ahead of where she expected me to be at this point, so I'm doing good there."

I hesitated, not wanting to betray Caroline's confidence by mentioning her concerns. It was better to keep it centered around my own experiences.

"The thing is, Piper didn't seem too happy to see me the other night, and I don't want to cause any problems."

"It won't be a problem," William said. "She's been staying at her cousin's, so she probably won't even be here. But if I changed my plans every time my daughter wasn't happy, I'd never get anything done. Now, that's not to say that I don't care if she's upset or that I don't take her feelings into consideration, but Piper has a penchant for drama. It's a delicate balance to be compassionate to her point of view but not fall prey to her every whim. I do better with it at some times than others."

"I hear what you're saying, but I don't want to be the reason she's upset. It's probably best if I stay away."

He paused, and I bit down on my lip, certain I was doing the right thing but disappointed at losing the chance to spend time with him.

"I don't want you to stay away," he said. "I want to see you. You let me worry about Piper. You just be here at one-thirty ready to ride."

CHAPTER 55
Caterina

I was relieved to see William walking toward the Jeep to greet me as I parked outside his house. I had dreaded ringing his doorbell in case Piper was home, but we got in his truck and left for the barn without any sign of her.

The horses stood saddled and waiting when we arrived, and I could barely contain my excitement. I'd had butterflies dancing in my stomach all morning, partly due to anxiety about Piper and whether or not I should be meeting up with William at all, but mostly pure adrenaline at the thought of being back on a horse. My butterflies flew into a frenzy as we approached the magnificent creatures.

"This is Sassy," William said as he handed me the reins to a gorgeous black mare. "Her official name is much longer and more dignified, but Sassy fits her better."

"She's beautiful!" I grinned as I smoothed my palm down her majestic neck, and she jerked her head up in response, as if to say hello. "Hi there, Sassy! You're not gonna send me flying off your back today, are you?"

"She's cooperative with a firm hand on the reins, but she's spirited and loves to run."

I turned to look at him with a raised eyebrow. "Is that why you chose her for me?"

He chuckled as he led his horse out into the sunlight. "I thought the two of you would get along well, yes."

We maintained a slow pace as we navigated the fenced enclosures around the barn, and then we sped up into an easy trot as we moved into the open field. Once we'd gotten past the fence lines, William looked at me with a nod.

"Go ahead. I know you both want to."

I laughed and nudged Sassy, and she was more than ready to go. We flew across the field in no time, her muscular legs pounding the earth as I braced my weight into the stirrups and synced my body's rhythm with hers.

Exhilaration coursed through my veins, and I laughed and let out a whoop of delight. I was drunk on the pure bliss of speed, and as always when I rode, I was in awe of the sheer power of the animal beneath me.

I knew at any moment she could easily throw me or choose to disregard my directions. Our partnership existed because Sassy was willing to honor it, and that knowledge made me admire and respect her strength even more.

When the distant tree line became close enough to make out individual limbs on the trees, Sassy and I slowed, and I turned in the saddle to look at William behind me.

He was grinning from ear to ear as he watched me, and he pulled up beside us with a laugh.

"Damn. I knew she was fast, but I didn't know she was that fast!"

Sassy snorted and did a little prance step, almost like he'd offended her with the statement, and I leaned down to pat her neck.

"I only gave her one nudge with my knee at the start, and that was all it took. You were right; she loves to run!"

"As do you! You should see your eyes right now. They're brilliant! The most beautiful shade of green I've ever seen."

Warmth flooded my cheeks, but then a coughing fit hit, and I doubled over the saddle, trying to catch my breath between spasms.

"Are you okay?" William asked, bringing his horse next to me as he reached for my reins.

I nodded as best I could and pulled the inhaler from my pocket.

When I'd caught my breath and the urge to cough had passed, I looked at William and smiled. He'd gone white, and his eyes were wide from fear or concern, maybe both.

"I'm fine," I said. "I just needed to open up my airways. They get a little tight sometimes." I looked away from him toward the woods. "Where to now? In there?"

"Yeah, unless you need us to turn back. You sure you're okay?"

"I'm fine! I swear!"

"We can ride another day, when you've had more time to

recover."

"William, I'm okay. I just overdid it a little. It's passed. We're good."

"If you're sure."

"I am."

He didn't look too certain, but he handed me back my reins and took the lead. "Follow me."

"We'll try to keep up," I joked, and he laughed in response.

We entered the thick forest and picked our way through the trees with no discernible path. I trusted that William knew where he was going and how to get back, but if we somehow got separated, I'd be screwed. My only hope would be Sassy knowing her way home for supper.

"How many acres do you have here?"

"Three hundred and fifty. We started with a small plot of land and then expanded it a few acres at a time as I convinced neighbors to sell. There was a company from Michigan that owned this wooded tract, the largest of the ones we bought. They'd planned to use it for lumber at some point, but that plan had never materialized, and when the company changed hands, the new CEO was willing to sell."

"What do you plan to do with it? I can't imagine that the woods would be beneficial for your horse purposes."

"No, but land is one thing they aren't making any more of, so I grab it when it's available. I've cut a few areas of timber here and there and reseeded them, but I also wanted to leave some of it untouched."

"I'm guessing we're in the untouched part," I said as I gazed around me at the tightly-packed variety of trees with its dense undergrowth. "You always did love the woods. You said in St. Augustine that you'd given them up, but you have them right here in your back yard. Surely, you must spend a lot of time out here."

"No. I haven't, and I should have." He frowned as he looked up at the canopy of treetops above us. "I should have been in these woods, wandering the trails that the animals have made. Exploring more. Communing with the solitude and peacefulness of nature. I'm outdoors all day every day, but this is different. This feeds my soul in a different way, and I need to find that part of myself again. To get back to my roots and who I was."

I smiled a sad smile, happy to hear he'd found joy in the forest again but bothered that he'd ever felt the need to give it up in the first place.

"It wasn't just because of us, mind you," he said, almost as though he could read my mind. "I don't want you feeling like you bear that burden. I got busy. Too busy. I spent all my time working and building and establishing. By the time we acquired this section of land, the farm was in full swing. Between training lessons, the rehab center, Revae's racing pursuits, and the business end of it all, there never seemed to be a free hour, much less a free day. I accomplished a lot, and I'm damned proud of what we have here, but looking back, I see where I could have done things differently."

He paused as he maneuvered his horse around a fallen tree, and then he sighed and rubbed the back of his hand across his chin.

"Revae and I were both work-oriented. We'd be out from sunup to sundown every day of the week and never think twice about it. I wish now that we'd gotten away from the farm now and then. Done more together while we were able to. Of course, we didn't know then how limited it would be. We thought we'd work hard and get it all built, and then once we retired, we'd travel. Relax. Do all the things."

His voice carried a wistful quality when he spoke of her. It was obvious her death still affected him deeply.

"I'm sorry you didn't get more time with her, William."

He looked at me and then straight ahead. "I'm sorry I didn't make more of the time I had with her." He drew in a deep breath and forced a bit of a smile. "But enough about all that. I didn't mean to get so morose."

"It's okay." I opened my mouth to add some comforting or insightful piece of wisdom, but nothing came to mind, so we rode in silence for the next little while until William abruptly stopped.

He stood in his saddle, turning left and right as he searched the woods.

"Are we lost?" I asked, alarmed at his seeming indecision.

"No," he said, shaking his head. "There's a particular spot I want to show you. Something I found when I was riding out here that first day I saw you at the hospital. We're getting close, but the rains this past week have the ground saturated. I'm trying to determine which way would be the least muddy for the horses to traverse."

He chose a direction and indicated that I should have Sassy fall in line behind him. She didn't seem to like the idea too much, and she tugged at the reins often as she tried to step to the side and assert her own path.

We bobbed up and down as she trudged along, and I hugged my thighs tightly against her sides and kept a firm grip on the saddle horn, not wanting to be pitched into the mud with her uneven steps.

William cut our path to the left, and the marsh gave way to an incline. The faint rush of water that we'd been moving toward grew louder as we climbed, but it wasn't until we'd gone over the top of the hill that the wide creek came into view.

I gasped at the sight of its winding beauty as it babbled and bubbled along.

"I thought you'd like this," William said with a wide grin.

"It's gorgeous!"

He led us down to the water's edge, and I slid off Sassy's back as she bent her head to take a cool drink.

"You said you'd just found this spot. You didn't know this was here before?"

"I knew there was a creek running through the property. More than one of them, actually. But I came across this spot where it's pooled so nicely that day, and there were ..." He paused as he scanned the area, and then he grinned and pointed. "Ah, there's one. See?"

My gaze followed his indicated direction downstream, and I laughed when I spotted it on a log that had fallen across the creek in one of its narrower spots.

"A turtle! You found me a turtle!"

He nodded, and then he turned in the opposite direction and pointed to another fallen tree that lay along the bank where the water pooled to its widest point.

"There were several on that log over there when I was here before, so when we topped the hill and it was empty, I thought this might be a bit anticlimactic. But that little fella saved me." He grinned as he turned back to the lone turtle.

Memories flooded my mind, and I resisted the urge to go to William and wrap my arms around him. He'd kept his promise to always find me turtles, even after everything that had happened and all the time that had passed.

We sat on a mossy knoll of grass along the bank and watched the water flow, content to be surrounded by nature and in each other's company. Unlike our trip to St. Augustine where the words came fast and furious, we were at ease in the silence, and there was no need to talk.

It was the horses that began to get restless after a while and signal we'd spent enough time in one place. William stood and stretched his arms high above him as he arched his back, and then he extended his hand to me.

Our eyes locked as he pulled me to standing and held my hand to his chest.

"Thank you," he said. "Thank you for coming out here with me. For making me remember how much I enjoy this."

"I didn't do anything. It was your idea. I just accepted your invitation."

He smiled and brought the back of my hand to his lips, and my heartbeat raced in response.

"I'm glad you did."

His gaze fell to my mouth, and I knew I couldn't let him kiss me. If I was ever going to stand strong and keep my distance, I had to make sure I didn't give in to him again.

Sassy neighed and pawed at the sand, and I used the distraction to pull my hand from his and step past him with a laugh.

"I think Sassy's ready to go," I said as I walked toward her. "I'm worried she might leave without us if we take much longer."

"She's not one for standing around, that's for sure. We'll head back and give her a chance to burn some energy."

The return trip seemed to go much quicker. Part of me dreaded the outing coming to a close, but another part of me was relieved that I'd been able to resist temptation. Perhaps if I kept seeing him and being around him in small doses, the urge would get easier to ward off. Maybe one day, I could be in his presence without feeling anything at all. Maybe I could condition myself and protect the ones I loved.

I looked over at him as he rode alongside me. His head was turned in the opposite direction as he stared across the field toward a fence in the distance, and I took the opportunity to have a good, long look at him. My gaze lingered on his muscular thighs outlined in the snug jeans before traveling up to his broad shoulders and the rounded bicep muscles that peeked from beneath his shirt sleeves. My perusal continued down his sculpted forearms to the strong and capable hands that rested on the saddle horn. Memories of those fingers on my skin replayed in my mind, and I shifted my weight in the saddle to ease the sensations they caused. He turned and looked at me, and my cheeks burned as I thanked the heavens above that he wasn't able to read my mind.

He smiled then, and my body betrayed me all over again by reacting in all the wrong places.

Yeah. It might happen at some point in the future, but the day when I felt nothing for William Ward was still a long way away.

CHAPTER 56
Caterina

O nce the horses were settled back into their stalls with fresh hay, William drove us back to his house.

"I'm starving," he said as he parked his truck in the space beside my Jeep. "I didn't realize how long we were out there. My cook, Gaynelle, went to her sister's in Gainesville for the day, but she left the fridge stuffed with leftovers for me. Wanna come in, and we'll see what we can scrounge up?"

"Sure," I said, telling myself it was purely for sustenance.

He had just pushed open the front door to the house when a man yelled his name from over by the two-story building.

"Yeah, Malcolm?" William shouted back.

"Sorry to bother you, Boss Man, but I got a man on the phone from Wilmington who's insisting he needs to talk to you today. Says he has to get his horse somewhere tomorrow, and he's running out of time to make arrangements. I happened to see you pull in and thought maybe you could talk to him. Seems pretty desperate."

William frowned and looked down at me.

I shrugged. "Don't put him off on my account. If you need to talk to him, talk to him."

"All right. Head on inside. Make yourself at home. I'll be back as quickly as I can."

"Take your time. I'm fine."

I pushed the door closed behind me and stood in his spacious foyer, immediately feeling like an intruder. I stared up at the crystal chandelier hanging above my head from the second story ceiling. I took in the double staircase winding up the walls on either side of me, and then I walked forward across the marble floor to look at the pictures that lined the hallway leading toward the back of the house.

The right side appeared to be pictures of Revae's family, and William's was on the left. I recognized Patricia and James right away in the older pictures, which made it easier to tell which families were theirs in the newer ones. I'd only met Helen and Henry once on the night William's mom had me over for dinner, but it was easy to pick them out in the photos as well. I smiled at the black-and-white images of William as a child, and then I stared in disbelief at a photo that was obviously William but looked like Ethan. I hadn't realized how strong their resemblance was until I saw it in the image.

As I walked farther down the hall, there were photos of Piper throughout her youth, and scattered among them were pictures of her with William and Revae.

His wife had been stunning, and I felt a ridiculous pang of jealousy as I stared at the happy trio.

She was petite, her figure a perfect hourglass in the snug riding clothes she wore. Her dark black hair was a stark contrast to her pale, milky skin, and her smile radiated warmth.

She was several inches shorter than William, and in later photos, even Piper towered over her, but she didn't in any way seem diminutive. She exuded confidence, and she had a fiery air about her that seemed to burn through the camera's lens. I suspected it was the same fire I'd seen in her daughter during the only encounter we'd had.

I wrapped my arms around my waist and stared at the photos as a maelstrom of emotions swirled inside me.

The selfless part of me who loved William enjoyed seeing him happy. It was impossible to deny he had been when I looked at his broad smile and the evident joy he wore as he stood with Piper seated on his shoulders or in another shot with his arms wrapped around his beautiful wife.

But a dark filter overlaid my glee.

I couldn't help but envy the woman who'd shared his house and his bed.

She'd gone to sleep in his arms every night and woken by his side each day. She'd built a home and a business with him, and she'd shared his dreams and helped make them a reality.

Like me, she'd carried his child, but he'd been there for it. I could picture his smile the first time he felt his daughter move within his wife's belly. I imagined him laying his head on Revae's stomach and talking to their baby as they waited for her arrival. Had he massaged Revae's back once her center of gravity had pitched forward and made her ache when she walked or stood? Had he been there when Piper was born? Had he held Revae's hand when she groaned in agony, and whispered affirmations to her in the lull between contractions?

Except for Nonna's loyal presence, I'd experienced pregnancy and childbirth alone. Banished. In exile. Shamed and tossed aside. How different it must have been to bring a child into the world together with the man you loved. The man you'd created that child with.

I reached to trace my finger over an image of Piper on a horse with William standing on the ground beside her. She couldn't have been more than two or three at the time. He'd probably taught Piper to ride. He must have been a wonderful father to grow up with. Perhaps he held her tiny hands as she took her first steps. He'd likely cradled her in his arms when she cried. And knowing his love for reading, I was certain he sent her to sleep each night with a bedtime story.

My heart wrenched for all my daughter had missed, and I cursed the universe for robbing the three of us of the life we should have had.

I turned away from the pictures, knowing that train of thought would get me nowhere.

It wasn't Revae's fault or Piper's that William and I hadn't lived our dreams together. But it didn't make it hurt any less to see proof that they had.

There was a small door open beneath the stairs, and through it, I could see a room awash with pink. I ducked beneath the arched frame to keep it from grazing the top of my head as I stepped inside.

Once I was in the room, the space opened into high ceilings with a pink crystal chandelier hanging in the center. An enormous leopard print chaise lounge dominated the floor space of the tiny room, and in the opposite corner sat an antique desk with a pink velvet chair behind it. Bright, colorful paperback titles filled the bookshelves that lined the wall on either side of the door where I'd entered, but my attention was focused on the massive painting that covered most of the far wall.

I walked toward it, captivated by its vibrant life-size image.

It was Revae standing next to a horse. She wore tight, brown riding breeches and a white collared shirt that was unbuttoned at the throat. A riding hat sat atop her raven locks, and she stood with one hand on her hip and the other resting on the horse.

I moved even closer to get a better look, drawn in by the chance to stand face-to-face with William's wife. Though she was fully-clothed, her expression and her stance were provocative. The artist had captured her sensuality and her confidence in the pose, and she stared at me from the canvas with a look in her eyes that seemed to issue a smug challenge.

"What are you doing in here?" Piper demanded from behind me.

I hadn't realized she was in the house, and I jumped at the sound of her voice. My hip bumped the small table next to me, and a tiny porcelain lamp crashed to the floor, shattering into pieces.

"Oh, God! I'm so sorry," I said, kneeling beside the mess as Piper rushed to my side.

"Get away from that! Don't touch it!"

I stood to face her as she looked down at the jagged shards.

"You broke my mother's lamp!"

"I-I-I didn't mean to," I stammered. "It-it was an accident. You startled me, and I—"

"What were you doing in here?" she asked, her eyes flaring with anger. "You have no business being in my mother's study. Who told you that you could come in here?"

"No one. The door was open—"

"And so you just let yourself in? Why are you in my house? What are you doing here?"

"Your father and I were riding, and he had to go take a call."

She stepped closer to me, and I could feel the heat of hurt and anger rolling off her.

"I want you to get out of my house. Now. I want you to leave and not ever come back. My father doesn't need your bullshit in his life. I don't know what game you're up to, but it ends now, do you hear me?"

My alarm at her unexpected arrival had begun to wear off, and my defenses kicked in gear in response to her attack.

"I'm not up to any kind of game, Piper, I swear. Your father invited me to come for a ride, and then he suggested we make something to eat. The door was—"

"I don't wanna hear it. I don't trust you, and I don't want you around my father. Haven't you already hurt him enough? Haven't you already done enough to screw up his life?"

"Piper! That's enough," William growled from the doorway, ducking to get inside the room. "Stop it."

"I'm gonna go," I said, stepping past Piper as William moved forward to block my exit.

"No, stay," he said. "I apologize for my daughter's behavior. I don't know what got into her, but she doesn't speak for me, nor does she make decisions for my life."

The two of them locked eyes like a couple of bulls staring each other down, each waiting for the other to make its move.

"I think it's best if I go," I whispered. "I don't want to cause any drama."

"You're not," he said to me, though his eyes never left his daughter's.

"I found her in here," Piper said. "What reason would she have to be in Mom's study?"

"The door was open," I said to William. "I shouldn't have—"

"This door is never open," Piper said. "Never."

"It was," I protested as I turned to her. "I swear, it was. I know I shouldn't have come in, but the door was open."

"She's right," William said, his steely gaze unflinching as he stared at her. "It was open. I came in here earlier with the new ranch hand's wife and their daughter. He'd mentioned they enjoy reading romance, and I invited them inside to borrow some of your mother's titles. They were the last to leave the room, and I intended to come back after I walked them out to shut it, but I forgot."

Piper's eyes darted from her father's to mine and then back to his as her full lips tightened into a grim line. She didn't seem to like being wrong.

"I still don't see why she had any business being in here."

"Enough," William said.

She moved past us both and out the door, and it felt like all the energy left the room with her.

"I'm sorry, William," I said when she'd gone. "I shouldn't have been in here, and then I bumped into the lamp and—"

I pointed in the direction of the mess I'd made.

He looked at the pieces of porcelain scattered on the pink carpet and shook his head.

"Don't worry about it. I'm sorry about Piper. She's having a hard time with everything, but that's no excuse for her behavior."

"No, please. I understand. She saw me in here, in her mother's space, and she had strong feelings about it."

"I'll have a talk with her."

"No," I said, pressing my hand to my forehead. "She's right. I have no business being here. It's complicated enough the way it is, and we've already discussed that it's best for everyone involved if we don't see each other."

I moved to walk toward the door, but he reached out to put his hand on my forearm.

"Cat, don't go."

I closed my eyes and drew in a deep breath, trying to ignore that his hand was like a torch on my skin and that my heart felt like it might shatter into pieces more irreparable than the porcelain lamp.

"Your daughter needs you, William." I pulled my arm from his grasp and forced myself to look at him as I exhaled. "She needs to know that she still matters, and that Caroline doesn't affect what the two of you share. She needs to know that you're not in any danger of being hurt, and she's not in any danger of being set aside."

"I'm—" He started to protest but I held my fingers to his lips.

"Shh. Go to her. Not to bitch at her and tell her you think she was being rude, though. Go put your arms around her, and tell her that you love her, and that you're not going anywhere. That you're going to be right here for her the way she needs you to be. The way you've always been. Piper's already lost her mom. She has to be scared that she's going to lose you, too. Make sure she knows she won't."

I held my head high and remained calm as I left Revae's husband standing in her study, and I didn't even cry until I was off her property and back out on the main road.

I kept telling myself it was enough that I had Caroline back in my life. It was enough that I had Eva and Ethan, and that William had forgiven me. It had to be enough, for it was all I would be allowed to have.

CHAPTER 57
William

A fter Cat left, I cleaned up the broken lamp and went to empty the pieces from the dustpan into the kitchen trash can. I had just hung the broom in its place in the pantry when I saw Piper sitting on the back-porch swing.

She didn't acknowledge me when I came outside, and she crossed her arms over her chest and looked away when I sat next to her.

"We gotta come to some kind of understanding with all this, sweetheart."

I rubbed my hand over the stubble of my beard and prayed for the right words to come.

"You know I love you. I have since before I laid eyes on you. There's nothing that could change that."

Her silence filled the air, and even the breeze seemed to stop blowing under the weight of her anger.

"Piper, the last thing I want is for you to be upset. I'd give anything in this world for you to never feel pain, but that's out of my control."

She didn't react or respond, so I took a deep breath and kept going.

"I suppose you might feel like I'm part of what's causing your pain right now, but I never meant for any of this to happen. I didn't know about Caroline, but now that I do, I need to do right by her. I certainly didn't expect Caterina to ever come back into my life, but she has, and I'm doing my best to figure out what that means. I wish you could understand that I haven't done any of this on purpose to hurt you or piss you off. This ball started rolling long before you were born."

She made a scoffing sound, and I turned to face her.

"Aren't you going to say anything? It's not like you to give me the silent treatment. Can't we discuss this?"

"There's nothing to discuss," she said at last, though she still didn't look at me. "You're going to do what you want to do, and everyone is going to be okay with it but me."

"I don't view this as me doing what I want to do. I view this as me doing the best I can with the circumstances I've been given. But to your point, if everyone else seems to be able to find a way to adjust and be supportive, why can't you?"

She turned to glare at me.

"Because everyone else isn't affected by this the same way I am, are they?"

She looked away again. I exhaled and wished her mother was still alive. Revae had always been so much better than me at handling Piper's emotions.

"Sweetheart, help me understand what it is you're so angry about. Is it Caroline? Or is it Caterina?"

"Both."

"All right, well, let's talk about it. There's not a thing I can do about Caroline being mine. She was conceived long before I even met your mother or had an inkling of you existing. But the fact of the matter is, she's here, and she's part of this family. I need you to realize that this doesn't change my feelings for you, and it doesn't make our relationship any less special. Now, I don't know what else I can say or what else I can do to get you to understand that. But this girl has come into our lives and brought Eva and Ethan into our lives, and we are going to make room for them. Plain and simple."

Piper continued to stare across the lawn toward the trees in the distance.

I took in a few more breaths as I considered what I wanted to say about the other issue she was upset about. That one was more prickly. With Caroline, it was pretty cut and dried. Black and white. She was my daughter, and that was that. There was no question in my mind of whether or not I would be a part of her life and the kids' lives moving forward.

Piper might be slow to warm to the idea, but I felt certain that once the shock wore off and she began to spend more time with Caroline and the kids, she would see the value in having a sibling and a niece and nephew. I had no doubt that Piper's heart would expand eventually to include them in her family circle, and then she'd protect them as fiercely as she did all of us.

But Caterina was a different story.

She herself had said that it would be best for everyone if we didn't get involved, and I knew that on many levels, she was right.

Having Cat in the picture made it harder for Piper to accept Caroline. My daughter couldn't see the two as separate entities, and she saw them as a double-threat working together to dismantle life as she knew it before they arrived.

Perhaps if I waited until Piper was over the hump with Caroline, then it might be easier for her to accept Cat in my life. But what if it never was easier? I'd already lost thirty-six years with Caterina, and I wasn't too keen on losing any more without knowing if what we felt for each other was real.

I felt like it was. I knew Cat felt it, too. Despite her protests and her attempts to keep everyone safe by putting distance between us, it was there. It was in her eyes when she looked at me. It was in her voice when she spoke of our past. It was in her kiss on the beach after St. Augustine.

There were no guarantees it would last, of course. No way to know if it could stand the test of daily life and all its stresses and complications.

What we'd shared before had been between two teenagers with no responsibilities, no commitments other than school and my mundane jobs, and no real obstacles other than our societal differences and her parents ruling over her life, neither of which would be issues any longer.

We were adults now. Both of us came with no small amount of baggage attached. We'd developed habits and quirks and ways of thinking that weren't likely to be changed at our ages. We both had scars that ran deep and hurts that shaped who we were and how vulnerable we'd allow ourselves to be with another human being.

I had no illusions that it would be easy to make a go of it with Caterina. But I'd already lost her once, and I'd be damned if I was going to let her go again without even considering giving it a try.

But how could I make Piper understand how important that was to me? How could I open my heart back up to the first woman I ever loved without hurting the woman I'd nurtured and adored from the moment I knew her mother carried her?

If only I could make Piper see that whether or not I pursued Cat held no bearing on my feelings for her or for Revae. Each of them had a separate compartment in my heart. They didn't have to compete. They had each carved out their own space.

A thought occurred to me, and I wondered if perhaps it might help Piper if I could put it into words.

"You know how when you go to the bank, you can open multiple accounts?"

She turned and looked at me as if I was nuts.

"What?"

"Go with me for a minute. I swear I'm getting to a point here."

She looked away again.

"Let's say you opened a savings account, and you put some money in it. Then let's say you open another one, and you put money in that one. And then you open two more, and put the same amount of money in them."

"What are you talking about?"

"Listen, and you'll see. Now, you can have the same amount of money in all those accounts. You don't have to take money out of one just because you open another one."

"Yeah, well, eventually you'd run out of money doing that. Why wouldn't you just put all your money into one account and not have to keep up with so many different ones? And why are we discussing banking all of the sudden? Where are you going with this?"

"Let's say you have plenty of money. Money's no object. You can put as much in the accounts as you want. The point is, it doesn't take anything away from one account for you to love another one. I mean, for you to put money into another one."

She turned in the swing and faced me. "Is this some really bad analogy that's supposed to justify you trusting that woman? Because illustrating that she can take all your money and put it in a separate account is not a good argument."

I groaned and rubbed my hands across my face. "Okay, forget the money! Let's say they're heart accounts. Like, savings accounts, but in your heart instead of a bank."

Piper stood and pressed her fingers to her temples. "This is ridiculous. I don't want to talk about savings accounts or heart accounts. I don't want to talk about anything, okay? I get it, Dad. I get that you have this other daughter, and she has to be part of our family. I get that you can't just turn your back on her, and that you want to get to know her and she wants to get to know you. But just because I understand it doesn't mean I have to like it."

She paced back and forth across the porch once as I leaned forward to rest my elbows on my knees, and then she stopped to face me again.

"I appreciate you trying to explain all this and reassure me, but no matter what words you use, it still sucks. I'm still not your only kid any more. There's always gonna be this other person now that was never here before. You have grandkids now. I always assumed I'd give you your first grandchild, but now? *Boom!* You've got two, and I had no part in it. By the time I find someone and get to the point of having kids, you'll be old hat at this. It won't even be special anymore."

"That's not true."

"And then, as if Caroline wasn't enough to deal with, you bring this woman into your life and suddenly, you're all gaga for her. What the hell? The only woman I've ever seen you with is my mother. I thought she was the only person you ever loved, and now I find out there's this other woman, this other daughter, this other life. I feel like I don't even know who you are. It's like you're kicking the life you had with us to the curb and trading it in for a life with these other people because you never got to have it. What about us? What about me and Mom?"

I stood and tried to go to her, but she took a step back, never one to be hugged or embraced if she was upset, even when she was a small child.

"Piper, this doesn't erase the life I've shared with you and your mother. It doesn't take anything away from that. You know, if I'd had my say, your mom would still be here. We wouldn't have lost her. But we did, and there's nothing I can do or say to bring her back."

"So, you're just going to replace her?"

"What? No. I couldn't do that even if I wanted to. No one will replace your mom. No one will even try."

She groaned in rage and walked toward the pool.

"So, that's what this is about?" I asked as I followed her. "Is that what you're thinking? That I'm replacing your mother? It's been four years, Piper. Four long, lonely, dark years. I've missed her more than I ever knew I could miss someone, but she's not coming back, and I have to go on with life. I can't just curl up out there in the woods somewhere and die with her."

"I don't expect you to," she said, whirling around to face me. "But I can't bear the thought of you loving someone else. I'm sorry, but I can't! It makes it feel like she's dying all over again, except this time, you're killing her."

Her words stunned me, and we stood staring at each other until she moved past me to go back inside the house.

I carried my own feelings of guilt about moving on, but Revae was gone, and there was nothing I could do to change that. Since cancer took her from me, I'd resigned myself to living the rest of my life alone. I'd never looked for anyone else, and I hadn't given any thought to what it would be like to find love again. I assumed I'd found it and I'd lost it, end of story.

But with Cat, it was like my heart had come back to life and was beating again. Suddenly, life held new possibilities that I hadn't dared consider. I wanted love in my life, Cat's love, and in all the heart-searching I'd done since I realized that, not once had I felt that it would be cheating on Revae or a crime against our marriage to pursue my feelings. It would have been different had Revae still been alive, of course, but she wasn't. I'd been faithful to her and to the vows we'd pledged, but those vows were until death do us part, and death had parted us far too soon.

Unfortunately, Piper obviously didn't see it that way.

I feared my daughter would never support me having a relationship with another woman. It would never be anything less than a betrayal in her mind. And although it was probably harder with Caterina than it would be with someone else because of our history and Caroline, Piper wasn't going to accept it no matter who it was.

But me staying alone for the sake of Piper's feelings wouldn't bring her mother back.

She was sitting on the bench by the front door pulling on her boots when I came back inside. I leaned against the stair bannister and watched her. In my mind, I could see her pulling on those boots at every age from two to twenty-four.

She'd always been a spitfire, and I'd loved that about her because it was her mother, through and through. Piper had been riding a horse since before she could talk in complete sentences. She'd earned praise and awards as the youngest show jumper ever to win in multiple competitions. She'd always sailed off the highest diving board, picked the biggest fight, and attempted the most difficult lessons.

She'd been fearless her entire life, but she was scared now, and I knew it was an unfamiliar feeling for her.

It killed me to think that she was scared because of me.

Revae and I had never coddled her. We'd never babied her or made a fuss when she stumbled or missed a mark. But I'd also never been the direct cause of her fears.

Was I neglecting her needs for my own? Or was this an instance where she should confront things head on and I should push her to do so and support her through it?

Her mother's death had been hard on us both, and it was obvious that Piper was still dealing with unresolved issues from that trauma. I needed to be sensitive to that, but at the same time, I didn't see where it would help either one of us if I fed into her insecurities and encouraged them.

She needed to face them, as she had every other challenge in life.

Or was I being too callous?

My thoughts whipped back and forth as I sought the right answer.

Was I justifying my own behavior to make myself happy at my daughter's expense? How could I know if the choices I made would be what was best for both of us?

She stood and stared at me, her eyes defiant.

I sighed and walked to stand closer to her, careful not to invade the wide personal space she required.

"How long should I wait, Piper? When will it be okay with you for me to see someone? It's been four years. If I wait one more, is that enough? If I wait five more, then will it not hurt? How long until it's okay if I feel again? Or am I ever allowed to love someone else?"

She turned and walked out the door without a word.

CHAPTER 58
Piper

My father's words and actions had enraged me, and I had to get on a horse and get away from everyone and everything as soon as possible. It felt like I was going to explode from within, and I needed wide open spaces to contain it if it happened.

Levi stepped out of a stall as I walked down the stable lane, and he swung his arm across my path and blocked me from passing with a huge grin on his face.

"Hey! Hold up! Where you goin' so fast?"

"Now's not the time. Let me go."

His grin faded, and his face filled with concern as he dropped his arm.

"Whoa, whoa, whoa. What's up, girl?"

"Levi, just leave me alone. Please?"

I moved past him to grab a saddle, gritting my teeth to keep from unleashing all my anger and frustration on him.

"You wanna talk about it?" Levi asked as he leaned against the stall door.

Any other time, I would have poured out my heart to him and welcomed his support and his advice, as I'd always done. But he had betrayed me, and he was a piece of my pain.

"Not with you, I don't."

"Wow. What does that mean? Did I do something to piss you off and miss enjoying it?"

He smiled, but I glared at him and his sarcasm as I walked back past him with the saddle.

"Don't act oblivious when you're part of the problem, Levi."

"I'm not acting anything. I just want to make sure you're okay."

"Really?" I lifted the saddle to set it on the horse's back and adjusted it on the saddle pad. "Because you haven't exactly been knocking down my door or blowing up my phone to check on me since I confronted you that night."

"You haven't been around! You've been avoiding everybody when you're here during the day and then staying at Lauryn's at night. Besides, you usually let people know when you have something to say. I figured you'd reach out when you were ready, when it was a good time."

"Yeah, well, now's not a good time." I reached beneath the horse for the front cinch, but he moved to grab it and hand it to me before I could get it.

"If you won't talk to me, would you at least talk to your dad? He's been awfully worried about you."

"We just had a conversation a few minutes ago."

"Oh, good, but I'm guessing from your mood that it didn't go well?"

I walked around the front of the horse and stared at him over the her back.

"Don't you have anything else to do?"

"Nothing more important than this."

"Right." I rolled my eyes and went back to preparing the horse for my ride.

Levi sighed and leaned back against the stall wall. "If you'd take a break from being so damned angry at everyone, you might see that the situation isn't nearly as bad as you think it is. No one's out to take anything away from you, and no one's scamming your dad. I don't know if you've noticed, but he actually seems quite happy. He's been walking around here whistling and telling jokes. I haven't seen him in this good of a mood since before your mom died. I'm thrilled for him. I think if you'd get out of your own head for a little bit, you might be, too."

"Well, of course, you're thrilled. You're walking around in a butterflies-and-rainbows trance of your own."

"Ooh, careful, P. You don't want to sound like a Bitter Betty."

"Piss off, would you?" I took the reins and led the horse out of the stall, not caring that the move penned Levi in the corner until we passed.

"Dammit, Piper," he said as he followed me toward the barn

door. "I know change is hard for you. I get that things feel out of control, which we both know you don't like. But some of us have good things going on right now, and would it be too much to ask that you not make everyone feel like asses for being happy?"

I stopped and turned to stare at him.

"Nice. I love how you ask if I'm okay when you know I'm not, and then you tell me to get over myself so you can be happy. Screw you, Levi. Screw you and your girlfriend. And her mama, too."

I clucked my tongue to the horse and exited the barn with Levi hot on my heels.

He moved past me and grabbed the bridle to halt the horse, and then he stood in front of me, his jaw tight and his brown eyes dark with emotion.

"You know, I've always defended you when people called you a brat or a bitch for speaking your mind and standing up for yourself. I've told them you're just confident and assertive, and that you were raised not to take any shit off anyone. But I've never seen this selfish side of you before. The Piper I know has a huge heart, and she'd do anything in the world for her family and her inner circle on this farm. I've seen you bend over backwards to welcome people when they arrive to work here, but you refuse to treat Caroline the same way you would anyone else who joined this motley crew, and she actually is part of your family now!"

"Just because we have the same father doesn't mean we're automatically family."

"Well, yeah, by definition, it sort of does. Even so—you've always said you consider me family, and Caroline means the world to me. Couldn't you find it in your heart to try and accept her for that reason if nothing else?"

"Are we done? I'd really like to get in a ride before the sun sets."

His lower jaw moved left and right as though he were grinding his teeth together, and then he released the bridle and stepped back.

"Ultimately, it's your loss, Piper. Caroline's a great lady, and you're missing out by not giving her a chance."

I swung myself into the saddle and left him standing there, but his words wouldn't stop screwing with my head.

How dare he insinuate that I was being selfish or unreasonable. Levi and my father had both gained something with the arrival of these women. I was the only one losing anything in the equation, and no one seemed to understand that. It seemed like Lauryn was the only one who cared how I was affected. Why should it be on me to welcome these women or pretend to be happy that they'd shown up and screwed up my life?

CHAPTER 59
Caterina

When my doorbell rang, I was in the process of writing an email to a senator to oppose a bill he was supporting. After the confrontation with Piper at William's, I'd come home emotionally spent but agitated and angry at the world. I'd done as many laps in the pool as my compromised lungs would allow, and then I'd fumed in the bath for a while. When my irritability still wouldn't subside, I decided it was the perfect time to take my frustration out on a lawmaker and I'd started typing.

The chime interrupted my train of thought, and I stomped down the hallway and peered through the peephole, ready to give hell to whoever had dared to bother me on a Sunday night. But when I saw who stood there, I flipped on the porch light and opened the door in surprise.

"William!"

"Can I come in?"

He looked tired, much more so than when I'd seen him just a couple of hours earlier.

"Of course." I stepped back to let him enter, and then I closed the door behind him.

"I hope it's not a bad time," he said. "I should have called first, but I didn't know I was coming. I've been driving around in circles and somehow, I ended up here."

"It's fine. I was just catching up on emails. Could I get you something to drink? Tea? Water?"

"No. I'm good. I just needed to talk to you."

He seemed nervous. He kept shifting his weight on his feet and rubbing his hands together, and his behavior only served to rev up the anxiety I already felt.

"Okay, have a seat," I said as I motioned toward the couch. I settled in the papasan chair with my legs folded beneath me as I crossed my arms and prepared for whatever may come next. "Is everything all right? Did you talk with Piper?"

He took a deep breath and rubbed his hands back and forth across the top of his head as he sat down, and then he looked at me with a timid smile.

"Yeah, I did. Which is why I had to get out of the house and drive. To be alone and think, to consider the decisions I had to make. I guess I knew all along what I needed to do, but I had to make sure I was thinking it through. That I was looking at it from all sides. Weighing the outcomes."

A sick feeling settled in the pit of my stomach.

I'd told him it was best if we didn't see each other again, and I believed that. But somehow, it felt completely different if he'd come to tell me he believed it, too.

I shouldn't have spent time with him. I shouldn't have allowed myself to get close to him. I'd left my heart vulnerable to be hurt, foolishly thinking I had some measure of control. Now, I would pay the price for it.

I braced for his words, ready to force a smile and agree that it was the right thing. It *was* the right thing, after all. I had to be okay with it. This was what was best for everyone else.

He sat forward to brace his arms on his thighs, clasping his hands together.

"You know, I never have been able to start a book without finishing it."

The statement was unexpected, and the reaction smile I'd planned faltered as he kept going.

"Even if I don't care for the story, or if it has holes in it, or if a character gets on my nerves, I have to finish it. I have to see it through. No matter how bad it gets, I just can't lay the book down and walk away from it. I have to know what happens in the end."

He smiled, but his blue eyes seemed somber.

"Our story had its share of conflicts, but it was a good story. I wanted to be in it. I wanted to know what happened next." He cleared his throat and looked down. "But then, it was like the book got ripped out of my hands, and I never had closure. I moved on to another story that was deep and fulfilling, but there was always this unfinished chapter, this open-ended narrative. Blank pages waiting to be written."

He stood and came to kneel on one knee beside me, taking my hand into his own.

"We didn't get to write the ending to our story, Cat." His smile widened, finally reaching his eyes. "I think that means it's not over yet."

I pulled my hand back and ran my fingers through my hair as his words sunk in. I'd been wrong about his conclusion, and the pain of losing him from moments before was replaced by a different kind of panic.

It would be so easy to buy into his narrative and get lost in it, but I had to keep a clear head. I had to think about the people affected by us and what price they would pay if we screwed up again.

"That sounds so romantic," I said as I met his eyes. "I wish I could just fall into your arms and tell you I'm ready to be your heroine, but life isn't a fairy tale, William. We don't get the guaranteed happy ending. We've got Caroline and the kids to think about. Piper, too. They've been through enough. We can't ask them to go through more."

"But don't you think their lives would be better if we were both happy? I think we could be happy together, Cat. We were before. We could be again."

"We don't even know each other," I said as I stood and walked across the room to put space between us. I couldn't think clearly with him smiling at me the way he was. "We had a summer fling decades ago, and we've both lived an entire lifetime since we parted. We had very little in common then, and I don't know that we have any more now."

He stood and turned to face me.

"I think we've gotten along pretty well so far. I can think of several things we have in common."

I put my hand on my hip and stared at him. "Counting our road trip the other day and our ride this afternoon, we've spent less than twenty-four hours together. Anyone can find common ground for one day."

"True. Did you say summer fling? That's what you think we had?"

"I, um, I just, well, I…"

He grinned at my discomfort, and I cursed under my breath as he stepped in closer. He didn't stop until we were only a couple of inches apart, his eyes darting back and forth as they searched mine.

"It wasn't a summer fling for me," he whispered. "I was in love with you. I planned to marry you."

"You were in love with Catherine. She was a foolish girl, and I've worked my whole life to be nothing like her."

I tore my gaze from his and walked past him.

"I see many similarities between Caterina and Catherine," he said. "You have the same sense of humor. The same free spirit. You're both rebellious, but you use it to help others. You buck the system, buck the law. You do whatever you have to do to cut through the bullshit and make things happen for the families and kids you work with. You're both passionate, and I see your dedication to these kids and these families as an extension of the passion you had for animals back then. It's that same desire to help the defenseless. To seek justice and be a voice for those who can't speak. You're both strong. Survivors. Fighters. Tough yet tender."

The portrait he painted of me felt so different from what I saw, and my throat grew tight.

He walked toward me, and I crossed my arms to form a barrier between us.

"Let me get to know you, Caterina. You're right; it's been a long time. But I want to know who you are now. How you like your eggs. What keeps you awake at night. What you order at a Japanese restaurant. What brings you to tears, and what would make you scream out my name in the surrender of passion. We have a second chance, Cat. Our paths have crossed again, and we'd be damned fools not to at least give this a shot."

I wavered.

Was it wrong that I wanted to give in so badly? Was it ridiculous to think that we might be able to do it?

I raised my hand to my throat, swallowing against the lump that just wouldn't go down.

"What if we don't make it?" I whispered.

He smiled and came a step closer.

"Ah, but Cat, what if we do? What if ours is destined to be a happily-ever-after kind of tale?"

He put his arms around me, and I pushed him away.

"I can't. I can't do this. I blindly pursued what I wanted before without considering the consequences, and it ended up hurting everyone around me. I can't do that again."

"I know you're scared. Hell, you think I'm not? I don't want anyone to get hurt either. That's why I was driving this evening, churning everything over and over in my head to figure out the right answer."

"And this is what you came up with?"

He nodded. "We have to try. We may fail, but we have to try."

I shook my head. "No. I won't put my own needs ahead of everyone else's. I can't."

"Don't you think you have the right to be happy, too?"

"No. No, I don't. I screwed everything up, William!"

"What's screwed up? Tell me. We have a beautiful daughter who is alive and happy and thriving. She has two fantastic kids who are smart and funny and eager to learn. Maybe we could have all gotten off to a better start if things had happened differently, but that's not how the cards got dealt. We're all fine now. Caroline is fine. She's in a good place. She's forgiven you. She wants you in her life, and she's not asking you to be miserable." He held his hand to his chest. "Look at me! I'm fine. I've lived a good life. I've been happy. I already told you I don't think I have anything to forgive you for. The only person having trouble forgiving you is you. The only person who wants to keep punishing you is you."

"It's not about punishment. It's about making different choices. It's about learning from my mistakes and putting others first."

"Okay, so what about me? Do I have a choice in the matter? I didn't have a choice back then, and neither did you, really. Are you going to give me a choice this time? Because I choose you. I choose love. I've lived with it and without it, and maybe I'm greedy as all hell for wanting more of it, but I choose to have love in my life, and that love is you. It's been you since the first time I saw you, and I'll be damned if I'll let you push me away when we have a chance to actually give this a go."

He moved closer again, and I closed my eyes to hold back the tears.

"I know you love me, Cat. Let me love you. Let me hold you. I learned the hard way that none of us are guaranteed tomorrow, and I don't want to waste another minute without you by my side."

I forced my eyes open and forced my question out.

"What about Piper?"

His smiled faded, and he rubbed his lips together.

"That's gonna be tough. She's dealing with some issues—some of which I didn't realize the extent of until now. I intend to do everything I can to help her confront them and work through them, but I'm not willing to lose us to her fears. Depriving myself of love and happiness won't ensure that Piper feels secure." His chuckle was uneasy as he shook his head and rubbed his hand over the back of his neck. "Hell, she's spent the past two years trying not to be my daughter, and at some point, she's going to have work through that, too. But she's tough as nails."

"Sometimes the people who seem the toughest are the ones who need our love the most."

"She has my love. She always will."

I walked to the couch and sank into it, pulling my knees up to my chest and hugging my arms around them.

"This whole situation is so precarious, William. Everyone's trying to merge lives, blend families, and juggle feelings. I just worry that if we do this, and then it doesn't work out between us, we've made it that much harder on them all."

"You know what? They'll be fine. Really. Life is messy. Relationships are messy, and families have drama. It just happens." He sat next to me and leaned back so that our shoulders were touching as he turned his head to face me. "But why not think positive? Think about how great it could be if we make it work. We get to spend the rest of our lives together with two beautiful daughters and our amazing grandchildren."

I laid my head back against the sofa cushions, and he reached to stroke my cheek.

"I love you, Cat. I know you love me, too. Say you'll give us a chance."

My head and heart both felt like they would explode with the conflict, and I closed my eyes and drew in the deepest breath I could manage, holding it for a moment before releasing it nice and slow. I'd hoped the action would lower my blood pressure and help calm my nerves so I could think more clearly, but it didn't work.

"You know what?" William said as he sat up and turned his body to face me. "You don't have to decide right this minute. Take your time; think about it. But I would ask one thing of you."

"What's that?" I said as I opened my eyes to look at him.

"There's something I've wanted to do since the first time I saw you. Something I never got to do before."

I tilted my head in curiosity. "What?"

"What are you doing tomorrow night?" he said, his smile so wide that it was contagious. It made me grin despite the circumstances.

"I don't have any plans. Why?"

"Because I want to drive to your house, ring your doorbell, and pick you up for a proper date."

I blinked a couple of times as I processed his request. "You're asking me out on a date?"

"I am. I want to take you out to a nice restaurant. I want to linger over a lovely meal and have dinner conversation as I gaze across the table at you."

When I hesitated to answer, he held up his hand as though he was about to be sworn in for testimony.

"No strings attached, no answers needed to the bigger questions. We won't even mention the future. I just want to spend an evening with you in a way we never could before when we were dating. Will you give me that opportunity?"

My heart pleaded with me to say yes, and nothing else in me was strong enough to say no. I wanted it just as badly as William did, and I reasoned that one date couldn't hurt anyone. It was only dinner, after all.

I nodded, and his smile grew even wider until it filled his face and created crinkles around his eyes.

"Yes?" he asked to confirm. "You're saying yes?"

"Yes." I nodded again. "I'll go on one date with you, William Ward."

CHAPTER 60
Caterina

"You look stunning," Patsy said as I turned in the mirror to survey the low-cut back of the little black dress.

"You're sure this dress is okay? I mean, he did say a nice restaurant, but it's Cedar Creek. It's not like there's some Michelin-rated place around the corner. Maybe the dress is too much."

"That dress is va-va-voom. It really showcases your legs."

"Do you think it's too short? And do I really want to go for va-va-voom? Maybe I should wear pants. I might be too old for this dress."

"Nonsense," Patsy said with a satisfied grin as she crossed her arms. "You have fabulous legs, and there's no reason you shouldn't show them off. Besides, it's not that short. I've seen some of these young girls running around with their butt cheeks nearly exposed. Your bottom is plenty covered, and you don't have your belly or your boobs hanging out. You look classy but sexy. I'm telling you, that's the dress. That's what you need to wear. That'll knock his socks off."

I tugged at the hemline to pull it down lower. "Is that what we're going for? Knocking socks off? I thought you were the one telling me to be cautious. This is not a cautious dress."

"Well, I do think you need to take things slow. I'm not saying to bring him home and take him to bed tonight, but I don't think it will hurt to make sure you have his attention."

"Oh, I'm pretty sure I have his attention. That's not an issue."

She began to hang up the clothes I'd discarded during our makeshift fashion show to choose the right outfit.

"When are you going to tell Caroline you guys are seeing each other?"

I sighed as I opened my jewelry box to select a pair of earrings. I hadn't told Patsy yet about my conversation with William the night before. She didn't know I was planning on this being only one date or that I'd told him we couldn't get involved with each other. She had no idea he'd already professed his love for me, and I didn't care to get into it with her just yet. That would only lead to a difficult discussion that I wasn't ready for yet. There'd be plenty of time for all that later. If I was only going to get one night with him, I wanted to go into like it was a real date and not a precursor to goodbye.

"We're not *seeing* each other," I explained. "It's dinner. Nothing more. There's no need to get anyone else involved."

"If you say so," Patsy said with an eyeroll and a dismissive wave of her hand. "I don't think anything between you two is *just* a meal, but whatever you need to tell yourself."

She came and stood behind me as I checked my hair one last time in the mirror.

I'd chosen to wear it up, and it seemed too rigid, so I reached and pulled a couple of tendrils out to hang loose.

"Should I wear it down instead? No, right? Keep it up?"

Patsy put her hands on my shoulders and smiled at our reflection in the mirror.

"You look beautiful. Don't change a thing." She gave my shoulders a light squeeze and sighed. "He should be here any minute, so I'm going to head out. If you need to talk when you get home, don't hesitate to call and wake me up. Otherwise, I'll see you in the morning."

I met her eyes in the mirror and grinned.

"Wake you up? We're just going to dinner. How late do you think I'm gonna be coming home?"

"Who knows where y'all will end up or what y'all will end up doing! I'm just saying that if we don't talk tonight, we'll talk tomorrow." She smiled, and when I turned to face her, she patted my cheek. "Have fun, love. Enjoy yourself. You deserve it."

"Thanks."

We exchanged a hug, and then she left.

William arrived a few minutes later, and the butterflies swarmed inside me as I pulled the door open.

His eyes widened as he took in my appearance, and he let out a low whistle.

"Wow. I think I must be the luckiest guy on the planet. Hello, gorgeous."

My entire body flushed with warmth, and I smiled.

"You don't look so bad yourself," I said as I checked out his charcoal gray suit with its pale blue shirt and patterned tie. I'd never seen him dressed so formally, and I was relieved I'd opted for a black dress that could keep up. He looked so damned handsome that it made me tingle from head to toe, some places more than others.

He held a bouquet of Gerbera daisies, and as he presented them, he also handed me a small gift bag.

"Thank you, but what's this?" I asked as I stepped back to let him enter.

"Oh, it's nothing, really. Something I saw at the hardware store earlier today. It made me think of you."

"At the hardware store? This should be interesting."

He took the flowers back so I could open the gift bag, and inside, I found a small metal wind chime with four bright green turtles dangling from its strings.

"Oh my goodness! How cute is that?"

"You like it?" he asked, his eyes bright with anticipation.

"I love it. Thank you! I'll ask George to hang it up out back."

"I don't think you have one like that already, do you?"

"No, I don't," I said as I inspected each turtle's individual facial expression. "I've looked at their wind chimes before in that store, and I've never seen this one."

William shrugged. "Perhaps it was fate."

I smiled as I laid the chimes on the table, and then I took the flowers and put them in a vase before we went out the door.

"So, where are we headed?" I asked as we walked toward his truck. I couldn't remember ever feeling so nervous on a date before. Not even a first date. Not even the first 'date' I'd had with William all those years ago.

He held open the truck door for me and smiled. "I'd like to surprise you if that's all right."

I'm sure my face registered that I was already surprised. Most men I'd gone out with had hit me with the '*Where do you want to go*' question as soon as we got in the car. The fact that William had already made plans and wanted to keep them to himself was intriguing.

"Sure, that's fine."

When we pulled away from my house in the opposite direction of Cedar Creek, I was even more intrigued.

"Are we not eating in town?"

"Hmmph. I said I wanted to take you to a nice restaurant. Nothing in town qualifies for what I had in mind."

As we drove through the rolling hills of Central Florida, we talked about the growth and expansion of the Orlando area and how much we both enjoyed Cedar Creek's quaint, neighborly feel. Before long, we arrived in Winter Garden, a small community on the western outskirts of Orlando's sprawl. The tiny former citrus town had become a mecca for those fleeing Orlando's crowded neighborhoods, and Winter Garden's historic downtown district had been revitalized and re-imagined with trendy shops and hipster coffee cafes.

Round twinkle lights were strung from the ornate lamp posts along the outer edges of the park that stretched down the center of the town's main street, separating traffic into one direction on either side of the grassy median. The sun had just dipped below the horizon, and the lights created a soft ambience for the families strolling with their dogs, the couples who sat on the park's benches, and the headphone-wearing teens underneath the large brick gazebo.

It was nice to see that some people still lived their lives outdoors in the evenings.

William parked in front of a large three-story brick building with a green-and-white striped awning that proclaimed it was the Edgewater Hotel, established in 1927. The ground floor of the hotel featured two restaurants, one that was clearly Thai, and the other that appeared to serve tapas-style entrees based on its window signage.

I wondered if either were as dressy as our attire, but I decided it really didn't matter. We were dressed for each other, not the other patrons.

He held the truck door open for me and offered his hand for assistance. I turned on the seat and stretched my foot toward the ground, but the sloping pavement was a bit farther down than I'd anticipated, making for an awkward, messy exit. I was pretty sure I gave William an unexpected crotch-shot in the process, but he was the perfect gentleman, never letting on my exit had been less than classy or graceful.

He put his hand on the small of my back to steer me toward the tapas place, and it lingered there as we walked, burning through the thin fabric. I'd told myself that it would be best to keep this date from getting physical since that would only make it harder to say goodbye, but he looked and smelled so damned good that it was going to be downright torture to follow through with that plan.

To my surprise, we walked straight through the tapas restaurant to a podium at the rear where William gave the hostess his name. She welcomed us and led us through a hallway to a small, intimate dining room that opened into a show kitchen.

Once we were seated at a table for two, a server came and introduced himself.

"Could we get you started with some wine?"

"Um, no, none for me," I said. "I'll have an iced tea with lemon, unsweetened, please."

"I'll have the same," William said as he smiled at me.

I smiled back. I was typically the odd one out in the group who didn't order a wine or an alcoholic beverage with dinner. It was nice to be with someone else who didn't drink and who didn't feel the need to discuss my choice not to.

The server had just departed when the chef came to our table for introductions and to explain the evening's menu selections.

There was almost a surreal filter overlaying everything as it happened. I'd promised myself that I wouldn't waste the evening questioning whether or not it was a good idea or worrying about what might happen after it ended. Any time my thoughts drifted in that direction, I forced myself to focus on the present and enjoy the moment as it unfolded.

As a result, it felt like I was in the center of a bubble, and everything in it with me was much more vivid and pronounced than it normally would have been. I was acutely aware of every single detail, hypersensitive to sounds, smells, tastes, lights, colors, and touch. Nothing seemed to escape me. My mind was on high alert, preserving the memories as accurately as possible for future recall.

The soft linen of the napkin in my lap. The texture of the warm soup as it rested on my palate. The hint of rosemary and the crispness of the truffle salt in the appetizer. The smell of the fresh bread in the basket, and the wafting woodsy scent of William's cologne as he reached to tear off the end piece. The flicker of the candlelight reflecting in his blue eyes. The way his head cocked to one side as he listened to me talk, his face relaxed and his smile ever-present. The sizzling sound from the grill behind me as the faint strains of jazz music provided a score underneath it all.

It had been a long while since I'd had a fancy evening out. Living in Manhattan and DC and spending so much time traveling, I'd had plenty of impressive restaurant experiences, and though some of those had been larger, ritzier, or more expensive than the Chef's Table at the Edgewater Hotel, nothing topped the feeling of being William Ward's date for one night.

CHAPTER 61
William

The last time I'd been on an actual date had been with Revae before we were married, and that was close to thirty years ago. I didn't count the time Cat and I had spent in St. Augustine and our day on the horses as dates. Those had been more spur-of-the-moment events that just sort of happened.

There was more pressure involved in planning to take Cat out for a real date, especially since it might be my best chance at convincing her we needed to go on more.

I'd chosen the Chef's Table because I wanted an intimate environment. In truth, I wanted Cat all to myself, but since it was impossible to get that in a restaurant experience, I figured the small number of fellow diners and the personal attention received at the Chef's Table was the next best thing.

The place normally booked far in advance, but I took a chance and called, and due to a cancellation, they were able to give me a same-day reservation. I chose to see it as another sign that the universe was working in my favor with Cat.

One night.

That was what she had granted me. I was determined to make the most of it.

I didn't want distractions. I didn't want background noise drowning out her voice and her laughter. I didn't want to be rushed to vacate the table for the next patrons waiting by the door. I wanted to bask in every single moment I could have with her, just in case she never allowed me the opportunity again.

I tried not to even consider that as a possibility. I had to convince her to give us a chance, somehow. I couldn't let her slip away when she held my heart so firmly in her grasp.

She'd damned near taken my breath away when she opened the door in that black dress. My mouth went dry, and something akin to an electrical pulse shot through my entire body, bringing it alive in ways it hadn't been for years.

It was damned near impossible not to fixate on the taut muscles of her calves as she walked ahead of me in those high heels with her legs on full display. Then, as if that wasn't already torture enough, when she stepped out of the truck at the restaurant, her skirt revealed she was wearing black lace underneath it. It was all I could do not to take her in my arms right then and there and let her know how much I wanted her.

But I had played it cool and remained a gentleman.

I knew that with any skittish, spirited filly, sudden moves or assertive behaviors only served to make them bolt or lash out. I had to be patient with Cat. I needed to stay calm and not push her into making decisions she wasn't ready for. I knew in my heart that we belonged together, and I was certain she felt the same way beneath all her fears. She just needed time, and I couldn't risk making her run by coming on too strong.

That should have been easy for me. After all, I'd built a career of taming wild horses and soothing their anxieties. It was what I did best. But Cat was a much more complicated creature than any I'd ever worked with, and none of my clients had ever held my heart, body, and soul hostage while I worked.

Her every movement undid me, and my body reacted like I was a teenager again.

She'd worn her hair up, and as we talked over dinner, her slender, exposed neck was like an invitation I struggled to resist. I wanted to taste her skin. I wanted to nibble at that spot just beneath her earlobe where she rested her fingers as she listened to the chef explain the dessert options.

But Cat was equally as fascinating to listen to as she was to watch. She was eloquent and well-versed in a diverse range of topics. Her passion for her cause was relentless, and I loved the charged fervor in her voice whenever we delved into the topic of adoption or foster care. She had an emotional intelligence that astounded me, and I admired her empathy for others and her ability to put herself in their shoes.

And Christ, was she funny! I couldn't remember a time when I'd laughed so much as I had since we'd reconnected. She was quick to laugh, and delightfully animated when telling a funny story.

It was like she had taken the best qualities of Catherine and refined them, honed them, and nurtured them. At the same time, she'd rid herself of Catherine's less desirable traits.

But she wasn't just a new and improved version of the Catherine I'd known and loved. She'd spent years as Caterina—as a person of her own choosing and her own making —and I was beyond intrigued by those facets of Caterina that were completely new to me. I couldn't get enough of her.

"So, how is it that you've never been married?" I asked as we waited for dessert.

"Oh, I don't think I'm really cut out for marriage. I'm a little too independent, I guess. I determined long ago that I never wanted to be like my mother. I never wanted to have to answer to someone else for everything I wanted to do. Every place I wanted to go. Every dollar I wanted to spend. To be told how to live, how to talk, how to dress. I don't know. I guess I was held under someone's thumb for so long that once I broke free of that, I didn't want to go back."

"And that's what you think marriage is? Being under someone's thumb?"

"I mean, I know there are other experiences in marriage out there. I see Patsy and George, and I admire what they have. I have friends who are happily married, and it works for them. But I don't know. I've never wanted to be in a position where I couldn't escape if I needed to."

"I don't think anyone would want to be in that position. What if you didn't feel trapped, though? What if it was some place that you didn't want to escape? Some place you wanted to be?"

"Well, if I found a place like that, then I guess I'd want to stay there, right?" She let out a nervous chuckle and picked up her glass of tea to take a big swallow, looking away from me to scan the room.

I'd veered off my intended path and into uncomfortable territory. Our conversation had taken a strange turn, and it left me feeling unsettled. I'd thought the only battle I was fighting for us to be together was getting past her guilt and her concern over the possible repercussions with Piper, Caroline, and the kids. But her response to the idea of commitment made me suspect that my uphill battle had just gotten steeper.

Luckily, the desserts arrived like the cavalry at that moment, and Cat's smile returned at the sight of the butterscotch *crème brûlée* with a pecan praline topping and the Nutella bread pudding with crushed pretzels and a *Frangelico ganache*.

Her eyes widened, and then she moaned and held her hand over her stomach.

"Oh my God! These both look delicious, but I'm stuffed! I can't possibly take another bite of anything right now. I'm already so full that I don't know how I'm going to climb up into that truck of yours."

"I can pick you up and toss you in the back like a bale of hay if that would be easier."

She laughed. "You might have to, so don't joke about it! You already saw how hard it was for me to get in and out of that truck, and don't even pretend you didn't notice the accidental flash. I know you saw it. You had to. But I did appreciate you being a gentleman about it."

I grinned and discreetly adjusted my pants as the memory of that black lace crotch came rushing back.

"I have no idea what you're talking about."

"Right. Okay. Thanks."

We both laughed, and I was struck yet again by how beautiful she was. Those green eyes that sucked me in and left me breathless. The high cheekbones. The perfect teeth. The delicate lips that I longed to claim again. God, she was perfect.

"What?" she said, her smile fading. "Why are you looking at me like that? Do I have something on my face?"

She picked up her napkin and wiped at her mouth and chin, and I shook my head and smiled.

"No. I was just thinking that you're every bit as beautiful now as you were the first day I saw you. Even more so."

She rolled her eyes and groaned before grinning. "Thank you, but I think the dim lighting in here must be hiding a lot."

"It's not the lighting. Remember, I've seen you outside in the bright sun, and I think you're a beautiful lady, Cat. Inside and out."

She looked down, and even in the soft candlelight, I could see a warm red flush creep into her cheeks. I wanted so badly to reach across the small table and touch her cheek. To stroke her skin. To hold her hand. To tell her how much I wanted her in my life, far beyond one night.

It didn't matter how steep that hill was. I was prepared to climb it. I'd do whatever it took to have her by my side.

"Are you going to try them?" she asked as she pointed to the desserts.

"I tell you what—why don't we have them boxed up for later? I have one more surprise for you, and maybe by the time we finish there, we'll be hungry again."

"Another surprise? You're going all out here. If I didn't know better, I'd think you were trying to convince me to go on another date with you."

"Let me know if it works."

She smiled, and then she stood and picked up her purse. "I'm going to visit the ladies' room. I'll be right back."

"I'll be right here waiting for you."

She paused, and I thought for a moment she was going to say something else, but then she gave an almost imperceptible shake of her head and walked away.

CHAPTER 62
Caterina

When I returned from the restroom, William had already paid the check and stood waiting with the bag of boxed desserts.

It felt bittersweet. I was sad to see our dinner come to an end, which meant the night was coming to a close. At the same time, I was excited to see what else he had up his sleeve.

It didn't matter what the surprise was, really. It didn't matter where we went or what we did. I was happy just being with him.

Nothing in my life had ever felt as right as William did. As he always had.

My mind kept replaying his questions and my answers. I'd promised him when we first started talking again that he could ask me anything and I'd be honest, and I had been.

But I'd also withheld part of the truth.

Marriage did scare me because of my mother, and I didn't know that I'd ever be willing to make that strong of a commitment to anyone if it meant giving up control over my own life.

But that wasn't the only reason relationships had never quite worked out for me.

I'd known some great men in my life, and several of them had tried to forge a path toward a future together. Unfortunately, there'd always been another person in my heart already when I met them, and no matter how hard they tried, no one could ever live up to the memory of the one I had loved first.

The bar had been set incredibly high, and everyone else paled in comparison.

I knew it was me causing them to fail. I'd built a wall around my heart when I lost William and Caroline, and that wall was strong and high. Damned near impenetrable. Few men had the patience or stamina to try and scale it, and for those who did make progress, it was usually me who bailed on them. I'd get tired of pretending when I realized the best I could get still wouldn't be as powerful as what I'd lost.

My therapist had told me again and again that I was seeing the past through rose-colored glasses. That I had created this standard in my mind that no one could possibly achieve.

Now, here I was with the man who had been the standard-bearer for love in my life. He was every bit as wonderful as I remembered, and he was asking me to enter into another relationship with him.

If anyone had said to me over the years that one day I'd get that offer, then I think I would have abstained from any attempt at love to wait for the real thing again with William.

But now that the offer had been made, I had to admit that I was more scared than I ever had been in any other relationship.

I was scared of hurting the people around us, for sure. But there was another fear at play. One I had only just begun to acknowledge as I felt myself opening up to the idea of being with William.

What if I finally got what I'd wanted all those years, and it didn't measure up either?

It was one thing to think that you'd already had the most powerful love you could ever experience, and no one could come close to it. But it would be another tragedy all together to discover that the love you'd placed on a pedestal inside the wall of your heart hadn't really been what you thought it was.

If I couldn't make it work with William Ward, I'd never be able to make it work with anyone. I was certain of that. So, if we failed, it would mean that I'd lost all hope for love.

It was definitely best if we didn't get involved. That way, I could protect the people we loved and keep William on the pedestal I'd built for him.

"You okay?" he asked as we reached his truck.

I forced a smile and pushed the conflict from my mind, determined to enjoy what little time we had left.

"Yeah, why?"

"You've been awfully quiet since you came back from the ladies' room. You sure everything's okay?"

I nodded.

"Yeppers. I was just thinking that I'm excited to see what you've got planned."

I was once again giving him the truth, but not the whole truth.

His eyes narrowed, and I hoped he wouldn't press the issue.

For a moment, he seemed like he was considering it, but then he moved to hold the truck door open, lifting his hand to cover his eyes as he grinned.

"Okay, I'm not looking. Do whatever you gotta do to get in here and let me know if you need any help."

I laughed as I climbed in, and then I took a deep breath and exhaled it slowly as I waited for him to get in on his side.

"So, what's this surprise of yours?" I asked as we left Winter Garden.

"If I told you it wouldn't be a surprise, now would it?"

As he drove, we talked, the conversation weaving in and out of topics as we did the same with the Orlando traffic.

When he pulled into the deserted parking lot of a large, dark building, I leaned forward to read the name on the sign.

It was a marine life center, and I smiled as I looked at him in confusion. His mischievous grin gave me no answers as he got out of the truck and came around to open my door. He turned his back to me so that I could exit without flashing, and then he shut the door once I stood beside him.

"Um, it's closed," I said, looking around the empty lot. "Did you know it was going to be closed?"

"That's the beauty of a surprise, isn't it? It keeps you guessing until all is revealed."

He pulled his phone from his pocket and dialed someone.

"We're here. Okay, yeah, I see it."

When he'd finished the call, he extended his hand for me to hold. "Ready?"

I nodded with a grin and took it, and we walked toward the building hand-in-hand. It felt natural. It felt right.

When we reached the sidewalk, he turned to go around the side of the building. There was a door toward the back with a light on outside it, and when William knocked, a young man opened it and welcomed us inside.

William and the man wrapped each other in a big manly bear hug, and then William turned to me.

"Cat, this is Trey. Trey, Caterina Russo."

We exchanged greetings, and William clapped his hand on Trey's shoulder and squeezed.

"Trey's father, Malcolm, has been part of my team pretty much since the beginning of Ward Farms. Trey was raised on the farm alongside Piper. You're, what, a year older?"

Trey nodded.

"And now, he's working as the night guard here at the marine center, and he's agreed to give us a private tour."

"Are you sure? Is that okay?" I asked Trey. "I don't want us to get you into any trouble."

"Oh, no. I told my boss Mr. Ward was coming. It's all been cleared. No big deal."

He led us to an employee elevator and up to the third floor, and then through a series of hallways past doors labeled as offices and labs. Finally, he opened the door to a spacious room with blue walls that appeared to be some sort of lab or medical center.

On the opposite side of the room was a rather large circular-shaped pool surrounded by a waist-high wall.

A woman in a blue T-shirt and white shorts with white sneakers squatted over the water on a metal catwalk that spanned the width of the pool, and she stood with a smile when we entered.

"Hi! You made it! Were you able to surprise her?"

"I think so," William said as he looked at me, his hand resting on my lower back as we walked toward her.

She came down the steps to greet us, and Trey stepped forward to make introductions.

"Mr. Ward, Ms. Russo, this is my friend, Molly. She's one of our biologists here, and she agreed to help us pull this off tonight."

Molly extended her hand to shake ours, and William thanked her for coming in so late.

"Are you surprised?" she asked me when the formalities were complete.

"Yeah, I'd say so. I still have no idea what's going on, though I have some hopes on what it might be."

William grinned, and he moved his hand lightly up and down my back, his touch on the bare skin sending ripples of sensation all over me.

Molly stepped closer to the pool and motioned for us to join her.

"I understand that you particularly like turtles, and we have a special friend here for you to meet."

As we neared the water, I was surprised to see that it was much deeper than I'd thought. It wasn't a pool after all, but a huge aquarium filled with rocks and plant life as well as a variety of fish. We were looking down into it, and though I couldn't see the bottom, it was at least a couple of stories deep and appeared to go all the way down to the ground floor.

Molly leaned over and tapped her palm on the water's surface.

"Shelby? You gonna come meet our new friends? You were just right here. Where'd you go?"

A large loggerhead sea turtle swam up toward us, and I squealed in delight as I grabbed William's arm and squeezed it.

Shelby surfaced, and Molly patted her head.

"There you are, sweet girl! You coming to say hello?" She turned to us and smiled. "This is Shelby."

The turtle was beautiful. I fell in love with her immediately, and tears of joy sprang to my eyes as I watched her bob and turn in the water.

"Oh, wow! We're in for a real treat tonight," Molly said. "The old guy wants to know what all the late-night hubbub is about."

A much larger turtle came swimming toward us with a deep scar cutting across the back end of his shell.

"This is Michaelangelo, but we call him Mike. As you can see, he got in a fight with a boat propeller several years ago, and he lost most of one back flipper and got that nasty gash in his shell. He gets around okay in here, but he wouldn't be able to navigate open waters, so he's a permanent resident of ours. Shelby, on the other hand, was struggling to eat due to a tumor. But that's been removed, and she has definitely gotten her appetite back, so we'll be transitioning her to return to the wild very soon."

Molly spent about twenty minutes with us, answering our questions and letting me geek out over Shelby and Mike. After a thorough hand washing, we were able to touch them, which sent me into a fit of girlish giggles and a few more squeals. Which, of course, made William laugh as he watched me.

When the turtles had tired of the attention and swam away, we thanked Molly for her time and bid her goodbye.

I assumed we were done, but instead of taking us back through the route we'd used to enter, Trey led us back downstairs a different way. We came out into the public side of the center, where Trey walked us through several of the rooms and exhibits for a private tour.

The last room was my favorite. It was the public side of Mike and Shelby's enclosure. We were at the bottom of their aquarium now, and one entire wall of the room was curved glass to offer a view of their living space.

"This is incredible," I whispered.

William chuckled as he leaned his shoulder against mine and spoke in hushed voice, though Trey had stayed by the entrance to give us privacy.

"I wanted to take you to see Albert, but I couldn't pull that off tonight. I hoped this might suffice."

My smile, already huge, grew even bigger. "This is perfect. It suffices. Definitely."

"I still feel bad about forgetting Albert's name."

"What you should feel bad about is teasing me for naming him in the first place." I playfully shoved my shoulder against his. "I mean, you got Mike over there swimming around. How is Albert any worse?"

"It's not," he conceded as he laughed. "Although, she said Mike is short for Michaelangelo, which everyone knows is a bonafide, official turtle name."

"Um, yeah. If you're a turtle who is teenaged, a mutant, and a ninja. Albert is none of those. He's dignified. Quiet. Scholarly. His name fits him perfectly."

"You may be right."

Shelby swam to the front of the tank and turned upward, exposing her belly to us.

I couldn't help but squeal a little, and William laughed when I did.

"What? Don't laugh at me. I can't help it! They're so adorable."

"I wasn't laughing *at* you," William said as wrapped his arm around my shoulders and pulled me in closer. "It just makes me happy to see you happy, that's all."

He kissed my forehead, and I smiled as I looked up at him, the warmth of his body next to me matched by the warmth in my heart. I *was* happy. Happier than I'd been at any point that I could remember.

Suddenly, everything I'd wished for was laid out in front of me, all right there for the taking. My health was on the mend. My career was fulfilling, and the foundation was primed to expand. My daughter would soon be living in the same town with me and working by my side. And the only man I'd ever loved was standing next to me, and he'd asked me to give our relationship another chance.

It all seemed too perfect, and that terrified me.

There was no way I could have everything I wanted. Was there?

CHAPTER 63
Caterina

As we followed Trey to leave the building, William's hand remained on my lower back, sometimes drifting just below my waist line, and sometimes moving upward across the bare skin exposed by the dress. It made it hard to pay attention to Trey's tour guide spiel. I was already anticipating the next chapter in our evening, and I couldn't wait to be alone with William for the first time all night. The fantasies playing out in my head were far more engaging than any marine life trivia or random facts shared by Trey.

We bid him goodbye when we reached the exit, and William put his arm around my waist and pulled me closer as we walked toward the truck. I'd fully expected him to kiss me when he opened the door for me to get in, but he shut the door with nothing more than a smile.

He had to be aware of the sexual tension between us. The air inside the truck was so charged with it that it seemed it might crackle at any moment. We were both more quiet than usual as he navigated us through the downtown Orlando traffic, and I was relieved when he turned on the radio to drown out the silence.

I'd rested my arm on the center console, and once we were on the expressway, he laid his arm next to mine. The proximity of skin so near skin only served to ramp up the energy, and I was certain I'd see sparks arc between us if we got any closer.

The first time his fingers brushed against mine, I jumped and pulled my hand back a bit, thinking perhaps I'd drifted into his space. But the second time he did it, I knew it was no accident. The casual brush was too deliberate. Too contrived. I didn't move away.

It happened again, and soon the contact was constant as our

fingers moved and stilled in a dance of flirtation. Neither of us acknowledged that it was happening. We both stared straight ahead at the road as though we had no idea what our hands were up to. We were like two teenagers in a dark theater, playing nonchalant despite being intently focused on the thrill of the touch.

As we neared Cedar Creek, our fingers had become fully intertwined, but we continued to move them together—stroking and teasing, squeezing and releasing, twisting and writhing. Very little pressure was applied, but the resulting sensations were powerful. It was as though tiny electrical currents were firing across my skin, and as a result, every nerve in my body seemed to buzz on high alert.

We'd both remained completely silent since that first casual brush, as if we suspected that words spoken or looks exchanged would break the spell. I didn't even dare breathe too deeply. What we were doing wasn't in itself overtly sexual, but the sensuality of the act and the secrecy we were pretending to cloak it in made it all at once intimate, tantalizing, and maddening.

By the time we reached my neighborhood, our fingers had expanded their explorations to include wrists and forearms. My body was literally aching with need, and I wanted William Ward to make love to me like I'd never wanted anything in my life. I feared I might explode from within if he didn't give me the release I so desperately craved.

He pulled the truck to a stop in my driveway, and then he reached across the steering wheel to put the shifter in park with his left hand, obviously unwilling to break our contact just yet. I suspected he didn't want to stop any more than I did.

We turned to look at each other at the same time, and I shivered when I saw the raw need reflected in his eyes. I shifted my weight in the seat and parted my legs slightly in an attempt to relieve the burning heat between them.

He gripped my hand and squeezed, and then he lifted it to his lips and kissed it.

"Are you ready for dessert?" he asked, his voice husky.

I damned near reached an orgasm right there on the spot, but then he released my hand and reached behind my seat to pull out the bag that held the *crème brûlée* and the bread pudding.

"I don't know about you, but I'm starving." His eyes twinkled with mischief, and a grin played at the corners of his mouth as he opened the door and exited the truck.

He came around to open my side, and once again, he turned to give me privacy for my dismount. My legs were like noodles when I put weight on them, and my knees gave a little, causing me to grab hold of him. He turned immediately and wrapped his arm around my waist to catch me, his face merely inches from mine.

"You all right?" he whispered, and I nodded, even though it was a lie. I was far, far from all right.

His gaze fell to my mouth and his arm tightened around me, but then he released me and took my hand in his to walk me to the door.

I fumbled with the keys, and he took them from me and handed me the desserts as he unlocked the door.

"I'll get some plates and forks for these," I said as I sat the bag on the table. I walked to the kitchen in a daze, still breathless and trying to recover.

What the hell was that? What had just happened? How could I have such an intense reaction to holding hands?

I realized I'd pulled open the wrong drawer in my own kitchen, and I shook my head and swore under my breath as I went to the correct one.

"Do you want it outside or inside?" William asked from behind me, and I jumped at the sound of his voice. "Did I scare you? I'm sorry."

"No, it's okay. I'm just … jumpy, I guess."

He grinned, and I swear the man knew the effect he was having on me.

How was he walking around as though nothing had happened? I'd seen it in his eyes. I'd felt it in his touch. I knew I wasn't the only one affected.

Yet, there he was, taking out the bread pudding and transferring it to the plate as though my entire body wasn't throbbing with every beat of my heart.

"I think I need a glass of water," I said. "Would you like one?"

"Sure," he said, seemingly oblivious. "That sounds refreshing."

I resisted the urge to throw the glass at his head, and I tried to ignore that my hand was trembling as I held it under the ice dispenser.

He had the desserts plated and set out on the coffee table when I came back into the living room, and I sat next to him on the couch and drained about half the glass of water.

"You must have been thirsty." He grinned. "What do you want to taste first?"

Did he intend for everything he said to have a double entendre, or was my mind just going there every time?

"The bread pudding," I said, and he took a fork full of it and lifted it to my lips. His eyes locked with mine as I closed my mouth over the decadent bite, and I detected the slightest tremble in his hand as he slid the fork back out.

Aha! I wasn't the only one finding it hard to maintain composure, though I'm not sure if that realization made things easier or harder.

After we'd sampled roughly half of each dessert, I put up my hand and shook my head. "No more! I'm too full."

"You sure I can't tempt you into having anything else?"

Okay, there was no way he didn't know what he was doing. And I was relatively certain he knew that *I* knew what he was doing, based on that ever-present mischievous twinkle and his ready grin.

"No. I can't be tempted," I shot back, deciding that two could play at that game. "I'm a fortress when it comes to refusing. Impenetrable."

He chuckled and took another bite of the *crème brûlée* as I reached down and slid off my shoes. I extended my legs and flexed my feet, wiggling my toes with a groan.

"Your feet hurting?" he asked.

"Yes! I don't wear heels much anymore since I'm mostly working from home. My toes are protesting my fashion choices this evening."

"Give 'em here," he said, motioning for me to give him my foot. "Let me see what I can do."

"No, they'll be fine, thanks."

"C'mon. Let me see your foot."

"No," I said with a laugh as I pulled my feet back toward the couch and tucked my toes under. "Didn't you watch *Pulp Fiction*? A foot massage is a very intimate act, you know."

He leaned against the back of the couch with his arm extended behind me, his expression something between a grin and a smirk. "Well, you already flashed your panties at me tonight, so I'm thinking at this point, we've reached foot massage intimacy level."

"That was an accident!"

We both laughed, and he motioned again.

"Gimme your foot."

I hesitated a moment longer but then swiveled on the couch to pull my feet up into his lap.

He lifted my left foot and placed my heel in his palm, and then his fingers began to knead the ball of my foot and the base of my toes as I laid back against the throw pillows.

It was ridiculous to feel shy about it. After all, we'd been far beyond foot massages plenty of times in our youth. Hell, we'd conceived a child together.

But there was something incredibly sensual about his hands on my body, no matter where he was touching me. I watched him as he worked his magic on one foot and then the other, his brow furrowed in concentration, and his eyes intent on the task. His hands were strong, and his technique was on point. I was certain it wasn't the first time he'd handled a woman's foot.

The thought brought Revae to mind, and I closed my eyes against the image, not wanting any intrusion. For one night, he was mine and mine alone.

One night.

Somehow, I'd forgotten all about my self-imposed time restraint as the evening progressed.

I'd let my defenses down, but rather than regret, I felt exhilaration. Being happy with William was intoxicating, and I was thoroughly enjoying the high.

He worked his way up to my ankles, my shins, and then slowly, oh so slowly, he reached my calves, and I gripped the side of the sofa and moaned in pleasure.

His hands faltered, and my eyelids fluttered open to find him watching me, his eyes dark with desire. His teasing mirth had disappeared, and I felt like I'd been laid bare in front of him for the taking.

My chest rose and fell as his hands began their circular massage pattern again, inching upward at a maddeningly slow pace. I couldn't tear my eyes from his, and I quivered beneath the intensity of his gaze as his hands moved higher. Once above my knees, the circles grew slightly larger, and I gasped when his fingers slid between my thighs for the briefest of moments as he completed a particularly wide rotation. His lips parted as he traced the same path again a bit slower, and I held my breath and bit down on my bottom lip to keep from begging him for more.

Suddenly, the ringing of his phone shattered the silence, and I sat up in alarm at the unexpected sound.

He pulled it from his pocket and looked at it, grimacing when he saw who was calling.

"I'm sorry, but I've got to take this," he said. "It's Piper, and she wouldn't call this late if it wasn't important."

"Of course."

He got up and stepped out the front door, and I lay back on the couch and covered my face with my hands.

The interruption had been like cold water doused on a fire.

What the hell was I doing?

I had to put the brakes on. I had to remind myself of all the reasons this couldn't work.

But for the life of me, I was struggling to remember what they were.

Piper.

Piper was one of those reasons. She wouldn't accept us being together easily. Her resentment and her hurt would drive a wedge between the two of them, and I couldn't bear being responsible for that.

Caroline was another.

She'd only just found us, and she was moving her family here with the intention of working for Turtle Crossing and spending more time with William and me both—as well as Levi, of course. We owed it to her to make sure we didn't do anything that would make that adjustment harder. If William and I became a couple, it would change the dynamic between the three of us. And then if we couldn't make it last, it would be increasingly awkward for Caroline. I would never want her to feel she needed to choose sides.

Then, of course, there was me and all my flaws. I had no idea how to be in a successful relationship. I had no idea how to mold my life to fit in with another person's. William was tied to the farm. His animals and his crew depended on him. His schedule held very little flexibility. If I tied myself to him, then I'd quickly be stuck. My travel time would be limited, and my ability to make plans at the spur of the moment would be greatly compromised.

I'd end up resenting that, probably sooner rather than later.

Besides, there was no way I could ever move into Revae's house. I couldn't live with the ghost of her memory, and I knew Piper would never allow me to feel at home in her mother's space.

On the other hand, William would never leave the farm to live with me here. It wasn't feasible. He had built everything he needed there, and it didn't make sense for him to leave that behind.

Not that I would want him to. My house was my sanctuary. My safe space. If I allowed someone else in, I'd need to give up my routines. My closet space. My control.

It had been a fabulous night. There was no denying that. But I'd gone into it knowing it could only be one night, and in the end, nothing had changed.

I squared my shoulders and told myself that when William came back inside from talking with Piper, I'd be strong.

CHAPTER 64
William

I stepped outside onto Cat's porch and took a deep breath as I slid my finger across the phone screen.

"Hi, sweetheart. What's up?"

"Where are you? Are you okay?"

I closed my eyes as I leaned my shoulder against the nearest porch post. "I'm fine. I'm at Caterina's. Why? Where are you?"

"At home, where I thought you'd be."

"Oh. I didn't know. You've been staying at Lauryn's, so I didn't know you'd be there."

"Yeah, well, I needed to talk to you about something. But it kept getting later and later, and when I didn't hear anything from you, I got worried."

"I'm sorry. I should have told you I was going out and that I'd be late. Like I said, I figured you'd be at Lauryn's. What did you need to talk to me about?"

She paused.

"So, are you coming home?"

I didn't want to. I wanted nothing more than to spend the night with Caterina in my arms, and we'd certainly been headed in that direction, but it was best if that didn't happen yet. It was too soon.

I'd fought with myself all night to resist the urge to kiss her, to taste her, to take her. I'd wanted to go slow and not allow our physical attraction to dictate the pace, but I'd been unable to refrain from touching her. So, I'd tried to give myself boundaries and limit it to her back, or holding her hand, or putting my arm around her. Something that seemed safe and manageable. But then that craziness in the truck had made even hand-holding dangerous, and I'd realized nothing about Cat was safe for me.

It had taken every single ounce of strength I had to keep from lifting her in my arms and taking her to bed since the moment we'd arrived at her house, and she'd given me no reason to think she wouldn't have welcomed the offer.

The foot massage had been a colossal mistake on my part. The sound of her moaning as a result of my touch and the feeling of her quivering beneath my hands did something to me, and I'd forgotten I was supposed to resist. The phone ringing had been like an alarm going off, clearing the foggy haze of lust from my brain, and it was all clear again. Despite her physical reaction to me, I knew Cat needed more time to be okay with us. I couldn't rush in for the sake of one night's pleasure and risk losing her for the long-term.

I had to go home.

"Yeah, definitely."

"Okay, when?" Piper asked. "Are you on your way home now?"

"Um, no. But I will be soon. How long will you be up?"

"So, you're still there. With *her.*"

The worry and concern in her voice had been replaced with anger.

I gritted my teeth together, not knowing how to be truthful but not hurtful.

"You never did tell me what you need to talk to me about," I said, choosing to ignore the issue for the moment.

She sighed, and when she spoke again, the anger sounded more like dejection.

"Never mind, Daddy. It's not important."

"Are you sure, sweetheart? I mean, I should be on my way soon. I can call you when I leave here if you want."

"I'm going to bed. I have a client coming for a training session early in the morning. Good night, Daddy."

I stared at the phone after the line disconnected, and then I sat on the porch steps and looked out over the immense blackness of the lake across the road in the dark of night.

It felt like I was walking multiple tightropes, and all of them were swaying in the wind.

Piper needed something from me that I wasn't giving her. Loving her and telling her I loved her was obviously not enough. She needed something more right now, and I had no idea how to provide it. What could I do to heal her hurts and help her be okay with where life was, as well as prepare her for where I hoped it was heading? How could I meet her needs and my own when they seemed so much at odds?

Caroline was an entirely different tightrope. It was new, and it was scary, and though I was excited about its possibilities, I didn't know what I was doing yet. At times, things seemed to be going well, but at others, it seemed I was fumbling in the dark without a clue. My mother was insisting on throwing this party for the entire family, and I wasn't sure it was the best thing to do. It was important to me that everyone know that Caroline and the kids were mine and that I wasn't ashamed of that. I wanted them to be welcomed into my family and know they were a part of it. But I also worried that such a large and public event might cause undue stress and pressure on both Caroline and Piper. I'd put it out there already, though, and everyone knew it was happening. If I canceled the event, would that send the message that I wasn't ready to welcome Caroline into the family?

She and the kids would be moving here soon, and I was determined to do all I could to help get them settled. The ex-husband would be an issue. I was certain of that. He'd threatened to take her to court. To tie up her funds in a lengthy custody battle. I was prepared to do whatever was needed to help her fight, but I couldn't protect her or the kids from the heartache such an ordeal was sure to bring.

I also had to be cautious about coming on too strong. We'd only just begun to get to know each other. I had to respect her boundaries as an adult who'd live her entire life without needing my counsel or my input. I couldn't barge in and take control the way I often did on my own farm, with my own team, or with my family who'd always known me to be that way.

And then, there was Caterina. This night had been every confirmation I could ever want that we were meant to be together. The connection was there. The desire was there. The love was there. For both of us. I'd believed that before, but I was certain of it now.

She'd let her guard down tonight. I'd felt it when the barrier disappeared. She'd allowed herself to be open, to relax, and to feel without questioning. I'd gotten a glimpse of what our life together could be like, and it had made me more determined than ever to fight for it and show her that it was possible.

I couldn't push her, though. I couldn't make any demands. She'd let me in on some level tonight, but we hadn't yet conquered her doubts or her fears, and I knew it was only a matter of time before they crept back in to try and steal her from me, to pull her back behind her wall.

All three tightropes required patience. I had to keep my cool and keep them all balanced. The stakes were unbelievably high, and the risks were plentiful, but if I could pull this off and make it to the other side with all three intact, my life would be fuller than I ever could have imagined it to be. And if I failed, I didn't even want to consider how painful that could be.

"Is everything okay?" Cat asked, when I came back inside.

"Yeah. It's fine."

"Is Piper all right?"

"Yeah. She was just worried. She's been staying with her cousin, so I didn't realize she'd be home. I should have told her I'd be late."

She nodded. "Well, if you need to go…"

It was back. The hesitation. The uncertainty. The distance. I could see it in her eyes. Hear it in her voice. It was visible in her stance, in the way she crossed her arms to keep me out. The way she held her back rigid and at attention. The way her eyes refused to meet mine for longer than a couple of seconds at a time.

She'd put up her guard again. Closed herself off.

I wanted to rush forward and wrap my arms around her. I wanted to plead with her to stay with me, to remain open with me. But the wall between us was so palpable that I feared I would slam into it if I got near her.

In the strangest way, I missed her, even though she was standing right in front of me.

I had to believe that something we'd done tonight had made progress, though. That something had broken through and planted a seed. I might not be able to see it right away, but I had to trust that if I could just be patient, if I could just keep nurturing it, then eventually she'd come around.

I knew from experience that the hardest ones to tame were the ones capable of the greatest feats, and Cat was more than worth the effort. Worth the fight.

"Yeah," I said with a sigh. "I probably do need to go."

She nodded, and I swear I could see both relief and disappointment in her eyes.

It killed me to leave, but I knew I had to. Piper needed me at home, and Cat needed space and time to recover.

I feared walking out the door, though, because once I left, I had no way of knowing if Cat would let me back in.

She'd given me one night. One night to prove my case. I could only hope that I'd done enough to earn another.

CHAPTER 65
Caterina

William came back inside from Piper's call in a changed mood. His jaw was tight, his mouth was set in a grim line, and his eyes had lost their softness.

With the ringing of that phone, reality had returned, and it burst the bubble I'd been in all night.

I asked if everything was okay, and he said it was. But as he explained Piper's concerns, I couldn't help but feel guilty that he'd been with me on the one night she'd come back home. I was certain that would cause further drama with her.

"Well, if you need to go…" I held my breath as I waited for his answer.

Part of me wanted him to say no. To say that he would stay. To insist that we finish what we'd started. I longed for him to take me in his arms and take me to my bed. I wanted to wake in his embrace and linger there between the sheets before having a lazy breakfast and coffee on the pool deck. Maybe return to bed afterward.

But another part of me was scared that if I allowed that to happen, I'd never be able to walk away again.

Tonight had been like a dream.

It had confirmed what I'd always known. My heart belonged to William Ward. It beat for him in ways it never would for anyone else.

And for a brief period of time tonight, I'd been able to fully experience how magnificent that could be without reservation, without guilt, and without fighting it.

But it was one night. One date. It was a meal and a fanciful encounter, far removed from the rest of the world and its demands.

I couldn't make life decisions that affected all of us based on one gourmet dinner and an intense hand-holding session before dessert.

He needed to go home, and I had to let him go.

"Yeah," he finally said, his sigh heavy and his face drawn. "I probably do need to go."

At least we were in agreement. I nodded, and I tried to ignore the panic that filled me.

What would happen next? When would I see him again? Or would I?

I'd told him one night. I'd agreed to one date. I couldn't go back on that, because I knew it was for the best. And he must think so, too, because he wasn't begging me to change my mind. He hadn't even asked if he could see me again.

The closer we got to the door, the more I wanted to throw my arms around him and cling to him, to plead for him to fight for me. To tell me once more that we were meant to be. I wanted desperately to hear him say he loved me again, and I yearned to say it back.

We couldn't just part ways at the door like this. There had to be more, didn't there?

He stopped with his hand on the knob, and then he turned to look at me. His eyes held a sadness that made my heart hurt. His mouth was still tight, and a muscle twitched in his jaw.

"I have something I want to say first," he said.

"All right."

I sucked in all the air I could and waited. Had he read my mind again? Would he make another plea? And if he did, what would my answer be? Would I have the courage to say yes, and follow my heart? Or would I have the courage to say no, and put others first?

He reached to twist one of the loose tendrils of my hair around his finger, and his expression softened. He even attempted a grin, though his eyes were sad.

"I wanted to thank you for agreeing to come out with me tonight."

"Thanks for asking me … and for planning it, too. It's been a lovely night. Perfect, really. The meal, the conversations, the turtles."

He gently tugged at the tendril and released it, and then he laid his palm against my neck and traced my jawline with his thumb. He'd been staring at my mouth, but then his eyes met mine, and the desire had returned to them in full force.

He stepped closer, and his lips parted, and I knew he was going to kiss me.

"I did promise you I'd always find you turtles," he whispered.

I swallowed hard, my entire body tingling as I anticipated his lips touching mine.

"Yes, you did," I whispered back.

He leaned toward me ever so slightly, and I braced for the contact. Longing for it. Aching for it.

His gaze fell back to my lips. "I kept my promise."

"Yes, you did," I said again. My voice was hoarse, barely even a whisper. God, why wouldn't he just kiss me already?

He leaned in a little more, our faces so close that our noses were almost touching.

"I also promised I'd always love you. I kept that promise, too."

Our eyes locked, and he moved his hand up to cup my cheek.

"And now, I'm making you a new promise."

He brushed his lips against mine so gently that it was like a feather tickling me. I leaned in, wanting more. Needing more. But he pulled back just enough to speak.

"I will never give up on you," he said, our lips so near that I felt the air of his breath when he spoke.

Then, another feather kiss as my body trembled.

"I will never give up on us," he whispered against my mouth.

Another feather kiss, and I wanted to scream.

"And that I promise you, Caterina." His words weren't even a whisper any longer. They were barely even audible as he moved his hand to the back of my neck and pulled me to him, closing his mouth over mine at last.

I was ready to go all in, to surrender, to succumb. To throw myself against him and throw caution to the wind.

But he released me without warning, and then he was gone, the door already closed behind him as I stood there in stunned silence, my body aflame.

CHAPTER 66
William

I rested my head on the truck's steering wheel as I sat in the driveway in front of my house.

It had been a roller coaster of an evening with highs and lows, and I was drained, but it wasn't over yet.

Driving away from Caterina had been hard and walking into the house for a confrontation with Piper was definitely not how I would have chosen to end the night, but it had to be done.

I'd called Piper's phone on my way home from Cat's, but it went straight to voicemail. She'd said she was going to bed, but she'd always been a night owl, so I suspected she was simply looking at the phone and refusing my call.

The downstairs lights were off when I entered the house, but when I reached the second-floor landing, I could hear the television on in her room.

I tapped lightly on her door, and I'd almost decided she might be asleep after all when she opened it.

She was in her pajamas, her fiery red hair hanging over her shoulder in a braid. She looked so much younger without make-up, and sometimes I had to remind myself that she was twenty-four, an adult who no longer needed or wanted my advice. Not that she'd ever much heeded it, but there had been a span of time when she was younger that she had sought it out before ignoring it.

"I tried to call you on my way home," I said as she stood in the doorway.

She glanced over her shoulder and back to me. "The TV was on."

It was a vague statement that neither confirmed nor denied whether she'd ignored my call.

"Can I come in?"

"Be my guest." She turned and walked into the bedroom and laid across the bed on her stomach, propping herself up on her elbows as she stared at the television.

The room had once been the master, and it was the most spacious and well-appointed bedroom in the house. But I couldn't bear its emptiness when Revae died, and so Piper and I had switched accommodations. She liked the feeling of being closer to her mother and the enormous closet and Jacuzzi tub that accompanied the master. Her former bedroom was plenty big enough for me, much larger than any bedroom I'd ever had before we built the house. It had its own en-suite bathroom, and more than ample closet space for my limited clothes collection.

I rarely came in the master any more, having no reason to visit it and preferring to avoid the reminders it inevitably brought.

I walked over to the windows on the far wall and looked down at the barn office and the fountain in the center of the drive, and then I sat on the edge of the double-chaise lounge that Revae had bought so we could read together at night. My eyes itched with the need for sleep. I rubbed at them and then cleared my throat and looked at Piper.

"What did you want to talk to me about?"

Piper's gaze didn't leave the television screen as she shrugged.

"I told you it's not important. Don't worry about it."

"Well, even so, I want to hear it."

"Are you dating her now?"

I picked at a small thread that was loose in the paisley print of the chaise. "Uh, no, I wouldn't label it as that. We did go out to dinner this evening."

She looked at me and back at the screen.

"On a date."

I shrugged. "Okay, I suppose it was a date."

She lifted the remote and flipped through the channels.

"Do you *suppose* you'll go on another one any time soon?"

She had no idea how much I wished I knew the answer to that one.

"I can't really say. But I hope so."

"So, is this going to get serious? Or are you just reliving your glory days?"

I scratched my head and moved farther onto the chaise so my back would be supported.

"I wouldn't call them *glory days*, and I don't think I'm reliving anything. I'm interested in this woman, I care about her, I enjoy her company, and I want to be around her."

She turned the TV off and stared at me.

"Why did you guys break up? I mean, back then, when you were dating."

"We didn't."

"What do you mean?"

"We didn't break up. One day she was here, and the next she was gone, and I never saw her again until I walked into that hospital room."

Piper rolled onto her side and wrapped her arm around a pillow.

"Why? Where'd she go?"

I leaned back and intertwined my fingers behind my head, anticipating a long conversation.

"Caterina—Catherine, back then—came from a very wealthy family. Her father had a lot of ideas about who she was supposed to be and how she was supposed to behave."

"Hmmph. Sounds familiar."

I raised an eyebrow and frowned. "Trust me when I tell you that your life has been nothing like hers. Her father was emotionally abusive, controlling. I realize you don't agree with everything I say or do, but I don't think I've been either of those."

"No, you haven't." She looked down for a moment and then back to me, her face expectant as she waited for me to continue.

"Catherine was rebellious, and she definitely made some choices that probably weren't the wisest she could make." I paused and tilted my head with my hand up to my ear.

Piper stared at me. "What?"

"Oh, I thought perhaps I'd hear another '*Sounds familiar.*' No?"

"Very funny. So, why'd she leave? Where'd she go? And why didn't she tell you about the child?"

I drew in a deep breath and exhaled, preparing to revisit the past once again. How funny that I went so many years avoiding any thought of it, and now it wouldn't stop resurfacing.

"She'd gotten in a bit of a trouble with her father, some of it typical teenage stuff—grades, parties, etc. Some of it was him having unrealistic demands and expectations, and just being a general ass." I wondered if I would ever be able to think of Phillip Johnson without anger and hatred seething inside me. "He'd threatened to send her to a school in New York. A girls' school. A boarding school. Her mother would beg him to let Catherine stay, though, and Catherine would walk the line long enough to appease him. But this one time, she had crossed that line in a pretty drastic way."

I thought back to the night Patricia had told me that Catherine was in the hospital. That she may die from an overdose. I'd been eating a bag of Fritos when Patricia came in, and to this day, I still couldn't stomach the taste of them. I recalled being immediately nauseous and overcome with feelings of rage, fear, and helplessness. It was the same feeling I got when we received Revae's diagnosis.

"So, he issued the threat again," I continued. "We should have heeded it. We should have been extra careful. We probably should have stopped seeing each other, even for a little while, just to let things die down and to wait him out." I sighed. "But we were young, and we were stupid. We were in love."

I glanced up to see Piper's reaction to that statement. It was the truth, but I hadn't thought about it hurting her until it had already come out of my mouth. She didn't seem bothered, though.

"Did her parents like you?"

"I never met them. They didn't even know we were dating."

"You're kidding! You, like, never went over to her house or anything?"

I shook my head. "No. Not while they were home. They would have separated us if they'd known."

"Is that what happened? They found out?"

"No. Things probably would have turned out much differently for all of us if they had. But her parents never knew about me."

"Who did they think Caroline's father was?"

"They didn't know. Catherine refused to tell them."

Piper's eyes widened, and her lips twisted as she chewed on the inside of her cheek, something she'd always done when deep in thought.

"So, is that why she left? To have the baby? Why didn't she tell you? How could you not know your girlfriend was pregnant?"

"Neither of us knew at the time she left. It had just, well, I mean, we didn't … look, it's complicated. But no, that's not why she left.

She didn't know about the baby until afterward."

"She didn't know? That seems weird. But, if that wasn't the reason, then why did she leave? Where'd she go?"

"He sent her away to that school." I brought my legs up onto the chaise and crossed one over the other. "Here's what happened. Catherine and I couldn't see each other during the day. Hell, we couldn't see each other at all. So, we'd been sneaking out at night—"

"Shut the front door! You? Mr. Rule-Follower? Oh my God! Did Grandma Abby know?"

"Sort of. She knew I wasn't home. I didn't literally sneak out of the house like Catherine did. I told Ma if I was gonna be gone, but she didn't realize I was driving your uncle James's truck to the East Coast."

"Dang! How long would y'all stay gone?"

"All night. We'd try to be back by four or five so I could get a couple of hours of sleep before work and so she'd be safely inside and asleep before her parents got up. But that night..."

Scenes from that night flashed through my head like a movie that was all at once happy, scary, and sad.

Catherine in my arms in the water as we bobbed in the waves. Catherine on that blanket in the moonlight. The intense emotion and pleasure of the first time. The weight of her lying on my chest as my mind got drowsy and my body slipped away into sleep. The panic of realizing what time it was, and the guilt of not being able to get her back home. Then, the rage on my father's face, and the pain on my mother's. And finally, Isabel's tears as she shoved that letter in my hand, and my own tears as I read Catherine's words of farewell.

"Daddy?" Piper asked, bringing me back to the present. "You okay?"

I cleared my throat and sat up, swinging my legs off the chaise lounge and planting my feet on the floor. "Yeah. I'm fine. So that night, we fell asleep, and by the time we woke up and got home, her father was awake. He flew her to New York that day, and I never saw her again. I didn't even get to say goodbye."

The remnants of resentment toward my mother for blocking the call came floating back, and I stood and walked to the window, working to shove all those emotions back in the mental box they'd been stored in until recently.

The room was silent as we both churned our own thoughts. It was

Piper who spoke first.

"Did you ever try and find her?"

"Of course. All I had to go on was some random girls' school in New York, though. I didn't even know the name of the place. You have to remember, there was no internet then. No Google. No Facebook. No email. We didn't even have cell phones. When someone left, if you didn't have an address or a phone number, you were out of luck unless they got in touch with you." I held my finger up and wagged it. "Don't ever forget how fortunate you are to have the internet, my dear."

"Why didn't she, then? Get in touch with you, I mean. Why didn't she call you or write you? She knew where you were."

That question had burned inside me for decades, and even now, even with it finally answered, it still hurt after all those years not knowing.

"She discovered she was pregnant pretty soon after she got to that fancy school. Her father was livid, and he would have punished me with great glee if he'd known who I was."

"But she protected you."

I nodded. "She did. And she paid a great price for it. She was kicked out of the school. She was disowned by her parents and tossed out on her own at the age of seventeen. Luckily, her grandmother took Cat in, and she was able to deliver Caroline while living there, but I can't imagine how difficult it must have been for her to go through that alone."

"It must have sucked. Why didn't she contact you later, though? After Caroline was born? I mean, you didn't meet Mom until you were, what, twenty-two? That's a long time. You guys could have hooked up and figured out a way to get your baby back."

I turned and sat on the corner of the bed, resting my back against the massive post at the foot of it.

"That's the million-dollar question, I suppose. Catherine said she never felt it would be safe. She always feared what her father might do. To me. To Caroline. To her. That's why she changed her name—to make it harder for him to find her. And she's probably right. I think the man was mentally unstable. There's no telling what would have happened."

I looked at Piper for the first time in a while, and all the anger had left her face. Her eyes were filled with concern, and her frown was sad, not mad. I had probably told her too much. I probably should have stuck to the main bullet points. I didn't want her to be upset.

"But hey," I said, forcing a smile. "Look at the bright side. I met your mama, and we fell in love and got married, and then we had you. My greatest blessing, and my biggest joy. Also, my biggest pain in the rump, but that's okay."

She didn't smile or roll her eyes as I'd expected her to. She was still deep in thought.

"So, if you had found Catherine—or, er, Caterina—you never would have met Mom. You two never would have gotten married, and I never would have been born."

The desolation in her voice cut into my heart, and I wished she was the type of girl that would let me take her in my arms and comfort her. Why was I destined to love women who fought being loved?

"But you *were* born, sweetheart, and I am forever grateful for that. Look, any of us could look back and wish that things had happened differently in our lives, but then we wouldn't be where we are, and we would have missed the experiences we had. Your mother and I had wonderful years together. We've had some great years as a family, and I wouldn't trade that for anything."

"Not even for Caterina and Caroline? What if you had been able to find them? Would you have chosen that life instead of Mom and me?"

"Piper, you're asking me questions that are impossible to answer. There was no choice. I didn't have a choice to make. They weren't part of my life, and you were."

"But now, they are part of your life. They're both back in your life."

I nodded, wishing I could see inside her mind to figure out her thought process and where it was headed.

"Yes, they are, and I'm thankful for that. But it doesn't change what you and I share—the life we've led together, the memories we have, the love we have for each other."

She'd been looking down at the bedspread, tracing the paisley pattern with her index finger over and over again. She stopped and looked up at me, her striking eyes dark with pain.

"Are you in love with Caterina?"

I swallowed hard and tried to consider all the ramifications of my answer. I refused to lie to Piper. I never had, and I never would. But I also didn't want to hurt her any further. I didn't want to push her any farther away.

"We're spending time together. We're getting to know each other again. Trying to figure out who we are and what we want at this stage of life. It's a lot different than it was before, you know."

"You didn't answer my question."

"Well, again, I think you're asking me impossible questions. I'm still trying to catch my breath in all this and figure out what's happening."

"Daddy. Cut the bullshit. Just answer me. Are you in love with Caterina Russo?"

I stared at my daughter and wished I could prevent her heart from ever having to hurt, and that I could ensure that I would never be the one inflicting the pain.

And then I told her the truth.

"Yes. I am."

CHAPTER 67
Caterina

"A re you up yet?" Patsy said when she called. "I've been on pins and needles over here all morning waiting to hear how it went. I've vacuumed and dusted the entire house and baked two dozen cookies. It's almost nine-thirty. I couldn't wait any longer."

"Yeah, I'm awake. Sorry. I've just been sitting out on the pool deck with my coffee."

"You okay? You don't sound right."

"I'm fine. Just tired. I didn't sleep well last night."

"Uh-oh. Did everything go okay?"

I took a deep breath and closed my eyes.

"Why don't we wait and talk about it whenever you get here? You coming over?"

"I'll be right there."

She came through the pool gate within minutes, coffee tumbler in hand, and then she pulled out the chair next to mine at the patio table and sat down.

"Good morning, love."

"Good morning."

We bumped our coffee cups together in greeting, and Patsy motioned for me to start talking.

"Spill the beans. What happened? And why didn't you sleep well? Please tell me it was because he was snoring beside you."

I smiled. "I thought you told me not to bring him home and take him to bed."

She rolled her eyes. "And when have you ever listened to me? So, did you?"

"No, no, no."

"All right, where'd ya go?"

"He took me for dinner at this little place in Winter Garden. Very intimate, only a handful of tables, and the chef comes to the table and explains the menu. It's *prix fixe*, you know, so a limited number of choices each night."

"Sounds nice. And you had a good time?"

I smiled and pulled my feet up into the chair with me. "Yeah. I did. It was a lovely dinner."

"And after dinner?"

My smile grew with the memory of Shelby and Mike.

"Oh my! Look at that blush!" Patsy said. "Maybe I don't want to hear what happened after dinner. I may not be old enough for such details."

"No, it's nothing like that," I said, laughing. "He took me to a marine life center in downtown Orlando for a private tour to see turtles."

"You love turtles!"

"That I do." I held my cup in both hands and took a long sip.

"So, he obviously knew you liked turtles, then?"

"Oh, yeah. He promised me once that he would always find me turtles."

Patsy's smile spread across her face. "It looks like he's kept that promise."

I thought of the other promise he'd kept and the new one he'd made, and the confusion and conflict that had kept me awake all night came rushing back.

"Honey, what's wrong?" Patsy leaned forward and put her hand on my knee. "You look like you're about to cry all the sudden."

"I'm fine."

"You don't look fine."

"Well, I am." I sat the cup on the table and pulled the elastic band from my hair. "Why don't we get to work? Did you get a chance to call that lady back who wanted to donate stuffed animals somewhere?" I ran my fingers through my hair as I talked, and then I pulled it into a tight ponytail and cinched it with the band.

"Caterina, what's going on?"

"Nothing." I looked down, hoping she wouldn't notice that my eyes had betrayed me by filling with tears.

"I thought you said you had a good time. What happened?"

"I did have a good time. I had a great time, in fact. And the whole situation is so screwed up that it doesn't even matter."

"What do you mean? What are you talking about? What's screwed up?"

I sighed and rubbed my eyes. "You know what? I don't even want to get into it. I've turned this over and over and over in my head, and there's just no right answer. I'm tired of thinking about it."

She stared at me for a moment, and then she frowned.

"I feel like I missed something big. You had a date last night with the guy you've been carrying a torch for most of your life, and you said you had a great time. But then we fast-forwarded to everything being screwed up and you being in tears. What happened after the turtles?"

"We came back here and had dessert."

"Dessert? Is that code for something risqué?"

"No, we had dessert. Bread pudding and *crème brûlée*."

"Okay, and then what?"

"And then he went home to his daughter and his big huge house that he built with his wife."

She rubbed her forehead and sighed.

"All right. I can tell you're gonna make this harder than pulling teeth with no anesthesia. If you really don't want to talk about it, we don't have to. But if it's bothering you enough to have you in tears and keep you from sleeping, then I think you should get it out. If you're not going to tell me, at least call your therapist."

"I did. First thing this morning. She's on sabbatical in Nepal."

"Oh." Patsy stared out over the pool and strummed her fingers on the table, and I finished what was in my cup and then stood.

"I'm gonna get another cup of coffee and get to work," I said. "You need a refill?"

"Sure." She followed me inside and leaned against my kitchen counter with her arms crossed. "Have you had breakfast?"

"No. I'm not hungry."

"You need to eat something. You want to come over to my place? I'll cook you eggs and bacon. I know you don't have that here."

"No, thanks," I said as I filled both our cups with coffee. "I'm fine."

"You're not fine. You're not sleeping. You're not eating. You're smiling one minute and crying the next. And you won't tell me what's going on. Do you want to land yourself back in the hospital?"

I went and stood side-by-side with her and put my arm around her shoulders, leaning my head against hers.

"No, of course not. Thanks, Patsy. I appreciate your concern. I really do. But eggs and bacon aren't gonna fix this."

My phone rang on the counter next to my cup, and I was surprised to see William's name on the screen. My heart leapt, and I grabbed the phone, eager to hear his voice.

"I'm gonna take this in my room," I said to Patsy. "Can you get started on the mailing list we talked about yesterday?"

"Sure."

I slid my finger across the screen as I walked toward my bedroom.

"Hey. What's up?" I hoped I didn't sound overly excited.

"Hello, gorgeous. How's your morning going?"

Hearing his voice sent tremors through me, and I sat on my bed with one leg tucked beneath me, my grin growing by the minute.

"It's just getting started," I said. "Patsy got here a few minutes ago, and we're about to tackle a few projects. What about you?"

"My day started hours ago. I've been out in the barn with a new horse that arrived yesterday, and now I'm on my way to Ocala."

"Busy."

"Yep. Hey, look, I'm gonna be coming back through Cedar Creek around two this afternoon. I happen to have a ladder in my truck, and I was thinking maybe I'd stop by and hang that wind chime if you'll be around."

My first reaction was joy, but then I remembered that this wasn't a good idea. I wasn't supposed to spend more time with him.

"Um, I can just have George hang it. He's got a ladder, and he's right next door."

I cringed at the silence on the other end of the line.

Why was it so damned difficult to do this if it was the right thing?

"Okay," William finally said. "Well, I don't mind doing it. It wouldn't be any trouble at all."

I looked to the ceiling and tried to referee the battle between my head and my heart. One said I needed to stay strong and think of the consequences. The other wanted desperately to see William no matter the costs.

The scale tipped in favor of my heart.

"I just remembered that George is working his part-time job at the theme parks today, so he won't be home until late. So, if you want to stop by … I mean, if you're sure it's no trouble …"

"Well, I think the forecast for the afternoon is breezy. You'd be missing some prime chiming time if you waited for George."

I laughed, and something in me released. It felt like I could take a full breath for the first time since he'd left the night before.

"I certainly don't want to miss any prime chiming time. I've already missed the morning breezes. Maybe you should have hung those chimes last night."

"I should have. I was a bit preoccupied with other pursuits last night, though. And unfortunately, I didn't have my ladder with me."

"Oh, and you just happen to have your ladder with you today?"

He chuckled, and I closed my eyes and pictured his smile.

"Yeah, for some reason, I tossed it in the truck this morning. Just in case someone needed something hung."

"Because you never know when that might happen. Or there could be a cat in a tree. A book on a high shelf. Ladders are handy to have for a variety of circumstances. Maybe you should carry one at all times."

"Maybe I will. So, I'll see you around two?"

"I'll be here."

I drew in a deep breath and held it as the call ended, trying to hold onto the high he'd given me. As it released, I cursed myself for being weak. I hadn't even made it twelve hours without seeing him, and I'd already given in.

It seemed I had a new addiction that I couldn't put down, and I wondered if it would be just as bad for me as the others had been. I pushed the thought from my mind and glanced at the time, ready to count down the hours until I got my next fix.

CHAPTER 68
Caterina

Patsy was in the office working when I came out of my room, and she looked at me with raised eyebrows as I walked to my desk.

"Sorry about that, but I'm back and ready to work." I sat in the rolling chair and swiveled it to pull a stack of papers from the priority box. "What task do we need to complete first?"

"I take it that was William?"

"Yes," I said, unable to contain my smile.

"Okay. So is the situation not screwed up anymore?"

"Oh. No. It's still screwed up. I've just decided not to care for the next few hours so I can see him again. I'm sure I'll still obsess about it, and I may even change my mind and tell him not to come, but for right now, I'm happy."

"I can tell. Your entire demeanor changed the moment you saw who was calling. Now, you're bouncing around with a light in your eyes that wasn't there before. So, if he makes that much of a difference, why would you tell him not to come?"

The paperclip holder was empty, and I pulled open the desk drawer and rummaged for a stray clip as I considered how to answer her question.

"Because, Patsy, this relationship can't happen. It can't. There's too much riding on it and too much that can be affected by it. So, no matter how happy he makes me, and no matter how high up on cloud nine he puts me, I have to think of everyone else and keep him at arm's length." I found a clip and slid it over the group of papers I was holding before tossing them in the file organizer on the corner of my desk. "But today? Today, I just didn't want to say no. I did say no at first, but then, I said yes. And it felt so much better to say yes."

"Why do you say it can't happen? What's riding on it and affected by it that's so much more important than this smile on your face?"

I took a deep breath and dove in. I explained the whole thing. The confrontation with Piper and the complications with her feelings. My fears for Caroline and the kids and how awkward it could be if things went badly. I touched on my relationship difficulties, of which she was already well aware, and I talked about William being on a pedestal and not even him being able to live up to my unrealistic expectations. Though, so far, he'd seemed to do just fine.

She rocked her chair back and forth as I talked, and surprisingly, she didn't interrupt. She nodded, she frowned, she smiled, and her facial expressions ran the gamut, but she let me pour it all out. Then, when I'd finished, she exhaled loudly with her cheeks puffed out and her eyes wide.

"That's a lot of weight to carry on your shoulders, Caterina. I don't think it's all your responsibility, though. What does William say about all this?"

"That he loves me. That he believes the universe has brought us back together for a reason. That he's not going to give up on us."

She blinked several times. "Wow. And you still think there's a problem?"

"Of course. He's ignoring the issues in order to have what he wants. I can't do that."

"Is he ignoring the issues, or does he just not see them as issues?"

I tilted my head and looked at her in confusion. "What do you mean?"

"Some of your concerns are valid, no doubt. But some of them, I think you're using as an excuse not to go all in. Take Caroline, for instance. She didn't know when she looked for you what she was going to find. She had no idea whether you were married or divorced. Whether you were with her father or not. She wanted to connect no matter what the situation was. Now, I think she'd be thrilled for the two of you if it was something that made you both happy. And if there came a time when it didn't make you happy any more, then she might be sad for you, but she'd be fine. It's not going to be life-altering for her. I think she'd be the first person to tell you to go for it."

"Maybe so, but what about Piper?"

"If William doesn't see it as a problem that should keep you apart, then I don't think you should either. She's his daughter. I think you let him handle that."

"But if I choose—"

"If you choose to be happy, then so be it. You choosing not to be won't guarantee that these girls will be any better off. And what about William's feelings? The man is telling you he loves you. He's telling you he wants to be with you. You're so worried about whether or not these other people are going to get hurt, but you seem to be disregarding his feelings. What about him?"

"Oh, I am worried about him. Definitely. What if I wig out like I have every other time I've gotten close to someone, and I break his heart again? I've caused him enough pain in his life."

"Again, if he doesn't see it as an issue and he's willing to try, why aren't you? Cat, I know you're scared, and I don't blame you, not one bit. But you have one life to live. You almost lost it, and you got a reprieve. You got a second chance. At life and at love, it seems. You have to decide what you want to do with that. Do you really want fear to rule your life? Or do you want to take life by the balls and wrench every ounce of joy you can out of it?"

My mouth dropped open. "Did you just say *take life by the balls*? I'm shocked."

"You shouldn't be. I married a sailor. You'd be surprised what words I know. Just because I don't use them doesn't mean they're not in my vocabulary. Now, listen to me. You keep saying *what if it doesn't work*. What if it does? If you'd take all this energy you're expending coming up with the worst-case scenario and put that toward the best-case scenario, you might find that things will move in that direction."

"And what if they don't?"

She rolled her eyes and groaned. "Then, you deal with it. No matter how carefully you weigh out what might happen, life can always throw you a curve ball. None of us get guarantees. We take it as it comes, and we figure it out. Do you think my marriage has always worked perfectly? Do you think George and I have always had an easy time of it? No. We haven't. But when something came up, we worked through it together. When a hardship arose, we got through it together. If we all refused to give relationships a chance unless we were guaranteed that they would work, no one would have a relationship. That's the beauty of love. It's something you put your faith in and your heart in without knowing the outcome."

I laid my forehead on my desk and made an exaggerated, fake crying sound.

"It all makes sense when you say it, Patsy, but it gets so jumbled in my head. How do I know what's the right thing to do when I can make both decisions seem right?"

"Let's do a little exercise that my mama taught me years ago. It's called head-heart-gut. Basically, when you need to make a tough decision, you need all three of those on board before moving forward. Close your eyes."

I did as I was told.

"Now, let's start with your gut. I want you to picture being with William. Being in a relationship with him. What's the first feeling you get in your gut?"

I drew in a deep breath and pictured the two of us together, walking hand-in-hand.

"It feels natural. It feels right. It feels like I'm where I'm supposed to be."

"Okay, now in your heart, do you believe you and William should be together?"

"I do, but—"

"No buts. Think about being with William. What does your heart tell you?"

I smiled as I pictured him, and I could hear his voice so clearly in my head.

"I love him. He loves me. That's what my heart tells me."

"Okay, now here's the tricky one for you, so I want you to listen to the question before you answer. Do you think it would be good for you to be with William? Now, I'm not asking if it's good for Caroline, or for Piper, or for anyone else. Do you think being in a relationship with William would be good for you?"

"Yes." My eyes opened. "But I have to consider them. That's what my head tells me."

"So, then consider them. Be considerate of them. But don't miss out on a chance to love and be loved because you think that would make it easier for them."

"You make it sound so cut and dried."

"It is. You're either going to give it a chance and see what happens, or you're not. That's all there is to it, really."

CHAPTER 69
Caterina

Caroline called around lunchtime to discuss the categories for the expense accounts, and once we'd finished business talk, she filled me in on the latest drama with Brad. He still planned to sue her for full custody, but he'd decided to stick with his original plan and move to Orlando instead of Miami.

"I'm glad for the kids," she said. "Miami would make it so hard for them to see him, and at least if he's in Orlando, the schedule as it is now is doable."

"I thought he wasn't really taking them that often on his weekends." I took another bite of my sandwich and put my hand over the phone so she didn't have to hear me chew.

"He doesn't, but I'm hoping that will improve once he gets settled in the new partnership. He's been juggling both offices during the transition, so most weekends he's out of town. He should be in one place soon, and if we're in Cedar Creek and he's in Orlando, he could still get Ethan to soccer practice on Saturdays or Eva to whatever she decides she's going to do next year. She's still on the fence on whether to continue with drama or go back to dance."

"Did you get the email I sent you about the dance school in Winter Garden?"

"I did, thanks. How you'd find it?"

I hesitated for a moment, not sure what I wanted to reveal, but then Patsy's words replayed in my head, giving me courage.

"William and I went to dinner in Winter Garden the other night, and we walked past it."

"Really?" Caroline said, her voice filled with intrigue and what could have been a bit of sarcasm. "That's interesting that you should say that. Levi and I were talking last night, and he mentioned that everyone on the farm is buzzing about William."

I stopped chewing and swallowed, washing down the potato chips with a drink of water.

"Oh? Why's that?"

"It seems that lately he's been in a great mood. Laughing. Joking. Whistling and singing. They say he's practically got a skip in his step." The humor in her tone made me smile.

"Is that so?"

"Yes, and the theory around the farm is that he's seeing someone. Romantically. Would you know anything about that, Cat?"

The moment of truth had come. If I owned up to it and told Caroline that William and I were interested in each other, then the ball would be set in motion. I wouldn't be able to pull it back easily.

"It's a long story," I said with an exhale. "It's complicated."

She laughed. "I'm sure it is. But I must say, I'm not the least bit surprised."

"You're not?"

"No. Of course not. I'm not blind. I've seen the way you are when you talk about him, and I've seen how he is when he talks about you. I don't think anyone could deny the attraction there."

"So, you'd be okay with it? If we were seeing each other, I mean. You wouldn't have a problem with it?"

"No. Not at all. You're both adults, and as long as it's what you both want, and it makes you happy, I say go for it."

It felt like a tiny weight was lifted off my shoulders, and I wished she was standing in front of me instead of on the phone so that I could hug her.

"Thank you. I appreciate that. I just worry about how uncomfortable it might be for you, for us, the three of us, if for some reason it doesn't pan out."

"Why wouldn't it pan out?"

"Oh, I don't know," I said as I swept the chip crumbs into a pile on my plate with my finger. "Any number of reasons."

"But it might pan out, and how awesome would that be! I guess you won't know until you try it, huh?"

"That's what Patsy said." I smiled at the thought of the two of them giving me the same advice.

"You should listen to her, then. She's a wise lady."

"She is. How are things going with Levi, by the way?"

I finished off the sandwich and got up to rinse my plate in the sink and put it in the dishwasher.

"Great. Wonderful. He can't wait for us to be there, though. He's been sending me realtor listings for houses around Cedar Creek. I need to nail something down soon. The closing for the buyers on this place is only a couple of days after school's out, so we have to start the moving process before then. That's good, though. That way we can get there, and the kids will have the entire summer to make new friends. Speaking of which, I need to run. I have to go pick up a birthday card and a gift for one of Ethan's friends who's having a party after school today. A party Ethan just told me about this morning!"

"Nothing like giving you advance notice."

"Right? He woke up with a runny nose this morning, and he was unusually concerned that I was going to keep him home from school. He didn't have a fever or any other symptoms, so I assured him he'd be going, but I had to ask why he was so worried about it. That's how I found out about the party."

"Poor bud. I hope he's not coming down with something. When is that party at William's? This weekend or next?"

"Next weekend. Ethan should be fine by then. Will you be there?"

I shuddered at the thought. "No. Definitely not."

"Why not? There's a ton of people coming evidently."

"All the more reason for me not to. No, you guys will have a great time meeting William's family. I'm sure of it. I think it's best if I sit that one out."

She paused a minute. "Is it because of Piper?"

I'd been walking from the kitchen to my office, but I stopped, nervous to find out what she'd heard.

"Why would you say that?"

"Levi said she's not being the easiest person to get along with right now. I guess part of that is because of me, and if you're seeing William, then I thought maybe part of it was because of you. But I could be wrong. I may be entirely to blame."

I continued to the office and sat on the corner of my desk.

"I think it's been a bit much for Piper with all the revelations. We need to be compassionate to what she's going through. Don't let her get to you. though."

"Oh, I'm not. I felt guilty at first, you know, but then I realized that I haven't done anything to her to feel guilty for. I'm dating Levi, which I know she doesn't like, but it's not like she should have the right to dictate who he sees. He's happy and I'm happy, so she can either be happy for us, or she can be sad. That's her choice. We're not going to let her steal our joy. And I'm sure she's not thrilled to find out she and I are related, although I can't say for sure since she hasn't spoken to me since that became public knowledge. But hey, William and I are getting along great, and he says not to worry about it. I figure he knows her much better than I do. Eventually, she'll have to talk to me because I'm not going anywhere."

I couldn't help but notice the similarities in our situations and the stark differences in how we'd chosen to deal with them.

As a result, Caroline was moving forward with her plans and with her life. She was filled with hope, despite the issues with Brad and Piper and the stress of relocating with her kids.

I needed to take a lesson from my daughter on how to be happy.

CHAPTER 70
Caterina

"How's that?" William asked as he held the turtle chimes from the ceiling for me to gauge the height. "You want them a little lower?"

"Yeah, a little lower. Maybe have them hang roughly the same as that seashell one. That one there. That way they're sort of staggered with the bamboo chimes."

"You got it, boss."

He'd brought everything he needed to hang the chimes—a screw hook, a drill, fishing line—and as soon as he arrived, he'd headed straight out the patio and to work.

I stood beneath him and held onto the ladder, which gave me the perfect excuse to check out his jeans from behind. It also gave me a nice view of the span of his upper back tapering down to his narrow waist and hips.

It only took him minutes to install the wind chimes, and when he climbed back down the ladder, we stood side-by-side gazing up at the turtles as they bobbed in the wind at the end of the chime's strings.

"They're not very loud," William said, holding up his hand to shield his eyes from the sun.

"They don't have to be. They're cute."

He dropped his hand and looked down at me with a smile. "So are you."

My cheeks grew warm, and I wondered if there was an age limit on being cute or on blushing when a guy told you that you were.

He folded the ladder and hefted it onto his shoulder.

"All right, well, you should be all set for the afternoon breezes, and I'll get out of your hair so you can get back to work."

I hadn't expected him to leave so soon, and I scrambled to figure out a way to delay his departure.

"I, um, uh, I made a pitcher of lemonade. Would you like a glass?"

"Lemonade sounds refreshing," he said. "Let me get the ladder back in the truck, and I'll meet you inside."

I went to the kitchen and prepared two glasses, disappointed that he'd been ready to go. I should have been relieved. I had at least twenty things on my must-do list for the day, and I'd already gotten a late start to the morning. But my mind had been consumed with thoughts of William since he'd left the night before, and now that Patsy and Caroline had planted matching seeds of doubt, my resolve to stay away from him had begun to waver.

"It's getting hot out there," he said as he came back through my front door. "We got spoiled with these mild temperatures the past few weeks, but the humidity is rising. Summer will be here with a vengeance before we know it."

I handed him his glass, and our fingers brushed together in the exchange, taking my mind back to the sensual encounter in the truck.

A little thrill of delight went through me with the memory, and I shivered in response and pulled my hand back.

"You okay?" William asked as he flashed a smile, his blue eyes playful.

"Fine. Never better."

His smile widened, and he turned up the glass and drained it.

"You must have been thirsty," I said. "Do you want more?"

"Oh, I'd love more! Wait, you meant lemonade, didn't you?"

I rolled my eyes as he laughed.

He seemed to be in a flirtatious mood, and as I took his glass back to the kitchen and refilled it, I wished we had the rest of the day to spend together.

We must have been thinking along the same path, because his next question was to ask what plans I had for the day.

"Paperwork, mostly. I do have a few calls to return, but I've been helping an adoption charity with grant-writing, and I need to have my portion of it submitted by tomorrow morning. So, that's going to be my main event for this afternoon and evening. Sounds exciting, doesn't it? What about you?"

"I'm gonna stick close to the barn. We've got a mare getting ready to foal, and the vet said this morning that she could go any time. Levi's there now, but he needs to head over to his sister Rachel's place for something she's got going on tonight, so I don't want to wander too far."

"Is this one of yours, or a client's horse?"

"One of ours. Well, our mare but someone else's stud. A good match, though. One I've been pursuing for a while."

I wanted to ask him if he'd like to have dinner. I wanted *him* to ask me to come out to the farm and wait for the foal with him. I also wanted him to put his arms around me and kiss me until I was breathless again.

But I didn't dare say any of that. I was still too uncertain of what we should do, and I didn't want to be the one to lead us down a bad path. It wasn't fair to him for me to move things forward if I knew I hadn't made up my mind whether I was willing to take the risk.

"I hope the delivery goes well," I said instead.

"Thanks. I should probably head back out there."

"And I should probably get to work on that grant."

Despite what we'd said we *should* do, neither of us moved. We just stood there in the middle of my living room and stared at each other.

"Okay, I'm gonna go," William said after a long pause. He turned to walk toward the kitchen with his lemonade glass, and I stepped forward to take it.

"Don't worry about that. I've got it." I reached for the glass and he handed it to me, our hands momentarily intertwined around it.

The touch lingered as we made eye contact, and then I pulled away to go and set the glass in the kitchen sink.

When I returned, he had walked to the door. He stood there with his hands in his pockets, and I came and stood in front of him, taking care to leave enough distance that it didn't look I was asking for a kiss, though I certainly wanted one.

"Thanks for hanging the chime," I said. "I appreciate it."

"No problem. I'm happy to help." He grinned. "I hope that prime chiming time this evening is everything you want it to be and more."

"I'm sure it will be, thanks to you."

We fell into silence again, and I wished I could tell him that I was reconsidering. That I thought maybe it was worth giving it a try if it meant we could be together. I wanted to let him know that I wanted this every bit as badly as he'd said he did, and that I was fighting with myself to find a way to let it happen.

But I didn't trust my mind not to change again. Too many doubts. Too many fears.

"Let me know if the horse has her baby," I said. "I'll buy you some bubble gum cigars to celebrate."

He grinned with wide eyes. "Ha! I'd forgotten all about those things. Do they still make them?"

"I have no idea."

"Well, maybe we can find some other way to celebrate then."

My pulse quickened. "Yeah. Maybe so."

"I'll talk to you later, Cat."

It was the perfect moment for a goodbye kiss, but he opened the door and left without one, and in doing so, he left me confused and perplexed.

I'd been certain the ladder in the truck was a ruse to come and see me, but he'd been so businesslike about the whole thing once he arrived. He went straight to work and was prepared to leave immediately after. He did have the mare to consider, and that might have been a factor, but what purpose did it serve for him to come over if it wasn't to spend time together? Did he really just stop by to hang my chimes and nothing more?

The night of our date, he'd pretty much kept a hand on me at all times. Whether he was stroking my back, holding my hand, or putting his arm around my shoulders, we'd been in almost constant contact. Today, other than the accidental brushes on the lemonade glass, he'd made no effort to touch me at all.

His manner had been playful and flirtatious, but then he'd left without even attempting a kiss.

Granted, it was I'd asked for. I'd told him we couldn't be in a relationship and that it was best if we didn't move things in that direction. Perhaps he'd decided that I was right. Maybe he came over to show me that we could be just friends and that he wouldn't pressure me into anything else.

But I wasn't sure that was what I wanted any more.

I found it hard to focus on the dry, technical aspects of grant-writing when my mind was in emotional overdrive. I worried that perhaps I'd pushed him away. He'd practically begged me to give us a chance, and I'd shut him down in every way possible. He'd promised when he left that night that he'd never give up on us, but what if he'd decided it wasn't worth fighting for? Why pursue someone who's made it clear they don't want to be pursued?

Except I did want him to pursue me. I wanted him to catch me, and then never let me go. I wanted him to want me.

I shuffled through the afternoon and evening in a fog, torn between worrying that I'd screwed up and convincing myself that it was still for the best.

When my phone rang with his number around eight that evening, the first thing I felt was relief. He had to still be interested or he wouldn't call. But the conversation went much like the encounter we'd had that afternoon. He asked how the rest of my day had gone and if I'd finished the grant I was working on, and then he updated me on the status of the mare, who still hadn't given birth.

A couple of times, I started to tell him that I didn't want us to be just friends. I formulated the sentences in my head to explain that it might still take me time to get used to the idea, but that I very much wanted us to be together in every sense. I desperately wanted him in my life, and not as a casual acquaintance. He was already in my heart, and I wanted him in my bed.

But each time I opened my mouth to speak, fear would steal my words.

Before I could make it happen, a colleague called him away, and we said goodbye without me telling him the truth.

I spent another night tossing and turning, unable to find peace with my thoughts and my feelings. When the sun finally rose, I got up and threw myself into work. By the time Patsy arrived later that morning, I'd gone through the priority box, cleaned out my emails, and cleared away the piles of papers that had been long-time residents on my desk.

"Holy cow!" Patsy said when she walked into the office. "What happened in here?"

"Oh, I did a little cleaning. A little filing."

"A little? It looks a giant vacuum cleaner sucked up everything in its path." She looked at me with a raised eyebrow and frowned. "Another sleepless night?"

I ignored the question and handed her a printout of an email request to fund playground equipment at a holding facility.

"I want us to look into them more before we approve this. I seem to recall hearing some scuttlebutt about mismanagement of funds at this place. I don't remember who told me, and it may just be rumor, of course, but let's be extra diligent in our homework for this one. Oh, and we got a submission on the website from a couple in Ft.

Walton Beach. They've got funds that their families and friends raised for an adoption, but they want some guidance in finding a good lawyer to help them through the process. Can you reply to them? Maybe recommend Terrance Lawson. We should have his contact information on file."

"Cat, this is ridiculous."

"What is?"

Her look turned stern as she set her coffee cup on her desk and laid down the paper I'd given her.

"Why are you fighting this so hard? You love the man and the man loves you. It's that simple."

"Nothing is that simple, Patsy."

She shook her head, and though I braced for her to continue, she remained quiet and settled into work mode.

All in all, it was a productive day, but I found myself checking my phone more and more often as the day wore on with no word from him. I even scrolled back through the notifications in case I'd missed a text or call somehow despite watching the phone like a hawk.

I even considered calling him a couple of times. I could ask how the mare was doing, and that way I'd know if being occupied with the new foal was the reason he hadn't called. I thought about texting him to say something cute and clever about the chimes, but that seemed so contrived that I couldn't bring myself to do it.

Patsy invited me over to their place for dinner, and I purposely left the phone behind so I wouldn't obsessively check it every ten minutes while I was there. It was the first thing I did when I walked back into the house from next door, though. I made a beeline for it, excited to see from a distance that there were notifications lit up on the screen.

I'd had three missed calls. One was a foster family in Ocala, who left a voicemail about setting up a time for a wellness check. The second was Caroline, but there was no message. Then, not too long after her call was William's, and he'd left a message asking me to call back.

My dour mood lifted, and I did a little happy dance right there in my living room. He might have decided we'd be just friends, but he was maintaining contact. That gave me hope that maybe I hadn't screwed it up beyond repair after all.

CHAPTER 71
Caterina

I wanted to call William back right away, but I was curious as to why Caroline had called, so I decided to talk to her first.

She answered on the first ring, almost like she'd been expecting my call.

"Hey," she said. "How are you?"

"Good! I was at Patsy's and left my phone here. Sorry I missed you."

"I thought you might be over there since it was dinner time. It wasn't urgent, so I didn't leave a message. I figured I could call you later once the kids were in bed."

"Is everything okay?"

"Yeah, it's fine. I just wanted to talk to you while they weren't around."

"Do you need to call me back? Or do you need me to call you later?"

"No. They're both occupied with other things right now. Let me step out on the back porch so they don't hear me."

I kicked off my sandals and tried not to worry about what she'd need to hide from the kids. Had Brad served her with papers? Had something fallen through with the sale of their house in Gainesville? Had she decided to get another job or perhaps reconsidered her decision to move to Cedar Creek?

"Okay, sorry about that," she said after a moment. "I don't want them to know anything until they have to."

It didn't sound like good news, and dread filled my stomach.

"Levi found a house that he thinks is perfect. He went to see it this afternoon, and he sent me pictures, and it really does seem like it has everything I'm looking for. It's a little out of my price range, but the realtor thought they might be willing to come down. It's got some issues, but Levi said he's certain it's nothing we couldn't handle on our own, and it might be good bargaining power."

"Okay!" I exhaled in relief. "Well, that's great news. Where is the house?"

"It's actually inside Cedar Creek's city limits, which is great, because the kids could walk to school next year. It's right by that little park. You know the one I mean? The one by the tiny lake. Lake Dot, I think he said."

"I have no idea, but Cedar Creek's not that big, so if it's in the city limits, it's got to be close to everything."

"Right! Levi said he drove around the neighborhood, and there seem to be other kids there. You know, basketball hoops in the driveways, bicycles laying in the yards, kid stuff."

I poured myself a glass of lemonade as she talked, pleased to hear the excitement in her voice. I knew she'd been stressing about not knowing where she and the kids were going, especially after Brad put their house up for sale and sold it out from under them.

"Hold on, Cat. Ethan has a question." She answered Ethan and told him she'd be back inside soon, and then she waited for him to go back in. "Here's the thing," she said when she returned to our conversation. "I'm going to drive down in the morning while the kids are in school so I can see the house. I'm not going to tell them, because I don't want to get their hopes up. We went and looked at a place the last time we were there, and it sold before I could even decide if I wanted to put an offer in. They were so disappointed, and I don't want to put them through that again. Once I find something, and it's definite, then I'll tell them."

"That's probably best," I said as I carried the lemonade outside to sit by the pool. All the chimes were tinkling and clanging above my head, and I smiled at the tiny turtles swinging in the wind.

"It's gonna be a quick turnaround trip because my mom went with her friends to Branson, Missouri, to see Tom Jones. I have to be back here in Gainesville to pick up the kids from school since she's gone. Levi's gonna meet me at the house to walk it, but I'd really like to have a female opinion. I know it's short notice, but is there any way you could meet us at this house tomorrow morning? Probably like eleven, I'm thinking. It shouldn't take long to walk through."

My heart soared and happy tears sprang to my eyes. I couldn't believe Caroline was asking for my opinion. That she wanted my input. She was basically asking me to stand in for her mom. What an honor!

"Of course. Yes, I'd love to see it."

"Awesome! Thank you so much. I've never made such a large purchase by myself before. Brad handled everything with the houses we owned, and this is technically my first house, you know, for me. Well, me and the kids. I just don't want to screw up. I don't want to make a mistake, and then be stuck in it. You've lived in so many places and seen so much and done so much. I'd feel better if you thought it was a good purchase."

"Well, now, I'm happy to give you my opinion on the layout of the house and its features, stuff like that. But I don't know how much I would know about issues the house may have. You know, structural or electrical or anything maintenance-related."

"Oh, I know! That's fine. Levi will be there, and I've asked William if he'd join us. He said he has to check his schedule and get back to me. He's supposed to let me know tonight. But he said either way, he'll go to the house and check it out, even if he can't meet us and be there the same time we are."

My heart began to race. This would be the first time the three of us were together other than those awkward encounters at the hospital. I'd spent time with both Caroline and William alone, but how would it feel to be with both of them at the same time?

Father, mother, and daughter.

It shouldn't have been a big deal. Parents weighed in on their adult children's decisions all the time, and we wouldn't be the first parents to accompany their daughter on a house-hunting excursion.

But we weren't typical. We'd never even had a conversation with all three of us present. I had no way to know what the dynamic would be like.

"That's okay, right?" Caroline said.

"What?"

"If William comes, that's okay, right? I figured since you guys are going out to dinner together and stuff, it's not going to be difficult for anyone, right?"

With things so undefined between us, I truly didn't know if it would be difficult or not, but I didn't want to put that on Caroline. If she needed us both there, we'd both be there.

"It's fine with me," I said to reassure her. "I have no problem with it, and I can't imagine that William would."

Would he? I didn't think so, but the push-and-pull, are-we-aren't-we nature of our relationship at the moment made it unpredictable. I didn't fully understand what he was up to the last couple days, but then again, I had no idea where I was at with it either. One minute I felt I couldn't live without him, and the next I was determined to avoid all contact.

"Good," Caroline said. "I didn't want to cause any problems."

"No problem here. Text me the address."

"Okay. Or maybe I should swing by and pick you up and we can ride together. That way we have more time to chat."

"That'd be great. I'll see you tomorrow morning."

When we'd said our goodbyes, I immediately dialed William's number.

"Hey there," he said when he picked up.

I closed my eyes and smiled at the sound of his voice, picturing him in my mind.

"Hey. I got your message so I'm calling you back. What's up? Do you have a new baby horse?"

"Not yet. Still nothing. She's restless, and she's shown some signs of the first stages, but nothing yet. I'm hoping she waits until tomorrow at this point. They usually give birth after dark, and I'm getting too old to stay up all night with a delivery. I need my sleep. Hey, have you talked to Caroline tonight?"

"I actually just got off the phone with her."

"Okay, so then she asked you about going out to see the house with her?"

"Yeah, she said she'd asked you too, but that you have to check your schedule. She thought you were going to let her know tonight, but I guess if the foal isn't here yet, you still don't know your schedule, huh?"

"I'm hoping for an arrival before then so it's not an issue, but I've already worked out who can be here in my absence so that Levi and I can both come to the house. That's not why I told her I needed to check my schedule."

"Oh?"

"I wanted to talk to you first. I didn't know how you'd feel about it, you know, with the three of us being there together. I didn't want you to be uncomfortable, so if you'd like, I will tell her that I'll go see the house before you guys get there and be gone before the two of you arrive."

Was he uncomfortable with the three of us being together? Or had he become so committed to honoring my wishes about not seeing each other that he thought it should apply in this situation as well?

"I'm fine with it if you are," I said. "Are you fine with it?"

"I'm fine with it."

I exhaled my relief. From the moment she'd told me he might be there, I'd been looking forward to seeing him, even though it might be awkward given the circumstances.

"Good. Then, I guess I'll see you tomorrow," I said.

He didn't reply at first, and I tried to think of something witty to keep the conversation going, not wanting to hang up just yet, but before I came up with anything, he spoke again. He sounded uncharacteristically nervous.

"I was thinking I could…that I might…well, if you wanted me to, I could pick you up and us ride together. Or do you think that's too much?"

I ran my fingers through my hair and silently swore. I'd already told Caroline I'd ride with her, and I very much wanted to do that. I was still blown away that she'd wanted me to tag along, and I didn't want to miss any opportunity to spend more time with her.

But if William was asking to pick me up, then that meant he would also drop me off, and that might give us the chance to talk. To connect. I might be able to summon the courage to tell him what all I was feeling. But then again, if he'd decided it was best if we moved on as friends, that might not be such a good idea for me to lay myself bare like that.

"Caroline's going to pick me up, but thanks. I appreciate the offer."

"No problem. It's pretty wild that she wants our opinions, huh?"

"Yes! I was surprised. Honored, to be honest. I'm glad she cares what we think and that she wants us to be involved."

"She's pretty terrific that way," he said. "Very considerate and thoughtful. She seems to have a good head on her shoulders, too, so I'm sure she'll do just fine making her own decisions. But I'm happy to lend her whatever advice I can."

"I feel the same way. I can't wait for them to be here in Cedar Creek where we can see them more often."

I'd said *we* without even thinking about it, but it was accurate. We both wanted more time with her and the kids. We shared our love for them and our interest in getting to know them better. We shared them.

We hadn't discussed sharing a daughter much, and it was a foreign concept in many ways. Usually if we were talking about her, it either related to my fears about us hurting her or it involved her beginnings, a painful topic for us both. It felt good to talk about Caroline together in a positive manner. I was certain it was an experience other parents took for granted, but we'd never had this opportunity.

For me, she'd always been a secret. For him, she'd been unknown. To be able to discuss her openly was in itself liberating, but to discuss her with the man I'd created her with was surreal.

I'd always known that William and I had a tangible product of our connection walking around the planet. I clung to the fact that even though we were destined to be separate, some part of us would live on united in the child we'd brought to life.

As I considered this new phase of life with the three of us in contact together, the full extent of that bond hit me in new ways, and it was like a revelation. William and I would never be just friends. We would never be categorized as merely casual acquaintances. We were parents together. We shared a daughter, and we shared grandchildren. We shared common interests and common loves.

I couldn't untangle myself from William Ward completely even if I wanted to. And more and more, I was accepting the fact that I really didn't want to.

"I don't think I've ever thanked you, Cat," he said, his voice breaking into the impromptu therapy session I'd been having in my head.

"Thanked me? For what?"

"For carrying my child. For bringing her into this world. For protecting her. Our daughter is incredible, and no matter what's happened in the past or what will happen in the future, I'm thankful for her, and thankful to you for having her. I know you had other … options … at the time, and well, I'm grateful to you."

My chest heaved with emotion and I swallowed hard to keep it from overcoming me.

"There was never any other option for me, William. She was ours. She was a part of you. A part of us. I'd have given my own life to protect hers."

We both were silent, as were the tears that streamed down my face. I wished he was with me. I closed my eyes and tried to imagine his arms around me. I tried to feel the comfort of his embrace, but the humid air surrounding me was empty.

Patsy was right. This was ridiculous. Why was I sitting there alone when he was only a few miles away? The only reason I wasn't in his arms was because I'd refused to let him hold me. I'd refused his offers of love, and I'd been too scared to admit how much I needed him.

I opened my mouth to ask him to come over, but he spoke before I could get the words out.

"I'm sorry, Cat. I didn't mean to remind you of painful times. I shouldn't have brought it up. I'm just tired and not really thinking straight. I'm gonna head to bed and try to get some sleep in case I get woken in the night by this foal. I'll see you tomorrow, okay?"

I sighed, and the plea on my lips fell away unspoken.

"It's all right. Get some sleep, and I'll see you tomorrow. Good night, William."

"G'night, Cat."

CHAPTER 72
Caroline

I made good time getting to Caterina's from Gainesville, and I was relieved when we pulled in at the little house to find William and Levi already there. The schedule didn't allow any time for deviations if I was going to be back before school let out.

"Oh, this is really cute, Caroline," Cat said as we got out of the car. "I love that huge oak tree in the front and the little screened-in porch."

"It looks older than it did in the pictures," I said, surveying the peeling paint and the lopsided angle of the porch.

"Hey, babe," Levi said as he came around the corner from the rear of the house.

My heart filled with warmth, just as it did every time I saw him, and I walked forward to wrap my arms around his neck as he picked me up and swung me around in a circle.

He gave me a quick kiss and then released me to say hello to Caterina.

"Hey, Cat. How are you today?"

"I'm good," she said. "Very good, in fact. It's a beautiful day. And how are you?"

As they continued to exchange pleasantries, I turned to inspect the house and saw William walking toward us, his eyes on Caterina. He smiled at her, and it was a full smile, which struck me as unusual since I'd grown accustomed to his melancholy half-grin.

She smiled back, and they did a polite hug as they greeted each other.

I'd never watched my parents interact other than in her hospital room. William had kissed her forehead the day she was discharged, and while that had seemed a tender moment, the evident affection between them now was something completely different. Their hug wasn't overly physical. It was one that could have been shared between any two friends or close acquaintances. But the way they looked at each other, the way they moved in response to each other, and the differences in their behaviors was telling.

Cat had been in a good mood since I picked her up, but when William came on the scene, it was like her entire being lit up. Her smile was bigger, her eyes were brighter, and she seemed to radiate beauty.

He seemed equally as smitten, if not more. In the short time I'd known William, I'd perceived him to be somewhat shy. Definitely quieter and more reserved than Cat. But even greeting her, he seemed more animated and engaged than normal, almost like she brought a different side of him to light.

At the same time, I was fascinated by how nervous William appeared to be. He'd always come across as confident and self-assured, but as they parted from their hug, he shoved his hands in his pockets, and he kept shifting his weight from foot to foot as though he didn't know what to do with himself.

It was bizarre, and at the same time, it made me all warm and fuzzy inside. If these two people could rekindle a love all these years later after everything that had happened, then surely, Levi and I could conquer whatever obstacles life put in our way.

"What do you think of the house?" Caterina asked Levi. "It's cute as can be, but Caroline said you thought there were some issues?"

"Nothing I don't think we could handle. I was just showing William some of the wood rot on the eaves, but that could be easily replaced."

"Why's the porch crooked?" I asked.

"It just needs to be jacked up and re-leveled," William said. "It's not a big deal. I haven't seen anything outside that seems major."

"I want to see the inside," I said, but then I realized someone was missing. I'd been so preoccupied with William and Cat that I hadn't even noticed. "Where's the realtor? She's not here?"

"Not yet," Levi said, looking at his watch. "You told her eleven, right?"

"Yes. I even confirmed it in a text." I pulled out my phone and scrolled through our conversation. "See?"

"Call her," Cat said. "She may be running late."

I dialed Ivy's number and she picked up right away.

"Ivy? This is Caroline Miller, and we were supposed to meet at eleven?"

"What time is it? Oh my gosh! I'm so sorry! I can be there in ten minutes. Fifteen tops. I'm sorry!"

"Okay, we'll see you soon." I hung up and exhaled in frustration. "Great. She can't be here for another ten or fifteen minutes."

"Well, we can walk around outside the house until she gets here," Cat offered. "It will be okay."

"I'm just worried about timing," I said as Levi rubbed his hand across my neck and shoulders.

"We can make it quick," Levi said. "C'mon, let me show you the back yard while we wait for her."

The back yard was fenced, and though Eva and Ethan were probably both too old for the wooden swing set and jungle gym, it was still a nice space. There were a few trees and a nice wooden deck that extended off the screened porch on the back of the house.

I tried to picture what it would be like. Would we put a barbecue grill on that concrete pad by the screened door? Maybe hang a hammock between those two trees? Would Ethan have friends over and pitch a tent in that corner?

"What do you think?" I asked Cat.

"It's a nice-sized yard. Plenty of room if you wanted to do a garden or some flowers."

"Please," I said with an eyeroll. "Even if I had the time for such activities, which I don't, I wouldn't know the first thing about how to keep a plant alive."

Cat laughed and put her arm around my shoulders. "Uh-oh, I think you may have inherited that from me. I've never had a green thumb."

"But your back patio and your front flower beds all look gorgeous! Like a tropical oasis!"

"Yes, they do, because I pay my landscaper to make them look that way."

We laughed, and then we put our faces up to the screen to peer inside the porch.

"It's small," I said.

"It's big enough for a table and chairs."

"Hey, Levi," I called out. He and William were over by the small shed in the back corner. "Did you see this ceiling on the porch? It looks like it's falling in."

The two of them joined Cat and me with all our faces pressed against the screen.

"That's nothing," William said. "This porch was added onto the house at some point, and they used sheetrock for the ceiling, which is common, unfortunately. The tape and mud they use between the panels tends to wear down in time with all the moisture and humidity of our Florida air. What you see there is just the tape falling down. It's an easy fix."

Once Ivy arrived and we'd walked the entire property inside and out, it seemed the house had no major issues, but plenty of those easy fixes. Levi and William both brushed them off as no big deal, but they felt like a big deal to me. I didn't know how to fix any of them, and I didn't want to rely on my boyfriend or my father to take care of it, even though they seemed more than willing to.

This was supposed to be my chance to stand on my own two feet. I couldn't do that if I was starting out already asking for help.

"What do you think, Cat?" I asked her as we stood in the kitchen. Ivy had gone outside to the shed with William and Levi, but the fear of snakes had squashed any curiosity I had about what was out there. "Be honest."

"I think it's a solid little house. It's got enough space for you and the kids. With that half bath in the back, you could each have your own bathroom, which will be nice as Ethan and Eva get older."

I sighed as I opened a cabinet door and closed it again. "Yeah, they already fight enough over everything as it is. I definitely wouldn't want them to share a bathroom."

"I guess the more important question is what do you think. Do you like this house? Do you see you guys living here? You don't seem too excited about it."

I took a deep breath and looked toward the ceiling, embarrassed to feel the tears stinging my eyes.

"I am so overwhelmed right now, Cat. I don't know what I'm doing. I look around this house, and I see that it's something I can probably afford and manage to take care of on my own. The house we're in now is too big. It's too much. But I also look around this house, and I see that Eva is going to complain that it's old and Ethan will probably say it smells funny. Neither one of them will like the bedrooms being smaller than theirs now, and Eva's going to stroke over the hall bathroom only having a tub and not a shower. In Gainesville, we have a living room and a family room, so with only one room here, they're going to fight over the television."

"Well, I think that everyone is going to need to make some adjustments, and that's part of life. So that can be a lesson and not necessarily a bad thing. But you don't have to get this house, Caroline. There's other houses, and you still have some time."

"No, I don't. Not really. By the time they do inspections, and closings, and all the paperwork and everything else, I'm running out of time. I've got to finish packing that house and get everything from there to here, but I don't want them to live in an empty space until the end of school, and we have to be out two days after school ends. Plus, I have to work, and—"

"Now, you know your schedule with me is entirely flexible. You take off however much time you need."

"Thanks, but I need to do the job you hired me for. You're not paying me a salary to pack and move. I just don't know how to make everything happen at once and feel confident that I'm making the right decisions."

Cat smiled and cocked her head to the side. "That's the age-old question of life, no matter what stage you're at. Look, if you don't feel like this is the right place for you, then we keep searching. Worst case scenario, you could put your stuff in storage and you and the kids could stay with me until you found something."

I shook my head. "No. I appreciate that you would offer that, but I definitely do not want to be homeless and camping out in someone's house. Besides that, I want you to like spending time with my kids, and if you had to live with them, that probably wouldn't be the case."

She chuckled and wrapped her arms around me, and I let myself relax into her embrace. My mother's embrace. Something about her holding me and comforting me made me even more choked up inside, and I began to cry.

When I'd set out on my search to find my birth mother, I'd hoped that we might eventually be able to have a relationship. That we'd be able to talk occasionally and perhaps visit now and then. What I'd found had gone so far beyond my wildest dreams that it was hard to wrap my head around it.

Here I was, uprooting my kids and my life to move to this tiny little town in the middle of nowhere. My immediate family—which had consisted of my mom, my kids, and me—had suddenly blossomed and grown. I had another mother now—and a father, too, for what felt like the first time in my life. And rather than being bystanders with occasional phone conversations, they were both eager to be actively involved with me and my children. My father was even throwing a party for us, which would expand my family circle even more.

And then, of course, there was Levi, who had taken my heart and who had become my rock and my other half in ways I'd never experienced before with Brad.

It was all good, but it was overwhelming.

"It's okay," Cat whispered as she held me in her arms and rubbed her hand up and down my back over and over again. "It's all right. You're carrying a lot of weight on these shoulders, but you're going to be okay. You're made of good stock, and you're a smart cookie. You've got Lorna in your corner, and you've got me, and Levi, and William. We all have your back, and we're here for you."

I heard footsteps enter the room, and I cringed with embarrassment, unwilling to lift my head from Cat's shoulder just yet.

"She's okay," Cat whispered over my head. "It's just a lot to take in. A lot to consider."

I raised my head and wiped at my eyes and turned to face William and Levi, both wide-eyed, looking bewildered and concerned. Ivy hung back behind them and looked like she'd rather be anywhere else.

"I'm fine, guys," I said as I rubbed my knuckle underneath my eyelashes to wipe away any stray mascara runs. "I'm okay. Sorry. Just got a bit emotional."

"You want us to give you a minute?" William asked. "We could wait outside."

"No," I said, shaking my head. "I'm fine. Really."

I looked at Levi and smiled, and he came and put his arm around me.

"Babe, if you don't like the house, it's okay. We'll find a better one."

"Um, I'm gonna step outside and return a call," Ivy said. "I'll give you guys some privacy, and I'll just be right out front if you need me."

Once she'd gone, I forced a little smile at everyone still standing there staring at me. "I bet I'll be the topic of her water cooler conversations this afternoon."

"Don't worry about her," William said. "You do what you need to do. If you need to cry, you cry."

I smiled at him, grateful for his kindness and his calming presence.

"So, is it the house?" Levi said.

"It's everything," I exclaimed with a sigh.

His brows raised, and I could see his concern level spike.

"No, no," I said as I reached out to lay my hand on his chest. "Not *everything*. Some things in my life are pretty great right now. Like you three."

They all smiled, and I noticed that William looked over at Caterina, though her attention was still on me.

I took a deep breath and exhaled loudly. "The house meets our needs. It's close enough to the school that the kids could walk next year. There's a park right at the end of this street. From what I read on the internet, it's a pretty safe neighborhood. It's at the upper end of my price range, but I could probably afford it, depending on what happens with Brad in court, of course. If I get tied up in a legal battle with him, I can't afford anything."

"Let's cross that bridge when we come to it, if we come to it," William said.

"So, yeah, it's got two and a half baths. Three bedrooms. A fenced-in back yard. Ethan's been begging for a dog, so that would be good in case I get suckered into that. It does have a lot of little things that we'd need to fix, though. And it's old. Which isn't bad, but I live in a relatively new neighborhood in a relatively new house. This has a different feel to it, for sure."

Levi took both my hands in his and turned me to face him. "Look at this way. Nothing says that if you buy this house now, you have to live in it forever. Think of it as the next step. The next chapter. You never know where you're gonna be down the road. This house is only temporary."

His eyes were so serious, and I wondered if he was somehow trying to communicate with me telepathically or something. If so, I wasn't picking up on the message. Was he hinting that we'd be in a house together? Was he saying that down the road I wouldn't need this house anymore?

We'd never really discussed logistics beyond me getting to Cedar Creek. He'd offered at first for the kids and me to move into his house, which was part of the Ward Farms property. But I knew that couldn't happen. I needed to be on my own, and the kids needed time to transition to a new life and a new town. Not to mention that our relationship had been a whirlwind, and it needed more time to grow and develop before we reached that level of involvement.

Maybe once the kids were older. Maybe once Eva was out of school.

School!

"Oh no! What time is it?" I asked, suddenly frantic.

"You're okay," William said. "I've been keeping an eye on the time for you. You're gonna need to head out soon, but I wasn't gonna let you leave late."

"Right. Okay. Thanks. I guess I need some time to think about this."

"Good idea," Cat said. "You don't have to make a decision right this minute, and if it's not available when you decide, then it wasn't meant to be."

I returned her smile, so thankful that I'd asked her to come and that she'd agreed.

"All right. Let's talk to Ivy, and then I need to get Cat back to her house and get on the road."

"I'll take Cat home," William said.

I looked at Cat as she looked at him, and I almost laughed at her surprised expression.

"If that's okay with you, of course," he said to her.

"Sure. That's fine. That would save Caroline time. Definitely."

When we'd bid Ivy farewell and waved goodbye to William and Cat, Levi opened the driver's door for me.

"You don't have to get this house. We'll find you something you like."

I smiled and slid my arms around his neck. "I already have something I like, and where I live is just a place. But hey, how about those two, huh?"

"What did I tell you? Could you see the difference in William?"

"Of course! Cat, too. I'm happy for them. You know, they were both alone and maybe lonely, and now to find each other again after all this time. I think it's awesome."

"Wouldn't that be funny if your parents ended up together because of you searching for them?"

"I'd be okay with that, if it makes them both happy."

He pressed his lips to mine and then frowned. "I want to see you happy. I want you to feel good about this move. About where you're bringing the kids to."

"I am happy. And we'll figure it out."

He kissed me again, and then he gave my bottom a pat as he pulled back.

"You need to get on the road. I don't want you driving fast trying to make up time."

"Yeah, I'd hate to have a blowout and need to get towed. Someone might steal my car or something."

He grinned and kissed me again. "I'm never going to live that down, am I?"

"Probably not."

CHAPTER 73
Caterina

William threw me for a loop when he offered to take me home. He'd seemed happy to see me when Caroline and I first arrived, but then we hadn't any contact or conversation after that. He and Levi had been in manly mode checking out the house, and I'd stayed by Caroline's side, trying to help her deal with the weight of the world.

"What did you think of the house?" I asked as we left.

"Much of what she's unhappy with is cosmetic," he said. "You paint that whole place inside and out, you get new appliances, new flooring, and new vanities in the bathrooms, and there'd be nothing wrong with that house."

"She doesn't have the money to get all that stuff, William. Instead of shelling out to remodel the entire place, she needs to find a different house."

"Levi said he's been looking high and low. As the suburbs creep more westward, demand is getting higher, and the prices are too. He said everything else he's seen in her price range has either been questionable in location or worse in issues."

"Maybe I could look at the numbers again and see if I can pay her more."

His phone rang, and though I couldn't hear the caller's words, I could tell by William's responses that the foal was on his way.

He swore softly when he hung up, and he accelerated our speed.

"You need to get back right away?" he asked as he rubbed his hand over his hair.

"Me? Um, no."

"I need to be at the farm, like, *now*. Her water broke, and she's in active labor. Would you be okay with riding along, and then I will get you home as soon as I can?"

"Sure. Whatever you need to do."

He made a couple more calls as we sped to the farm, and when we arrived at the barn, there was a group of people on the scene, including Piper.

I followed William inside, but then I hung back near the entrance, not wanting to be in the way.

Levi arrived at almost the same time, and he said hello and flashed me a smile as he walked past, as did a few of the other people who saw me. I smiled back and tried to look like I was completely at ease, though I was anything but. I stood out like a sore thumb in my white capris and white sneakers against the sea of denim and cowboy boots, and the fact that I had no purpose or reason for being there only intensified the feeling of being a fish out of water.

The barn was buzzing with excitement, and the air was fraught with nervous energy as everyone stood around talking, helpless to speed up nature's process.

After about ten minutes had passed, William walked toward me with a smile.

"You okay?"

I nodded and grinned bigger than I felt. "Yeah, I'm fine. Don't worry about me. Do whatever you need to do."

"There's nothing I can do, really. We're all on her timetable. His head and shoulders are out, so she's resting until it's time for her to push again." He shoved both hands in his front pockets and leaned closer, his voice quiet as though he wanted his words to be for my ears alone. "It figures that the one hour out of the day that Levi and I both are out of pocket, that's when she chooses to get on with the show."

I smiled. "Timing is everything."

He was so close, and it was impossible to ignore the way my body reacted to his proximity. I shifted my weight onto my right foot and leaned into it, which gave me a tiny buffer of space between us.

"I'll get you home as soon as possible," he said. "I just want to make sure there's no issues."

"You're fine. I'm good. I may step outside to return a couple of calls, though."

"Sure, yeah, whatever you need to do. I can have someone run you up to the office if you need privacy or a computer or something."

"No, I'm good. I'll just go over by the truck."

He smiled, and his hand came up to rest briefly on my elbow before he turned to go back to the mare's stall.

As I watched him walk away, I felt eyes upon me, and I turned to see Piper staring in my direction. She didn't look angry like she had that day in her mother's study. Instead, she looked sad, and though she was looking right at me, she seemed to be elsewhere, not seeing me at all.

I attempted a smile and gave a brief nod before I turned to walk outside, and she looked back toward the stall with the group.

I'd been pacing back and forth by William's truck for a little while, checking my voice mails and returning calls, when cheers erupted from the barn. I walked back inside the entryway as several members of William's team came out. William saw me and hurried over, his face lit up with joy.

"Is he out? Is she all done?" I asked, my smile wide as a result of seeing him so happy.

"He's out! He's a beauty. It will be a while yet until the process is complete, but for the most part, we're good. I want to stick around a little longer and make sure they're both doing well, and then I'll get you back home. I feel so bad that I've kept you from your work all this time."

"Take however long you need," I said.

"I can take her," Piper said as she walked up to join us.

William and I both looked at her with stunned surprise, and she gave her father something between a smirk and a smile.

"What?" she asked. "You need to be here, she needs to be there. I'm not doing anything right now, so I can drive her home, and you can finish up here." She turned to looked at me, her eyes issuing a clear challenge. "If that's okay with you, of course."

I would have rather walked home, but conscious of appearances and not wanting to escalate the situation, I nodded and forced a smile I hoped would pass for genuine.

"Sure. That would be great. Thanks."

William looked at me, and he reached to put his hand on my lower back as he stepped in closer. "You sure that's okay? I won't be long if you'd rather wait."

"God, Daddy! You make it sound like you're sending her off with the executioner. I think I can handle getting Cat home safely."

William's eyes searched mine, and I could feel Piper staring at us. I had no doubt she was playing her cards, waiting to see how I would react and how William would handle it.

"Really, it's fine," I said to him before glancing in her direction, my smile still plastered in place. "It will give us a chance to chat, right, Piper?"

"Yes," she said. "We haven't really had time to do that yet."

William looked about as uncertain as I felt as his eyes darted back and forth between us, his exuberant smile long gone.

"If you're sure," he said to me, and then he turned to her. "I'll expect you to be on your best behavior."

She did an exaggerated military salute, and then she looked at me. "You ready? We'll take Dad's truck since it's right here."

I moved to follow her to the truck, but William put his hand on my arm and held me back as Piper kept walking.

"You don't have to do this," William whispered. "I can take you home."

"It's okay! Maybe she's trying to make peace, and if so, I don't want to refuse the offer."

He frowned and released my arm. "All right, but you let me know if she says anything at all out of line to you. Anything!"

"It'll be fine. I can take care of myself, I promise. I'll talk to you later."

She was already in William's truck waiting, and I took a deep breath and hoped for the best as I climbed in the passenger seat and shut the door.

"Don't worry," she said as we pulled out of the gate. "I'm not going to knock you in the head and leave you on the side of the road or anything."

Her voice was light, and I knew she was joking, but there was an undercurrent of tension between us that couldn't be ignored.

"I wasn't worried, but I wouldn't have gone down easily, either."

She chuckled as she navigated the truck around a curve.

"I believe you. You strike me as someone who can stand up for herself, and I like that."

My eyebrows rose as I took in the compliment, surprised to hear her acknowledge something positive about me.

She glanced over at me, and I was surprised to see that her expression had softened somewhat.

"My dad told me a little about what went down with you guys. You know, with Caroline and all. I wanted to say that I'm sorry that happened to you. It sounds like it really sucked, and it sounds like you were put in a pretty messed-up position."

She looked at me again, and I swear I saw genuine compassion in her eyes. There was no challenge, no threat, no anger at all.

"Thank you. It wasn't the best time in my life, for sure."

She stared at the road ahead, and her hands twisted back and forth on the steering wheel. I got the feeling there was a lot going on in her head, a lot of decisions being made about what words she'd put forth next.

"I think it's cool that you chose to protect my dad. That took a lot of guts from what he told me, and … I don't know … I just wanted to say … I guess, thanks … on his behalf."

I was unsure of what to say. The statement felt like it should be acknowledged, but I didn't want to say anything that would upset her or shut down the unexpected flow of conversation.

"Your dad meant a lot to me. I cared very much about him, and it was never my intention to hurt him."

"What about now?" she said after a while. "What do you feel about my dad now? God, that sounds like he's in high school and I'm interviewing his prom date, doesn't it? *What are your intentions for my father, Ms. Russo?*"

I smiled at her attempt at humor, but the weight of her question was uncomfortable, and I shifted in my seat as I considered my answer and how it might be received.

"I still care about William." It seemed a safe choice.

"You care about him? Or you love him? Because those are two entirely different things."

Whoa. I'd never in my life been so put on the spot, and I had no idea how to take it. My first reaction was to tell her that it was none of her business, but that wasn't entirely true. How I felt about William affected her life, and I understood that she'd want to know.

What struck me as odd was her tone. I didn't sense any of the anger that had been on display when she walked in on me in Revae's study. Her voice was calm, but it held a wistfulness, a sadness. It felt as though she hadn't liked the question and dreaded its answer, but for some reason, she was compelled to ask it anyway. It made me wonder what the purpose was, and where the conversation would head next.

"I'm not sure it's entirely appropriate for us to be having this discussion." I paused to think about my words before continuing. I was certain that one way or another, they'd come back to haunt me. "But since I understand how close you are to your dad and I get that you're concerned about him, I'll answer your question. Before I do, though, I want you to know that I would never do anything to hurt William, and that includes anything that would cause problems between the two of you. He loves you so much, and I know it's scary for you to think of someone coming into his life."

She looked over at me again, and her eyes flared for an instance before she looked back to the road. I'd hit a nerve.

"Piper, I don't mean anything negative by saying that. I just want you to know that the relationship he has with you isn't in any danger. Not from me! I have no desire to come between you and your dad, or to make you feel in any way threatened."

"I'm not threatened" she said, a bit of the steel returning to her voice. "I know what I have with my dad. You didn't answer the question."

"Again, I'm not sure it's a good idea for us to discuss this."

"You already said you'd answer the question, but then you didn't, and I have to wonder why."

"I guess because it feels like we're talking about things that are personal between William and me, and I'm not sure how he would feel about me revealing that."

We pulled up to a stop sign, and she took the opportunity to turn and face me, her expression a mask of determination.

"Do you love my dad?"

I exhaled slowly and tried to determine the best route to take with the line of questioning.

A car honked behind us, and Piper repeated the question, her tone more impatient.

"Do you love my dad?"

"Yes. Yes, I do. With everything in me. With all my heart and all my soul. I've loved him since I met him, and he's the only man I've ever loved."

She turned her attention back to the road, driving away just as the car behind us honked again. I wondered if the answer surprised her. Had she expected me to say that I cared for him but not go so far as to profess love? Had she thought I wouldn't answer? Was she upset by my admission, or was that what she had sought?

Piper sighed and tapped her fingers on the steering wheel. "I know the general vicinity of your house, but not the exact address, so you're going to need to tell me."

I pointed to the road up ahead. "Turn left up here, just past that sign. Then we'll curve around the lake for little bit."

Silence hung in the air between us, and I had no way to gauge her reaction to what I'd said. I'd been truthful, but now that the words were out there, I wished I could take them back. I felt exposed and vulnerable, like I'd given away an important piece of me to someone who might wish to use it for my harm.

"It's coming up," I said, relieved that the ride was almost over. I'd never been so happy to see my house. "It's the one with the orange tiles. The one with the mailbox that looks like a house and has orange tiles, too."

She pulled William's truck into my driveway and put it into park as I reached for the door handle, ready to make my escape.

"He loves you, too," Piper said as she turned to face me. Her eyes held hurt, and her mouth turned downward in a frown. "I want my dad to have love in his life, and I want him to be happy. I think you could make him happy, but I wanted to know if you thought that, too. If you loved him the same way he loves you."

I didn't know what to say to that, so I didn't say anything. I wasn't at all sure I could make William happy. I wasn't even sure I could be happy in a relationship, but I did think my best shot at it was with him.

She sighed and looked out the truck's back window toward the lake.

"Cat, I'll be going away soon. I haven't told my dad yet, and I'm not entirely sure why I'm telling you, but it's important to me that he's going to be happy when I'm gone. I want to know that he's not going to be lonely." She looked at me, and her eyes flashed with the fire that I'd seen the first time I met her. And the second. "I also don't want you to think for one minute that I'm leaving because of you. You don't have the power to make me leave my dad or my family. No matter what happens between the two of you, he will always be my daddy, and nothing will change that."

I nodded in agreement, still reeling from the secret she'd confided. Where was she going? Why didn't William know? How would he react when he found out? And to echo her own comment ... why was she telling me?

"Where are you going? Or ... is that none of my business?"

"I think my dad should probably get those details first, and I intend to tell him tonight. Well, if he's not with you, that is. It seems every time I need to talk to him lately, he's otherwise occupied."

"I don't have any plans with him tonight."

Her lips twisted as she chewed on the inside of her cheek and stared across the hood of the truck, her mind somewhere else for the moment. "I should probably get back to the farm so he won't be worried that we killed each other or something."

She gave me a crooked grin, and I saw William in her face. I smiled back.

"I'd like to think that we could get along, Piper. I don't think we're all that different, you and I. I grew up wanting to escape, too, and I know how hard it is to want to be someone else. Someone other than who you are."

"Yeah, well, I don't think we're to the point of having heartfelt therapy talk yet, but I needed to know that my dad was going to be okay."

"He is," I said. "I mean him no harm."

"All right. Hey, I know he's gonna call you and ask if I behaved. I'd really appreciate it if you could keep my plans between us for now. It'd probably hurt his feelings if he knew I told someone before him."

"Sure. I understand." I groaned inside even as I agreed, not wanting to be responsible for hiding something from William but knowing that she was right. This news needed to come from Piper.

I opened the door and got out, and then I smiled at her. "Thanks for driving me home. It was ... nice ... getting to know you a little better."

"I suppose I owe you an apology. I overreacted the other day at the house, and I'm sorry for that."

I shrugged. "I had no business being in there, so I understood you being upset. I'm sorry about the lamp."

She waved her hand and rolled her eyes. "It wasn't like an antique or anything. Don't worry about it."

"Will I see you before you go? When are you leaving?"

"Are you coming to this shindig my dad's throwing for Caroline this weekend?"

"I wasn't planning on it, no."

"Lucky you! Well, if not then, I'm sure our paths will cross somehow before I leave. I still have to firm up some details on exactly when that's happening. But either way, take care of my dad, okay?"

"I will. You have my word."

CHAPTER 74
William

Piper had always been full of surprises, but her offer to take Cat home came out of left field, and I wasn't sure what my daughter was up to. If Cat had seemed more reluctant, then I would have insisted that I take her myself. But when she agreed to go with Piper, my refusal would have caused a scene and likely a rift with my daughter. I only hoped that she hadn't done or said anything that would hurt Cat.

I'd watched the clock until enough time had passed for them to reach Cat's place, and then I'd given them ten minutes leeway before dialing Cat's phone.

"How'd the ride go?" I asked once we'd said hello.

"It was fine. I told you it would be."

"Was she polite?"

"She was," Cat said. "I mean, Piper has an edge to her; you're aware of that, I'm sure. But compared to our past two encounters, yes. She was polite."

"She hadn't set the bar very high in those encounters. Did she say anything I need to be concerned about? Anything I need to address with her?"

Cat hesitated, and I swore under my breath, certain that Piper had either accused her of something or insulted her in some way. She was just being too nice to tell me.

"She did, didn't she? Cat, tell me what she said, and I'll have a conversation with her. It's not okay with me for her to speak to you disrespectfully."

"She didn't speak to me disrespectfully, William. She conveyed that she had some concerns, and I understood those concerns and where she was coming from. We had a lovely conversation, so there's nothing you need to chastise her for on my behalf."

"You're sure?"

"I'm sure."

Levi motioned for me to come back inside the barn, and I frowned. I'd looked forward to seeing Cat that morning at the house with Caroline, but I'd been so focused on the task at hand that I didn't get to interact with her much. I'd thought we'd have time to connect afterward, but I'd been called back to the barn and then Piper had stepped in.

I longed to see her one-on-one, just the two of us.

"Are you busy later?" I asked. "Now that our little guy is here, I'm not so tethered. Would you like to grab dinner?"

She paused, and I sensed she was going to say no. I'd expected an uphill battle, but that awareness didn't make it any easier. I wanted to be with her. I wanted to talk to her without guarding my words. I wanted to taste her lips and feel her skin beneath my fingertips. I wanted to wake up with her in my arms.

"Tonight's not good for me," she said. "Maybe another night."

I looked toward the clouds above me and silently cursed. I wanted to hear the last part as a sign of hope, but she was probably being polite.

"William!" Levi called from behind me, and I threw him a thumbs-up to let him know I was coming.

"I gotta go." I closed my mouth to keep from asking if I could call her later. I had to have patience. I had to remember that the long-term goal was more important than the short-term gratification. I couldn't pressure her.

"All right. Talk to you later," she said, and though it may have been wishful thinking on my part, she sounded sad that the conversation was ending.

"You betcha."

When we'd wrapped up things in the barn and the mare and her foal were happily bonding, I headed back to the office to check emails and return calls. My truck had been parked outside the barn when I came out, so I knew Piper had returned, but I hadn't seen her.

She didn't come into the office the rest of the afternoon, and I figured I'd seek her out before dinner so we could talk alone without everyone else listening in.

I texted her to ask where she was, then told her I'd meet her at the stables when she said she was coming in from a ride.

"Hey there," I said when I found her checking the horse's hooves. "Did you have a client this afternoon? Or am I not remembering correctly?"

"It was supposed to be the Sackett girl, and she canceled again. That's the third time in two months. I told her mother she's not going to be ready for that event if she doesn't start showing up."

"Is she ill? What's causing the cancellations?"

"No, she's not ill. She's lazy. She doesn't want to follow directions. She gets mad when I call her out on not making progress, and then she doesn't show up."

She began to brush the horse as we talked, and I leaned over the fence with my arms propped on the top rail.

"I was surprised that you offered to take Cat home. Thank you. I appreciate you making the effort. She said the two of you had a nice chat and that you were polite. That means a lot to me."

Piper stopped and looked at me. "Did she say anything else?"

"No. Why? Should she have?"

"Nope." She went back to brushing.

I thought about saying more, but I decided it was best to take what I'd gotten with her and Cat and be satisfied with it. Now, if only I could get her to put forth a little effort with Caroline.

"You'll be here Saturday, right?" I asked. "For the party?"

"Of course," she said, her voice dripping with sarcasm. "I can't miss the opportunity to welcome the new family members into the fold."

"Piper, please. Isn't there any part of you that can see this as a good thing in our lives?"

She glared at me and moved to the other side of the horse. "Caterina said she's not coming. Did you not invite her?"

"I haven't mentioned it to her. I wasn't sure she'd be interested."

"Why wouldn't she be? Caroline's her daughter."

I turned and leaned back against the fence rail, stretching my arms across it.

"It's complicated. I don't think Cat would come, not because she doesn't want to, but because she'd probably feel like it took something away from Caroline and the kids and their time with our family. She tries to think about others and how she's affecting them."

"Nice. How very considerate of her."

"She's trying to be. She's trying to consider everyone else's feelings, including yours."

Silence.

I walked forward so that I could see her, though she didn't look up for eye contact. "I'm trying to consider your feelings too, sweetheart. I just wish you would consider mine."

"How am I not considering your feelings, Daddy? I'm coming to the party, aren't I? I drove your girlfriend home today, and she said I was polite, right?"

"I wouldn't say she's my girlfriend, and yes, you're coming to the party, but you're obviously not happy about it."

She tossed the brush in the bucket and stood with her hands on her hips, her eyes flashing and her jaw tight.

"What if I can't be? What if I've tried—like, I've really, seriously *tried*—and I just can't be happy about all this? I want to be. I want to be thrilled that I've got this instant family out of nowhere and that you've fallen head over in heels in love and lost your shit over some woman you knew in high school." She crossed her arms and took a step closer to me. "I think what happened to the two of you and how you got split apart is awful, and I *want* to think it's great that you're back together and you have another chance. I know you want me to be just as excited as you are, but I can't." She came another step closer, and I could see her pulse pumping her anger through the base of her neck. "I don't want to hurt you, Daddy. I don't want to disappoint you. And I don't want everyone thinking I'm a spoiled brat who only thinks of herself. But I don't know how to pretend to feel something I don't, and I don't how to stop feeling the way I feel."

She picked up the bucket and grabbed the lead rope to walk the horse back to his stall.

"I'm not disappointed in you," I said as I followed her. "I understand what you're saying. What you're feeling. Maybe it's just going to take some time."

"Time?" She stopped and turned to face me. "Time isn't going to make me want to pretend it's all fine when it isn't. This doesn't feel like home to me. I don't even want to be here anymore. I don't want to watch you and Cat making fools of yourselves like a couple of teenagers. I damned sure don't want to walk in my house and see the two of you making out or something. And I'm sorry, but I don't want to be somebody's sister or somebody's aunt. I don't even know how to be me."

She clucked her tongue at the horse and continued walking him until they'd reached his stall.

"What am I supposed to say to that, Piper? How am I supposed to help you with this? I can't make this okay no matter what I do. I can't love Caroline without feeling like I'm betraying you. And I can't love Cat without feeling like I'm hurting you. Not that it matters that much anyway, since she doesn't want me to be in love with her, but tell me how to fix this between me and you! What do you expect me to do? What can I possibly say or do to make this right for you?"

She removed the horse's halter and closed the door of the stall, and then she faced me. The pain in her eyes took my breath away, and I walked forward, even though I knew she wouldn't let me hold her.

She took a step back, and I halted.

"Piper, please. The last thing I want is for you to hurt. Please tell me what I can do. What do you want me to do?"

"There's nothing you can do, Daddy." Her voice trembled, and the fact that she was upset enough to reveal her emotions even in such a small way was telling. That combined with her words nearly crippled me. "So, I'm gonna make it easier for everyone. I'm leaving Ward Farms."

"What do you mean? Where are you going?"

She squared her shoulders and took a breath, and when she spoke again, she'd regained her composure and her voice was steady.

"I've accepted a position with a ranch in Puerto Rico. The owner was injured recently, and she needs a trainer to help her get ready for a big race coming up. It's a limited-time contract with an option for permanent employment based on the decisions of both parties at the end of the agreement."

"Puerto Rico? A contract? You already signed a contract and you didn't even tell me?" I took a step back, stunned. "Why would you do this without even discussing it with me?"

"I tried. I came home the night I got the job offer to talk to you about it, but you didn't come home."

"That was what you needed to talk to me about? You said it

wasn't important. I did come home. I called you on my way here, and I came to your room as soon as I got back. I tried to talk to you, but you told me not to worry about it. Again, you said it wasn't important. I'd say your career and your future and where you'll be living is pretty damned important."

She looked down and kicked at the dirt with her foot.

"You're right. I should have told you. I was upset that night, and I signed the contract the next day and sent it off." She lifted her eyes to look at me. "I'm sorry. I should have discussed it with you. I felt like you were preoccupied and that you didn't have time for me."

"So, that's what this is?" I asked, waving my hand in the air. "This is to punish me? You're taking a job God knows where and moving to an island to punish me because I wasn't sitting home alone when you decided to tell me about it?"

"No, that's not the reason. I applied for this job before I ever knew about Caroline or Cat. I did it online when I was in Denver and found out that was falling through. I created a user name on this job site using Mom's maiden name so I wasn't tied to Ward Farms as a family member. That way I knew if I got an interview, it was based on my credentials and my educational background, not my last name or my father's reputation."

I was so upset I wanted to spit. I wanted to hit something or kick something. I wanted to yell in rage. But I couldn't do any of that. She was an adult. She could make her own decisions. She'd been wanting to leave for a while. Since a year or so after her mother died, at least. I'd known it was a possibility, but I'd always hoped she'd come to terms with whatever was driving her to abandon her heritage before it took her away.

"So, they've hired you? It's a done deal? You've signed a contract."

"Yes. I told him I wanted to give my employer two weeks' notice, so I leave a week from Tuesday."

"Your *employer*? Nice. Don't you think they're going to notice that your last name is Ward when they process your employment paperwork?"

"They already know. I told the guy that I hadn't used my real name online because my current employer didn't know I was seeking a new job. All the official paperwork and documentation has my legal name."

"And they hired you just like that? You haven't gone there for an interview. Or at least, I'm assuming you didn't fly to Puerto Rico in the last two weeks without telling me?"

She shook her head and stuck her hands in her back pockets.

"No. We've done the interview process via email. The owner's son handled the interview and hiring part of this. He asked questions, and I replied with answers."

"Via email? So, you haven't met these people at all? You haven't even had a phone conversation?"

It was the first time she'd looked anything less than confident since she'd started giving me details.

"I talked to the son on the phone a couple of times. He lives in New York, and his mother lives on the island."

"How do you even know this is legit, Piper? You can't fly off to move to some ranch somewhere without knowing what you're getting into or who you're working for. Come on. You gotta use your head. Why are you doing this?"

She lifted her chin at what I'm sure she perceived as criticism.

"I needed to get out of here, even before everything imploded. I figured this was a way to get something new on my resume, get experience under a different ranch, and get me the hell away from here. And hey, how rough can it be to work on a tropical island where I can go to the beach whenever I get time off? The pay's good, not what I'm making here, but my father is known to be a rather generous employer. It includes housing on the ranch—which is in a rainforest, by the way—and it's for six months. So, by my reasoning, worst case scenario, I hate it and I stick it out for six months and come home. Best case, I love it, and it turns into something permanent."

I laid both hands on top of my head and stared at the wooden beams of the ceiling.

"What kind of ranch hires someone without meeting them, Piper? How do they know that your style will fit theirs? How do they know how you treat the animals? For that matter, how do you know how *they* treat their animals?"

"I did my research, Daddy. I looked her up. I looked up the ranch. They've never had any complaints or anything filed against them. And she's won a lot of races. It seems like she's a pretty big deal down there. Just because you haven't heard of her doesn't mean she doesn't know what she's doing."

"That's not what I meant." I gritted my teeth together and swore. "I can't help feeling like you're doing this to get at me instead of doing this because it's the right thing for your career. If it was a great opportunity, I'd be all in for it." I paced up and down the stall lane, trying to keep moving to keep from exploding. "I supported you going to Denver to work for Warren, and I supported you talking to Harrison Jones about joining his team. So, it's not like I'm trying to hold you back or prevent you from leaving if this is not where you want to be. But you have to be smart about career moves, and I don't see this one as a good move. I think this is a dumb decision. I really thought you were smarter than this."

Her eyes were all fire and flame, and her face flushed red, which I knew meant she was about to blow.

"I'm not asking for your permission or your approval. I'm simply giving my employer notice of my departure."

She moved to walk past me toward the exit of the barn, but she turned just as she reached the door.

"Oh, and Daddy? You were wrong. Cat wants you to be in love with her. So, quit screwing around and make your move already."

"What? What are you talking about?"

"I'm not blind. I can see that you're happier with her in your life. You deserve to be happy, and I want that for you, even if I can't bear to watch it or be a part of it. I asked Cat this afternoon if she loved you, and her answer left me with no doubt. You have a future with her if you want it, and I'm stepping out of the way."

She turned and left, and I slammed my palms against the railing and cursed my life.

CHAPTER 75
Caterina

I'd just stepped out of the tub a little after nine when my phone rang. It was William, and despite the leap of my heart, I almost let it go to voicemail. I didn't know if Piper had talked to him yet, and I couldn't carry on a conversation with him knowing I was hiding something of that magnitude.

My finger hovered over the screen as I wavered, but the thought of hearing his voice proved most persuasive, and I answered the call.

"Hey," I said as I wrapped my robe around me and pulled the sash tight.

"Are you busy?"

"No. I just got out of the tub and was about to brew some tea and do some reading before bed. What's up?"

"I swear I'm not trying to make a habit out of showing up without calling first, but I'm sitting in your driveway. Can I come in?"

I looked in the mirror and frowned at my reflection. My skin was flushed and blotchy from the warm bath. My hair had been loosely piled on my head, but it had escaped in several places and gotten wet. I was nude beneath the robe, not having had a chance to put on my pajamas before he called.

"Um, yeah. Give me a minute."

"I'm almost to your door. Take your time."

"Oh. Um, okay. I'll be right there."

I didn't take the time to change, figuring I'd let him in and then excuse myself to do so.

He looked like hell when I opened the door, and I wanted to wrap my arms around him and make him okay.

"What happened? Are you all right?"

"I've been driving again, and somehow when I do that lately, I always end up here."

"Come in. You want something to drink?"

He walked in and sat on the couch in a slouched position with his head laid back against the cushion. "Funny you should ask. I was thinking maybe I should start drinking. I've heard whiskey's nice." He smiled and waved his hand to convey he wasn't serious. "I'm kidding. Probably not funny, I realize."

"I never liked whiskey, personally." I sat sideways on the couch so I could face him, taking care with the robe to ensure I didn't broadcast my nudity as I tucked my leg beneath me. "You wanna tell me what happened?"

I feared it may have been Piper's announcement that put him in a funk, but since I wasn't supposed to know about it, I couldn't very well ask about it.

He looked up at me, his eyes bloodshot and haggard, and he lifted his hand to my face and caressed my cheek.

"I do, and I don't. Part of me wants to pour my heart out to you, and another part of me just wants to pick you up and carry you in there and climb into bed with you."

"Whoa. Okay. Are you sure you haven't been drinking?"

He grinned and dropped his hand to rest on my thigh. "I'm positive."

"How about I make us a pot of tea, and you can tell me what's going on?"

"The bed option's out?" His eyes seemed a little brighter, and I could see that he was teasing.

"Let's start with tea."

"Foreplay. I like it."

I filled the kettle and put it on the stove, and then I came to sit next to him. He put his right hand back on my thigh where it had been with no hesitation. He was in a strange mood, for sure. The past few days he'd been so reserved around me, and now it was like all the pretense was gone, and he was comfortable touching me without reservation.

"What set you off?" I asked. "What made you drive?"

"Where should I begin?" He crossed his left arm over his forehead and closed his eyes. The lines in his face seemed deeper than they'd been earlier in the afternoon, and I wanted to smooth my fingers over them and ease his tension. "Piper got a job and put in her notice today."

I swallowed hard and tried to have no reaction at all. Should I tell him I knew, or would that hurt him like she said? Should I feign shock, or would that be a level of deceit beyond withholding information?

I opted for neither. "Where's she going?"

"Puerto Rico. To some ranch there that she's never seen to work for people she's never met. Because evidently, working for the top facility east of the Kentucky just isn't good enough for her."

"You said the other day that she's trying to get out from under your shadow and make her own way. So, maybe it's not that Ward Farms isn't good enough. Maybe it's that she needs something else that's just not Ward Farms."

He picked up my hand and intertwined his fingers with mine before laying them back on my leg.

"I never have known what to do when she gets upset. Even when she was a little kid, she rarely cried. If there were tears, there was either blood or something very wrong. She's never wanted to be held. To be hugged. She wasn't one to snuggle or sit on a lap. Couldn't stand to be carried unless it was on my shoulders where she could see the world. And even then, she didn't want me hanging onto her legs." He smiled at his memory as he recalled it. "She used to say '*I do it, Daddy*' and brush my hand off her knee. *'I do it, Daddy. I hang on.'* And you can't just let go of a little kid on your shoulders, you know, so I'd have to kind of put my hands up by my shoulders and leave them there in case she started to fall."

He sighed, and I pulled my right foot up on to the couch and tucked it beneath me.

"Piper and Revae clashed pretty much from the day that child was born. They butted heads on damned near everything. I think they were too much alike, but Revae could handle Piper's fire. I guess she understood it. She always seemed to know what to do. I never did." He'd been staring straight ahead, lost in his thoughts, but he turned and looked at me as he squeezed our hands together. "I'm a fixer. You fall down, I help you up. If something breaks, I make it work again or replace it. So, I guess I parented by giving her whatever I thought it would take to keep her happy. Piper needed a job, I gave her a job. She wanted a car, I gave her a car. Whenever she's faced any challenge in life, it's always been my instinct to step in and fix it. To try and make it right."

He sighed and closed his eyes again. "But she doesn't want that. She never has. She has always wanted to do everything on her own, on her terms, from the very beginning. And I try to understand that. I try and respect it. But it drives me nuts to see her make everything harder for herself when she doesn't have to."

His eyes opened, and he turned to focus them on me.

"I don't know how to fix this, Cat. I don't know what to do to make this okay for her. Me and Caroline. Me and you. Piper not wanting to be a Ward. And I've been trying to stay hands-off. I've told everyone not to worry about her. That she'd work things out in her own way in her own time. Because that's what she's always done! That's the way she had to do it. But this…this job. This could be a really big mistake."

I watched the emotion come over his face, and I wanted so badly to wrap my arms around him.

"What if it's not safe for her, Cat? What if they're not good people? What if she gets there and she's miserable?"

"Then she comes home," I said with a shrug. "I have no doubt that if she needs to come home, her daddy will get her home, and I guarantee you Piper doesn't doubt that either."

"And career-wise? She could have her pick of top facilities. She doesn't want to work for me? Fine. But with our connections and her abilities, she could work anywhere she wanted to. Why is she picking some no-name farm so far out of the circuit? How will that further her career?"

"Maybe this decision isn't about furthering her career so much as furthering her life. Piper's trying to spread her wings. She's trying to figure out how to fly on her own without your help. Without you needing to fix it every time she falls. Maybe she figures that some no-name far-removed farm is the best way to do that. You just said she could work anywhere she wanted to. What if this is where she wants to work?"

"I just can't help but think that she's doing this to punish me. To get back at me. For Revae dying. For Caroline. For you. For any multitude of reasons."

I ran my fingers across his hairline just above his forehead, smoothing the strays.

"Maybe. And maybe it isn't about you at all. Maybe it's about her."

"So, what am I supposed to do? Just let her go?"

I smiled and laid my hand on his cheek. "What choice do you have? Are you gonna lock her up in a barn? She's an adult, sweetie. She has to find her own way and make her own mistakes. And it just might take going away for her to learn who she is, and then, who's to say? Once she figures that out, she might find her way back home."

He turned his face to kiss my palm as the tea kettle blew its whistle.

I got up, but he grabbed my hand and held me.

"Thank you," he said. "I appreciate you letting me in."

I squeezed his hand and pulled mine from it as I walked backward toward the kitchen.

"What was I going to do? Leave you out there in my driveway all night? Have my neighbors think you're some kind of stalker?"

I made the two cups of tea, calling out to ask if he wanted honey, sugar, and lemon, and smiling when he said all three, just like me.

When I returned, I handed him his tea and sat on the opposite end of the couch with my feet propped against his thigh.

"Why so far away?" he asked. "Isn't foreplay supposed to be a close-up activity?"

"Very funny. I want to drink my tea without spilling it all over me, so I'm sitting with my back against the end of the couch."

"It feels so good to be able to talk to you," he said. "I feel like I can tell you anything. Like you know me inside and out, and I don't have to hide."

Guilt riddled me as I considered all I hadn't shared with him. I tried to put myself in his shoes. Would I want him to know something major and not tell me he knew? There was a risk of it hurting him that Piper had confided in me before she told him, but there was also a risk of him finding out I knew and didn't tell him. I felt he'd be understanding of why I didn't say anything before she did, but once the cat was out of the bag, it was like I was pretending that I didn't know. It felt wrong.

He sipped his tea as he traced his finger over the turtle tattoo on the top of my foot, and then he looked at me with a grin. "I love that you got this tattoo. I love that we share it."

I couldn't remain silent. I had to tell him.

"In the interest of full disclosure, there's something I need to tell you."

"Okay." He'd slouched down pretty far against the back of the couch, and he sat up straighter as he put his teacup on the end table and turned back to face me. "Shoot."

"Piper told me this afternoon that she was leaving. She asked me not to say anything until she'd had a chance to tell you. It was her news to give, so I obliged, but I can't sit here knowing that I knew and act like I didn't know. I promised you I'd always be honest with you."

"Well, that is not the disclosure I thought you'd be making, but thank you for telling me. I appreciate your honesty, and I understand why you didn't say anything before."

"Wait, what disclosure *did* you think I'd be making?"

He lifted my feet off his thigh and moved closer to me before pulling them back onto his lap.

"It's the damnedest thing. Here I've been, trying to find any excuse to get to see you. Coming up with any reason I could think of to call so I could hear your voice." He leaned a little closer, and his fingers began to caress the top of my foot. "I've been shoving my hands in my pockets every time I'm around you to keep from touching you." The contact was so light that it tickled and at the same time, it was intense enough to make me tingle inside. "I've bitten my tongue damned near in half to keep from saying, *I love you.*" His fingers crept higher, just above my ankle. "And why was I doing all that? Because *you* told me we couldn't see each other."

I sat motionless, not wanting to do anything to make him stop touching me, but also not understanding what he was saying.

"You told me a huge part of the reason for that was Piper and Caroline. You didn't want to make it hard for them. You didn't want things to be awkward."

His fingers had caressed their way up, and as he slid his hand beneath my leg to massage my calf, I began to squirm a little, from both his touch and his words. Where on earth was he going with either one?

"It *was* because of them," I said. "I was trying to protect them from our mistakes."

"Really?" he asked as he inched higher.

As his hand came over the top of my knee, the robe fell away from my leg, exposing it all the way to my upper thigh. I reached to grab the robe, but he blocked my hand and moved it away. He leaned forward and pressed his lips to the bare skin of my thigh, and the sight of his head going down toward that general region of my body set me on fire.

I sucked in a breath and fumbled as I tried to get the cup of tea on the coffee table without spilling it. William grinned as he reached to take it and set it on the table for me, and then he stared into my eyes as he shifted his weight forward and moved my legs so that his body leaned over mine.

"You see, that's interesting that you say that, because Piper told me that when the two of you talked, you indicated to her that you were in love with me and wanted a future with me."

He nestled his nose against my neck as he braced his weight on his knee between my legs, and I gasped as his tongue darted out to taste my skin. His words echoed somewhere in my head, and I knew I should respond, but just then his hand began to loosen the sash of my robe.

"And then, I talked to Caroline." He took my earlobe between his teeth. "Do you want to know what she told me?"

At that moment, I really didn't care who told who what, and the only thing I wanted revealed was our bodies to each other, but I obliged him by asking.

"What?"

"She had called to chat about the house, and she mentioned how nice it was to see the two of us together." He paused in his seduction to raise up and look at me. "It was nice, wasn't it?"

I nodded, and he situated himself alongside me on the inside of the narrow couch as he propped his head on his elbow.

"Then she congratulated me and told me how happy she was that we were seeing each other. She said it was inspiring how we were giving our love another chance."

I knew I should be upset. I knew I should be freaking out at the words he was saying, but he had completely undone the sash of the robe and was beginning to spread it open.

"So, tell me something, Caterina," he said as he laid my breasts bare and my stomach began to quiver. "Why is it that you've told both of my daughters that you love me, but you haven't told me?"

CHAPTER 76
Caterina

William's words registered, and I opened my mouth to protest, but he began to trace a circle around my taut nipple with his index finger. My body jerked in response, and my ability to formulate words became limited.

He leaned forward to rub his nose against mine and tease my lips with his as he moved his hand to the other breast and brought that nipple to attention, too.

"Tell me," he whispered against my mouth, his tongue flicking across my bottom lip as I opened up to him. "I already know it's true, but I want to hear you say it, Cat."

I thrust my fingers into his hair to pull him closer, to try and make him kiss me rather than tease me, but he pulled back.

"Ah-ah-ah." He took my wrists and laid my hands on the pillow above my head. "I want to hear the words come out of your mouth." He kissed my cheek. "I want to hear them over and over again." He slid his lips to the corner of my mouth. "And the only reason I want to stop hearing you say you love me is because you are screaming out my name as you surrender to me."

His face was just above mine, and our eyes were locked. His hands stilled, and neither of us moved.

"Say it."

"I love you," I whispered. "I have always loved you. I will always love you. You are the only love for me."

He crushed my mouth with his as his tongue plundered and laid claim to me. It felt as though his hands were everywhere all at once, as a multitude of sensations washed over me.

I lifted my arms around his neck and grabbed hold of his

412

shoulders as the kiss became wilder and wanton. We both explored with abandon as we sought to become part of each other in every way possible.

We'd spent so much time suppressing our desire, fighting our impulses, and ignoring our attraction, and suddenly, all that pent-up passion had been loosed and freed.

I don't remember him lifting me from the couch, and I barely remember us staggering to my bed, our mouths never parting and our hands tearing at clothes to rid any barriers between us.

He laid me back on my bed and knelt beside me, looking down at me with those beautiful blue eyes that seemed to see right through my soul.

The last time he'd seen me fully nude, I'd been sixteen years old. My breasts had been higher and firmer, and so had my ass. My belly was still flat, but it wasn't as taut as it used to be, and the skin of my chest had begun to thin from a lifetime soaking up the sun.

But beneath his gaze, I'd never felt more beautiful than I did in that moment.

"I can't believe I found you again," he whispered. "You've haunted my dreams, even when I forbade you to be there. I'd wake and taste you on my lips, and in that moment before I realized it was a dream, I'd feel such complete bliss. But then as I became more aware, I'd accept it for what it was, and I'd feel guilty for my subconscious mind's betrayal."

He laid on his side next to me and leaned in to kiss me, gentle this time, and then he held my face in his hands.

"I will never take for granted that we've been given this second chance, and I know it's going to be complicated, and it won't be easy to merge our lives at this point, but I believe we can do it because I believe we belong together."

"Why the hell are you still talking? Shut up and make love to me, William!"

It was as close to an out-of-body experience as I'd ever come. A whole lotta time and way too much pain had dimmed my memories of what it was like between us that summer night on the beach, but there was no comparison between seventeen-year-old William and fifty-three-old William.

He knew his way around a woman's body, and he took his time to explore every inch of me. The man had techniques that I can't even describe, and he'd predicted correctly that I would scream out his name over and over again.

He brought me to ecstasy the first time with skilled hands between my thighs and expert oral attention to the various erogenous sensitivities of the upper body. As I lay quivering and shaking in the aftershocks, he took each of my fingers into his mouth and alternated between suckling lightly and biting with enough pressure to make me writhe.

When I protested that it was too much sensation, he stopped, but his hands never left my skin. He touched each scar and asked its origin, and he counted each mole and freckle, kissing a few here and there.

He waited for my breathing rate to calm and my body's spasms to cease, and then he brought me across the finish line a second time with nothing more than his tongue as I dug my fingernails into his scalp and squeezed his shoulders with my thighs.

There was no pause or rest after that one, for he couldn't wait any longer, and he reached beneath me to cup my ass in his hands, spreading me and lifting me as he buried himself inside me and cried out my name.

We moved together in a frantic rhythm as we consummated with the physical what we'd already expressed with our hearts.

When I reached release for the third time, he came right along with me, and then he collapsed upon me as though his muscles had all gone weak.

It was some time before either of us stirred, but then, William lifted himself on his elbows to look down into my eyes.

"Well, that was intense," he said with a grin.

"That's some powerful foreplay tea. I didn't even drink that much."

He laughed as he kissed me, and I smoothed my hands over his face and cupped them beneath his jawline.

"So, Cat, you never did tell me why you told other people we were officially dating without telling me."

"I don't recall ever using those words."

He raised an eyebrow. "What words did you use?"

"Piper asked if I loved you, and I told her the truth. I do. With all my heart and all my soul. With Caroline, I think I mentioned that we'd been to dinner together, and she sort of asked if we were seeing each other."

"And what did you tell her?"

"I'm pretty sure I said it's complicated."

"That it is," he said as he planted a kiss on my nose and rolled from me to lay on his back.

I moved to my side with my head propped in my hand, and then I leaned to kiss the turtle tattoo on his arm, almost identical to mine.

"When did you get this?"

He glanced down at it and rubbed his hand over it. "On your eighteenth birthday. That's what you'd said you were going to do, and I'd planned to do it with you as a surprise. When you didn't come back, I took the drawing I'd done of your wooden turtle before I carved it and got the tattoo anyway. I figured it was a way to always have you with me. To carry you on my skin."

I lifted my leg in the air and flexed my foot up and down as I wiggled my toes.

"Look," I said, pointing at the turtle on the top of my foot. "When I do this, it looks like he's swimming. See?"

William laughed and lifted his arm, waiting as I raised my head so he could slide the arm beneath me. I nestled in closer and lay my head on his chest with my knee slung across his thigh, much like we'd been that fateful night years ago.

He kissed the top of my head and squeezed me to him.

"I don't ever want us to part again, Cat. I don't ever want to be without you like that."

I leaned my head back to look into his eyes.

"Then don't ever let me go."

"I won't. I will never let anything or anyone tear us apart again."

I yawned and laid my head back on his shoulder, and then I fulfilled a lifelong dream and fell asleep in William Ward's arms.

CHAPTER 77
Caterina

I woke with the morning sun streaming through the windows and the sensation of something heavy across my leg.

I looked down in a sleepy fog of confusion, momentarily surprised to see a man's arm flung across my naked torso.

William was sound asleep on his stomach with one arm and one leg holding me in place.

So, this was what it was like to wake up with him.

I smiled at his sleeping face, and then I moved as slowly as possible to extricate myself from his embrace. I picked up my robe from the floor and slipped into it, tying the sash as I went to the kitchen to get the coffee brewing.

He was awake when I returned, and he held his arms open wide to welcome me back to bed.

"Good morning, beautiful," he said as he kissed the top of my head and held me tight against his chest. "I wanted to wake up with you in my arms, but when I opened my eyes, you were gone."

I nuzzled his neck with my nose and pressed my lips against his warm skin. "I went to get the coffee going so it would be ready when you got up."

"Mmm." He rubbed his hands up and down my body. "You feel so damned good. I wish we could stay in bed all day like this. I'd love to do some encore performances of making you scream last night, but unfortunately, I've got to get back to the farm this morning. I don't think anyone even knows where I'm at, although I'm sure they could wager a good guess if they needed me. And I have my phone here …. somewhere. I have no idea where it is."

"I think it's on top of your jeans, which are on the floor beside the bed."

I got up from the bed and looked back at him. He looked so damned handsome lying there nude twisted up in my sheets, his bare chest exposed and his muscular arms spread across my pillows.

"God, you look sexy right now," he said.

"Me? You've got to be kidding." My hand went to my tangled hair.

"I'm not kidding at all." He rolled to the edge of the bed and sat up, and then he reached to pull me between his knees as he reached up to brush my hair back from my face. "Your skin's a bit flushed, and your hair's wild, and your eyes are so green that they seem to glow." He tugged the sash of my robe free and then parted it to slide his hands around my hips and pull me closer. He buried his face between my breasts, and I gripped his head with my hands. "You're making it difficult for me to remember why we can't stay here all day." He took one nipple in his mouth and suckled just long enough to make it firm, and then he moved to the other one and did the same before looking up at me with a grin. "Maybe we could stay long enough for one encore performance."

I laughed and pulled myself from his grasp.

"I have to get in the shower and get on the road. I have a meeting in Ocala at ten-thirty with a couple and their adoption attorney. Can I get a raincheck?"

He stood and bent to grab his jeans from the floor.

"You have a standing invitation, my love. The offer can be claimed at any time."

I started to walk toward the shower, but then I stopped. "Do you normally eat breakfast when you first get up? I just realized I have no idea what your morning routine is."

He shrugged. "I like breakfast."

"Hmm. Let's see what we can find. Come with me."

He followed me to the kitchen and stood behind me with his arms around my waist and his chin on my shoulder as I opened the fridge and stared at the lack of options.

"Wow. Talk about the cupboard being bare."

"I don't normally do much for breakfast," I said.

"Or any other meal, it would seem."

"Yeah, I pretty much hate to cook, and I avoid it whenever possible."

He turned me in his arms to face me.

"Lucky for me, I happen to have a cook."

"There was yogurt in there. You want a yogurt?"

"I think I'll have a banana if that's okay," he said pointing to the two lonely bananas hanging on their little metal tree on the counter.

"Sure, knock yourself out."

"I have something I need to talk to you about," he said as he peeled his banana on the way to the table.

"Uh-oh, that doesn't sound good. Waiter," I joked. "Check please!"

"Hear me out before you say anything, okay?" He took a sip of his coffee and tossed the banana peel in the trash can. "Caroline might have told you already, but I'm having a little get-together at my house tomorrow to introduce her and the kids to my family. My parents are coming. My brothers and sisters. Nieces. Nephews. Levi's mom and dad will be there, too, and his sister, Rachel. My brother-in-law Dax is bringing his smoker and doing barbecue. It'll be casual. Nothing fancy. I was wondering if you'd like to come."

"Absolutely not. I can make toast. Do you want toast? One slice or two?"

"Two. Could you at least think about it before you shoot me down?"

"I'm not shooting you down. I appreciate the invitation, but I don't think it's appropriate that I attend."

"Appropriate for whom? It's my house, it's my party, and it's for our daughter. Who needs to approve?"

I put the bread into the toaster and turned to face him with my hand on my hip.

"William, thank you for including me. It means the world to me that you would. But this is a pretty big deal for your family, and I want them to welcome Caroline with open arms and open hearts. If I'm there, I think it will be a distraction."

"If you're talking about Piper—"

"Piper. Your mother. Your siblings. All of them. I'm not stupid, William. You weren't the only person who didn't know why I left you high and dry without a word. And I can't imagine that finding out it was because I gave birth to your child and never told you improved their opinion of me very much." The toast popped up, and I grabbed each hot piece with my fingernails and threw them on a plate. "To your family, I'm still Catherine Johnson, and I may always be."

"No, you're wrong about them. They'll be fair. They'll see how happy I am, and they'll see how you've changed, how you've grown, and they'll get to know you as you are now. They'll love you, just like I do."

I'd buttered the toast as he protested, and I brought it to the table and set it in front of him, sliding the strawberry jam his way.

"Maybe so. But that takes time. That won't happen the first time they see me, and it won't be accomplished over the course of an afternoon barbecue. The best chance Caroline has at endearing your family is if I'm nowhere around. I don't want them to associate her with what they think of me."

He frowned as he opened the jam jar.

"You're part of my life now, and they will have to accept that. I'm not going to hide our relationship from anyone. We had to do that before, but never again. I love you, and I will shout that from the rooftops of every building in town. I refuse to hide it."

"I'm not asking you to. But there's a difference in hiding it and throwing it in people's faces. We can still see each other and spend time together without other people having to witness it before they're ready to."

"How is it not hiding if I'm not able to have you by my side for a family function?"

I peeled back the lid from my yogurt container and sighed.

"I'm not going anywhere, William. We have all the time in the world for me to attend a family event with you. But let's not rush them. Give them time to adjust. Let them accept Caroline and the kids first. Then, in time, if you're happy with me, they'll be able to see that when they're around you. If I bring good to your life, then maybe it will make it easier for them to see me for who I am instead of who I was."

He swallowed his bite of toast and stared at me. "I feel like we have a role reversal. Wasn't I the one who was always trying to talk common sense into you, and you the one who was making decisions based on emotions?"

"Yeah, well, working with troubled youth has taught me a lot about giving people time and space."

He leaned forward to kiss me, his lips flavored with a delightful hint of butter and strawberries. "I don't know if I've said this in these words yet, but I admire the hell out of the woman you've become."

"Thank you. You were the catalyst in shaping the woman I've become."

"Is there any chance you'll change your mind about the party?"

"Nope."

"All right. I'll try to respect that."

"Thank you."

When we'd finished the makeshift breakfast, he departed, and I stood at the door and watched him pull away.

I closed the door and waltzed my way to the shower. It felt like the years had been erased, and I was a giddy teenager again. I smiled at my reflection in the mirror. He was right about my skin being flushed, and my lips seemed fuller than normal, swollen from his vigorous kisses. The scratch of his beard had left red blotches on my chin.

My body still tingled and pulsed from his touch, the sensations he'd awakened within me hours ago still stirring even after he'd gone.

When I pulled my robe off to step under the water stream, his scent wafted up from it, and I buried my face in it to breathe him in.

I was done resisting. I knew there were risks, and there was a chance it might end in disaster. But there was nothing I wanted more than to love him, be loved by him, and be a family with him.

I just hoped that I would never tire of it. That I would never become disillusioned and bored. As much as I prayed that he'd never leave me, I also hoped I'd never do that to him.

CHAPTER 78
Caterina

When I'd finished my meeting in Ocala, I was starving, and I stopped in a little cafe to grab lunch before heading home. A woman approached my table as I sat checking my email on my phone.

"Catherine? Um, I mean, Cat?"

I looked up to see Abigail Ward. I recognized her from the recent pictures I'd seen in William's house, but her smile was as warm as I remembered it to be. Her hair was completely gray, and she was a bit rounder than I'd known her. Her eyes were still the same though, their color an identical shade to William's.

"Hi," I said, my brain unable to come up with anything more elaborate in its state of shock.

She smiled wider and adjusted her purse on her shoulder.

"I don't know if you remember me—"

"I do." I also remembered our last conversation, though I didn't say that. I'd begged and pleaded with her to let me talk to William, to let me say goodbye, and she'd refused to call him to the phone.

"I thought it was you," she said. "I was sitting over there having lunch with a friend when you came in, and the longer I sat there, the more convinced I became. William had told me you were back in town."

I nodded, unsure of what else to say to that.

"May I join you?" she asked, pointing to the empty seat across from me.

If there had been any way to politely refuse, I would have. But like it or not, eventually I was going to have to be around this woman. She was important to William, and I wouldn't be able to avoid her forever.

"Sure."

She hung her purse on the seat back before sitting, and then she crossed her hands on the table in front of her. We stared at each other for a moment, each of us studying the other, or sizing up more likely.

Finally, she spoke. "I'll cut right to the chase so I don't waste your time."

I braced for whatever might come next, the chicken salad sandwich feeling like a rock in my stomach.

"I believe I owe you an apology," she said.

The shock of seeing her still hadn't worn off, and that sentence stunned me so much that I had no reply.

She looked down at her hands and back up to me. "That morning when you called, I wasn't aware of what was happening. My son had been missing for hours, and I was worried to death for him. My husband had been called home from work and was giving William the what-for, and I was in such a state that I couldn't think beyond making sure William was safe and that he knew what he'd done was wrong."

She took in a breath and picked up the paper wrapper from my straw, and she began to roll it up from one end to the other. She looked down at the paper as she rolled it, and when she spoke again, her voice was heavy.

"If I had known why you were asking, if I had understood the situation, I would have let you talk to him. It took him years to forgive me, and I don't know if he ever fully did, but I asked him to. And now, I have the opportunity to ask you." She looked up at me again. "I'm sorry that I didn't get him to the phone. That I didn't allow you to say goodbye. I don't know how much it would have helped, you know, with everything that happened the way it did, but I hate that I was the cause of you not getting to tell him goodbye. Could you ever forgive me?"

What the hell was I supposed to say to that? How could I look this poor woman in the face and refuse to give her peace over a split-second decision made in a moment of stress thirty-six years earlier?

"I know you didn't know." I rubbed my lips together and tried to choose my words carefully, aware not only of the role she held in William's life but also the role she would likely play in the future of my daughter and grandchildren, as well as possibly my own. "You couldn't have known. I look back on that time, and I appreciate that you were always kind to me. Here I was, an unruly, obnoxious, stuck-up teenager who was keeping your son out until all hours of the night and showing up at your house crying in the dark. I can't imagine how worried you must have been about him. I'm sorry for the stress I put you through, not only that night but in the weeks and months leading up to it. And, of course, in the time after I left."

The waitress came and asked Abby if she needed anything, and she told her she'd already eaten but would love a glass of water. She set the straw paper aside as the woman left, and then she looked at me again.

"I won't lie and say that I wasn't angry with you then. More angry than I knew what to do with. I prayed and prayed for God to remove it from me. William was a wreck when you left. His father and I thought if we could just get him settled at school, at the college, then he'd be okay. We thought he'd meet people, he'd make new friends, and he'd move on from it. But he didn't. He told me he couldn't concentrate. That he couldn't focus. Couldn't study. His father said William had to stay. That he'd earned all that money for an education and he needed to get one. But the boy was gonna flunk every class. What was I to do? I let him come home."

She paused as the waitress set her water in front of her, only continuing after she'd thanked the woman and waited for her to depart.

The guilt I'd long struggled with came back with a vengeance, and I fought the urge to get up and run. I wanted to get as far away from her words and my actions as possible. Even though William had forgiven me, it killed me to think of what I'd done to him, and by extension, what I'd done to his family.

"I never intended to hurt William," I said, my voice shaky and my skin hot with perspiration.

"I believe you," Abby said, and her face softened into a smile. Not a big, joyful grin or anything. Just a small, compassionate gesture that went a long way. "William has explained what happened, and why you felt it was best not to contact him. He told me what you sacrificed, what you went through, to protect him and keep him safe. I think that took a lot of courage on your part, and you must have cared for him deeply to do that."

"I did, and I still do." I laid my hand on my stomach to calm it as I blinked back the tears threatening to fall.

Her smile faltered, and she slid her hand across the table toward me. "I can see that I've upset you, and that wasn't my intent. I simply wanted to apologize and perhaps clear the air between us to make it easier moving ahead."

She took a sip of her water, and then her eyes brightened, and her voice was lighter.

"I very much look forward to meeting Caroline and the children tomorrow. William can't say enough positive things about them, and I'm excited to get to know them for myself."

I was thankful for her attempt to change the subject.

"Caroline has William's eyes ... your eyes."

Her smile was the broadest it had been in our conversation, and she nodded. "William told me she does. His red hair, too. That also came from my side of the family, but mine started getting lighter with every baby I had. Will you be joining us at the party?"

I shook my head and looked down at my hands. "No."

"Why not? Surely, William invited you."

"He did," I said as I looked up to meet her eyes.

"Well, I'd like to personally invite you myself. We'd love for you to come."

"Thank you, but I'm gonna sit this one out."

She stared at me for a moment, and then she opened her mouth and closed it, perhaps thinking better of what she was going to say. She sat back in the chair and crossed her arms as she tilted her head to one side. Then she opened her mouth again but didn't close it. Instead, she launched into another of her speeches.

"I don't know if William ever told you this, but his brother Henry was conceived before his father and I were married. I was just sixteen years old when I found out I was gonna be a mama."

My eyes widened at the revelation. I hadn't known.

"My parents were devastated, of course," she said. "That was not what they'd envisioned for their daughter. I think it nearly killed my papa. But Denny's parents, why, you would have thought I'd given him a death sentence! His mother Matilda begged him not to marry me. She told him that we should put Henry up for adoption. Denny was just a couple of months shy of graduation, and she offered to send him away to a college out-of-state to get him away from me. He

424

was the only boy, the baby of his family, and he was her pride and joy."

My nausea began to subside as I focused on her story.

"Do you know that woman actually told me to my face that she hoped I would miscarry? This was her own flesh and blood. Her grandchild. And she would rather have that baby die than me marry her son and deliver our child!"

I shuddered at the thought, but unfortunately, I could relate. My father would have easily had me abort Caroline if he'd been able to force it to happen.

"Now, as you know, Denny and I did marry, and we did have Henry, and went on to have four more."

"Did your mother-in-law ever apologize?"

Abby smiled, but her eyes held a glint of hardness.

"No. She never did. Nor did Matilda ever forgive me for ruining Denny's life, in her words. She went to her grave still convinced that he would have been much happier and much better off if he'd never met me."

"Even after all that time? After years of the two of you being married? Having your kids?"

She nodded. "Even after all that time. She was vindictive, too. She'd forget to invite me or my kids to family functions. She'd buy the other grandkids gifts, but not our children. She'd tell Denny lies about me in the beginning, but he never believed her."

"I'm surprised the two of you still had a relationship with her."

"She was Denny's mama. The only one he had. I didn't want to ask him to give her up and risk him resenting me for it. He always stood up to her for me, and I always knew he had my back. I never doubted his love for me."

She leaned forward and crossed her arms on the table.

"I have to tell you, that when I saw how hard William worked after he dropped out of school, how carefully he planned and prepared, how focused he was on having a place for you to come home to, I knew that it wasn't any crush I was dealing with. William loved you. I didn't understand how much at first, but as months and then years went by and he refused to give up, there was no doubt in my mind about what he felt for you. So, I told myself that when you returned, I would set aside my own feelings for his sake and do whatever it took to forgive you. That I would embrace you as the woman my son loved and welcome you into our family."

A passerby spoke to Abby, and she smiled and nodded in greeting before looking back to me.

"Now, I didn't tell you all this so you would feel bad, and I didn't tell you so you'd think Matilda was a bad person. She wasn't. She was a sick person, and I'll leave it at that. I told you this because I want you to understand that I'm no Matilda. I know how much my son loves you, and if he's choosing to make you a part of this family, then you're part of our family."

She stood and gathered her purse, and then she tapped the table with her knuckles. "I'd love to see you at that party tomorrow." And she was gone.

CHAPTER 79
Caroline

E va groaned for what was probably the fifteenth time since we'd left Gainesville.

"Please tell me this isn't going to be one of those parties where old ladies pinch our cheeks and tell us how cute we are."

"Mom!" Ethan whined from the back seat. "I don't want my cheeks pinched. I don't want to go to this stupid party. Can't I just go to the barn with Malcolm?"

"Thank you, Eva," I whispered to my daughter before making eye contact with my son in the rearview mirror. "Malcolm is going to the party, Ethan. And so are we. William wants us to meet his family. Our family. Our new family."

"Aren't you nervous?" Eva asked. "What if they don't like us? What if they think it's weird that William never knew about you?"

I gripped the steering wheel tighter and tried to reassure her of something I had no assurance of.

"You've seen how nice William is, baby. These are his family members, so I'm sure they'll be nice, too. He wouldn't ask us to come if he thought people weren't going to treat us well."

"Are we gonna ride horses at this party?" Ethan asked. "I want to ride the horse again."

"No, dimwit," Eva chastised. "It's a barbecue. We're not all gonna be holding paper plates while we sit around on horses."

"Eva, please. He's ten. Cut him some slack."

"There were horses at the other barbecue we went to here. The Farm Day barbecue."

"That was different," Eva said. "This is a party for people to look at us and decide whether or not they like us."

"Eva, that's not what it is."

"Isn't it?"

I turned into the entrance of Ward Farms and drove under the arched gate. It was still so bizarre to me to think of it as *my* family farm. I wondered if I would ever truly feel like part of William's family.

"I'm gonna run inside and get Levi," I said as we pulled into his driveway. "You guys stay here. I'll only be a minute. Eva, can you get in the back seat and give Levi the front?"

"I still don't understand why he has to ride with us. He has his own truck, and he lives, like, literally right here. He could practically walk if he wanted to."

"Well, he doesn't want to, and it's a big farm, so that'd be a long walk. He's riding with us because I asked him to, okay?"

I got out and shut the door, not wanting to explain to my daughter that I needed Levi with me to face all these strangers.

"Well, hello there," Levi said when he opened the door. I rushed forward and wrapped my arms around his neck, nearly knocking him backward. He tightened his arms around my waist as he steadied us. "Hey, hey, hey. You okay? What's wrong?"

I shook my head and just held on tight, not wanting to let go and risk tears falling to mess up my make-up.

"It's gonna be fine, you know," he whispered against my hair. "They're gonna love you. You're going to be surrounded by love and by the end of the day, you'll be a Ward."

I made a scoffing sound and released my grip just enough to allow me to face him.

He kissed me, and then he bumped our foreheads together and grinned.

"Caroline, these people have been nothing but kind to me for years, and I was a total stranger who just happened to get a job here."

I sighed and ran my fingertips up his neck into his hairline.

"I'm just so nervous to meet everybody. It would be bad enough going to a party full of strangers for any reason, but I feel like they'll be judging me, or judging William. Or both."

"I'm telling you, they're gonna love you. You're William's daughter, and by having this party, he's laying down the law for how you, Eva, and Ethan should be treated. It's gonna be fine. Besides, it's not all strangers. You already know Malcolm and Gaynelle, and several of the guys. Mom, Dad, and Rachel are coming, and you've met them before."

"Once."

"Okay, but they're not strangers. They're coming to be here in support of you. They're on your side. Not that there are sides."

"But there might be. What if Piper's been talking to people in the family and turned them against me? What if there's people who *are* on her side in all this?"

He scrunched his face with a look that said he found that ridiculous.

"Piper doesn't have a *side*. No one has done anything to her. And trust me, the entire Ward family knows how Piper can be."

"Mom!" Eva screamed from the car. "Ethan farted in here, and it smells like death. Could you guys hug later and come now so we can go, please?"

I'd forgotten my children were watching us as we stood in the doorway, and I released Levi like a hot potato.

He laughed and pulled the door shut behind him. "I'm just excited about getting some of Dax's barbecue. You're gonna love Dax. Maggie, too. She's a redhead, like you." He suddenly stopped walking, his grin gone. "That reminds me … I need to tell you something because I don't want you to be caught off guard by it, but I also don't want you to take it personally. And I'm afraid you will."

"What am I supposed to say to that? And why would you tell me something awful right before we go to this party?"

"It's not awful, but you're going to see it at the party, and I just figure I should give you a heads-up."

"Okay," I said, wary.

"Piper dyed her hair blonde."

"Okay. Why would I take that personally?"

"Mom!" Eva yelled again. "Come on!"

I started walking again but then turned and looked at Levi.

"Wait a minute! Did she dye her hair so people wouldn't think we looked alike?"

His grimace told me I'd hit the nail on the head.

"I don't know that for sure," he said. "But she's never dyed her hair before as long as I've known her, so the timing's a bit suspect. It's stupid, really, because the two of you don't even look that much alike. Especially not for anyone who knows either one of you.

There's not a lot of similarities."

"Except the hair."

"Yeah. I guess. I just didn't want you to see her or somebody say something about it and it hurt your feelings."

"Thanks. I wish she would just talk to me. Do you think she'll try to avoid me all day at the party like she has on the farm?"

"I would expect that, yeah. She knows William wouldn't want any confrontations today, so I'm betting she'll keep her distance. But hey, this party isn't about her. It's about you and William. Let's go see your father and meet your family."

He took my hand and led me to the Tahoe, which did indeed smell like death.

CHAPTER 80
Caroline

When we arrived at the main house, William gave each of us a big hug and thanked us for coming. There were only a few people there already, and I knew several of them from the farm. As other family members began to arrive, we were greeted with hugs and handshakes, and I began to feel like a long-lost relative who'd just come home with amnesia. They all seemed to know who we were and what our story was while I knew nothing about them.

William's siblings had a menagerie of grandchildren at various ages, and it didn't take long for Ethan to be running wild outside with the younger ones and for Eva to be huddled out by the pool with the older teens.

Levi did his best to stay by my side, as did William, but both of them would get called away into conversations, leaving me open to some well-meaning person coming up to introduce themselves and give me a summary of their connection to William and therefore me.

It was a whirlwind of faces that all looked remotely similar, and I struggled to keep up with names and who belonged to whom.

At some point, I'd excused myself to go to the restroom, and when I came back outside, I didn't see Levi or William right away. I went and stood under one of the large oak trees and took in the entire scene.

People were scattered all over the yard and underneath the lanai, grouped together in small animated vignettes of laughter and boisterous conversation. Kids ran to and fro as they chased each other for tag or fired Nerf darts at each other. Smoke billowed up from the large, black cast-iron smoker, and a large group of men stood gathered around it.

I noticed a woman smiling at me from where she sat a few feet away. I was fairly certain she was one of William's sisters, and as she stood and walked toward me, I tried to remember whether she was Helen or Patricia.

"You're probably wondering what my brother's gotten you into, huh?" she said as she came to stand by my side and watch the party from my vantage point.

"You're … Patricia? Right?"

"Yes! The youngest sister, and the prettier one, but don't you dare tell Helen I said that!" She laughed at her own joke, and I laughed with her. "I would think this is all a bit much to take in at once."

I wasn't sure what to say to that, and I shrugged, not wanting to offend.

"Oh, it's fine. It's been a fun day."

She arched one eyebrow and leaned in closer to speak in a low, conspiratorial tone. "I know that's probably what you feel like you should say to be polite, but here's one thing you need to know about me. I shoot straight from the hip, and I'm perfectly fine with you doing the same. Don't ever feel like you have to sugarcoat anything with me, and don't expect me to either. Deal?"

She lifted her plastic cup in some sort of high-five invitation, and I accepted with a bump of my cup against hers.

"Deal."

She took a drink from her cup as though that sealed the deal, and then she sighed.

"I told my mom this was a bit over the top. I thought a family dinner with just her, Dad, and William with you and the kids would have been more appropriate to start with. Ease you into the crazy in small chunks. Then you could expand, little by little, you know? Have dinner with Henry and his family. Then, dinner with Helen and hers. Then, eventually you'd work your way over to my place and realize you'd saved the best for last." She grinned and bumped her elbow against mine. "But, Mom felt strongly that we needed to rally the troops. Gather round and show support. Make sure you knew you were welcomed."

Two kids ran past us squealing and screaming, and she admonished them to watch where they were going. She glanced over at me with an eyeroll and a chuckle.

"So, tell me, Caroline. Do you feel welcome? Because your smile is still on-point, but your eyes look a little shell-shocked and glassed over. And that's okay! Hell, my eyes look like that at pretty much every family function we have, and I've known these people my whole life."

Something about her tone and her manner put me at ease, and I began to relax a little.

"It's been great," I said. "Really, it has. My mom, Lorna—well, my adoptive mom, I guess I should say. That's hard to get to used to since she's always just been my mom—but she has a big family. So, some of this feels familiar, and I've always loved going to family parties and being around everyone. Feeling like I belonged, you know? But this feels more like I'm a stranger who got invited to the party. I mean, not that everyone hasn't been nice! They have! But you all know each other, and I'm the odd man out."

She looked at me for a moment, and then she pointed across the yard to a tall, slender woman with blonde hair. "Do you see that girl over there? That's Melissa, James's wife. That poor girl didn't say a word at any family event until they'd been married probably two years. The first time she spoke, we all nearly fell out in shock. I'd wondered if James might have married a mute." She scanned the crowd again, pointing when she found her target. "And do you see that guy there? The hipster-looking dude with the beard?"

I nodded.

"His name is Elroy. Kid you not, someone named a baby Elroy and thought it was a good idea. But Elroy there is from Seattle. He's the nicest guy, and he's been dating Henry's daughter for about a year now. Elroy's as granola-crunching, tree-hugging, vegan-eating, organic-cloth-wearing as you can get. My nephews gave him quite the hard time when he first started coming around, but now? He's the life of the party, and I guarantee you by the end of the night, people will demand that he take his guitar from the car to serenade us all." She turned to face me, and the kindness in her eyes matched her smile. "My point is, it's always daunting to join a family and figure out where you fit in. But eventually, you find your spot. You find where your piece fits in the puzzle, and soon, you're part of the whole picture, and no one remembers a time when you weren't there yet. It's like until you come along, there's a gaping hole, and then you fill it as only you can."

"Thank you," I said, feeling such warmth from her that I wanted to ask her to stay by my side the rest of the day.

"And there goes my newly-blonde niece," Patricia turned to watch Piper walk across the yard and into the house. "How are the two of you getting along these days?"

"Hard to say. We actually haven't had any interaction since we found out we're related. The few times I've been down here to the farm since Cat got out of the hospital, Piper either hasn't been home or has been out of sight. Levi said she's not doing so well with the news. I'd really like to talk to her about it, but William told me to hold off. He said it's probably best to give her some time."

"Hmmph. Piper, Piper, Piper. I love that girl, but she can be a handful. Her mother, Revae, was so caught up in horse racing that she didn't have much time for parenting. She was gone often, and William was busy, too, so Piper was pretty much on her own. She roamed around this farm with a team of surrogate uncles looking over her, and they all let her do whatever she wanted and indulged her every whim. The last few years have been a rude awakening for her. Life hasn't catered to her like her parents and William's crew always did."

"I feel bad. It had to be a shock to suddenly have me come out nowhere. I just hope she's not angry with me about it. I think she already didn't care for me much, even before all this."

"She's particular about who she gets close to, for sure. But she has no reason to be angry with you, and if she is, that's her problem. It's not like you had any say-so in who your parents were. I disagree with my brother on this one." She turned to face me. "If you're going to be a member of this family, then you'll need to deal with Piper like the rest of us do. Be direct and don't take any crap off her. Uh-oh," she said as she looked past me. "There's Mom. Looks like I'm being summoned to work. I'll see ya around. It was nice talking to you."

"Nice talking to you, too. Should I come help out?"

"No, she wouldn't let you this time. You're the guest of honor. She won't put you to work today."

As Patricia walked away, I scanned the crowd for Eva and Ethan, and when I saw that they both appeared to be happy, I decided to walk inside in search of Levi or William.

As I walked down the hallway from the kitchen toward the front of the house, Piper came down the stairs.

"Piper! Hi. I haven't seen you much today. I'd hoped we'd get a chance to chat."

She stopped on the bottom stair and looked at me, her face impossible to read.

"I've been hanging out upstairs with my cousins," she said.

I decided to take advantage of the moment, not knowing when I might get another chance.

"Could we talk somewhere? Somewhere private?"

She didn't look enthused about the prospect, but she didn't turn me down.

"Sure. Follow me."

I followed her into William's study, where she leaned against his desk with her arms crossed.

"What's up?"

Now that I had her alone, I realized I had no idea what I wanted to say.

"I just, well, I felt like you and I hadn't really had a chance to talk lately. So much has happened. It's been a whirlwind, and I guess I wanted to see where you're at with everything."

"Where I'm at? I don't know where I'm at, to be honest."

Her eyes were hard, and her jaw was set, and my palms got all sweaty at the prospect of conflict.

"That's fair," I said. "I mean, I know I'm a little overwhelmed with it all, and I'm sure you are, too." I moved forward to stand a bit closer, and I reminded myself that I'd done nothing wrong. Her glare and her stance made it hard not to feel guilty. "Look, Piper, I get that this was probably not something you wanted to hear—that your dad had some other kid from before that you didn't know about. I can't imagine how I'd feel in your shoes. But you and I, we both got tossed into this situation through no fault of our own. I think we need to just try to make the best of it. You know? We have an opportunity here to get to know each other and build a relationship—a friendship. Growing up, I always wanted a sister—"

"I didn't," she said, cutting me off. "I rather liked being the center of attention. I liked being my father's only daughter. Daddy's little girl. It was part of what made me feel like me." She stood and walked to the center of the room before turning. "I know none of this is your fault, and I appreciate you reaching out and all, but I'm not okay with things right now. And if you notice I'm avoiding you, it's not because of anything you've done, all right? I have nothing against you personally, Caroline. I have nothing against Eva or Ethan. I just don't know how to accept things as they are, and so I stay away from everyone rather than being a raging bitch to everybody all the time. Who knows? Maybe someday I'll be up to having some kind of sisterly chat where we bond and become friends. I'm not there yet. So, please just do me a favor and give me my space."

She left the room, and I followed not long after, bumping into Levi as I stepped into the hallway.

"Hey, you," he said as he wrapped his arms around me. "You okay? I got trapped in a conversation with William's uncle, and I just escaped to come looking for you and saw Piper fly out of here like a bat out of hell. Everything all right?"

"It's as good as it's gonna get for now. I spoke my piece, and Piper spoke hers. And now we both know where we stand."

"I've told you not to worry about her, babe. She'll come around."

"I guess. I thought maybe if we had a heart-to-heart, it would do some good. But life isn't like a soft-focus Hallmark movie, right? People feel what they feel, and sometimes you just have to move on with your life. And that's what I intend to do. I've had probably sixty people come up to me today and tell me they're glad I'm here. I'm not going to focus all my energy on the one who isn't."

Levi grinned and pulled me closer.

"I, for one, am very glad that you're here," he said between kisses.

CHAPTER 81
William

I'd lost sight of Caroline, and I walked through the crowd outside to find her. The last time I'd looked up, she'd been with Patricia, but my sister was helping my mother bring out all the cold dishes and Caroline was nowhere in sight.

I knew she'd been nervous about the day, and I'd tried to make sure she always had either me or Levi with her as a buffer against my well-meaning family.

Thinking perhaps she'd gone inside, I walked through the throng of people in the family room and kitchen, searching for any sign of her red hair.

Piper came storming through wearing a dark scowl, and I started to reach out to her, to stop her and ask her what was wrong. But she looked hellbent on being miserable, and I decided I didn't want her mood to ruin my day.

I continued into the hallway and found Caroline wrapped in Levi's embrace as they kissed.

"Hey, hey, hey," I called out to tease them. "Get a room, you two. But not until after the party."

The three of us laughed, and I smiled at the joy on Caroline's face.

"You doing okay? Having a good time?"

"Yeah, I am," she said. "Thanks."

Relief came over me, and I relaxed a bit. I'd had my reservations about Ma's party, but judging from what I'd seen of Eva, Ethan, and now Caroline, they all seemed to be having a great time.

It was hard not to notice that part of my heart was missing, though, and I wished I could have convinced Cat to come.

The doorbell rang, and the three of us turned to look at it, and then I went to pull the door open.

She stood there in a pair of denim capris and a fitted lime green T-shirt that made her eyes sparkle like emeralds.

My heart raced, and my entire body felt lighter.

I rushed forward to scoop her into my arms, lifting her off the ground.

"You came! God, I'd hoped you would!"

She wrapped her arms around my neck and laughed, and I covered her mouth with mine, reveling in the taste of her.

Levi stepped up behind us, never one to miss an opportunity to tease back.

"Hey, hey, hey. Get a room, you two! But not until after the party!"

I laughed as I turned to face him and Caroline, my arm firmly around Cat's waist.

Caroline's smile lit up her whole face, and she and Cat held their arms out to each other as they embraced.

"Hey there!" Cat said to her.

"I'm so happy you're here," Caroline said. She looked back and forth between the two of us, and her eyes filled with tears. "I can't tell you how much it means to have you both here." She looked to Cat then, her brows close together. "I thought you said you weren't coming, though."

Cat smiled and looked up at me as she put her arm around my waist and squeezed, and then she took Caroline's hand in hers.

"I decided I wanted to be with my family."

The three of us embraced, and then Levi joined in the group hug.

When we'd finished our lovefest, we made our way through the house, stopping for introductions along the way. By the time we reached the back yard, my mother was announcing that the meal was ready to be served.

Ma came walking up to us once people started getting in line, and before I could say anything to reacquaint them, Ma and Cat shared a hug and a smile.

"I'm happy to see you here," Ma said as she squeezed both of Cat's hands.

"Thanks for inviting me," Cat replied, and I raised an eyebrow in question of what I'd missed.

"What was that all about?" I asked once my mother had walked away.

"I'll tell you later," Cat said as my sister Patricia approached to say hello.

When the meal was finished and the sun had dipped closer to the horizon, Cat and I sat in the swing underneath the lanai, looking out onto everyone's smiling faces.

"What a lovely day," Cat said.

"Yeah, it has been. But you know my favorite part?"

She looked at me with bright eyes as she pulled a stray strand of hair away from her mouth.

"Let me guess … the barbecue!"

"No," I said with a grin. "Although that was top-notch. Dax never disappoints. No, my favorite part of this day hasn't happened yet."

She smiled, and a sensual glint crept into her eyes.

"Oh, do tell me more. What's your favorite part?"

"Knowing I get to take you home."

Cat giggled, and my insides went to jelly, like only she could make them do.

"And what happens when you get me home?" she asked.

"That's up to you. I'm yours for the taking, my love."

She reached up to kiss me, and then she laid her head on my shoulder.

I pulled her in close as I buried my face in her hair and breathed her in.

My heart felt like it had been made whole again, and it was bursting at the seams with happiness. I closed my eyes and thanked my lucky stars for stolen cars and crossing paths.

Want to spend more time in Cedar Creek?

Read The Ghost in the Curve,
Volume 1 in Cedar Creek Mysteries.
Romance, Suspense, Humor, Mystery, & a Ghost.

CHAPTER 1
Sloane

I never believed in ghosts before I met her. Ironic, I realize, since my entire career was based on my role as a ghost slayer. Those on-screen opponents weren't real, though. They were movie magic, added in post-production. Truth is, I never even saw them.

I'd like to think it speaks to my brilliant acting abilities. I mean, I could make an audience believe I saw the same thing they did when all I was doing was staring into thin air against a green screen. Occasionally I got to play off an actor stand-in who'd be replaced in digital editing. But it was all special effects. Smoke and mirrors. An illusion not grounded in reality.

Sort of like my life.

I don't know when I lost sight of who I was and who I wanted to be, but I know that all I wanted that night was to escape who I'd become—a washed-up scream queen who'd passed her point of expiration.

I never knew twenty-nine could feel so old.

"The desired demographic can't relate to you anymore, Sloane," Douglas had told me as my trembling hands held the letter explaining my release of contract. "You were sixteen when your first movie hit the big screen. The girls who idolized you for kicking ass with the after-lifes have grown up. They've gotten married, had kids. They're watching animated Disney flicks now. And the younger generation sees you as too old. You don't have an audience."

"But you're my agent. Can't you tell them to find me something new? I have two more movies left in my contract. Can't we option that for a different script? Maybe a comedy? I could do comedy."

Douglas sighed and crossed his arms as he leaned half-sitting, half-standing against his large oak desk. "You don't have a contract anymore, babe. They've exercised the opt-out. You get one lump sum payment, and they're no longer obligated to you."

"But...I...but...you..."

The words died away in my throat.

I guess I should have seen it coming. Numbers for the last two films had been down, but I'd blamed the scripts. The marketing efforts had been lackluster. We'd opened against some strong contenders.

Douglas had talked to me after the last film wrapped production—was that a year ago already?—about branching out and seeking new projects, but I'd felt safe in my world. I knew how to be a scream queen. I knew how to navigate those waters. Put me in charge with some supporting characters backing me up against pissed-off, misplaced spirits, and in the end, I always saved the day.

I didn't know how to be any other kind of actress. The mere thought of being a small player in some ensemble cast where I'd have to show the world I could really act was far more terrifying than any digital ghost I'd encountered.

So I'd done nothing. And now I had nothing to do.

"Take a vacation, babe," Douglas had suggested as I sank back in the chair and let the letter fall from my hands. "It'll do you good. Take some time off. Lay on a beach somewhere. Find a hot guy to hook up with and generate some tabloid attention. I'll look for script opportunities and if I find something, I'll send it to you right away. You can read it in a lounge chair with an umbrella drink in your hand."

Then he'd ushered me out of his office with a brief squeeze of my elbow and an air kiss.

I didn't want an umbrella drink. I didn't want to lie on a beach somewhere contemplating my future, or lack thereof. And I certainly didn't want any tabloid attention. I could see the headlines flashed across the stands already.

Washed-up Scream Queen Drowns Sorrows in Aruba
Ghosts' Worst Nightmare Faces Nightmare of Her Own
Sloane Reid Does Best Acting Yet Pretending Not to Care about Her Future

So I begged my publicist to keep the story from surfacing for a few days, and I called my Aunt Virginia to see if I could use her remote Florida cabin to hide out and lick my wounds. I worried she might ask too many questions about why I suddenly wanted to hole up by myself in the middle of nowhere, but if she wondered, she didn't ask.

"Of course, you're welcome to stay there! Why, it would actually be a godsend for you to open up the place and air it out. I don't make it down there much since your uncle Ted died. I'd say it's been three years at least. I have a man who keeps the outside tidy, but the inside will need some sprucing when you get there. Dust and such."

"I'm sure it'll be fine, Aunt Virginia. I just need some peace and quiet. A few days' rest."

"Oh, you'll find it there! Most peaceful place on earth, Ted used to say. So you're in between films, then?"

That was one way to put it. In between. I just had no idea when the next one would come. Or if it would.

"Yes, ma'am. Just taking a little break."

"We all need that from time to time. Let me give you the security code for the alarm system. You gotta pen?"

For the life of me, I don't know why she bothered to install an alarm system. I doubt any burglars could find the place to rob it.

They'd built the house high upon a hill overlooking Cedar Lake with the small town of Cedar Creek in the distance across the water. Dense woods lined both sides of the narrow, winding road that led from the town to the property, and the cabin was completely blocked from view behind tall, thick pines that surrounded its perch at the top of the hill.

The driveway was at the end of a sharply banked curve that hugged the lake, and if you weren't looking for it, you'd never know it existed. Hell, I *was* looking for it and I still missed it, even as the GPS was announcing that I had arrived. Navigating the hairpin curve took my focus away from the road ahead, but I don't think I would have seen the driveway anyway, hidden like it was by the overgrown bushes on either side.

Of course, it didn't help that it was pitch black out. I hadn't wasted any time leaving L.A. after my meeting with Douglas and my call to Aunt Virginia. I took the last flight out to Orlando, anxious to get out of town and leave it all behind. In hindsight, I should have gotten a hotel room near the airport when I landed and waited to find Cedar Creek in the morning light. My mind had fixated on one goal, though. I had to get to the cabin so I could have my nervous breakdown in private.

When I'd finally found a place to turn around in the dark and make my way back toward the curve, I held the GPS in my hand on the steering wheel and still almost missed the drive again. No markers. No mailbox. No way to find it if you weren't seriously looking.

As I made my way up the twists and turns of the steep gravel drive with the light from my headlights bouncing off the pine trees, it looked more like one of my movie sets than a welcoming retreat.

"I swear, Aunt Virginia," I said aloud. "Would it have hurt to invest in some outdoor lighting?"

When I finally reached the cabin, I fought the urge to turn around and head straight back into Cedar Creek. The prospect of finding a hotel in a town with one traffic light was slim, but the dilapidated, rundown building trapped in the beam of my headlights didn't look promising.

Truth be told, I'm nowhere near as fearless as my on-screen alter ego. Lucy Landry would have bounded out of the car without a moment's hesitation, spectral sword drawn and ready for action. But she has the advantage of being on set surrounded by cast and crew. I was alone, and I wasn't overly eager to exit the car and venture inside a dark cabin that had been all but deserted for the last three years. I switched off the engine and sat to contemplate my options.

I could see nothing around me but trees and night. Lots of trees and a whole bunch of night. Wispy tendrils of Spanish moss hung low from the branches above me, swaying and dancing on the evening breeze. As the popping and sighing of the cooling engine subsided, a chorus of crickets and frogs serenaded me.

Weighing the fright factor of sleeping in the car against venturing inside the house, I was leaning toward the car. I even fumbled with the levers to see how far back the driver's seat would recline, but I'd opted for the value rental, and it was short on amenities.

I took a deep breath and another quick look around. It wasn't getting any less spooky.

"This is ridiculous," I called out. "I make a living off other people's fears. I'm the Spectral Slayer. I'm not scared of anything."

The feeble attempt didn't accomplish much bolstering. After all, technically, I'm *not* the Spectral Slayer. Lucy Landry is. I'm just Sloane Reid, and she's scared of plenty of things. Including dark, deserted cabins in the middle of dense woods.

I exhaled loudly and looped my fingers through the handle of my suitcase in the passenger seat, wishing I had a few weapon props from the set to brandish and make me feel less defenseless. The last thing I wanted was a headline saying *"Washed Up Scream Queen Sloane Reid Dies in Suitcase Battle"* with an accompanying article detailing how my body was found amid my T-shirts and undies.

My hand hovered over the door handle a moment more before I swung it open and stepped out into the night. The loud chime from the open door rang out obnoxiously, and I shut it quickly. The interruption had quieted the frogs and crickets, and the air hung heavy with the lack of sound. I didn't dare turn off the headlights before heading for the cabin's porch, and every step toward the house I prayed the lights wouldn't suddenly go off on their own as they would have in the movies.

I found the key under the flower pot where she'd said it would be. It turned easily in the lock, and though I had pictured a swarm of bats overtaking me as I opened the door, it was surprisingly anticlimactic. With a flip of the switch, the room was immediately awash in light.

Sheets covered every available piece of furniture, lending an eerie ambience that did nothing to welcome me or assuage my uneasiness. I reminded myself again that this was the quaint cabin my aunt and uncle had enjoyed for most summers of their marriage, and not the horror movie set it resembled. I half expected to turn and see a camera crew off to one side, or at the very least, wires and boom mics.

The headlights blasting through the front window blinds only added to the spooky decor, so I flipped on the porch light and went to the car to turn them off. Just as I shut the car door, a stick cracked in the woods to the right of me, piercing the silence. My mind immediately conjured an image of the heavy step that caused it. I took off running as though my life depended on it, sure in that moment that it did. My heart pounded as I covered the short distance between the car and the porch, refusing to look back in case something had emerged from the shadows and was closing in on me as I took the porch steps two at a time.

I slammed the cabin door behind me and slid the deadbolt in place just as I heard the alarm trigger.

"Oh no! The code! Dammit! I forgot to put in the code." I ran across the living room to the kitchen where the alarm panel was flashing, its siren near-deafening in its intensity. I frantically punched in the four numbers, but nothing happened. The shrill pitch stabbed through my eardrums as I tried the code again. No result.

I clapped both hands over my ears and tried to replay the conversation with Aunt Virginia, conjuring up the numbers in my mind, but my brain was tired and already spent from the world crashing around me in L.A. and too much time to think on a cross-country flight. The alarm reverberated throughout my body, threatening to break the precarious emotional dam inside me and flood the spooky little cottage with my tears.

It occurred to me that I'd written the code down and put it in my purse, which I'd left in the car. I was almost to the front door when I realized I could hear a second siren coming from outside the house. I stepped out on the porch to see red and blue lights flashing their way up the drive. If I'd thought the day couldn't get any worse, I was wrong.

ORDER THE GHOST IN THE CURVE AT YOUR FAVORITE ONLINE RETAILER!

A NOTE FROM THE AUTHOR

I hope you've enjoyed this story from Cedar Creek Families. I have several more books planned for this collection, including Piper's story, Lauryn's story, and a story with Levi's sister, Rachel, who has a key role in The Glow in the Woods, the second volume in the Cedar Creek Mysteries.

All of The Cedar Creek Series novels feature recurring characters who live in this quaint community. The Cedar Creek Mysteries are stories with suspense, romance, humor, mystery, and a ghost or two. The Cedar Creek Families are stories of love, laughter, family, and friendships.

For more information about future books set in the small town of Cedar Creek, visit www.violethowe.com to sign up for my newsletter or you can join my Facebook reader group, the Ultra Violets, for all the news about upcoming releases.

Happy Reading!

Violet

Want more Romantic Women's Fiction?

Follow wedding planner Tyler's funny and poignant diary entries as she encounters crazy bridezillas and outlandish blind dates in her journey to find her own modern-day Prince Charming. Along the way, Tyler discovers that real-life love is often more complicated than the fairy tales she grew up believing. A lot happens between Once Upon a Time and Happily Ever After.

Learn more about the Tales Behind the Veils series at
www.violethowe.com.

ABOUT THE AUTHOR

PHOTO CREDIT: I. ARMAGOST

Violet Howe enjoys writing romance and mystery with humor. She lives in Florida with her husband—her knight in shining armor—and their two handsome sons. They share their home with three adorable but spoiled dogs. When she's not writing, Violet is usually watching movies, reading, or planning her next travel adventure.

www.violethowe.com

Facebook.com/VioletHoweAuthor

@Violet_Howe

Instagram.com/VioletHowe

NEWSLETTER/READER GROUP

Sign up at www.violethowe.com to receive Violet's monthly newsletter with updates on new releases, appearances, prize drawings, and info on joining the Ultra Violets Facebook Reader Group.

THANK YOU

Thank you for taking the time to read this book.

I sincerely hope you enjoyed it! If you did, then please tell somebody! Tell your friends. Tell your family. Tell a co-worker. Tell the person next to you in line at the grocery store.

One of the best compliments you can give an author is to leave a review on BookBub, Amazon, Goodreads, or any other social media site you frequent.

Made in the USA
Middletown, DE
15 February 2020